YOUNG BESS

By the same author in PAN Books

ROYAL FLUSH

THE PROUD SERVANT

THE STRANGER PRINCE

THE GAY GALLIARD

THE BRIDE

YOUNG BESS

MARGARET IRWIN

UNABRIDGED

'Such incredible fierce desire'
NAN BULLEN

PAN BOOKS LTD : LONDON

First published 1944 by Chatto & Windus Ltd.
This edition published 1968 by Pan Books Ltd.,
33 Tothill Street, London, S.W.1

330 20258 8

2nd Printing 1968
3rd Printing 1969

PRINTED AND BOUND IN ENGLAND BY
HAZELL WATSON AND VINEY LTD
AYLESBURY, BUCKS

To
Lucy Bell

My thanks, 'first and foremost on the list,' to J. R. M. And to Lady Helen Seymour for the lively help she gave me, with the papers and household books of the Seymour family.

Chapter One

SHE HAD BEEN allowed to come out to the royal flagship, and had been eating cherries and strawberries dipped in wine. All round her the sea was a flaming white glitter, the air was hot high summer, the wind in a mad mood; she was twelve years old, and Tom Seymour, who was Admiral of the Fleet and her favourite step-uncle, was talking to her as though she were rather more; he was joking and chaffing her, but then he did that with all women, even with the Queen.

And he went on talking to her, looking down at her with wickedly merry eyes half shut against the sunlight, watching her as though he really wanted to know how she would answer.

'And what will you do when England is invaded?' he asked her. 'Will you raise a regiment and ride at the head of it? Will you be Colonel Eliza or Captain Bess?'

'England won't be invaded. She never has been.'

'Not by the Normans?'

'Five hundred years ago! And they were us, or they couldn't have done it.'

'There speaks the proud Plantagenet!'

She stamped like a wilful pony and tossed her head, and the wind seized a strand of her smooth hair and pulled it out from under her little jewelled cap, tossing it like a wisp of flame, teasing her just as he was doing; but it was a bad joke to mock the thin strain of royal Plantagenet in the Tudor blood – and with her father on board.

'It's lucky for you I'm no tell-tale-tit.'

'No, you'll never be that.'

'How can you tell what I'll be?'

All her egoism was agog. What would she be? At twelve years old anything was possible. And so he seemed to think as he scanned her, and the wind flicked the wisp of hair into her eyes and made her blink.

7

'How can I tell what you'll be? You may become anything. Elizabeth the Enigma. Will you be beautiful? Will you be plain? You might so easily be either. Will you have a pinched whey face and carrot-coloured hair and a big peeled forehead like a pale green cooking apple? Or will you suddenly be mysteriously lovely, with your hair aflame over that white face, and that quick secret look of yours? What *will* you become, you strange secret little thing?'

'I *will* be beautiful, I *will*!'

But how astonishing that he should dare to talk to her like this. The man could be afraid of nothing.

He saw her thought and laughed again. The light reflected from the sea rippled up and up over them in a ceaseless wavering pattern. Their faces were still in that moment of silence, and their eyes looked steadily at each other; but all the time the flickering movement went on, a current of sea-light weaving its web over them both, over their bright, stiff clothes, the golden point of his beard, the red lights in her hair, the soft gleam of her bare neck and shoulders. For the moment they seemed quite alone on board the *Great Harry* on the summer sea, the sails soaring above them like big white clouds, and the other ships careening and skimming past them, trailing their blue shadows over the sparkling water. They were here to defend the English shore, the long line of emerald downs behind them, and in front the golden shimmer of reeds that surrounded the Isle of Wight.

At any moment the enemy fleet might heave into sight out of the blue distance, the biggest fleet ever gathered together against this country. It was, as she had frequently heard of late, the most fateful moment in all their history. And she had been allowed on board the royal flagship! So great was the privilege, so lovely the day, so bright the air, so dangerous the moment, that perhaps it really did not matter what one said. She gave a swift glance behind her; no one was near. She said, very low, the thing she must not say; she spoke of the person who must never be mentioned.

'My mother – was she beautiful?'

The air still quivered in the sunlight, the deck shone

8

smooth as satin; even the flighty wind had dropped for the moment as if to hold its breath. But her step-uncle still stood and looked at her; he did not turn away muttering some excuse to leave her as fast as possible; he did not even turn pale nor pull at his elegant little foreign-looking beard. He answered, without even lowering his voice, as though it were quite natural that she should speak of her mother.

'No, she was not beautiful. But she was clever enough to make anyone think so whom she wished.'

The child drew a deep breath as though they had stepped past a precipice.

'Well, I am clever, so all my tutors say. I too will make people think I am beautiful.'

'Who do you want to think it?'

She looked up at him and a deep mischievous smile stole over her pale little face. Tom Seymour was certain that the answer would be one swift monosyllable – 'You!' But it was not. With an odd mixture of childish coquetry and passionate sincerity she replied, 'Everybody!'

'What! Do you want the whole world for your lover?'

'Yes, or at least the whole country. I don't mind so much about foreigners.'

He flicked her cheek. 'What a wanton! And I thought you a modest little maid. There's another puzzle. Will you be good? Or will you be naughty – like your mother?'

There again. Yet the deck did not open and let him fall straight into the sea.

'You remember her?' she just breathed.

'As if I had this moment heard her laugh. "Ha, ha!", that was how all the Londoners read it when your father had his initial and hers intertwined over the gateways. H.A. – HA HA! They read right, for she laughed at everything and everybody.'

'Even at—'

'Yes, even at him. She was clever, but not wise. She danced herself into his favour and laughed herself out of it – to her death. And she went laughing to that death. The Sheriff was shocked.'

He fell silent, hearing once again across the years an echo of the shrill mocking note, clear as the call of a bird, and as wild and void of human meaning, that had made men call Nan Bullen a witch. Well, she had used her witchcraft on the King, enslaved him, scorned him, held him off from her for six long years, while to suit her plans he wrecked the whole structure of the English Church, and built it up anew with himself as Pope in England. The King himself said he had been seduced by her sorcery to marry her, but that was after little Bess was born and no boy for heir, and the King had by then turned to Tom Seymour's meek little sister Jane, Plain Jane her brother rudely called her, though she was pretty enough, but with a prim mouth and pale eyes and no charms that could vie with Nan's, except the charm of being wholly unlike her. Unlike Nan, she was a gentlewoman by behaviour as well as by good, though not noble, solid county family birth.

That had brought Bess's first step-uncles on to the scene; the eldest, Edward Seymour, newly created Earl of Hertford, tall, sparely built, keen-faced, of the kind that goes on being called a rising young man even when rising forty; fiercely and coldly intellectual in his pursuit of his ideals, or, some said, of his ambitions. He had married one sister to the King, another to the grandson of a blacksmith, but both, it was thought, to the same purpose, for the blacksmith's son had been Thomas Cromwell, the King's greatest minister, and his heir a catch even for a rising earl.

His second brother, Henry, flatly refused to rise. He had heard enough of public life to prefer to remain a simple country squire, declining all honours and even invitations to Court.

The youngest, Tom Seymour, acclaimed the handsomest man in England, was the complete opposite of Edward – a wild rascal whom no semi-royal responsibility could sober, and with a proficiency in swearing so picturesque that he had said it was his chief qualification for the post of Admiral of the Fleet. That he had others was evident from the work entrusted to him at this dangerous crisis; he and his ships had been stationed at Dover to defend the Kentish coast against the French invasion, and had now joined up with the main fleet, under his command, at Portsmouth. Soldier, sailor, and foreign diplomat, Tom Seymour had had a brilliant career in all three professions, and had started it well before his sisters' marriages had helped on the family. He had been abroad for the best part of the last seven years, on embassies to the French Court, to the King of Hungary, and to Nuremberg; he had been in Vienna for two years and seen a good deal of the war against the Turks; he had exchanged the job of Ambassador to the Netherlands for that of Marshal of the English army fighting against Spain, and done it so well that he was appointed Master of the Ordnance for life in reward for his military services.

His reckless courage had given rise to a score of wild stories; so had his attraction for women. His good looks were the least part of that attraction; it was his careless talk, his great infectious laugh, his good-humoured gaiety and utter lack of premeditation or caution, in a Court growing paralysed with these things, that made him irresistible. Though nearing the middle thirties, he had managed to evade all his matrimonial pursuers, and they were many. The Duke of Norfolk's beautiful daughter had been desperately anxious to marry him for years, but her brother, the young Earl of Surrey, declared the Seymours were upstarts and wouldn't hear of it. His father, the old Duke, was as harsh and intolerant an aristocrat as his son, but not when it suited his self-interest, and he had rather favoured the match, since the Seymour brothers were now the most powerful men in the country, next to the King; it was not merely that they had provided him with one of his wives, but that she had provided him with his only male heir, Edward, the little Prince of Wales. There were no 'steps' in that relationship; they were the flesh-and-blood uncles of the undoubted heir to the throne. Prince Edward was legitimate by all counts and all religions, whereas nobody could be quite sure how the King's two daughters stood; so often had their father bastardized them by turns. 'The Little Bastard' had been the most frequent informal title given to the Princess Elizabeth at her birth; nearly three years later her father had himself endorsed it by Act of Parliament.

And now the Little Bastard herself asked about that title. Standing by Tom Seymour, leaning over the gunwale, the light from the water rippling up under the soft childish

11

chin, her head turned sideways towards him, her eyes, so clear and light, taking their colour from the sea, fixed themselves upon his face. She said in a voice that he could only just hear above the creak of the ropes and the wash of the waves against the boat's side:

'The women are no use. They answer what they think one ought to think. Can you tell me who I am? I once heard my sister Mary say to another woman that she did not believe I was even the King's bastard – I was just like Mark Smeaton, the handsome musician that was beheaded with my mother, – and the woman laughed and said there was choice enough, since three other men had been beheaded too, and one of them her own brother.'

Tom Seymour gave a startling exhibition of his choice of oaths. 'Your sister Mary is a sour old maid, poisoned with hate and jealousy of your mother.'

'But she doesn't hate me – or at any rate she is very kind to me. She did not know I was listening.'

'And well whipped you should have been for it – and would have been, had I been there. But never mind that, or her. I tell you, by God's most precious soul, you are the King's daughter every inch of you, and none could doubt it who looks at you. Can you doubt it yourself, standing here on his flagship, the *Great Harry*? And by God,' he muttered on a sudden drop in tone, 'here comes Great Harry himself.'

Yes, here he came, rather like his own ship, she thought, as he swung portentously into their line of vision, a ship with huge bellying sails ('bellying' is good, she thought, with a pert snigger concealed behind the grave mask of her face as she sank to the deck in a deep curtsy), his silks and jewels flashing in the sunlight and his great hot red face beaming and glistening like a painted block of wood carved on a ship, while beside him Edward Seymour, Earl of Hertford, stalked earnestly like a lean shadow.

Now the King was in front of her, towering over her, blocking out the sunlight, with his silly little flat cap squat on top of all that bulk, and his finger and thumb, hot and sticky as a pair of sausages and yet with surprising force beneath all their fat, pinched her chin and pulled her upright from her curtsy; now she must look him in the face and smile, for he couldn't abide sullen, scared children; they should be frank and fearless as he had been himself. So she stood straight and looked him squarely in the eyes and gave him a charming, ingenuously admiring smile, while he playfully tugged at the loose strand of her hair, and tucked it back under her cap, and she thought: was this enormous being before her, man or monster or god?

He himself did not quite know, for with his arm flung round the nervously smiling Chancellor Wriothesley he was talking of his last Chancellor, jolly Tom Cromwell, and lamenting that he had not got him here now – a pack of rascals had schemed against 'the best of his servants' and so brought him to the block, the more's the pity. Terrible, jovial, at his nod the greatest heads in the kingdom fell, struck by Jove's thunderbolt, – and then he seemed astonished and annoyed that he was not sufficiently a god to put them on again. She had seen him weep brokenheartedly over his first wife, 'the best of women', over his last one, Cat Howard, 'the lovely little wretch' – he'd done them both to death but he still loved them. (But no one had ever heard him mention Nan Bullen since her death.)

His present wife, Catherine Parr, had been a widow almost as often and as briefly as King Henry had been a widower. One could not imagine her without a husband, it would have been such a waste of gentle, humorous, infinitely tolerant benevolence. She put a hand on Elizabeth's arm as the child stood there watching the Ship of State surge on, having laid his grappling arms on Tom Seymour now; you could almost hear the young man's wiry frame crack as that obese giant flung his free arm round his shoulders.

'Why so pensive, Bess my sweetheart?' asked Queen Catherine's pleasant smiling voice.

Bess said demurely, 'I was thinking, Madam, of the story of the fisherman my nurse used to tell me.'

'And what was that?'

The royal procession was well past now.

'Oh, there was a flounder in the sea that promised the poor fisherman three wishes, and his wife made him go down night after night to ask them, though the wind rose and the waves roared and at the last he had to bellow through the storm:

13

> *"Flounder, flounder in the sea*
> *Come and listen unto me,*
> *Come, for my wife Isabel*
> *Wishes what I dare not tell."*

For she made him ask first to be King, and then Pope, and then God.'

Catherine shook her head, but the little face remained as blankly innocent as a baby's. You could not even see that she was frightened, but she was. ('Dear God, have I gone too far this time again? No, not this time, not with nice soft Pussy-Cat Purr. She'll see no further than's good for me – or her.')

The two were great friends. Elizabeth had a pretty knack with stepmothers. The four that she had known had all been fond of her, one after the other; she had written letters to them in French, Italian and Latin, and this present one made as much a companion of her as if she were grown up. They read French and Latin together, and with little Edward, so much younger than Elizabeth but already the cleverest of the family, and with Mary, so much older, but, in Elizabeth's opinion at any rate, so much the stupidest. Catherine Parr, a born homemaker, was in fact succeeding almost miraculously in making a real home for the King's three ill-assorted children by different mothers.

Family life was a difficult affair with a father who had repudiated two of his six wives, beheaded two others, and bastardized both his daughters; yet Catherine managed to bring to it some sense of coherence and even security. She rescued Edward on the one hand from being utterly overlaid by tutors; and on the other, instead of discouraging Mary from reading in bed at night as did everyone else because it was bad for her very weak eyes, she suggested her translating Erasmus's Latin treatises. The poor girl, no longer a girl, badly needed other occupation than fussing over her clothes and other people's babies, and it might flick her pride to read in Udall's preface the praises of modern learning in 'gentle-women who, instead of vain communication about the moon shining in the water, use grave and substantial talk in Greek or Latin.'

There had been no such need to flick little Bess's mental energy into action. Last New Year's Day the child had given her latest stepmother a present of a prose translation she had made herself of a very long religious poem by the present Queen Marguerite of Navarre, sister to King François I, that brilliantly learned and witty lady. Yet she could perpetrate the 'Mirrour of a Guilty Sowle,' which ran, or rather limped, to a hundred and twenty-eight pages of the Princess Elizabeth's childish but beautifully clear and regular handwriting, and of Queen Marguerite's edifying sentiments expressed in a profusion of confused dullness. But no one could doubt the suitability of the little girl's choice; it would never have done to present a new stepmother with a translation of one of the merry and improper stories in Marguerite's *Heptameron*. Nor were learning and propriety the only qualities displayed in the gift; Elizabeth had made the canvas binding of the book and embroidered it with gold and silver braid and silken pansies, purple and yellow, and one tiny green leaf; it was the part she had most enjoyed doing – at first; though she got tired of it long before the end, and the stitches went straggly.

She liked to make her own presents, and had always insisted on her own choice in them. At six years old she had flatly refused to give her baby brother Edward any of the jewels or elaborate ornaments that were offered to her as suitable gifts for his second birthday; no, she would have none of them, though tempted momentarily by a bush of rosemary covered with gold spangles, which, however, on reflection she decided to keep for herself. And she carried out her determination of making the baby a cambric shirt.

A small girl so practical and independent was wasted in a royal household, the women decided; Bess was clearly cut out to be a good wife and mother in a poor household with a host of children. But Bess did not agree, though she did not say so. Even at six years old she had become something of an adept at not saying things, though she could not always keep it up, for she was also an adept at pert answers. And nothing could alter her quick and imperious temper, which had shown itself so masterfully before she was quite three years old that her distracted governess had written long garrulous letters to the Lords of the Council about the difficulty of controlling 'my lady's' princely demands for the same wines and meats that her grown-up companions were having at table. Bess's state had been far from princely then; her clothes were all outgrown and there were no new ones for her; she had been sent away into the country with no provision made for her, and her governess at her wits' end as to how to clothe and feed her.

Yet only a very short time before, her father had tossed her up in his arms, and crowds of gorgeous strangers had thronged round her, uttered ecstatic little cries at the sight of her, bowed down to her and pressed glittering toys into her hands.

There was a winter's evening when she was just two and a half years old (she always remembered it, though people said she could only have remembered hearing of it) when that enormous figure, not nearly as stout as now but seeming even taller, and dressed from top to toe in yellow satin like a monstrous giant toad, hoisted her up on to a vast padded shoulder, where she clutched at the white feather in his flat cap, and carried her round at that dizzy height, showing her off to everybody, shouting, 'Thank God the old harridan is dead! Here is your future Queen – Elizabeth!' And all the courtiers shouted back, and the dark crowds in the street below the window where he stood with her, in a terrifying exciting roar, 'God save the King! God save the Princess Elizabeth!'

'The old harridan' was her father's first wife and her half-sister Mary's mother, Queen Katherine of Aragon, that noble Spanish princess who had been hounded to death at last by her husband's six-year persecution. That was at the end of January, and by the following May Bess's mother too was dead, her head cut off by her father's orders; and by the next morning he was wedded to Jane Seymour.

Bess did not know that at the time, only that she went away into the country, that there were no more crowds nor shouting for her, that her clothes grew shabby and uncomfortably small for her, and no one was in the least excited or pleased to see her.

> 'Here we go up, up, up,
> Here we go down, down, down,'

so the children sang, playing on the see-saw on the village green, but she was not allowed to play with them either. The time of neglect and poverty passed; she went up again, though never to the dizzying height of her first two and a half years; she went back to Court, where, however, a new baby, a tiny boy, was now the centre of all the swaying, bowing crowds, carried aloft on that towering shoulder.

It was he now whom the giant King would dandle and toss in his arms by the hour together, and stand at a window showing him to the crowds below; and their roars would surge up in rugged waves of sound, 'God save King Hal!' 'God save the Prince!' 'Long live Prince Edward!'

The baby's mother, Jane Seymour, was not there. She had died in giving birth to him, – 'my poor little Jane,' the King said occasionally with a sob.

He did not seem to like Bess now, he was odd and uncomfortable with her; sometimes she would catch him looking at her with a strange intent gaze, and then when she looked back he would turn away and talk to someone else. And he never again called her Elizabeth, but only Young Bess, which should have sounded more affectionate, but did not. Long afterwards she guessed that he had ceased to feel her worthy of the name, for he had bestowed it on her in memory of his mother, that gracious and beloved princess, last of the royal Plantagenets, who had given him his most legitimate claim to the throne.

But at the time Bess only knew that she must be very good and quiet and not thrust herself forward. Her half-sister Mary, a grown-up woman, said: 'It is your turn now to learn to be silent, as I have done.'

She said it on a note of acid triumph, for she had been forced to agree to the Act of Parliament that declared her mother's marriage illegal and herself illegitimate, forced to acknowledge this baby sister's prior right to the throne over herself, to let her take public precedence to her everywhere, and even to serve as maid-of-honour to her. That had been when Elizabeth was 'up, up, up'; now she too had been bastardized and was 'down, down, down,' where Mary had been for many years now. She looked cowed and dull. She was a good woman and did not seek to revenge herself on her small half-sister for the agonies and humiliations she had had to suffer on her behalf; instead she tried hard to be kind to her, but Bess knew she did not like her.

The King talked about finding a new mother for his poor motherless children, and then something opened in Mary's dull face: in one instant it had shut again, but in that instant Bess felt she had seen into hell.

It was not so easy a task by now to find a new Queen for England. The foreign princesses were growing wary. A Danish one said that if she had two heads she would be delighted to lay one at the English King's disposal; a French one, tall and stately, of the House of Guise, was told that Henry wished for her as he was so big himself, he needed a big wife; and she replied, 'Ah, but my neck is small.' And Mary of Guise had the effrontery to marry his nephew instead, that young whippersnapper King James V of Scotland. Then Tom Cromwell, the 'best of his servants,' engineered a German Protestant alliance and a marriage with the Bavarian princess, Anne of Cleves, whose portrait was very pretty, but not, Bess decided, as quick and chic and merry-looking as that of her own mother, Anne.

But when the new bride arrived, and all the Court went to meet her with the King (Bess, now six years old, by the side of her twenty-five-year-old sister, Mary), then everybody saw with a shock that the bride was not pretty at all. Fat 'Crum' was bustling about with a staff in his hand, sweating with energy and anxiety – 'just like a post boy,' Tom Seymour whispered wickedly, though Bess thought him much more like a panting ox. He acted as interpreter between the King and the large raw-boned German princess, who beamed effusively and said 'Ya, Ya,' for she was as stupid as she was plain, she could speak no language but her own, to the shocked amazement of Bess, who had never heard of a princess who couldn't speak at least six languages including Greek and Latin. Crum remarked to the King that she looked 'very queenly,' but he did it timidly, 'as though he were offering a coin to an elephant,' said Tom Seymour.

The elephant rejected it; he shot one red glance at the best of his servants and trumpeted two words: 'What remedy?' In six months he had found it; annulled his marriage with Anne, and beheaded Cromwell.

Elizabeth heard of it a month before her seventh birthday, while she was stitching at the shirt for her baby brother. She knew by now that this ox, who could pounce like a tiger, had got her mother beheaded, after making her Queen; and now he was beheaded himself. 'Here we go down, down down.'

Anne of Cleves lived on in England; she said she would 'always be a sister' to Henry, she was kind and friendly to his daughters, and she did not even mind (perhaps she was relieved) when he married Cat Howard, an enchanting creature not quite eighteen.

Mary was cold and haughty to Cat, a flighty girl, seven years younger than herself, who had scrambled up to womanhood in the careless modern fashion among a host of boys and girls as wild and reckless as herself. She said Cat was of inferior rank and not at all fitted to be their father's wife. In her scorn of Cat, Bess could see what this daughter of the Spanish kings had felt for Bess's mother, Nan Bullen, whose family had lately started to spell their name Boleyn to make it sound grander. They were relations of the Howards – but of far less noble stock, and Nan was the granddaughter of a mercer and Lord Mayor of London, as Mary once blurted out to the child when provoked by her to one of her hysterical rages.

It was perhaps the worst shock to her self-esteem that Bess had received in her childhood. There was no disgrace in having some of your family executed; it was a thing that might happen to anybody, and frequently did; and under the Tudors, the more noble the family, the more likely it was to happen. But a mercer, a Lord Mayor! She flung an inkpot at Mary, called her a liar, and rushed screaming with fury to her beloved governess, Mrs Ashley, who soothed her with reminders of her mother's Howard uncle, the great Duke of Norfolk, of one of the oldest families in the kingdom. But

Bess was not impressed; she thought her great-uncle Norfolk a vulgar old man who said very rude things, and she had heard that he was always ready to do the King's dirty work for him; this she imagined to be something to do with cleaning his horse or his boots when on an expedition together.

Mrs Ashley was worrying about something more important; Bess must be very careful never to quarrel with her half-sister, the Lady Mary, 'for one never knows – And she had good reason to hate your mother, Queen Anne, who was, God forgive her, very unkind to her and to her poor mother, Katherine of Aragon, – and *she* was a saint if ever there was one.'

Bess said mutinously, 'Well, I'd rather have a witch for my mother than a saint – and an Englishwoman than a Spaniard, – and anyway, why should Mary turn up her nose at Cat Howard?'

She adored the lovely warm impulsive creature, the Rose without a Thorn the King called her, who insisted on giving Bess the place of honour next herself, as she was her cousin. She brought gaiety into all their lives; she coaxed the King with such endearments as 'her little pig,' for he was growing very stout; but, determined to defy it, he rose at five or six and rode and went hunting and hawking with her every day and often all day, sometimes tiring out nine or ten horses in a single hunt. King François's sister, the fascinating Marguerite, kept asking flatteringly but tactlessly for his portrait, and he hoped to give Holbein a chance to show how young he'd grown in body as well as heart, – but alas he was still 'marvellously excessive in drinking and eating,' so people noticed; and also that he often held quite different opinions in the morning from those he held after dinner.

And the months went on passing and Cat gave no sign of bearing a child.

But on the whole he was in a sunny humour, so much so that he quite forgot his awkwardness with Bess and treated her once again as his especial favourite, so that the child came under his wayward, extraordinary spell, and saw how it worked on others; they might be baffled, thwarted, exasperated, even terrified or loathing, but, when he chose, they could not resist him. Nor could Bess. She tingled with triumph when he laughed at her bright answers and quoted them to the Court as remarkable specimens of childish wit. It was a thrilling sport, this answering back; she knew that she must go about it as warily as if 'offering a coin to an elephant,' for she could never be sure if the offer would be accepted with a slap of his thigh that sounded as though he were thumping a cushion, and a delighted roar that he would write and tell that to old Foxnose François himself, by God so he would! or else a sudden terrifying knitting of those infantile eyebrows, a pursing of the little slit of a mouth, a narrow glance like the thrust of a stiletto, and the sharp command to get out of his presence for an impudent little bastard. 'By God you go too far!'

There came a dreadful day when she went so far that she never came back for a whole year, and never knew what she had said to put him in such a lasting rage. But that was after he had become indifferent again, sunk in gloom and fat, his cheeks grey and flabby, and had a horrible tendency to burst into tears in front of everybody, – for it was after he had had Cat Howard beheaded for adultery.

'It is no more the time to dance,' they told Cat when they came to arrest her, and sent away her musicians. They took her to the Tower, the royal palace, fortress, prison, where she had slept before her Coronation, as her cousin Nan Bullen had slept before hers; but this time she went in by the Traitors' Water Gate, as Nan Bullen had done the second time she went there, and like Cat, left it only for the block.

'It won't be hard to find a nickname for me,' Nan had giggled with desperate gallantry; 'I shall be called Anne Sans-Tête!' and she had put her hands round her long slender throat and promised the executioner an easy task. 'They might make ballads of me now,' she said, 'but there is no one left to make them now they've killed my brother. Oh yes, there is my cousin Tom Wyatt – but he is in the Tower too.' There had been a vein of wild poetry in Nan herself, a living echo to the art of her brother and cousin.

But the people did not make ballads of her, they did not like her enough. Their legends of her were not pretty; they said she had tried to poison the Princess Mary; that she had a rudimentary sixth finger on her left hand, though so tiny that few ever noticed, and that it was a teat to suckle her devil's imps who told her how to bewitch the King. In any case, she was an upstart who had worked and schemed and waited for six years to oust the Good Queen Katherine of Aragon and her daughter Mary, the true heir to the throne; she had been hard and sharp and tyrannized over everyone, even the King; had loved to crack her whip at him and show her power; she had met him at a dance, and a pretty dance she had led him ever since – so they said when, for her too, it was no more the time to dance.

She had been unpopular, and that was the real reason she died; and her daughter knew this by the time her gay, kind-hearted cousin Cat Howard met the same fate, while still in her teens.

Bess was eight when this happened; nine when she offended her father and was sent away from Court; ten when she returned again at the entreaty of yet another stepmother, another Queen Cat, no wild heedless kitten this time, but her motherly Pussy-Cat Purr, as Bess instantly called her.

Would this one stay? Bess passionately hoped so. She had stayed two whole years by now, a record in the child's experience. She never flirted with anyone else, she was wise and kind and tactful, but could anyone ever be tactful enough with the King? She had found that she herself could not; and Bess had a good opinion, and with reason, of her own tact. And Queen Catherine had given no sign of bearing him an heir, and everyone hoped for a baby Duke of York to follow the little Prince of Wales – 'in case.' It was the lack of direct male heirs to the throne that had torn and ruined the country with the Wars of the Roses in the last century. To secure the Succession, Bess knew this to be the one unswerving purpose behind her father's murderous philanderings.

She had noticed the sudden hush, the shiver of excited apprehension that seized the gay rollicking girls of the Court when the King's gaze fell on one of them a trifle longer and more weightily than it was wont. 'Was the King about to seek a new wife?' The whisper would run like wildfire through the Court, and following it in the minds of all, though unspoken, – how soon would yet another Queen be told that 'it was no more the time to dance'?

She watched her stepmother with a solicitude that was positively maternal; she was watching her so now, on the deck of the royal flagship, as they walked up and down in the wake of Great Harry. The men were talking of the danger of invasion – a nice safe subject, she considered; one could hardly go wrong over that. In fact, it put all the men in a good humour, as usual. Her magnificent Howard cousin, the young Earl of Surrey, the soldier-poet, blazing in scarlet from head to foot, was saying in his cool insolent drawl that all the men between sixteen and sixty had been called up along the coasts, and could be called out at an hour's notice; his father, the Duke of Norfolk, that lean old wolf, was snapping his jaws in a hungry grin as he told how all his stout fellows of Norfolk had sent a deputation to him begging him that 'if the French come, for God's sake bring us between the sea and them that we may fight them before they get back to their ships.' God's body, that was the spirit!

Tom Seymour said it was sheer folly of the French to bring galleys from Marseilles, and barges – they would all be boarded as easily as jumping off a log. At which Edward Seymour drily remarked that they had three hundred tall ships as well.

Tom flung back his head and shouted with laughter, 'D'you think I'd forgotten their tall ships? They'd no reason to forget ours when I sailed slap through their blockade and revictualled our garrison at Boulogne under their noses.'

'Braggart!' muttered Edward, and for an instant the two brothers looked daggers at each other; but just then the King's voice boomed out like a foghorn:

'We whipped them by land and sea last year, and by God we'll do it again.'

Certainly an invasion was the best thing to talk about. And next to that, the Scots. The King had beaten them last year too. But the Scots were not quite so good, for they would not stay beaten. He (or rather Norfolk) had smashed their whole nation years ago at Flodden, where his brother-in-law, King James IV, had got killed together with most of his nobles; he had smashed them again about a couple of years ago at Solway Moss when his nephew, young King James V, died of a broken heart from his defeat; and since then Edward Seymour, Earl of Hertford, had destroyed Melrose Abbey and Dryburgh, and 7 monasteries, 5 market towns, 243 villages, 13 mills and 3 hospitals in one district alone. But still the unspeakable villains would not stay smashed; though ruled only by James's French widow, Mary of Guise, that very same tall lady who had had the effrontery to refuse King Henry's offer of marriage with an unseemly joke about the smallness of her neck, and to prefer his red-headed rascal of a nephew to himself. She was now refusing his offers of marriage for her infant daughter Mary to his little son Edward, or rather (for she would have agreed to the marriage without his conditions) she was refusing to send her baby away from her to be brought up at the English Court under the charge of her great-uncle who had caused the death of that baby's father and grandfather; such ungrateful, unnatural, unwomanly behaviour made Henry purple with rage every time he issued orders to his armies to raze Edinburgh and all the Border cities to the ground, exterminate every man, woman and child in them, and above all seize the person of the infant Queen of Scots. But she had not yet been caught, although she had had to be hurried away into lonely mountain fastnesses to escape. It was early to begin adventure, very early to be a queen, almost as soon as she was born. Elizabeth felt a thrill of envy for the tiny mountain princess whose mother was guarding her so indomitably.

Here came the gentle Archbishop Cranmer, his heavy sagging cheeks more yellow even than usual, for he had just been seasick. Bess detested his soft voice and nervous eyes, even as her mother had done. He had helped Nan Bullen to the Crown, but done nothing to hinder her from the block; his 'former good opinion of her prompted him to think her innocent,' so he wrote to the King; but then 'his knowledge of the King's prudence and justice induced him to think her guilty.' Such balanced casuistry had echoed down the years, even to Nan's little daughter.

Henry flung out a great wave of charm at the Archbishop's

approach, and a padded arm like a silken bolster round his shoulder, sweeping him in his stride ahead of the others.

'Aha, my chaplain, I've news for you. I know now who is the greatest heretic in Kent!'

The Archbishop's eyes seemed to bolt out of his head like a startled rabbit's. For an instant Bess thought he was going to be sick again, on the royal sleeve. And no wonder, for Henry, watching him sideways with some amusement out of the poached eyes set flat on his cheeks, was twitting him with his own words; had he, or had he not, burst out to his Chapter at Canterbury, 'You will not leave your old Mumpsimuses, but I'll make you repent it!'

'Old Mumpsimuses,' the King pointed out, was not the way an archbishop ought to refer to the ancient holy forms of religion; it was small wonder that the Chapter had retaliated by sending out an accusation of heresy against him and his chaplains. And from the very sleeve that was now enfolding the victim's neck in the affectionate grip of a grizzly bear Henry produced the paper of the accusation, while in a jocular aside he reminded his friend that three heretics had lately been burned alive on Windsor Green: 'And what do you say to that, my old Mumpsimus?'

Cranmer had so much to say that the King quickly cut him short, and Norfolk seized his chance to cut in. He shared Bess's feelings about the Archbishop. Cat Howard had been Norfolk's niece as well as Nan Bullen, he had worked for her marriage to the King as hard as he knew. And then that sneaking Lutheran fellow, who had picked up a wife in Germany, as well as a lot of these poisonous new revolutionary notions, had gone and destroyed all his work by getting poor Cat beheaded, just as Nan had been, and the whole family had shared in the disgrace for a time.

'For my part,' he growled virtuously, 'I never read the Scriptures and never will. It was merry in England before this new learning came up, but now every ploughboy thinks he's as good as the priest – and maybe he is, – seeing what some priests are!'

He glared at the Archbishop, who weakly averted his gaze. Henry, cocking an amused little gooseberry eye at Norfolk, called out, 'Paws off there! Down – good dog, down! You got your teeth into a Cardinal when you shogged off Wolsey must you worry an Archbishop too?'

'God's body, Your Majesty, I only meant that I wish every thing were just the same as it used to be in the good old days. New ideas indeed!' His glare had swivelled round on to Edward Seymour, who was of the advanced party and eager for reform in politics as well as religion. 'New ideas – and a brand-new peer to lead 'em! All this fine talk of the rights of the people – rank revolution, that's all it amounts to,' he snarled at Seymour, but the King clapped a hand on his shoulder.

'No more of that now, or you'll be giving us one of your Council speeches till we all get lost in your thirdlys and fourthlys.' He turned to his anxiously waiting Archbishop, but only to deal him some heavyhanded chaff about his wife. Was it true that Cranmer had had her smuggled from Germany into England in a packing-case which some careless porter had placed upside down, so that she had had to scream to be rescued? 'There's a fine tale of a wife tails up! Well, well, I owe a couple or so of my wives to your services, so no doubt you think I should wink at yours, but it's a big wink that will cover an archbishop's wife boarded up in a box. Old Wolsey had as fine a mistress as money could buy, but that was all correct and above-board – not under the boards!'

Cranmer became incoherent in his denials and protestations; he would not dream of evading the law against married clergy, he had never seen his wife since he came to England to be Archbishop – at least, not, not—

'Not in a packing-case, hey? Or did you send her packing?'

Like some huge cat with a shivering mouse, he played with the terrified little man, enjoying his discomfiture and the roars of laughter from Norfolk and the others. Just as Cranmer was certain that the blow would fall on him both for heresy and illegal matrimony, Henry suddenly returned to the former charge and rumbled out, 'That little matter of your Chapter's complaints is easily handled. I'll appoint a commission to examine the charges – and put you at the head of it! *And* help you with the answers. I've not forgotten my theology. That will cook their goose for them. So whichever goose roasts, it won't be you.'

His hearty friendliness made Cranmer almost blubber with thankfulness; it made his small daughter grow thoughtful. The Queen was still with the two men, though Henry had outstripped the rest of the company, but he had beckoned her on, so he must wish her to hear this conversation. Bess they did not notice; she was, indeed, at some distance and looking out to sea as though absorbed in the other ships, but her sharp ears had been listening acutely. Why was her father so kind to old Mumpsimus? (Yes, that was the perfect name for him and his meek bag face – a mouse with the mumps!) Henry had, as it happened, a warm and affectionate respect for Cranmer's disinterested love of learning and his lack of ambition, but as these qualities did not appeal to Bess, she discounted them. And the King had been angry enough, so she had heard, when he had first received the accusation of his Archbishop's toying with heresy. But then someone had said Cranmer was too useful for the King to lose him. How useful?

Was it because he had already got rid of three wives out of six for the King, and might be required to get rid of a fourth? The notion came to her on a sudden heartstop of dismay as she realized what prompted it, for she could hear her father's and stepmother's voices – arguing! How could the Queen be such a goose? 'Whichever goose roasts' – The King always said he liked nothing so well as a good theological argument; that he liked women to be intelligent, – but surely anyone would know that he only liked an argument when he got the better of it; and however intelligent a woman might be, she must be less so than himself. Queen Catherine was arguing the case for translating the Bible into English; Henry was shouting that, in consequence, 'that precious jewel, the Word of God, was being disputed, sung, and jangled in every alehouse and tavern,' which showed how he was getting the worst of it, for he was only quoting from his last speech in Parliament, since he could not think of a fresher answer.

Catherine evidently began to get some sense of her danger,

for without any crude change of subject she adroitly introduced some flattery on the great and beneficial changes Henry had made in England's religion. But that wouldn't do; couldn't she see that the King had never wanted to introduce any changes in religion, that he was as ardent and conservative a Papist as anybody – with this one exception, that he alone was to be Pope.

And behind all Bess's anxiety was the terrifying fact that the Queen's friend, Lady Anne Askew, had been arrested for denouncing the Mass, and had been tortured in the Tower more than once. Was it an attempt to make her implicate the Queen? Whatever happened, Catherine must not plead the cause of her friend now, – let her be tortured, racked, burned, but if the name of Anne Askew were mentioned now, it would be the death-knell of Catherine Parr.

It didn't look as though Catherine would get the chance to mention it, for Henry was doing all the talking now, watching her out of the corner of a hot, intemperate eye while he threw out some ominous chaff: 'So you've become a learned doctor, have you, Kate? You're here to instruct us, we take it, not to be instructed or directed by us?'

Kate quickly protested, but, unheeding, he began to roll his great head and mutter, 'That's a pretty business when women turn clerics; a fine comfort for me in my old age, to be taught by my wife!'

It was going to happen – it was happening now – nothing could stop it. Bess shut her lips tight to keep from screaming aloud. Could nothing else happen to prevent it? Why couldn't the French sail up now and attack? More fervently than any stout fellow of Norfolk, she prayed silently for a sight of their foes. 'Oh God, let them come and invade England now, quick!'

'Anne Askew!' The fatal name had been spoken, it crashed on the air like the crack of thunder. But it was not the Queen who had uttered it; it was the King, accusing her of having sent the condemned woman money and promises of help, of having received heretical books from her in times past, of – would the next word be – 'Treason!'?

Bess opened her lips and screamed.

They all turned towards her, hurried towards her, cried out

what was the matter. Now she would have to find an answer.
Had she twisted her foot? seen a mermaid or a sea-serpent?
She would only be scolded and sent below, and the King's
rage increased by so momentary an interruption. She
screamed again, on a high note of childish excitement, and
pointed : 'The French! Their ships – far out to sea – coming
up like clouds!'

So intense was the conviction in her voice that for an instant they believed her. Then, as no confirmation came from
the crow's nest, they said she must have imagined it and
taken the white clouds on the horizon for the sails of the
French fleet. Her best retreat would be to look childishly
stupid and sulky, admit she had been frightened, perhaps even
shed a few tears. But she decided to brazen it out. 'I *did* see
the ships – for a moment. They've disappeared now. Perhaps they saw us and sailed away.'

Henry's infantile eyebrows puckered in his vast face. His
just anger had been interrupted by this false alarm, and now
surged back, redoubled. 'The girl's lying!' he roared; 'the
French have been reported miles away. She could never have
seen them.'

He looked at his daughter and saw her mother's face, the
big forehead, the clever bright eyes, the silly little rosebud
of a mouth that had smiled so sweetly at him – and at others.
'Take the little bastard away!' he shouted.

But at that moment Elizabeth had one of those stupendous
strokes of luck that were enough to accuse her as well as her
mother of witchcraft.

A shout came ringing over the sea and was echoed by another. The alarm had been raised in good earnest, the French
fleet sighted, sailing straight towards Portsmouth.

Chapter Two

ELIZABETH WAS disappointed in her first invasion. She had thought they would stay on the flagship, that she would have a first-hand experience of a sea-fight, that somehow she would manage to dress up as a sailor and save Tom Seymour's life. Then for once he would take her seriously, he would take her hand, and look deep into her eyes and say – what *would* he say?

It didn't matter, for it didn't happen, none of it happened.

That glittering July sea and the proud ships floating over it all vanished like sea-spray as far as the royal family party were concerned; in no time they all bustled off the flagship and on to a very fast pinnace and made for the shore and then inland. It was not Bess's idea of the way to take an invasion. She had seen her father ride off to the French wars last year, in a suit of armour that two slight young men could easily have got into together, and hoisted on to an enormous dapple-grey Dutch stallion, seventeen hands high, with white feathered hoofs and flowing white mane and a little angry red eye, not unlike his rider's. They had needed no army behind them, she had thought, to strike terror into the foe.

But now – was this the way he had fought when he got there? She was told that Kings and Queens must not adventure their persons like common soldiers and sailors. She was not convinced. She told Tom Seymour with a sniff that the flagship had better be re-christened 'The Great Hurry'!

He scrutinized her narrowly. 'How could you, on deck, have seen the French fleet before any lookout in the crow's nest had seen it?'

'I don't know. My eyes are better than theirs, I suppose.'

'Even your bright eyes couldn't see them before they came up over the edge of the horizon. Haven't your tutors taught you that the world is round?'

'Then they must be wrong, and the world is flat.'

'So that's flat. You'd shape the whole world differently to suit yourself!'

'Why not? My father does.'

'You're his daughter, no doubt about that!' he chuckled.

'I'd have stayed and seen the fight,' said Bess. 'I'd not have let the French land on the Isle of Wight.'

But the French accomplished nothing by that; they soon had to take to their ships again, and after a short engagement were driven back out to sea. The fortune-tellers were now saying they had known all along that this was not the invasion England had to fear; her real danger, worse than any she had faced since the Normans landed, would not come for more than forty years, in the summer when there would be four noughts in the date, for an 8 is a double nought, one on top of the other, so the year '88 would be quadruply unlucky. Bess asked why the unlucky noughts shouldn't be for the invaders; 'anyway it's naught to me,' she said, for who cared what would happen more than forty years hence, when she would be an old woman, if indeed she could bear to live as long as then? And anyway there could be small danger from foreign ships since the great French Armada had such poor success; everyone was boasting of England's security behind her sea-walls; a blunt fellow even said as much to the Emperor Charles V in Spain, and his son, that cold, formal youth, Prince Philip.

'Young Cheese-face,' Henry still persisted in calling the Emperor, the nephew of his first wife, ever since Charles's visit to England, to be betrothed to the Princess Mary, then a pretty child of six, who had not shared her father's view of her prospective bridegroom's long pale face and wedge-shaped chin, very like a slab of cheese. She had given an ardent hero-worship to her cousin, the young monarch on whose lands, her mother had told her, the sun never set; and who, still more important, was a very devout Christian. But the betrothal came to nothing; all that was over twenty years ago, and now the Emperor Charles was mobilizing against the Protestant princes in his Empire, so that, in spite of his confidence in England's splendid isolation, Henry was finding orthodoxy advisable, and the Queen's broadmindedness untimely. (Besides, she had not borne him an heir. 'Impossible!

she is so virtuous!' said the wags.) So Anne Askew was burned for denouncing the Mass; though the following month Henry tried to get the King of France to join with him in abolishing it. Bess found politics difficult to understand. Anyway, they were now at peace with France, and the King spoke so beautifully on charity and concord to his Parliament that they all wept.

But Parliamentarians' tears, and the King's charity and concord, did not lessen Bess's anxiety one jot, and there came a moment in the garden when the confirmation of it stared her in the face, stared up at her from the path, a sickly white paper scrawled with black writing which told her at one glance that the King had finally given over his faithfully devoted wife to the power of the beast. It was an indictment of Catherine Parr, and Henry had set his name to it.

No sooner had Bess seen it than the Chancellor Wriothesley, who had been Chancellor Cromwell's secretary and helped work his fall, came hurrying back between the clipped yew hedges.

'A paper!' he panted, 'a scrap of paper – has Your Highness seen it?'

Bess shook her head, lifting wide blue eyes to his, and pointing at what she had apparently all this time been staring – a butterfly that had perched on her bright shoe, mistaking it for a flower.

'Oh, you have disturbed him!' she exclaimed reproachfully as it flew away. 'A paper, did you say? Is it important?'

Mr Wriothesley had already stuffed it into his sleeve, violently cursing the tailors who could not invent any safer receptacle in men's clothes, while women went hung round with pockets.

He departed as fast as, or rather faster than courtesy permitted; a beast padding away in his soft broad velvet slippers, and the little slits of satin over the toes like claws in the sunlight, Bess thought, standing there stock still until he disappeared.

The garden was all still round her, cut into sunlight and sharp shadows, and the bees hummed loud, or was it the blood throbbing in her ears?

Then, with a glance to right and left of her, she picked up her skirts and ran, ran into the Palace to her stepmother and gasped out what she had seen.

Catherine Parr sat stunned; she neither moved nor spoke nor wept. Bess despaired. No silent grief would move the King. At last, through blue lips, Catherine moaned, 'What shall I do? What shall I do?'

Bess told her.

'You must cry, cry, cry, and loud; so that he'll hear, so that he can't hear anything else. Do it in the room next his. Shriek. Be hysterical, mad. Go on for hours and hours and hours.'

Catherine did. A clamour of weeping and howling next door disturbed the King; he sent to stop it, but it went on; he sent to ask the reason for it, and was told the Queen was distressed because she feared she had displeased him.

That brought him himself; he told her he could not bear her to cry, which was true, especially after three hours. But he spoke kindly; he got her to stop; then, after a little more comforting, he went on with their last theological argument. But the mouse avoided the cat's paw this time; his wife would not discuss religion; she referred it and all other questions to his omnipotent wisdom; if she had ever seemed to do otherwise, it had only been to pass the time and take his mind off his bad leg.

'Then, sweetheart, we are perfect friends again!' said Henry; and the Chancellor was sent packing with a flood of abuse when he called about the Queen's arrest. There was no arrest. The crisis had passed, and Henry yawned, when he did not swear at his bad leg. Perfect friendship is not as stimulating as discussion.

Life was growing dull and depressing. Old enemies were dying, and that is often worse than the death of old friends. Martin Luther died, far away in Germany. When Henry was a brilliant young man he had written a theological treatise confuting Luther's heresies, and the low fellow had replied with his usual bad taste. 'Squire Harry wishes to be God,' wrote the miner's son, 'and do what he pleases.'

The Pope, on the other hand, had shown his appreciation by giving Henry his title 'Defender of the Faith': 'F.D.' He thought of putting it on all the coins of his realm. Now there was no one to confute – except the Pope, whose latest title for him was the 'Son of Perdition and Satan.'

Worse even than Luther's death, they said François I of France was dying. Ever since he could remember, Henry had been an envious rival, a frequent foe, an occasional boon companion of Foxnose François. It was impossible to imagine life without this peppery stimulus.

Worse still, François was three years younger than Henry, was as tall and strong, had lived as well (though it was doubtful whether he or any other man had ever eaten as much), and yet here he was, petering out, surely long before his appointed span of years, like a feeble old man, a premature death's-head warning at the feast of life. For if life were not still a feast, what was it? Luther was dead, François might be dying, and he wasn't feeling very well himself; but thank God there was still good eating and drinking, and not all his doctors could keep him from it, especially when it came to the Christmas and Twelfth Night feasts.

All the Royal Family were together for these festivals, and most of the cousins too, with one notable and, to Henry, infuriating omission. The Queen of Scots, four years old this December, was still absent from the hospitable board of her great-uncle who had offered his only son in betrothal to this fatherless brat, Queen of such a beggarly kingdom that his Ambassador had nearly burst out laughing at the poverty of the baby's coronation in Stirling.

But there was one bit of news from Scotland that had put Henry in high good humour; the new Scots leaders of the Reformed Religion had at last succeeded in murdering the great Cardinal Beton, the right-hand man of the French Queen-Dowager, the Regent of Scotland. Henry had been giving advance payment for this work for years; now at last, in his palace of Greenwich just before Christmas, he heard from the murderers' own lips how they had stabbed the enemy of Christ as he sat in his chair, and hung his body over the wall of his castle at St Andrews.

Henry, as he made his final payments, reflected that it had been well worth the money. Much as he disliked these 'ministers of the true religion,' they would work for Scotland's alliance with England against the age-old Franco-Scottish alliance favoured by Cardinal Beton and his Regent of Scotland, that damned obstinate, suspicious-minded Frenchwoman who would not entrust her little daughter to his tender avuncular care.

Edward, now nine years old, a pretty boy with smooth flaxen hair, did not want to be betrothed to a baby. He would rather, if he had to have a cousin, marry the Lady Jane Grey, a year older than himself, though much smaller, who often helped him with his lessons. But Jane in her turn thought him more suited to one of her little sisters. She was undergoing a rather solemn adoration for Elizabeth, so much older, by three years, than herself, and wearing her cleverness with so gay and insouciant an air.

Jane was King Henry's great-niece, standing in the same relationship to him as the baby Queen of Scots. For Henry had had two sisters, the Tudor Roses they were called when in the splendour of their sumptuous white and red, their blue eyes and golden hair. The elder, the Princess Margaret, had married that strange, beautiful tortured creature, James IV of Scotland, and made a few gallant efforts, but only briefly, to live up to it. When he was killed on Flodden Field, her son, James V, was a year old; when he in his turn died broken-hearted from defeat by the English, his daughter Mary had become Queen of Scots at five days old.

Henry had been much fonder of his younger sister, Mary Rose, who was lovelier and merrier than Margaret, and did not grow too fat like her; nor did she plague him with long tearful letters and demands for money. For all that, he had made Mary Rose, at eighteen, marry the invalid old French King Louis XII instead of the man of her choice. But Mary had the Tudor way of getting what she wanted; in a few months she had danced the adoring old Frenchman into his grave, avoided the proposals of his young successor, François I, and married her beefy English duke.

Her granddaughter Jane Grey had inherited none of the glowing colours and bouncing vitality of the two Tudor Roses; she was tiny and pale, with some fair freckles on her straight little nose, which her mother unavailingly scrubbed with all sorts of concoctions, but they remained, with something of Jane's own persistency. Her eyes and forehead gave promise of a certain grave beauty, and beneath it an unexpected force of character.

Her younger sisters, Catherine and Mary, were so small that their mother was afraid they might be dwarfs.

Taking Elizabeth's hand before the banquet, Jane whispered as demurely as if she was saying grace, that thank God her parents were away, for it was hell when they were at home. Many children might think it dashing and modern to refer to their parents' company as hell; not so Jane, that best of all good little girls. Elizabeth was as startled as if a mouse had sworn. 'The creep-mice' was her name for the three little Grey cousins; could this one be a shrew-mouse? She looked down at the meek little face under its smoothly parted hair, and saw it set and tense.

'Your mother is very strict, isn't she?' Bess whispered back sympathetically.

'She never stops scolding, pinching, and slapping me. However hard I work, it makes no odds. You are lucky to have only a stepmother.'

And a murderously inclined father? Yes, on the whole Bess thought she was, since he forgot about her for long spaces together, whereas Jane's mother never forgot her eldest daughter; in fact, the Countess of Suffolk never stopped thinking; it was a mistake. The Grey mare, Tom Seymour called her, and said she stood two hands higher than her little weak mule of a husband, – also broader, for she had the Tudor tendency to fat, and hunted like fury to escape it, and not, like her uncle, King Henry, for love of the sport. But nothing that she did would be for its own sake. She rode ambition harder than any horse, and had great plans for Jane, that was evident. No doubt she had determined to marry Jane to Edward and make her Queen of England, thought Bess with a sharp twinge of exasperation that she had not been born a boy, and then she would be King before Edward or Mary, who had been put back into the Succession, after Edward, a year ago; and then, too, her mother would not have been beheaded, 'and *she* would not have slapped and pinched me, especially if I had been a boy.'

Aloud, she told the younger child to come and look at the

Christmas present Mary had given her – five yards of yellow satin to make a skirt, and Mary was keeping it to have it made up; 'it cost seven and sixpence a yard,' said Bess proudly, and then winced at the sound of her own words; would Jane recognize in them the tang of the Bullens' draper grandfather?

But Jane was far too nice a little girl to do anything of the sort; she smiled with unenvious pleasure, while her younger sister Catherine, hugging a doll almost as big as herself that Mary had given her, uttered rapturous squeaks at sight of the shining stuff.

But the person it gave most pleasure to was Mary as she showed it off to the children; she loved children, and fine clothes, and she loved giving presents; nearly all her allowance went in these three things. Her room was strewn with patterns of glowing carnation silk and blue and green brocades for yet more dresses, and a roll of some spangled Eastern stuff to which she had already treated herself, and a dozen pairs of fine Spanish gloves. 'When *will* she wear them all?' Bess wondered, and wondered more that at thirty years old a woman should care what she wore.

'I have something pretty for you too,' Mary said to Jane, pleased that the little girl had evidently not expected anything for herself; and she stooped to put a gold and pearl necklace round the thin childish neck; 'it's a very little neck,' said Mary as she fastened the ponderous clasp, and Bess repressed a faint shudder, for wasn't that what her mother had said in the Tower, when she put her hands round her slender throat and laughed that the executioner would have an easy job?

She turned her attention hastily to the present moment; it was her chance now to feel envious, and she promptly took it. Why should Mary give anything so gorgeous, and worth far more than five yards of satin even at seven and six a yard, to their small cousin, who did not at all appreciate it? She was too young and too much of a bookworm to care about clothes and jewels, and was even rather critical of Mary's doing so. She had said Mary overdressed; probably she had heard her mother say so, but anyway it was a foolish thing to say.

37

'Anything might happen,' Bess's governess had said, warning her to keep friends with Mary. But the 'anything' might be Jane marrying Edward and becoming Queen of England; in which case it was sensible and far-sighted of Mary to give her the necklace, so Bess finally excused her, – though indeed she could not believe in Mary being sensible and far-sighted.

But she forgave her even this lack when Mary paid up the forfeit Bess had won from her at 'Bonjour, Philippine' last week. A gold pomander ball with a tiny watch dial in it was a fascinating prize, as curious as it was magnificent. All Bess's careful respect to her elderly half-sister exploded at the sight of it, and she flung her arms round her neck.

'My ball, my golden ball! I will carry it always at my girdle and never be late. I could never have got anything half so beautiful for you if you had won. But you will win next time, won't you?'

'Oh no,' said Mary with a rather bitter little laugh, 'you will always win.'

There was a moment's uncomfortable pause. Why did Mary say these things? There was no answer one could make to them.

But Queen Catherine, looking in to tell them to come and play Blind Man's Buff, made everything seem happy and smiling again, as her dear Pussy-Cat Purr always did. She discussed Mary's patterns and advised the goose-turd green rather than the brilliant new colour, popinjay blue, that Mary hankered after; 'the goose-turd would be far more becoming to your delicate fair skin,' she said tactfully, and they all giggled when Mary wrinkled up her round button of a nose and objected that it had a stinking name!

Catherine took her arm as they left her room and chaffed her about all those gloves. Had the King of Poland sent them? He was the latest suitor for Mary's hand; King Henry was encouraging him, and the Queen was really hopeful.

But not Mary. There had been too many suitors ever since her early childhood: the Emperor Charles; James V of Scotland; François I, who had gallantly preferred her to the Princess of Portugal 'with all her father's spices'; even her own half-brother, the illegitimate Duke of Richmond, suggested by the 'advanced' Pope Clement as a means of securing the Succession – but found Henry less broad-minded. And now there was the danger that a foreign Papist husband would press her claim as the Papist heir to England: but still her father used her as bait. 'A bride in the hand is worth two in the bed,' he said.

'As long as he lives,' she broke out, 'I shall be only the Lady Mary, the most unhappy lady in the world.'

She burst into tears, dragged her arm away from her stepmother's, ran back into her room and slammed the door.

'Poor woman!' said the Queen, and turned to Jane and her small sister Catherine, who were looking profoundly shocked. 'I pray you will never know such unhappiness as your cousin's,' she said. Something told her that it was no use saying anything of the sort to Bess, whose little pointed face had shut itself up in an inscrutable expression. 'Come,' she cried gaily, 'we mustn't miss the Blind Man's Buff. The Lady Mary will join us at the banquet.'

The Blind Man's Buff had already begun, and Tom Seymour was Blind Man. Staggering and groping absurdly, his black sleeveless coat, lined with cloth of gold, swinging in a wild circular movement from his shoulders, he swooped and swirled and spun round on his heel, round and round like a gorgeous spinning-top, and the men thumped him on the back and then dodged away, and the girls pulled his coat and then fled shrieking as he darted on them. Bess flung herself into the game, plucked at his sleeve, then, more daring, pinched his hand and ran away, but he was after her; so directly that he must be cheating; she nearly called 'A Cheat! A Cheat!', but why should she? She wanted him to catch her, and in spite of her dodging he did. Now he had to guess who it was in three guesses; his hands stroked her face, her hair, her thin bare shoulders; he was an unconscionable time in guessing.

'The Lady Mary,' he said, and there was a shout of laughter, but it was not too absurd, for Mary was short and Bess was already the same height. 'The Dowager Lady Dorset!' he said, to a louder yell of laughter, for the Dowager was past seventy. He must make very sure now or he would lose his guess. He pinched her ear, and gave a tweak to her nose. 'The Lady Elizabeth!' he said. 'I'd know that nose in a thousand.'

And he pulled off his bandage and tied it round her eyes while she said low, 'You are a poor Blind Man not to have caught anyone before.'

'Ah, but you see I didn't want to – before.'

Now it was her turn to clutch at the air, and swing round and run while hands pulled and touched her and voices called and tittered all round her.

The King sat in his great chair with the new seat embroidered by his daughter Mary for his Christmas present. The seats of Henry's chairs were apt to wear out; this one was so ample that the materials had cost Mary £20. He was spread over every stitch of that labour of filial love as he sat staring at all those glittering young figures prancing, dancing, running here and there. Usually he chuckled and cheered them on, but now he stared without seeming to notice them; only, once or twice, his poached eyes rolled round between the folds of his cheeks to follow the antics of the pretty young widow of his old friend Charles Brandon who ran with tittering shrieks to escape the blindfolded pursuer.

Would she be his seventh wife? It had been whispered. But there was another whisper that said the King would never have a seventh wife.

Now came the real importance of the evening, and his flat eyes opened with the gleam of a hawk's as a host of silver-clad pages carried in long tables and set them up on trestles in the hall; roasted Peacocks in their Pride with spread tails and swans re-invested in their snowy plumage were perched on them, waiting to be carved, and a few of the lately discovered turkeys brought to breed in Europe from the New World by a Spanish adventurer, Pedro Nino. 'But it will take more than Nine Pedros to make us English take to such poultry, tasteless as wood,' proclaimed King Henry, who, however, liked to show these novelties among the old Christmas dishes; mince pies in the form of the Christ Child's manger, boars' heads whose jellied eyes glared between their tusks as fierce as in life, shepherds and their flocks made of sweetmeats, and flagons of cock ale, a mixture of ale and sack in which an old cock braised with raisins and cloves had been steeped for nine days and the liquid then strained and matured.

Henry was hoisted by four men out of his chair and into one that fitted his stomach more accommodatingly against the table.

The buzz of talking and guzzling rose higher and higher as the wine circulated; when it had soared almost an octave, music took up the note, and the voices of choristers clear and piercing sweet. They sang a song that Henry himself had composed, words and music, when he had just come to the throne, a youth of eighteen, in the full flush of his cherubic beauty and athletic vigour, 'rejoicing as a giant to run his course.'

> *'Pastime with good company*
> *I love, and shall, until I die.'*

The little eyes blinked and closed; the vast padded figure in the chair sat like a dummy, apparently insensible, as he listened to what he once had sung. It was still true, he told himself, it always would be, – pastime – good company – none had had better. Odd that of all that brilliant company it was only those that he had enjoyed long ago who now stood out vividly in his mind, so much more vividly than all these scattering, chattering young apes he had just been watching, even that brisk young widow of Charles Brandon's – the half-Spanish girl – what was her name? He could not trouble himself to remember. The notes that he had once plucked out for the first time on his lute were teasing him with older memories.

Charles Brandon himself seemed nearer now than his widow, so did all those other vigorous young men with whom he had once played games and practical jokes and exchanged low stories with roars of laughter and thumps on the back: that young rascal Bryan whom he had nick-named the Vicar of Hell – Buckingham – Compton – Bullen – all dead; some, it is true, by his orders, but that didn't make it the less pitiful for him that there were now so few of the old faces round him, so few to remember him as he once had been.

41

There was that tough old ruffian Norfolk, of course, he'd always been there from the beginning of time, – where *was* Norfolk? He stared at all these new young upstart whippersnappers, seeking Norfolk's grizzled peaked beard and wiry hair, still black, somewhere among them. 'Where —' he began aloud, then checked; he had remembered, just in time, that Norfolk was in the Tower, awaiting sentence of death. He had already signed the death-warrant for Norfolk's son, the Earl of Surrey; in a day or two now the insolent conceited lad would lay on the block the handsome head that had dared compose verses against his King.

> *'Whose glutted cheeks sloth feeds so fat*
> *That scant their eyes be seen.'*

Was it possible young Surrey had intended that for his Dread Sovereign? But anything was possible with these Howards. Two nieces Norfolk had wedded to him, and both had to be beheaded. Now Cranmer and Ned Seymour said that he had conspired to put his son on the throne. He denied it, of course. 'When I deserve to be in the Tower,' he had exclaimed, 'Tottenham will turn French!'

Just like old Norfolk! Told George Lawson once that he was as good a knight as ever spurred a cow! Useful fellow, Norfolk, always ready to run and pull down whoever he was set on; – how he'd chased Wolsey from town, swearing he'd 'tear the butcher's cur with his teeth if he didn't shog off!' Pity you couldn't tell with the best wolf-hound when it mightn't turn and bite its master.

He took a deep drink, with a glance at his watchful physician. 'Let every man have his own doctor,' he wheezed. 'This is mine.'

This was a good song of his. Surrey, the lazy cub, was writing verse without rhyme and calling it a new invention, blank verse. Blank it was. His own was the real thing.

> *'Youth will needs have dalliance,'*

sang the choristers.

His youth had had all that youth ever dreamed of, once his dreary lonely boyhood had passed, and his stingy old

42

father in the shabby fur cloak had died, and young Prince Hal found himself one of the richest kings in Europe. He had turned everything to gold with his Midas touch; the foreign visitors could not believe their eyes, they had to finger all the tassels and cups and jugs and horses' bits, to be convinced that they were solid gold. He had been the most splendidly dressed king in Europe. What feasting there had been, unequalled by Cleopatra or Caligula, the ambassadors said; what spiced game and venison cooked in sour cream, what flowing of fulsome wines.

It was the same now, but it had tasted better then, after his father's diet of porridge and small beer; and with the zest of youth, an appetite as voracious for fun as for food, that pie he had carved, full of live frogs that leaped out over the table and floor, making the girls scream and jump on the benches, lifting their skirts above their knees – what a roar of laughter from him and all the other young fellows had volleyed and tumbled round the hall, echoing back to him now after all these years.

The lids of those lowered eyes just lifted; the grey lips moved. 'Another cup of wine,' they mumbled.

'Every man hath his free will,'

sang the choristers from Henry's early song.

What masquerades there had been then, what pranks and dressing-up as Muscovites or Saracen robbers, surprising the Queen and her ladies into delicious alarm and then laughter! What dancing, he himself leaping higher than any, and long, long into the night, and that after he had played a hard game of tennis, wrestled in bout after bout, run races and leaped with the long pole, or been in the saddle all day riding at the gallop after hounds, riding in the lists and unhorsing all his opponents. There was no one could beat 'Sir Loyal Heart', the name he always took in those tournaments of his youth when he cantered up on his great war-horse with his wife's Spanish colours on his sleeve in defiance of the fashion (for a knight should wear some other lady's), into the pavilion that was all spangled with gold Tudor roses and the pomegranates of Aragon, and H.K. intertwined.

43

H.K. everywhere for Henry and Katherine.

'As the holly groweth green and never changeth hue,
So I am – ever have been – unto my lady true.

For whoso loveth should love but one,
Change whoso will, I will be none.'

That was another song of his, but he never cared to hear
it sung after the 'H.K.' was all changed everywhere to 'H.A.'
for Henry and Anne. 'HA HA!' shouted the rude Cockney
boys, and they were right – the common people always were
in the long run – right to mock and distrust that accursed
whore who bewitched Sir Loyal Heart and led him into
captivity, unrewarded for six long years. What torture of
desire he had undergone for her, what abject letters he had
written her – and then the reward, good God, another girl!

He blinked down the table at the girl, as lithe and whippy
as a greyhound puppy, and the light glinting on her red-gold
hair. 'Nan Bullen's brat!' he muttered to himself, 'a whey-
faced scrap of a thing like her mother, a green apple, a
codling,' he drooled on, regarding her with a fixed and
menacing eye.

She looked back at him; for one instant he saw himself
reflected in the dreadfully dispassionate eyes of a very young
girl. But the image was quickly blurred; the light seemed
oddly dim tonight, as it had been in his father's day when
they cut down the number of candles and saved the candle-
ends.

What did that girl matter – or all the other girls either? –
though it was enraging the way the Tudor stock had run
to seed in a crop of females: first his own two daughters;
and then the only grandchildren of his two fine strapping
sisters were those three diminutive Grey brats, and the baby
in Scotland who might well become the most dangerous
person in Europe.

But he had the boy, his son Edward, yes, he had got a
legitimate son at last. He turned his great stiff head slowly
and stared at the pale child beside him; nothing like as big
and strong as he himself had been at his age; he was much
more like what Henry's elder brother Prince Arthur had

44

been, but that Henry could not bear to recognize; for the slight boy whom he could scarcely remember had died at fifteen of a consumption. No, Henry would see no likeness to Arthur in Edward; for one thing, Edward was far cleverer, already he knew more than lads twice his age. 'I wish I had more learning' Henry had sighed when a youth, as greedy for the beauty of great minds as for rich food and drink, for pleasure and sport and glory and conquest.

He had welcomed Erasmus to his Court, he had been proud to count him as a friend; and witty ironic Thomas More too, with whom he had walked so often in More's garden at Chelsea, watching the river flow past and the sea-gulls swoop and swirl, while they discussed everything under heaven and in it too as they walked up and down, his arm round his friend's neck. But his friend had betrayed him, defied him, tacitly refused to recognize the righteousness of his divorce with Katherine of Aragon, turned stiff-necked in resistance to his will, until there was nothing for it but to cut off his learned and witty head. Tom Cromwell had urged him to it. 'More must go,' he had said; and then in his turn Crum had to go. Crum was a knave if ever there was one: when Henry held a knave in his hands at cards he used to say 'I hold a Cromwell!' But he was a witty devil and a good servant.

The best of friends, the best of his servants, the best of women, how was it that all had failed him? He needed friendship, he needed love, he needed a wise, tender, in-finitely understanding companion who, while giving him all the glowing admiration that was his due, would also know just where to throw out a hint in guidance of his judgment, where to encourage and where to still the doubts that often stirred deep down within himself, so deep that even he did not always recognize them until too late.

But he had never had such a companion; never since— Was there a strong draught that made the candles gutter and sway, and the smoke swirl in wreaths from their flicker-ing flames? Through the blue and shifting mist he was see-ing pictures he had not seen for over forty years – a fair Spanish princess of sixteen, all in white, with long hair down her back, seated in a litter hung with cloth of gold, and himself riding beside her, a cavalier of ten, entrusted to escort his brother Arthur's bride through the roaring cheering flower-strewn streets of London. He, who was never allowed all his boyhood to be with any girl except his sisters, had then his first taste of the pageantry of chivalry that he adored in the romances; and was so intoxicated by it that, that evening, to show off to Katherine, he danced so hard that he had to tear off his hot coat and caper in his small-clothes. And after Arthur had died a few months later, and Henry had married his widow a few years later, he went on showing off to Katherine, finding her the perfect audience, through twenty years of marriage, – until he found to his rage that she too claimed to take a part in the play herself.

Muttering something to himself, he reached forward to take another helping of sugared marchpane, felt the marble edge of the table pressing into his belly, and squinted down at it resentfully. How long had he been in labour with this huge paunch? Tonight it seemed so short a time had turned that splendid young athlete, with flat hard stomach and limbs clean as a whistle, into this mountain of pain and disease, in labour with – was it death? The choristers sang:

> *'To hunt, sing, dance*
> *My heart is set.*
> *All goodly sport*
> *To my comfort*
> *Who shall me let?'*

There was no one to offer let or hindrance to his pleasures; except himself. *'Every man hath his free will,'* but what use was that? since a vast aching body told one, as sternly as any gaoler come to arrest a quaking girl, that 'it is no more the time to dance.'

There was no pleasure now left to that body except to cram it further with food, with deep stupefying draughts of wine, cloying the palate, mercifully dulling the senses. He reached forward for his cup. *'Who shall me let?'* Neither his anxious-eyed physician nor his fearfully watching wife dared offer let or hindrance.

And suddenly he began to talk. His great voice swayed gustily to and fro, a storm wind rising and falling in the hall that a moment since had been full of music and pattering chatter, and now was paralysed into silence with the resurgence into life of the figure-head, monstrous and moribund at head of the table.

He talked of the French and how he had so lately beaten them; he had made the Narrow Seas English for all time; no other foreign invaders would ever dare come sailing up the Channel. Once indeed he might have turned the tables the other way and conquered the whole country of France after winning a yet more glorious Agincourt; he had in fact conquered and now held Boulogne. When only twenty-two he had taken the Chevalier Bayard prisoner and shown them that an Englishman could be every bit as much a 'very perfect gentle knight' as any bowing Frenchman. ('Now,' thought Bess, playing with the nutshells on her plate, 'now he will say, "Stout fellow, Bayard, a very fine fellow." ') Sure enough he said it, and with episcopal authority – 'Old Gardiner showed sense, for a bishop, when he said Bayard is a stout fellow.' He always had to say that when he mentioned Bayard, to remind himself that he did not really bear the noblest man in Europe a grudge for knighting François on the terrible battlefield of Marignano when the young French King and his armies had fought 'like infuriated boars.' Henry had never been in a battle like that; even now, when François too had grown old and cautious, it irked him to think how the Foxnose had once fought his own battles, where Henry had only paid the Emperor to fight them.

Well, it was something to have had an Emperor in his pay. And once he had planned to make himself Emperor when his servant Wolsey had aimed to be Pope – Wolsey the butcher's son, a fellow that had once been put in the stocks for a brawl at a fair, but whom he had raised to be the greatest priest and statesman in England, and, almost, in Europe. Yes, he had brought England back into the Continent, he had made her a power to be feared and courted.

'Look at the Field of the Cloth of Gold!' he shouted suddenly. *That* showed Europe was at his feet – and with what a show! The English had outvied the French at every point; François alarmed at the competition, had sent anxiously to him beforehand to ask him to forbear making so many rich tents and pavilions. François had shown him with great pride a portrait of a woman called Mona Lisa that he had bought from the old painter Leonardo da Vinci who had died the year before; he had paid four thousand florins for it, a ridiculous sum for a picture, and of a rather plain woman too.

Henry could retaliate with Holbein, whom he had honoured with his patronage and an income of £30 a year (less £3 for taxes) apart from the sale of his pictures. The new Dutch School was coming far more into fashion than those old Italians.

They said François was as tall as Henry, but it was only because the Frenchman's wretchedly thin legs made him seem taller than he really was. If only he could have matched his knightly prowess against François in the tourney, which cautious royal etiquette forbade, he would have proved himself the victor, he was sure of it. He had overcome all his opponents in it, and killed one of his mounts from sheer exhaustion (François had overcome all his too, but they had probably thought it wise to let him win). Henry had excelled even his crack English archers at the long bow; the French had gasped with admiration of his aim and strength. Certainly he would have been more than a match for François.

'Remember how I threw him in the wrestling bout?' he chuckled. 'What a to-do there was! Kings mustn't be thrown! Why, Kate, you and the French Queen had to pull us apart, d'you remember, hanging on to our shirt-tails like a couple of fishwives parting their husbands in a brawl!'

The hall seemed to rock to the sound of that mighty guffaw, and echoed it back in a frozen silence. No one knew where to look, what to say. The King heard and saw the emptiness all round him, a herd of sheep staring, but not at him, not at anyone, a wavering cloud of white foolish faces, scared and averted, and among them a very young red-headed girl playing with the nutshells on her plate. Who *was* that girl? She was always cropping up, baffling, frustrating, charged with some hideous memory.

The scene grew thicker, more confused. 'Kate!' he called in sudden terror, '*Kate!*' A woman was hanging on to his arm, imploring him something. She seemed to think it was her that he had called – why, he did not even know who she was! Some fellow was loosening his collar, the woman put water to his lips.

He stared at the red-headed girl and knew now she was his daughter – but not by Kate. There had been other Kates, Annes, Jane, – but the Kate who could remember him at the Field of the Cloth of Gold, as King and bridegroom at eighteen, as a child of ten riding beside her, that Kate had gone for cvcr, and would never come back.

Not Katherine of Aragon hung on his arm, but Catherine Parr, who knew him only as an obese, sick old man.

He made a mighty effort and guffawed again. 'Why, how I've scared the lot of you!' he gasped out. 'Who do you think I took you for, Kate? I was asking only if you remembered hearing the tale. You were only a little girl when it happened.'

But he spoke with difficulty and his lips had gone blue, and his twitching hands where the great jewelled rings were sunk in fat.

Bess, holding on to her nutshells so tight that they cut into her hands, stole a glance at him under her down-dropped eyelids and thought his face looked like a glistening suet pudding. Then, even as she glanced, it sagged, a deflated bag, turned a greyish purple, and a tight smile twisted it as though trying to hold it together; the eyes opened for one instant in a puzzled, frightened stare, – and then the crash came. He fell forward over the table, into clattering plates and knives and cups, and a great red pool of spilt wine pouring over and drip-dripping on to the floor like drops of blood.

Women shrieked, men sprang up, Edward Seymour rapped out a sharp order, and servants surrounded the King, bent over him, more and more of them, until at last they succeeded in hoisting the inert mass into a poled chair, and staggering off with it through the wide-opened doors.

Bess unclenched her hands and saw the palms were bleeding. She looked at Tom Seymour, and saw he was looking at her. She looked hastily at her brother Edward, and saw he was finishing Jane's marchpane. Edward liked sweets.

She slipped out and found her governess, Cat Ashley, who had already heard all about it.

'But, Ashley,' said Bess, 'I though it was François who threw the King.'

'Sh-sh-sh,' said Ashley.

Chapter Three

THE KING lingered nearly a fortnight. His mind did not again wander. With Herculean courage he bent it to his will, though his face had gone black with agony, and his legs, which had had to be cauterized some time before, were plunged in a perpetual fire. Yet he forced all those last hours of his long torture to the service of his son, and the constitution of the government that might best safeguard his minority.

There was no time now to brood on the past; that company of long-forgotten comrades that had stepped forward as he began to lose his grip on life were driven ruthlessly back into the shadows. They were dead and done with; there was nothing to be done about them. With the hand of death heavy on him, every nerve and impulse in that fast decaying body reached forward to the future. His dying urgency was fiercer far than that of youth and hope.

For thirty-eight years he had worked tirelessly to secure his kingdom both on and from the Continent; to secure it at home in England, both from Papal interference and the revolutionary dangers of the New Ideas; and to secure its uncertain sovereignty over Wales, which now he had definitely incorporated with England by Act of Parliament ten years ago; over Ireland, where the sovereignty was far more uncertain; and over Scotland, where, he had to admit in rage, it still did not exist.

With failing, gasping breath, he urged on his brother-in-law Edward Seymour, Earl of Hertford, the necessity of his completing Scotland's conquest, as the first work to be done in the new reign.

Edward Seymour, as Prince Edward's uncle, would be on the Council of Regency which Henry appointed; and with him fifteen of the wisest of his Ministers: a judicious mixture of the 'New Men' who inclined to reform, and conservative elements to act as a brake; such as Chancellor Wriothesley, a heretic-hater, to pull Cranmer's lawn sleeve when it flapped too urgently at 'Old Mumpsimuses' – so he said with the ghost of a smile before it twisted into a grimace of pain. And he added Edward Seymour's younger brother Tom to the Council, a lively fellow after his own kidney, with none of Edward's priggish and possibly dangerous earnestness; – he might act as a check on it, for the two brothers couldn't abide each other.

Henry knew that Edward Seymour, beneath his stern exterior, was white with eagerness for him to die. He had accused Norfolk and Surrey of aiming at the sceptre – well, the pot may have accused the kettle. One could trust no one. The nobles were always ready to conspire, the commons to rebel. The nation itself had a proverb that the vice of the French was lechery, but that of the English, treachery. He had to leave his life's work to a child of nine – and to what busy and ambitious schemers? What chances of treason and murder? 'Woe to the land whose King is a child' – woe also to the child! The skeletons of his own boy-uncles, murdered sixty years ago in the Tower by their uncle, Richard III, would raise their little heads through his fever to warn him how near the fate of Edward VI might be to that of Edward V and his small brother. But *this* uncle, Edward Seymour, virtuous, high-principled, was no Richard Crookback : – or was he?

Anyway, he could do no more. And he had to see about dying. He left command that he should be buried at Windsor beside the body of Jane Seymour, his third wife, the only one who had given him a son. And that his soul was to be prayed for, and masses said for it, to release it the sooner from Purgatory. He had abolished Purgatory; he had intended to abolish the Mass; but no matter, one might as well be on the safe side. Henry had never learned that he could not eat his cake and have it; there was no time to learn it now.

Bess spent the days in terror lest she be summoned to his sick-chamber. But he did not send for her, nor for Edward. It had become indeed no place for children. He sent for his wife Catherine, and for Mary, separately. They both came out weeping uncontrollably.

Bess gazed in wonder at her stepmother. She would be free now and unafraid, yet she was crying as if for the loss of a child. Had he been sorry? What could he have said to move her so? He had said, 'It is God's will that we should part.'

Bess could recognize the simplicity of greatness; and its practical quality. It was no good looking back; he had looked forward, told Catherine he wanted her to keep all the jewels and ornaments he had given her, and not to hand them back to the Crown, and that he had 'ordered all these gentlemen to honour you and treat you as if I were living still.' Yes, Bess conceded inwardly, as she listened to her stepmother, it was something for Catherine Parr to have been made a Queen.

And Mary, of course, was always ready to cry.

Mary had, in fact, cried so much at the interview with her father that he could not bear it, and had signed to her to leave him, for by then he could speak no more.

He had tried to talk to her of the councillors he had appointed, but she would only beg him not to leave her an orphan so soon. To which he made no answer. But presently with deep earnestness he had asked her to try and be a mother to her brother Edward, 'for, you see, he is little.'

It was that last request that tore her heart. Catherine Parr owed him royalty, honour and jewels. Mary's debt had been otherwise; she had been dispossessed from her royal and legitimate inheritance, and dishonour cast on her birth and on her mother; she owed him years of loneliness, sometimes imprisonment; insult and ill treatment both from himself and his servants; worst of all, separation from her adored mother all the last years of Katherine of Aragon's life; a refusal even to be allowed to go to her when she was dying and afraid, as even her stout heart admitted, that she would have to die alone and abandoned, 'like a beast.' Did Mary not remember how she had been forbidden her mother's death-chamber, when she came out of her father's, sobbing as if her heart would break?

So Bess asked herself with the clear-cut logic of thirteen, and a horror of the father who had killed her own mother four months after he had at last worried Mary's to death.

She could not guess how much else Mary remembered.

The huge decaying body Mary had just seen had not appalled her as the corruption of his soul had done, long years ago, when he became rotted with power and the lust of life.

The thirty-year-old woman who met the child's astonished gaze, all her pent-up passion in these repressed years broken loose by an agony of pity and desire for what might have been, had one of her violent irrational impulses, and tried to tell her what her father had been; like the Sun himself when he 'cometh out of his chamber like a bridegroom.'

'You never knew him as I did,' she burst out, 'you never saw him as a young man, glorious, gay, doing everything twice as hard as other men. He made everyone else seem a ghost. You should have seen him as I did when I was a child, on board his ships in a common sailor's dress, short trousers and vest but all of cloth of gold, and blowing a whistle so loud it was like a trumpet. But he was kind and tender too, tender even in teasing.'

A flood of tears choked her as the memory swept over her of his pulling off her hood at some solemn State function, so that her hair came tumbling over her shoulders. The schoolboy prank had been partly due to his pride in her long fair hair – she had known that, even at six years old. He had loved to show her off to the grave courteous foreigners who had come to ask her hand for their Sovereigns of France or Spain. 'This girl *never* cries,' he had told them proudly.

'She has made up for it since,' Bess thought, in acute discomfort at her half-sister's emotion. It only made her hate her father worse than ever; why couldn't Mary be sensible and hate him too, and then she would be glad instead of sorry that he was dying?

'You will be able to marry now,' she said in desperate

attempt to comfort or at least turn her thoughts, 'and then you'll have your own children instead of just Jane and the other silly little Greys – you know you said that as long as he lived you'd only be the Lady Mary.'

But Mary's re-discovered appreciation of Henry could not go so far as to admire the forward-thrusting mind he had bequeathed to Bess. She only wanted to look back, to forgive, and if possible excuse her father.

'He would have arranged a marriage for me if he could,' she said eagerly. 'He spoke of it to me just now and how sorry he was that fortune had prevented it. You are too young to understand – but you will – how difficult and dangerous a thing is a royal marriage. The fate of a whole nation may depend on it.'

Her eyes narrowed; her face grew strained and terrible; 'the fate of a nation,' she repeated. 'Yes, and its soul, its living soul. That is what one marriage may destroy.'

She was thinking how the King's marriage to Nan Bullen had done that; had torn the nation's soul away from Christ's Church to the pagan worship of the State; had imposed a revolution from above on to the people, so that they were persecuted, not for a new idea, but for believing in the faith of their fathers; had robbed and desecrated the tomb of Saint Thomas à Becket who for three hundred years had been a national saint and hero and was now declared a traitor for having opposed his King, his bones thrown on the common dust-heap by royal command. Henry had, in fact, pulled down the whole structure of the Church just as he had pulled down and robbed the monasteries, and built it up anew with himself at the head of it – in order that he might marry Nan Bullen.

And of Henry himself, and 'the terrible change' that the foreign ambassadors had noticed in him at that time, Mary could only think as of the destruction of a soul. Only a year or two before, they had reported that 'Love for the King is universal ... for he does not seem a person of this world, but one descended from Heaven.'

But so had Lucifer descended from Heaven, to become Lord of Hell. Mary had seen her gay affectionate father, a conventionally pious man, disintegrate before her eyes into an irresponsible ogre; or else, even more disillusioning, into the ridiculous figure of a man driven between two women, living for a long time under the same roof with them both, helpless, angry, even frightened.

Yes, he had been frightened of his Nan; she had taunted him and told him what to do and what not to do.

She had told him not to argue with Katherine of Aragon, for he 'would always get the worst of it'; not to see his daughter Mary when he went to visit his baby daughter Elizabeth, for his 'weakness and instability' might let him soften to her.

Once – it was on an autumn morning and all the fields and trees were gold under the wide still sky – Mary had met him by chance walking in the open country, and he stopped and spoke kindly to her, telling her he hoped he would soon be able to see her more often, and then, abruptly, he moved away, and she saw it was because two of Nan's servants were sidling up to overhear.

Mary knew that her desperate loathing and jealousy of Nan was not only on her mother's account; it ran like a withering fire through her veins. The image of Nan had burnt into her eyelids so that whenever she closed them she saw the slight supple figure enthroned in the amazing black dress that her daring French taste had dictated. It had cost more than five times the amount of Mary's dress allowance for the whole year; thirty-two yards of black satin and velvet, and the King's jewels gleaming out of all the blackness; and framed in it a thin white face, bold forehead and scarlet lips and black eyes that sparkled and, the ambassadors said discreetly, 'invited conversation.' 'The Night Crow,' Wolsey had called her; the She-Devil, Mary called her, as did all decent women, knowing the danger of her and her like to safe, ordered matrimony; she had been chased by a mob of women several thousand strong who yelled their curses on 'the goggle-eyed whore,' – and Nan had told of that herself, with shrill shameless laughter.

Would Mary ever forget her laugh? Never, never, never, she told herself in agony when she woke in the night to hear it ringing in her ears, hearing that laugh alone, and everywhere else the night-long silence. No more the sweet familiar sound of bells from the chapels where the monks had prayed for men's souls at their appointed hours, the bells that had always comforted her childhood when she woke afraid of the dark. That laugh, ringing down through the years, had silenced them, it seemed for ever.

It was on an evening in early spring that it had sounded their doom; when the wind and slanting sunlight were sharp as thin steel and all the little thrusting flames of the crocuses in the garden at Hampton Court were tossed this way and that with the light shining through them, and out swept 'the Lady' (not wife yet nor Queen) from the Palace, into the bowing, curtsying company on the terrace, out she swept all in one flashing movement, chattering and calling, greeting first one and then another, and cried to Sir Thomas Wyatt, whom all the world knew to be mad for love of her, 'Lord, how I wish I had an apple! Have you such a thing about you, my sweet Tom? For three days now I have had such an incredible fierce desire to eat apples. Do you know what the King says? He says it means I am with child. But I tell him "No!" No, it couldn't be, no, no, no!'

And then out rang her laughter, sharper, wilder than the early March wind; and her thin nervous hands flew up like fluttering white birds to peck and clutch at the King's pearls round her throat, pearls bigger than chick-peas, and she stared at all the shocked dismayed faces, and suddenly turned and fled from them, still laughing, back into the Palace, leaving only a ringing, mocking, frightened echo in the appalled hush she had created.

Now everyone knew. The six-year siege that the King had laid to Nan had been raised at last, the fortress yielded, which she had held through all his furious importunings while living under the same roof, his showers of gifts and titles, even through the general belief that she had long since been his mistress. It had been yielded at the exact moment when, his patience strained to snapping point and his resentment mounting to fury at the way she treated him, it had become necessary to apply the final spur.

Now Henry and his new servant Cranmer would have to

stir themselves in good earnest to get Nan's child born in wedlock. They did.

On the last day of that March of 1533 Cranmer was consecrated Archbishop of Canterbury and had to swear allegiance to the Pope before the high altar, – but, four days earlier, he arranged another and more private ceremony before the altar of the Palace Chapel in Westminster, where he forswore this sacred oath in front of a notary and other witnesses, declared that he put the King's will above the Pope's, and that whatever he would have to swear at his consecration was only an empty formula. He did not like being consecrated in deliberate perjury, but Henry had another word for it, which was 'compromise.'

It took Cranmer under two months of the Sacred office thus achieved to find the marriage of Henry to Katherine of Aragon to have been 'null and void from the beginning.' That was just before the end of May, and on the first of June he crowned Nan Queen of England; King Henry was excommunicated that summer; and on the 7th of September Elizabeth was born.

Just when and where Nan's marriage to Henry occurred in this sequence nobody quite knew: but Cranmer pronounced it to have been 'good and valid.' Its lack of ceremony was made up for at her coronation, when all London was draped in scarlet and a conduit ran claret and white wine through Cheapside all the day, – but, so the seventeen-year-old Mary heard with delight, in all those gaping crowds there were few heads bared, and fewer still to shout 'God save the Queen.'

But Nan still held her head high, and did so until just three years later she laid it on the block. That altered nothing – to Mary. Nan had won.

In twin birth with her child, Elizabeth, the Church of England was born; and the break with Rome, with the Pope and the monastic orders, made complete. The bells were silenced.

Nan had won. Her daughter would win. Mary's despondent nature was certain of it. But one comfort she could clutch to herself; she had been born of a woman who loved the King, and Elizabeth had not.

57

She looked up from her brooding reverie to speak to Elizabeth, perhaps to say that very thing, she did not want to, but often words came out of her mouth and hung on the air for her to hear them, aghast, before she knew she had spoken them.

But it did not matter now if she spoke them or not, for Elizabeth had tiptoed softly away.

* * *

Bess went to find Edward. He was reading St Paul's Epistles in Greek with Jane Grey, while their tutor, pretending to correct their exercises, snored murmurously near the fire, its light flickering upwards over his finely cut nose.

She sat down on the bench beside them, and the three fair heads bent together over the book and talked in whispers.

'They've sent for old Mumpsy-mouse,' said Edward in his even little voice. (Bess's nickname had at once become the children's name for Cranmer.) 'He'll be coming down by water. That means *he's* not likely to last the night, and I shall be King tomorrow.'

Bess, callous enough herself about her father's death, was startled, not for the first time, by Edward's lack of feeling, for Henry adored his son. She longed to tell him he was an ungrateful cub, but one doesn't say these things to a boy who will be King tomorrow. Probably Jane had influenced him, since she openly hated her parents.

But Jane was not interested in current affairs, she was wrestling furiously with a tough passage of Greek prose; 'I think,' she said, 'Paul got it wrong himself.'

'Very likely,' said Bess. 'Pope Clement told the theological students at Rome never to read him, as it would spoil their style.'

Both the younger children froze at mention of the Pope. It was not done. 'Have you been talking to Mary?' Edward asked severely.

'Yes, but not about religion. She is very unhappy at the King's dying.'

'Why should she be?' said Edward. 'I shall see to it that she is properly treated, even though she is a Papist.'

'If we don't finish this epistle,' said Jane, 'we shall be whipped tomorrow.'

'*I* shan't,' Edward reminded her. 'Barnaby might.'

'Yes, Your Highness has a whipping-boy. It isn't fair,' she added under her breath.

'What is the day of the month?' Bess asked suddenly.

'The 27th,' they told her, and knew why she had asked. If the King lived till tomorrow morning, the Duke of Norfolk would die. His execution had been fixed for dawn on Friday, January 28th. But if the King died tonight, then Norfolk would live. His son, Henry Howard, the Earl of Surrey, had been beheaded nine days ago, after a speech of furious defiance when like a stag at bay he had stood and gored the King and Council with his words.

None of the children spoke of him, for they had worshipped him from afar as a scornful god who had scarcely noticed their presence; they had yelled with shrill delight as they watched him at tennis, winning game after game, or in the tilt yard, charging down on his horse White Cherry, as he wrote himself, on

'*The gravel-ground, with sleeves tied on the helm,*
On foaming horse, with swords and friendly hearts';

they had sung his songs, all in the modern Italian manner which made other verse seem so tame and old-fashioned; and envied the Irish girl, Fair Geraldine, to whom he had written them.

But his father Norfolk, a grumpy fierce old man, they did not like; it was therefore possible to discuss his chances.

'Mary will be sorry if he lives,' said Edward, who had heard how Norfolk had tried to bully her into submission to her father's divorce. 'He told her once that if she were *his* daughter he'd knock her head against the wall till it was as soft as a baked apple.'

'It's that already,' said Bess, and they all giggled. Somehow it was irresistible to make a butt of Mary when they got together, but she felt guilty and uncomfortable in doing so; poor old Mary, it wasn't fair, especially just after she had been talking to her almost like a sister, – well, a half-sister.

59

'Why are you always rubbing your nose?' Edward asked his sister suddenly.

'I'm not,' she said indignantly, and then in self-contradiction, 'it tickles.'

Ever since Tom Seymour had tweaked it in that game of Blind Man's Buff she had felt anxious about her nose. Why did he say he'd know it in a thousand? Did he think it would be big or bony? She could feel just the faintest hook in the bone, but then all the heroines in the romances had aquiline noses. Still—

'You'll make it red if you go on,' said Edward, and buried his own in St Paul again.

Silence fell on them all except for the gentle rhythm of Mr Cheke's faint snores and the sudden spurts and crackle in the fire.

It was a wet windy night. The draught blew the wood-smoke down the chimney and the candle-flames this way and that. Bess noticed a winding-sheet of wax forming in one of them; was it for her father or for Norfolk? She shivered, and glanced at the others, but they had noticed nothing; they were deep in their Greek. 'They're only children,' she thought.

Mr Cheke woke with a snort as a puff of smoke blew into his face; he jerked up, saying, 'Well, well, well!' and tried to pretend that he was exclaiming at something he was correcting in the exercises and that he had not been asleep at all. The little girls smiled slyly at him; they had a great admiration for him – Jane because he was the best Greek scholar in Cambridge; Bess because he was so handsome and aristocratic looking that no one would guess his mother kept a small wine-shop in a back street there.

'A forfeit!' she cried, in what Jane thought a very pert way. 'Whoever falls asleep must tell a story!' And instead of reproving her, as Jane thought he would and should (again it wasn't fair), he laughed in a shy pleased way as though she had paid him a compliment. So they all sat beside him, hunched on the hearthrug, with their hands held out from their wide sleeves to the spluttering blaze of the logs as the rain fell down the great chimney, and he told them the story of Saint George of Merry England and the Dragon. He told it well and dramatically, making Saint George speak in Latin in a very grand voice, and pointing out a great dragon with fiery eyes that they could all see in the fire. The girls listened with grave attention, but Edward startled them all by bursting out laughing. It was the more astonishing as no one had ever heard him laugh before; a pale little smile was the most he had ever achieved. Nor could he tell what he had found so funny in the story; he just went on laughing in that shrill childish treble, to their consternation, for no one in the Palace should do it on the night the King was dying, and for Edward of all people to do it was so odd as to be uncanny.

Jane said in her sedate fashion, 'They say Crassus laughed only once in his life, and that was at an ass eating thistles.'

'But St George isn't an ass,' said Elizabeth rather sharply.

'Hee haw! Hee haw!' brayed Edward weakly, wiping his eyes; then began to laugh again.

Was he bewitched? He looked as though he had been suddenly transformed into a goblin, with that small mouth stretched from one to other of the immensely long ears that peaked up above his straight hair, and the little round button of a chin turned to a sharp point. Was he really a changeling? Bess asked herself with a twinge of childish fear.

Mr Cheke in his kind way said he was over-tired, excited, he had got another of his colds, and had better go to bed and he would tell Mother Jack to bring him a hot posset to drink. Mrs Jackson had been Edward's nurse 'as a child,' he would explain gravely, but he still called her Mother Jack and got her to tuck him up in bed on every possible excuse; Bess said it was why he had so many colds.

She decided to go to bed too; it was better than doing nothing. She left the room with exaggerated grace, for she thought Mr Cheke was looking at her.

But in bed she could not sleep. She lay watching the firelight through her bed-curtains, hearing the rain drip-dripping, and all the time the minutes too were dripping past; old Mumpsymouse was slipping along down the black rain-drummed river in his barge, landing at Westminster, coming up to Whitehall Palace, coming into that awful room where the King lay already unconscious, the greatest King England had ever had, people said, and there he lay, a rotting hulk, with the life drip-dripping away from him.

She shivered and huddled the blankets more closely round her. All the warmth imparted by the silver warming-pans seemed to have gone chill; the sheets were cold as cere-cloths to wrap the dead in, so she told herself with an almost enjoyable thrill in working up her own fears.

The great clock outside tolled out midnight: one, two, three, four—; if that hulk still kept its fierce hold on life, by eight o'clock tomorrow old Norfolk, listening to the rain, and the minutes dripping past, would then be beheaded. Would they go down to hell together, the King's hands gripping his servant's throat?

She did not care for old Norfolk, but he was in 'that very narrow place, the Tower, from which few escape except by a miracle,' and that place exercised a terrifying spell on her imagination; was it because of her mother's last hours there? or because – because somewhere in the unwritten future she might find herself floating down the rain-drummed river to the Water Gate that is only opened to admit traitors?

Past and future, death and life, the air all round her was full of forces struggling together in the dark, and behind them, flowing on endlessly, relentlessly, the dark river of Time, bearing them all away.

With a sudden panic-stricken movement she leaped out of the bed, pulled on a long fur-lined bedgown, thrust her bare feet into a pair of heelless embroidered slippers, and went hastily, stealthily out of the room.

The Palace was alight, silent, waiting. She ran along the passage and paused as she saw at the end of the long gallery the armed halberdiers standing at attention like statues against the tapestry that moved in the wind so that its patterned figures looked more alive than they. What use were they? They could not hope to bar Death from stalking down the gallery, in through that door at the end. She slipped back behind the corner of the passage as she heard the faint sound of a voice, very low, but fast, urgent, almost desperate, coming near, then further away till lost in silence, then back again, up and down, up and down the gallery. She peeped round the corner again and saw Edward Seymour, Earl of

Hertford, walking there with his friend Sir William Paget, the Secretary of State, and talking, talking as if he would never stop, flinging out his arm every now and then in an abrupt, angry gesture; sometimes Paget would lay a hand on it as if to restrain him, and once he spoke, clearly, – 'Too many irons in the fire,' she heard, but that was all, and indeed he had little chance to speak through that low persistent torrent of words. Their shadows ran up against the wall as they advanced, Paget's thick nose and two-pronged beard sticking out of his great fur collar in absurd exaggeration, while Edward Seymour's face ran into a long narrow point; the shadows grew, then dwindled, then came again, then away.

The clock boomed out a single note. It was one o'clock, it was morning, it had only to strike seven more times and then—

The door at the end of the gallery opened. The two men walking up and down stopped dead, their faces turned towards the open door and the little close-knit group of figures that came out of it, walking very slowly with bent heads and a faint intermittent murmur of voices, just as though they were mumbling in church, Bess thought. Old Mumpsy-mouse was in the middle of them, his face yellow and glistening with sweat under the waving torches; and, yes, with tears; he drew his sleeve across it and mopped it as he came up to Seymour and his friend, and said on a beautiful low yet clear note like the toll of a bell:

'All is over. His Majesty has died in the faith of Christ.'

They were all coming on now down the gallery towards her. Bess had slid back behind the shadowed corner of the passage and now fled noiselessly down it. Had they seen her, were they coming after her? She dared not look back, she turned down a little stairway of only three or four steps, sped along another corridor, swung round a corner and fell against a man. She began to sob and gasp something about a nightmare.

'Steady now, steady. What's all this?' said Tom Seymour's voice.

She looked up wildly into his face with incredulous relief, and flung her arms round him. He pulled her back through a doorway into a little bare room where the firelight flickered on new wooden panels all over the walls and ceiling. He thrust a taper into the fire and lit a couple of candles on the table, took her by the elbows and turned her face to the light, while she stared, fascinated, up at those square, humorously cocked eyebrows, so unlike his brother's fretted brows, and saw how his short hair curled towards them at the side of his head.

'Now,' he said, 'what's the to-do?'

'The King is dead.'

Tom Seymour drew a soft whistle through his lips.

'So-o-o! I've won a thousand crowns.'

She swung sharply from him. 'How dare you bet on the King's death?'

'Not so, my Princess. I bet on old Norfolk's life. Always said there's no axe long enough to reach him.'

'Yes, he'll live. I'm glad.'

'Are you fond of your great-uncle?'

'No. But I'm glad that someone who has gone to the Tower will get out again.'

He nodded, with understanding. 'Tell me, how did you know this of the King?'

'I heard old Mumps—the Archbishop himself say it. He came out of the King's rooms and told your brother – he was there walking up and down, talking, talking, talking.'

'Trust Ned for that!' he exclaimed with an unpleasant laugh, and added eagerly, 'Did you hear what he was saying?'

'Only one word – "Liberty." ' ('Oh, that!' said Tom contemptuously.) 'He was talking very excitedly – like this,' she imitated the sawing movements of Seymour's arm and the fierce solemnity of his face, in a way that made his brother chuckle – and she added, 'but very low.'

'Can't trust his own shadow as usual – that's the worst of these damned virtuous fellows, they never dare speak out. Well, he's got his chance to now, – it'll be a great day for him and all his new notions. May he ride 'em safely, that's all – and maybe he won't!'

He had forgotten her, his handsome angry face was sparkling with malicious interest as though he were looking on at some play she could not see; but suddenly he turned from it, looked sharply at her and asked:

'What were you doing running about the Palace in your shift?' and gave a pull at her bedgown, which she quickly hugged round herself again.

'I was frightened. I heard the clock strike. I had to know – or anyway do something.'

He bent suddenly forward, paused, then put his arms round her, kissed her swiftly on the chin and cheeks, and at once let her go as she struggled.

'I'm thirteen and a half,' she said indignantly. 'I'm too old to be kissed.'

'Too young, more's the pity. Now run back to your room, or to your maids if you're frightened, but don't say you met me. Child, are you crying?' He cursed softly under his breath. 'I daren't keep you here, it's too dangerous, for you as well as me. Go to your Mrs Ashley.'

She shook her head, gulping back her tears. 'I don't *want* women. I don't *like* them. They always say the correct things and expect one to say them too. I shall say them all tomorrow, I shall cry then for my father. I am not crying for him now – I don't know who it's for – me, I think.'

He took her by the shoulders, very gently this time, and began to shove her out of the room, but she twisted round to look up at his face. 'One thing I must ask of you before we part,' she said earnestly. 'I may never have so good a chance again.'

'Ask away then, but quickly.'

'How is it you'd know my nose in a thousand, and just by feeling it?'

'By feeling it,' he replied, and kissed her again, this time on her nose.

Chapter Four

NEXT DAY BESS waited to hear the news of her father's
death as if for the first time – but nobody told it to her. Nobody seemed to know of it; the doctors went to his room as
before, the guard was changed outside his doors, all just as
though he were still alive. The Palace was full of whisperings
and hurryings, the street outside of troops marching; on the
day after, Saturday the 29th, Parliament met, but still nothing
was said and no one announced the King's death.

Bess had to nurse her secret knowledge until Monday the
last day of January, when Edward Seymour, Earl of Hertford, with a long, grave, anxious face, told her and her
brother together that their father was dead, and that he
would now be a father to them. The Council had appointed
him the King's guardian and Lord Protector of the country.

So that was why he had delayed the news, – in order to
make all his arrangements safely first, and take the supreme
power before the country knew what had happened. Bess,
mustering her tears, and gazing up at his noble countenance
(he had a finer head even than his brother Tom's, but few
noticed that), swiftly calculated what steps he must have
already taken.

So that was what he had been talking about with Paget in
the midnight gallery, with their shadows going up and down,
up and down, – no wonder Paget had tried to restrain him!
'Too many irons in the fire' – how many?

Even little Edward, without her clue to his uncle's actions,
could see something of what had happened; he began to cry
and say he didn't want a Lord Protector, and if he must have
one he'd rather have Uncle Tom, and where was Uncle Tom?
Edward Seymour looked grim at mention of his brother and
did not answer; when he spoke again it was about something
else and in a severe, repressive voice.

Edward began dimly to realize that he would never see
his father again, and that nobody else would ever make so

66

much fuss over him; he put his head down on his arms and sobbed: 'I don't want Protectors, I want – I want my father.'

Bess, who had begun to cry dutifully for her father, found herself doing so in good earnest. She put her arm round the little boy, they clung together and ignored their uncle, who hovered uneasily over them, trying to find something comforting to say, and failing, even to his own ears. It was odd, he reflected scornfully, his delicate eyebrows shooting up into his already worried-looking forehead and making a sharp network of new wrinkles – it was very odd how much better his rascally younger brother would have succeeded. Children must be as undiscerning as women, for they all alike adored Tom. But he had more important things to see to, and at last, to their relief, he went away, and as everybody else seemed too busy to attend to them at the moment, they were left alone.

Sitting there huddled together like a couple of forlorn fledgelings, they heard the trumpets sound outside and the long strained shout of the heralds: 'Le roi est mort. Vive le noble roi Edward.'

'I don't want to be King,' sighed Edward, his flaxen head still tucked into Bess's shoulder.

She gave it a little shake. 'Yes, you do. You're going to be a great King like your father. Uncle Edward won't last long. You'll grow up soon and do what you want, and not what he wants.'

'He wants me to marry that baby, the Queen of Scots, and *she*, Aunt Anne, wants me to marry Janet, and I don't want either.'

'How do you know?'

'Janet told me so herself. She heard them talking when they thought she was asleep.'

Janet was Edward Seymour's pretty, clever little daughter, and Bess was not at all surprised that her mother planned to marry her to the King. Edward grumbled on, – 'All these cousins – all these nasty little girls – I don't want any of them. Janet is not royal, she's my subject. When I marry, I'll have a princess, a foreign one, well stuffed and jewelled.'

'Stuffed?'

'With money, silly, and lots of fine clothes, and perhaps a province or a navy. I'm not going to be fobbed off with a cousin and no proper dower. The Seymours are a beggarly lot, they haven't enough clothes to go round. They can't have, or they wouldn't have taken Surrey's when they got him beheaded.'

'What *do* you mean?'

But it seemed it was true. Edward had heard that too from Janet (in whose company he had been thrown by her mother), that her parents had seized not only the dead Earl of Surrey's house and possessions and splendid horses – 'Yes, even White Cherry whom he would never let any one else ride' – but all his clothes down to the very caps and stockings. A vision rose in Bess's mind of the gorgeous scarlet dress Surrey had worn on board the *Great Harry*, and she broke into horrified, hysterical laughter at the thought of it on Edward Seymour, who always wore the plainest dark clothes. It wasn't possible. Of course it must have been his wife, their Aunt Anne, who had done this horrible thing – a vulgar rapacious woman, as handsome as an Arab hunter, but with an eye like a gimlet and a mouth like a steel trap. It was all the more horrible because Surrey, though hating Edward Seymour as an upstart, had been attracted by the flashing vigour of his wife and paid her attentions which she prided herself on rejecting; he had written her an ode, 'On a lady who refused to dance with him,' a title that fascinated Bess, for how could any woman have refused to dance with Surrey?

She was their thin aunt; Jane's mother, the Lady Frances, their fat aunt; sometimes they argued which was worse; Bess thought she knew.

But thank heaven there was no more time for thinking. Edward had to be dressed in his best clothes and ride in state through the city to the royal Palace of the Tower, where all new Kings had to stay for the few weeks before they were crowned. And as soon as he had ridden off on his white pony, looking very small and solemn among all the attendant nobles, the Queen pounced upon Bess, and carried her off with her, with hardly any preparation or packing, to the

Manor House at Chelsea, which King Henry had had built as a nursery for his children and then presented to Queen Catherine.

Oh the relief of getting there! Catherine and Bess hugged each other and ran straight out into the garden to see if there were an early snowdrop – 'after all, it will be February and spring tomorrow!' said Catherine, on such a note of ecstasy that you would have thought she had been longing for the spring all her life – as indeed she had.

At Whitehall, the King's body lay in state. Bishop Gardiner had a hot encounter with Lord Oxford's company of players, who were going to act a grand new play at this unsuitable moment; he advised a solemn dirge instead, and finally had to appeal to the Justice of the Peace, swearing that if he couldn't prevent the play he would at least stop people from coming to see it.

The players in revenge chalked on the walls of his palace:

> *'As Gardiner such he is,*
> *He spoils so all our plants*
> *That justice withers, mercy dies,*
> *And we wronged by their wants.*
> *A priest only in weeds*
> *And barren all his seeds.'*

But they had to give in, grumbling, illogically that if only Old Hal were alive he'd be the first to tell them to go on with the play. Much *he'd* have cared for a solemn dirge! What bluff King Hal liked was a good show with plenty of dancing and jolly songs, and a fine performer he'd been in them himself when he was younger; so all the older players reminded each other, shaking their heads over their mugs of ale and complaining that nothing would be the same now Old Hal was dead, there'd never be another King like him, a bit hasty maybe, chopped off heads like cabbage stalks when he'd a mind to – but they were generally the nobles' heads, mark that, and no doubt they deserved it, – he kept those proud bullies in their place, made them kneel when they addressed him as 'Majesty', a grand new title for a King, but the common people always found him as jolly and friendly to talk to as one of themselves, and almost as easy to get the chance to talk to too – you only had to step out beside his horse when he went riding and pull off your cap, and he'd rein in and chat with you as though you'd known him all your life.

Pity he couldn't have lived till the young one was in the saddle, instead of their having one of these new jumped-up nobles as Protector, a strange new-fangled title, though very old men like Martin Whitehead, who was kept in the Company to work the fireworks in the jaws of the Hell-fire dragon, could remember the time when there had been a Protector before in England. For that was what Crookback called himself for a few weeks before he called himself King Richard III – until he got killed by Old Hal's father.

And at the Crookback's name they all said 'A-ah' and took a deeper drink, for which they had to pay, although this very day the Protector had led the little King in a grand procession through the city and everybody had turned out to cheer them and run along beside their horses up Tower Hill. But not a drop of free drink did the Protector order for them, and no pipes of wine were laid in the streets; he rode along beside his nephew, looking very fine and noble but cold as a statue, and harried-looking too; he might take all he could get, but he'd never get any pleasure of it, nor would anyone else.

'Old Hal would have given us a drink,' grumbled the young ones as they turned away in disappointment: 'Young Hal gave us a drink,' mumbled the old ones, remembering that golden youth riding in triumph to the Tower, and added, 'God rest his soul!' with more feeling than Bishop Gardiner, whose sonorous voice was saying daily masses for his dead master, while his indignant mind absorbed the discovery that he had been cut out of his Will.

Seven other bishops assisted him in his thankless office, and Archbishop Cranmer was present though he would not celebrate High Mass, which showed the way the wind blew and that the new Government would now go all out for the new austerity in worship. But until the old King was buried, his masses had to be said, and they went on for a fortnight in Whitehall Chapel, where the King's body lay in state, and all day the nobles and gentry filed past it, and the ladies of the Court sat up in a separate gallery to pray.

The King's widow, the Dowager Queen Catherine, came up to Whitehall from Chelsea, and at first she brought the Princess Elizabeth with her to the Chapel, in her purple mourning, holding her new pomander firmly to her nose. It contained a dried orange stuck with cloves and impregnated with other perfumes; the watch set in the filigree case also served its purpose since she could watch the time without seeming to do so.

But she quickly discovered that she had a cold, and did not come again before the coffin was moved in the middle of February to its burial at Windsor. She made up for her remissness by a very stilted letter in condolence in beautiful handwriting to her young brother, which tied itself up in such tortuous expressions that she herself could not quite make out what she had meant to say; but they greatly impressed Edward, who wrote back compliments on the elegance of his 'most dear sister's' style. He added that there was evidently 'very little need of my consoling you' and 'I perceive you think of our father's death with a calm mind,' which made his most dear sister give a rather lary eye at the paper. Such common paper too! Was Edward Seymour going to be a skinflint guardian?

Bess liked being at Chelsea better than anywhere else. The house was a pleasant, fair-sized mansion, with no pretensions to a palace, built in the modern fashion of red brick with chimneys and turrets clustering together, and plenty of tall windows so that the rooms were filled with light and one could watch the endless busy movement of the boats sailing up and down the river and hear the cries of the watermen. She felt safe and snug as a kitten being looked after by two motherly cats, her stepmother, Pussy-Cat Purr, and her governess, or rather her lady-nurse, Cat Ashley, whom her royal charge regrettably called her Ash-Cat, a nickname which it must be admitted suited Mrs Ashley, a thin sallow woman with a casual strolling air and a roving eye always ready to twinkle with entertainment over any scraps of news she might pick up, and they were many.

She told her charge, sitting in the window-seat looking

71

out on the river, something of what she had heard at White-hall of King Henry's last hours, how he had stared into the shadowy corners of the room and muttered 'Monks! Monks!' But none knew whether in remorse at having turned them out of their monasteries, or because at the eleventh hour he had wished in vain for their ministrations. And at the end, when he had lost consciousness and none had thought to see him move even a finger nor hear him speak ever again, he had started up in bed so that all were amazed at his strength, and cried out in a clear voice, 'Nan Bullen' – 'Nan Bullen' – 'Nan Bullen.'

'Yes, three times he called her, and his eyes wide open, staring as if he saw her there, standing before him, and that's the only time he's ever said her name since – since—' and Cat Ashley's eager voice broke on a sob.

Mr Ashley was related to the Bullens, and his wife, dazzled from the first by that lively, go-ahead, essentially modern family, had been as devoted to Nan as she now was to her daughter.

Now at last it was safe to speak of her, now that King Henry, having spoken, had died.

And after his funeral, followed by a procession four miles long, had left for Windsor, Cat Ashley picked up a grisly tale of the coffin having burst the night before the burial and how the plumbers had to come and solder it up again; and this she knew for a fact, for one of them was engaged to her own chambermaid, but of course it was kept quiet, and scarcely any knew of it who attended the magnificent ceremonial next day when Bishop Gardiner preached his most moving sermon on 'the loss to both the high and low of our most good and gracious King,' – 'as well he might,' the Ash-Cat declared, her twinkling black eyes rolling round at Bess, 'seeing that it's meant the loss of all his hopes from the Will!'

Bess sat hugging her knees, staring at the rain-scuds flying down the river from the west, feeling very grown-up to be told so many things that she knew she should not be told. But one of them startled her worse than even the horrifying tale of the coffin, and that was when Cat Ashley, pulling a long purple thread through some mourning garment she was making for her, said lightly, 'It's my belief your stepmother will be a widow for even fewer days this time than the last. She must make haste with all her mourning clothes if they're to be ready before she's ordering her wedding dress for the Admiral.'

Bess's knees went taut as whipcord in her grasp. If she did not hold on to them tight she would be springing up to fly at the Ash-Cat, shake her and scream that she was a liar.

She kept silent. Cat Ashley, disappointed in her lack of interest, said, 'Well, and I thought you would be pleased. He'd be your step stepfather then, and your guardian as like as not.'

'*I* don't want him as a stepfather,' said Bess, loosening her grip on her knees with a jerk. 'I don't believe the Queen wants him as a husband either. Why should she?'

It was a good move, for Mrs Ashley at once poured out a protesting flood of all the reasons, among them some very flattering to the Admiral, which Bess heard with little painful stabs of pleasure – the finest man in England, so handsome, tall and splendid in his bearing, with none of his brother's cold stateliness but all the more imposing just because he didn't trouble about it; there was a careless magnificence about him, like that of a man born to be King. Fierce as a lion in battle, yet as merry as a schoolboy, and that grand voice of his, it would put courage into a mouse.

'But the Queen – isn't she rather old for him?'

'*That* she's not, at just thirty-four, and he a year or two older, though they neither of them look it. Besides – this had to be a secret while your father lived – I don't know that I'd better even now—'

'Now, my Ash-Cat, hand up your titbit; I'll never stop twisting your tail till you do.'

Bess had seized Ashley's little finger and was pulling it round and round. Laughing and jerking her hand away, Ashley disgorged the titbit; Catherine Parr and Tom Seymour had been privately betrothed before her marriage to the King. When he signified his choice of her as his sixth wife, there was nothing for her to do but to give up Tom, for to have married him against the royal will would have only meant utter ruin and probably death for them both. She had been a faithful wife and devoted nurse to Henry for three and a half years, and he had been the third elderly widower she had had to marry.

Now at last she was free to take her own choice and still young and pretty enough to enjoy it. She had already been having some confidential meetings with the Admiral in London even before the funeral – though that was all quite correct and above-board, since he had been a member of King Henry's household and was now one of the Council of Regency, and had many things to discuss with her about her royal charges, – 'but depend upon it, they've found time to discuss their own affairs too, and what I say is, the sooner the merrier : she's a sweet kind creature and deserves her luck, and I wish it with all my heart – don't you too, my Lady Bess?' she added, suddenly surprised by the child's grave silence.

But Bess, having got all she wanted out of Ashley, was quick to assume a reproving air. 'It's a serious matter,' she said, 'and you oughtn't to talk of it, Ashley, – Oh, to *me*, yes,' she put in quickly, at Ashley's indignant movement – besides, she might want Ashley to talk again. 'But not to anyone else. The Council may not approve, and I know Edward Seymour hates his brother—'

'So do I, *and* I know why. Jealous!'

'Jealousy is a dreadful thing,' said Bess virtuously.

Ashley gave a quick look at the demure face. 'That's too good to be true. Are you mocking me, my Lady Mischief?'

'No, only myself,' murmured Bess, but went on rapidly, 'At the least, they'd make a horrible scandal if it were talked about so soon after the King's death.'

'Talk? *I* talk! It was only to please Your Highness, and I've found you are to be trusted. You can be sure I would never talk to anyone else, never, on any dangerous matter.'

'Can I, Cat? Can I?' She said it slowly, reflectively, and those clear, light-coloured eyes of hers seemed to Cat to be looking right through her. Was it a child who spoke and looked thus? It was more like some ageless Sibyl.

Cat had flushed to the roots of her hair; she took her young mistress's hand in both of hers and said, as though she were giving the oath of fealty, 'I swear to Your Highness, you can be sure of me.'

Bess leaped up, flicked Ashley on the nose, cried, 'Silly old Ash-Cat, what are you so solemn about? Look! the shower is over and the sun's come out!' and dashed into the garden.

Chapter Five

IT WAS A large and charming garden, enclosed within its high red brick wall that was only ten years old, but already mellowed to a warm rosy hue, and had small fruit trees splayed against it. Some old trees and shrubs had been allowed to remain, though they interrupted the symmetry of the formal rectangular flowerbeds and knot gardens and paths edged with box hedges a few inches high. In the wall at the far end was set a postern gate which opened on to the reedy marshy fields, bare of hedges but with outcrops of scrub and forest, that spread away into a blue distance of low wooded hills, the heights of Highgate and Hampstead.

And across this open country, by the single road that led through the village of Chelsea to the Manor, Tom Seymour came riding this windy stormy sunny afternoon in late February.

He saw the bright sails of the boats on the Thames scudding as if on dry land beyond the trees, which were still bare and purple-black, but flushed here and there with the palest glimmer of gold; it might have been the willows budding, or only wet twigs in the sunlight. The square stone tower of the church on the riverbank looked almost white against a blue-black stormcloud, for the sun was shining on it, and the golden weathercock flashed through the tossing branches as if some exotic bird had strayed up-river with the seagulls that squalled and swirled around it, making wheels and arrows of white light.

He came to the new red wall of the Manor garden, dismounted and gave his horse's bridle to the groom that rode with him, opened the postern gate with a key that he pulled out of a little purse in his belt; and there he stood for a moment, quite still. The formal flowerbeds were glistening with wet earth, but along the borders crocuses pierced them with little flecks of coloured light. Some hazel shrubs dangled their catkins in the wind in a shimmer of faintly yellow tassels, and a blackbird shouted its early song as it balanced itself precariously on the topmost twig of a taller tree, swinging and bowing to the wind. The small stone fishpond reflected the sunlight in a mirror of gold. Round and round its edge a childish figure in purple silk was running, dancing, leaping, tossing a golden ball high into the air, and catching it again. A gleaming cloud of hair blew out from under her cap as she danced, and she shrieked as the wind blew her ball all but into the pond, retrieved it in a wild, sideways leap, and all but fell in herself, laughed on a note that seemed to answer the blackbird's, and pranced on.

At first glance it was as though one of the crocuses in all its sheen of purple and gold had sprung into human stature and movement. Crocuses and the early song of birds, and a laugh as shrill and wild, and those darting movements, erratic as a dragonfly, – what was it they were all bringing back to him? In an instant he had it – an evening in early spring just fourteen years ago, as vivid as if it were this month, and Nan Bullen's slim form flashing out upon the terrace at Hampton Court, swirling and trailing her bright plumage as she turned from one to another – and then laughed. 'Lord, how I wish I had an apple! ... Such an incredible fierce desire to eat apples! Do you know what the King says? He says it means I am with child. But I tell him "No!" No, it couldn't be, no, no, no!'

And again that laugh that had rung on and on in his ears, so that he still seemed at times to hear it, especially on these cold spring evenings so like herself, sudden, harsh, brilliant, changeful.

Thus unceremoniously had the advent of this girl, the Princess Elizabeth, been announced to the world six months before her birth – in a woman's 'No'; not meant to be believed.

And here she was herself dancing on the verge of womanhood, and till this moment he had not perceived it.

Suddenly she saw him standing there, stopped dead, letting

her ball fall to the ground, while she stared as if at a ghost, swooped to pick it up in an action like the plunge of a long-legged foal, and then at last advanced slowly towards him.

'How did you get there?' she asked, almost in a whisper. 'The garden was empty, and now – you've appeared.'

'By magic. You were thinking of me, and I obeyed your wishes.'

'I was *not*!' she exclaimed indignantly.

'No need to toss your head. All those golden catkins on it are tossing hard enough without your help.'

'I call them lambs' tails.' She flung away from him and broke off a couple of their branches. He noticed how abrupt and angular her movements had become again as soon as she ceased to dance, and yet there was still something of that wild grace in them. But what had happened to her manners, and was she angry just because he had startled her? He at once became the magnificent courtier, sweeping his hat to the ground in a low bow.

'I implore pardon for not recognizing Your Highness earlier. I took you for a wood nymph and now I see my mistake. You are a great princess – are you not?'

She swung round to him again, her face flaming.

'I won't be mocked,' she said, 'I won't, I won't!' and stamped her foot, all the more like a wilful colt.

He put a hand on her shoulder. 'What's the matter, child? Here's a nice welcome for me after these weeks! I'd hoped day after day to see you at Whitehall, but no, you had a cold and had to keep your bed – your flowerbed I should say,' as she stepped back from him inadvertently over the little box hedge. Even Bess's indignation had to break up in laughter as she shook the wet earth off her heel.

'It was only a church cold,' she said.

'Now do you know I guessed as much! What's your golden apple, my Lady Atalanta?' and he took the pomander ball from her hands. 'Remember that if, like her, you embark on a race for glory, you must never turn aside, as she did, for golden apples.'

Turning it round, he saw the watch-dial set in it and exclaimed, 'Is this how you kill time?'

'It won't go anyway. It stopped' – she paused and stole a look at him under drooping white eyelids, then finished on a note of exquisite melancholy – 'on the night my father died.'

'What a shocking little liar you are! Do you ever say a word you mean, or that you mean anyone to believe?'

'Not often. What is the use?'

He put the pomander back into her hand and his own hand over hers, holding it and the golden ball together, and she shivered at the warm strong grasp. His voice too was warm and strong; what had Ashley said of it – that it would put courage into a mouse? But it did not put courage into her; she wanted to burst into tears, to fling herself into his arms, to fasten herself tight up inside his coat and never have to face the world again; and go on feeling those deep tones tingling through her like the throbbing low notes of a harp.

'What has hurt you, little Princess?'

She struck away his hand and ran from him, turned at the edge of the pond and flung her pomander at him with all her force.

'Catch!' she cried on a high, merry note, but her face was that of a little fury, and she had thrown the hard gold ball to hit, not to be caught.

He dodged it and dashed after her, seized her by the shoulders and swung her round to him. 'You little wild cub!' he exclaimed, laughing, but like her his face was in earnest. And he held her a moment before he spoke again.

'Are you so much a cub after all? It won't be long before you're grown up. Bess, will you marry me?'

'You're laughing at me again.'

'And why not? Can't one marry and laugh?'

'Then you've only just thought of it this moment.'

'What of that? Everything has to have a beginning.'

'It's monstrous, – why you're—' No, she must not say she had just heard he was practically betrothed to her stepmother. She finished – 'You're nearly three times as old as me.'

'But in ten years I'll be only twice as old.'

'Ah, you *have* thought of it before! You couldn't have done that sum in your head on the instant.'

'Witch! Will you have me?'

'No.'

'Why not?'

'I'm too young.'

'Not yet husband-high?'

'Oh, as to that!' – She had nearly said, 'I'm already as high as the little Queen,' but she changed her ground. 'I shan't think of marrying for years yet, if ever, and I'm in mourning for my father – for two years at least.'

'Tell that to the Merchant Venturers!'

She was casting wildly for her reasons. Suddenly she remembered what she had said to Ashley of himself and the Queen – an objection of even more force in her own case. 'I couldn't marry without the Council's consent – I'd lose my place in the Succession.'

'As much as your place is worth, hey?' He was grinning, but not very pleasantly. 'And why shouldn't they consent?'

'Oh well, there's your brother—'

'There is indeed my brother. I'll see about that. And now answer for yourself. Wouldn't you like me for a husband when you're a little older? Wouldn't you, my tawny lion cub? No claws out now!

> *"Noli me tangere, for Caesar's I am,*
> *And wild for to hold—"* '

'Who said that?'

'Tom Wyatt, of your mother. And now another Tom is saying it of you. God's soul, it will be a work to tame you!'

'I'll not be tamed by you or any. I'll be myself alone, always, I—'

He put a hand under her chin and forced it up to shut her mouth. Then he bent slowly, his eyes laughing down into hers, his face came nearer and nearer, she knew he was going to kiss her on that forcibly closed mouth, and she stopped trying to move her head this way and that; she stood breathless, her whole body stiff and taut in expectation.

A woman's voice came ringing out into the garden, soaring on a clear high note of happiness, calling to them, laughing at sight of them, winging towards them, and Queen Catherine came running into the garden.

Bess wriggled furiously, trying to get her chin free of that grip of his finger and thumb, but it held like a vice and the Admiral never stirred.

'Come here, my Pussy-Cat,' he called, 'and tell me how to deal with this vixen of yours.'

He had even taken her nickname for the Queen! Bess was aghast at his impudence – and his duplicity, for here he was laughing with Catherine and telling her practically all he had just been saying to herself, as though it were nothing but a joke, or – far more horrible thought – was it *not* duplicity? Had it really all been only a joke, which she had been fool enough to take seriously?

'I've been asking if she'll have me for a husband when she's older, but she'll have none of me. What's more, she's flung her watch at me – there's a fine way to pass the time!'

He let go of her at last and strolled over to pick up the pomander and show the broken watch in it to Catherine, and Catherine scolded Bess lightly for her carelessness with her possessions, just as though she were a child. But then she *was* a child again now; they both seemed to think so; they did not mind her being there while they chatted together with gay friendly intimacy that sometimes dropped on to a tender note and sometimes pranced into flirtation. Yet Catherine did not want her to leave them, she kept her arm round her as they walked, and though she did not bother to bring her into the conversation, she turned to her sometimes with a smile of such happy goodwill that it gave Bess a throb of awed envy, not for what Catherine possessed, but for what she was – so naturally good and kind and unsuspicious, as she herself could never be.

The wind was too cold for sauntering; they went indoors, and Catherine gave the Admiral a posset of mulled wine and spices to warm him after his ride, and still would not let Bess leave them, so she sat on a cushion by Catherine's chair near the fire and played with her new greyhound puppy, and listened to their assured, easy, grown-up voices as they talked on and on, forgetting her (yes, he had even forgotten she was there), and felt unutterably miserable that she was only thirteen and a half.

They talked over Edward's coronation last week. Thank heaven, Catherine said, that Mr Cheke had shown some sense, in spite of being a great scholar, by insisting that the service in the Abbey should be shortened so as not to exhaust the child more than was necessary: as it was, he had been sick from sheer nervousness all over his beautiful pearl-embroidered white waistcoat, even before the procession had started; and after it was all over he had had to go straight to bed instead of sitting up for the splendid banquet Tom Seymour had given to all the Court in his grand new house at Temple Bar – and here she went into a fit of giggles.

'I can't help it,' she gasped out, 'it looked so funny, you and your brother sitting on either side of his empty throne like a couple of watchdogs and glowering at each other across it! My Lord Protector had reason to glower, certainly,' she added with quick tact, 'for you outshone him completely in the procession. What a shout they raised as you rode by. It was like the roar of the sea.'

Tom looked pleased. 'Ah, he laid down plenty of wine for them in the fountains this time, but they'll never shout 'Good Old Ned!' for him as they did for 'Good Old Hal!' – nor for the boy either,' he added without even troubling to drop his voice, which made Bess certain he had forgotten her presence, for surely even he could not be so incautious as to criticize her brother in front of her?

She had stuck her two branches of lambs' tails into a silver jug on a table and was watching the ghostly shadow of their dangling tassels that the pale sunset light had thrown on the wall. She thought of Edward being sick on his gorgeous Coronation dress, – why couldn't he have waited for a basin? Boys had no control. So they wouldn't ever call him 'Good Old Ned.' Would they ever shout 'Good Old Bess' for her? But she didn't like the sound of that, – it would be better if it were 'Beautiful Bess' or 'Our Glorious Bess.'

The city children would dress up as angels for *her* then, and sing, as they had done for Edward:

Sing up, heart, sing up, heart,
Sing no more down,
But joy in (King Edward) that weareth the crown.'
(Queen Bess)

It had reminded her of the children playing on the village green at Hatfield:

'Here we go up, up, up.
Here we go down, down, down,'

and she thought that one day her turn might come, and she would be up, up, up, not on a see-saw but on a white pony riding to her Coronation, and a tinsel-winged angel would come flying down (but you could see his wire ropes in the sunlight) from a triumphal arch in Cheapside and give her a purse of a thousand gold pounds, and *she* wouldn't just drop it like a toad as Edward did because it was so heavy. But even Edward had shown pleasure at the tightrope dancer who greeted him with such amazing antics on a cord slung from St Paul's Cathedral to the Dean's door. It was grand sport being crowned; but her envy was the more painful for a throb of pity that Edward had been too tired to enjoy it as she would have done.

Her elders had settled down into a rich comfortable grumble; it was comfortable because they were sharing it so wholeheartedly, but they were both angry and indignant; Tom kept exploding into more and more surprising references to different parts of the Deity's person, and Catherine kept beginning her sentences with 'I should have thought—'

All the arrangements for the new régime seemed to have been just what the late King did not intend. The Council of Regency that he had ordered was being set aside as a completely subservient body to Edward Seymour, who had at once taken supreme power as Protector and got himself created Duke of Somerset, while Tom had been fobbed off with a couple of empty titles, for he was now Lord Sudley and Lord High Admiral – 'God's beard, what's that to me who have been Admiral of the Fleet in good earnest?' And of what account was an extra title or two at a Coronation when everybody got them? Even his bashful second brother, Homely Harry, had had to accept a knighthood to bring him slightly more into line as one of the King's uncles.

But Tom had been given no working share in the Government nor personal control of the King, although, or no doubt because, the King liked him far better than his Uncle Edward. Catherine too had had good reason to expect a share in the Government, for King Henry had once appointed her Queen Regent during his absence in France; the only time a Queen Consort had had the title formally conferred on her. But what she really wanted was to be made personal guardian to the King; she had looked after him more closely than anyone these last few years, nursed him through illness and read his lessons with him; she knew how fond he was of her in his odd way, and that King Henry would have wished her to continue her charge of him.

'It isn't what Hal wished that counts now,' said Tom, 'it's what our precious pious Ned wishes.'

'I should have thought he's pious enough to carry out Hal's wishes. He was there when the King told his nobles to treat me always with as much honour as when he was alive – when he said I was to keep the jewels he'd given me.' And suddenly she gave a sharp cry, 'Oh, the jewels! I've just thought! I left them at Whitehall.'

'God's blood, why didn't you keep a hold of them?'

'I didn't think of them, or anything else except getting here as fast as we could. I could hardly wait for my maids to pack. All those horrible whispers at Whitehall—' she shuddered and hid her face in her hands. 'You know they say the King was dead three days before' – she broke off and laid a hand on Bess's shoulder.

'Yes, I knew that too, Madam,' said Bess, and looked across her in cool challenge at Tom Seymour.

So he had not told Catherine how she had met him on the night the King died. But he paid her no attention; the jewels were worrying him far more.

'You were mad to leave them behind,' he said. 'I'll get them for you at once, before my sweet sister-in-law puts a claw on them.'

'She *could* not, Tom. They're the King's jewels.'

83

'Couldn't she! You don't know our new Duchess, our Lady Protectress! She'd say she's protecting them for *this* King. And Ned would back her.' His blue eyes were brilliant with anger under their dark brows; he sprang up, swearing torrentially, and looked round for his cloak.

'Where are you going?' she cried in distress.

'To Whitehall and the whole Protectorate pack. I have a deal to say to them.'

He strode over to Bess and patted her head. 'What else shall I say to them, my Lady Bess? Shall I ask them for your hand?'

She swung up her arm with a slap at his face, and he caught it by the wrist.

'So here it is, you've given me it already.'

He lightly kissed her hand and then the top of her head, and in another moment he was gone, Catherine pattering out beside him, plucking at his sleeve, begging him to be cautious, her tone half laughing and wholly loving.

Bess was left alone. She raised her eyes to the wall and saw the shadowed pattern of her branches fade fainter and fainter as the light died, until it disappeared and the wall was blank.

Chapter Six

FOUR DAYS LATER, Catherine told Bess that she and Tom Seymour would marry as soon as it was possible for her, so recent a royal widow, to do so. They had just become formally betrothed, with rings and a written contract of marriage, but this would have to be kept the closest of secrets while Tom set about getting the consent of the Council to it. She had written to him to wait two years, but he had scratched out 'years' and changed it to two months.

She looked anxiously at the wooden little face in front of her, pale, with the mouth set in a determined line and the eyes regarding her so steadily yet blankly; Catherine could not see what lay behind them. Surely she liked Tom; Catherine could not imagine any woman of whatever age failing to do so, and he was so charming with her, teasing her so gaily, and really fond of her too. She did want this odd difficult girl to be glad of their marriage, to know that her home would be with them for as long as she wanted it. She said this last, and Bess thanked her, and then remembered to smile and said she could not imagine any home as home without her Pussy-Cat Purr on the hearth. Catherine, feeling baffled, admitted that it was indeed extraordinarily soon for her to be planning her next marriage, only a month after the King's death had been made public; she told her of her previous betrothal to Tom and how all thought of it had had to be laid aside at the King's command to her to be his wife.

Bess thought, 'Why does she tell me all this, and of her betrothal now, when if I were foolish or treacherous it might bring ruin to them both?' How silly women were, always telling each other things, however dangerous! *She* would never tell any woman anything; even if it were not dangerous, what was the use? You never knew what the other might be thinking about it. Here was she thinking all sorts of angry, contemptuous things about Tom Seymour, while her stepmother prattled on in her artless fashion about his wonderful loyalty and constancy in having waited for her these long three and a half years, and never wanting to marry anyone else, though he might have made such brilliant matches.

'Such brilliant matches,' thought Bess – 'to a King's daughter and second in succession to the throne'; yes, he had wanted that; and if she were as foolishly girlish as her stepmother she would now be telling her so, and causing all sorts of mischief for all of them.

But had Tom really wanted it, or had he only been playing at it?

Her questions tormented her. Catherine, looking down at her shut face, asked her what she was thinking.

'That I should be happy, Madam, ever to find a tenth part of the happiness you deserve.'

It was far too good to be satisfactory.

Catherine with a sigh went over to her little Italian escritoire and began to write to Tom. Within three minutes she had forgotten that odd difficult girl as she scribbled in hot haste, her face flushing and her breath coming faster in delicious excitement.

'I pray you be not offended with me in that I write sooner to you than I said I would, for my promise was for but once in a fortnight. Howbeit, – the weeks are shorter at Chelsea than in other places.' She smiled broadly at the excuse, and indeed she had a better; she must tell him that his brother Edward had said he would answer all her requests about her jewels, etc., when he came to see her, which he had said more than once he would do, and had not done; 'I think his wife has taught him that lesson, for it is her custom to promise many comings to her friends and to perform none.'

Then, having signed it in a hurry, she remembered all the things she really wanted to say, and a P.S. followed, longer than the letter, telling him how she had always wanted to marry him, 'before any man I know.' She had had to give up her will, and now God had given her it again, – 'God is a marvellous man.'

And then she remembered that she must tell him if he visited her here in secret he must come so early in the morning as to be gone again before seven o'clock when anyone was about, and to come always by the postern gate in the garden and the lonely marshy road across the fields over the foot-bridge that was ominously named Bloody Bridge from the number of murders committed there by highwaymen, – a terrible precaution, when he must ride alone in the dark hours to preserve their secret, but the danger from highway robbers to such as Tom was nothing to the danger of the Council – and the Duchess, his brother's wife.

But God would protect him, God was a marvellous man, the birds were singing their mating songs high and glad through the sunny window, and Catherine felt no fears as her quill pen scratched on; and behind her her stepdaughter sat on her low stool with her face cupped in her long hands, and listened to that scratching and the songs of the mating birds and wondered whether, if she had been a woman grown, Tom Seymour would have deserted his loving Catherine for herself.

* * *

The weeks were short at Chelsea, and elsewhere. Everything seemed to move twice as quick now the old King was dead and men dared to put their plans into action as fast as the changes in nature. The spring rushed on, the flowers rushed on, the birds picked off the heads of the crocuses, but the daffodils shot up in their place, the birds built nests, and the nobles houses.

Edward Seymour decided that as Lord Protector and Duke of Somerset he must have a London palace worthy of himself, and pulled down the north aisle of St Paul's Cathedral (which contained the elder Holbein's pictures of the Dance of Death), the Priory of St John of Jerusalem at Clerkenwell, and a couple of Inns of Court, all in order to furnish space and materials for Somerset House.

So of course his brother Tom was not going to be outdone in the housing matter, which had hitherto given him no concern, for he had always preferred to live in lodgings when in London, changing them frequently, but always taking his adoring old mother to keep house for him wherever he moved. But now he too decided that his dignity as Lord Sudley and Lord High Admiral demanded a fine house in his name, though characteristically he could not wait to build one. His brother for once was really sensible and pleasant about it, for 'good old Ned' promptly turned a bishop out of his house and confiscated the best part of his property, so that Tom should have a huge mansion all ready to hand, with stables, tennis-courts and bowling-greens in the Strand, orchards and meadows and terraced gardens leading down to the river, and call it Seymour Place. He was already installed in it a fortnight after the proclamation of Henry's death, and the whole vast place was humming with activity and gaiety, banquets, sports and water-parties.

Spring was in the air; even tutors and bishops, even vice-chancellors, even archbishops, bore testimony to it, and with them half the clergy. Bishop Parker, Vice-Chancellor of

Cambridge, rode off to get married to the young woman who had waited patiently for him for seven years. For Cranmer had at once pushed forward Parliament's edict to legalize matrimony for the clergy, and produced his German Frau in the open, to everyone's rather malicious curiosity. It was extraordinary how difficult it was to avoid references to packing-cases in her presence. Tom Seymour did not try; he at once asked her what she thought of that little box of a palace at Lambeth.

Curates and parish priests all over the country were rushing to get married, but the results were not always as happy as the bridegrooms, for their parishioners frequently sent in complaints of their choice: that these new young wives were either too frivolous and got their husbands into debt, or else they poked their noses into the affairs of the parish, in which they should have no business. Finally it was decided to pass another edict, declaring that all clergymen's prospective wives should first have to be passed as suitable by a bishop and two Justices of the Peace.

It was well they had not also to be approved by the Duchess, for her antagonism to poor John Cheke's new wife would have lost him his place as the King's tutor had he not written letters that fairly crawled in apology for her, both to the Duke of Somerset and his exigeant lady.

Among all these mating and nesting plans, those of Tom Seymour, both for himself and others, threatened more upheaval than those of all the clergy. For a boy-King's uncle who married the Queen Dowager of England would form a great counter royal house which might well bring about another civil war. His elder brother had already taken on a practically royal authority, given himself powers to act independently of the Council's advice, used the royal 'we' even in his private correspondence, and alarmed everybody by his presumption in addressing the new French King as 'Brother'. (For Foxnose François died at the end of that March, having been as much dashed by Henry's death as Henry had been by François' dying illness; the lifelong rivalry had ended without either of them finally succeeding in getting the better of the other.)

Somerset House and Seymour Place already looked like

dividing not only half London but all England between them;
'You *must* go warily,' Queen Catherine told Tom Seymour,
who wagged his finger against his fine nose and promised he
would be as wily as the serpent and as gentle as the dove, –
which gave her more amusement than hope.

But he was being more wily than she knew. One proof of
it, though not to her guileless eyes, was that little Lady Jane
Grey came to stay at Seymour Place with her tutors and her
servants and her personal possessions, in charge of Tom Seymour and his mother. Catherine was delighted, for this
would mean her having the charge of Jane's tuition as soon
as she was openly married to Tom; the child was far from
happy at home; the country air of Chelsea with the sea-
breezes coming up the river, and the companionship of her
gay playfellow Elizabeth, would do her a world of good. In
fact, Jane had already grown a whole new crop of freckles
in her first week at Seymour Place, and her small nose was
quite covered by them, so much more time did she spend
out of doors.

Jane's freckles were not Tom Seymour's prime motive;
nor, when Catherine demanded with ingenuous admiration
how he had managed to persuade Jane's parents, did he confide to her that he had paid Jane's impecunious father a
lump sum down of £2,000 as an extra inducement to place
his daughter in Tom's care.

And he had bigger bait than that to offer: the opportunity
and influence he would have as Edward's favourite uncle to
push forward a match for him with Jane Grey. The Protector
might succeed at any moment in marrying the boy either to
his own daughter Janet or to the little Queen of Scots; nobody
was sure which he favoured most; he was indeed not quite
sure himself, for his desire for England's peace and prosperity
and unity with Scotland was sometimes almost as strong as,
sometimes even stronger than his desire for his own personal
advancement.

So, as Tom was quick to point out to Jane's anxious father,
with the odds against them on not only one but a pair of
fillies for the matrimonial stakes, they must move quickly
to get Jane into the running. He would work it with the boy,
he could do anything with him, he told Henry Grey, a

nervous pallid little man, overshadowed by his stout Grey mare, the hard-eyed, hard-riding Lady Frances, with the red hardening to purple in her fat cheeks (King Henry's niece, so that it was she who gave Jane her claim to the throne, and never let her husband forget it). He trotted along in the terraced gardens by the river in vain effort to keep step with the Lord High Admiral's long strides, and peered up at the wagging point of his burnished beard, at the gay blue eyes, and warmed himself in the ringing confidence of that great voice; while Tom, looking down at the thin moustaches, the long nose and absurdly high collar, longed to tell his fellow-conspirator that he looked like a seedy mule peering over a wall.

The Admiral's first step was to introduce a valuable servant of his own, not inappropriately named Mr Fowler, into the King's household, and was pleased to hear that Edward often asked about him and when Fowler thought he could see him. Fowler, under instructions, asked if the King didn't think it strange that his younger uncle had never married. Edward, not having thought, did not answer. Fowler then asked if he would like him to marry.

'Oh, very much,' was the bored reply as he tried to tie his spaniel's ears over the top of its head.

Well, then, to whom?

'Anne of Cleves,' said Edward automatically. It was always a safe answer.

The spaniel yelped. So did Mr Fowler, almost. 'Your royal father called her a Flanders mare,' he said reproachfully.

'What's wrong with a Flanders mare? I wish I had one. I'm tired of ponies.' Then an impish gleam came into his eyes and he swung round from the spaniel, who at once leaped up for more teasing. 'No, d'you know what? I wish he'd marry my sister Mary and get her away from her old Mass.' And he gave a shrill crow of unaccustomed laughter that suddenly robbed him of his chill bewildered royalty and turned him into a mischievous schoolboy.

'Poor brat!' Tom exclaimed in a burst of pitying affection when he heard of it. '*I'll* make him laugh when I get at him!'

He could do anything with his nephew – if he could get at him. But that was the difficulty. Edward was being kept at his lessons harder than he had ever been kept before. Even when he was not at them, the Protector or one of his most trusted intimates was always with him; his own sisters could hardly ever see him by himself, and to Elizabeth, on one of the very rare occasions when they managed to give his guardians the slip, he burst out in fretful annoyance that he was scarcely ever alone for as much as half a quarter of an hour. And this particular occasion was won only by a glorious adventure.

She had been allowed to come and see him, but an excuse had been found to prevent Queen Catherine coming too to visit her stepson as she had wished, and Mrs Ashley was in attendance on her. The two children conversed solemnly in front of her and a couple of under-tutors (not Mr Cheke) and a major-domo of the Protector's. Then Elizabeth showed off for a bit in Latin, and Edward first matched her easily in it, then branched off into Greek, at which she fell rather behind and made an attempt to catch up in Hebrew, but again the honours were easy, so she shot into Italian, wherein she was really fluent and Edward far behind. The tutors, applauding her, excused themselves for the King's backwardness by declaring that they had nothing to do with his Italian lessons and made no pretence themselves of proficiency in the language.

On this assurance Bess slipped in a sentence or two in a 'little language' that they had long ago made up together out of a mixture of baby-talk, private slang and Latin or Italian-sounding endings to the words. It would not carry them far, but enough for her to ask him if they could not talk alone, and for him to tell her that he might manage it with his fellows if she would get rid of Mrs Ashley. He then said in English that he would like a game of shuttlecock with her, and they went out into the courtyards at the back of the Palace. He would not play in the closed-in tennis-courts; it was a lovely evening and he wanted to be out of doors. On the way there Bess had whispered to Mrs Ashley, who now said she had a cold and must not dawdle about in the raw evening air and went indoors. The major-domo had not come out, and the tutors walked up and down discussing the scandalous innovation of the modern pronunciation of Greek which Mr

Cheke, as Greek professor at Cambridge, was bent on introducing. It was said that Archbishop Cranmer backed him up – that showed what excesses Reform could lead to!

Suddenly Edward drove the shuttlecock far over their heads into a tree, and then found it was the only one he had brought.

'Fetch me more,' he shouted to the tutors, who began to call to a page who was passing, but Edward stamped his foot and roared, 'Fetch them yourselves! You'd have done it fast enough for my father.'

That sent them scurrying, each trying to outrun the other, and as they whisked out at one end of the courtyard Edward seized Bess's hand and ran out at the other, into a yard where there was a mountainous woodpile. He clambered over it, she followed unquestioning, and into a hollow that had been cleared among the logs, where they squatted down completely hidden.

'I've come here once or twice with Barney,' he told her. Young Barnaby (Barney at home) Fitzpatrick, three or four years older than Edward, was the son of an Irish peer, Lord Ossory; he had left the wild hills of Donegal some years before and become Edward's favourite school- and play-fellow, and on rare occasions his whipping-boy. The gay coolness and lack of resentment with which the Irish boy took the beatings that were beneath the dignity of his royal master seemed to Edward the perfect example of knightly valour and endurance; it was entirely fitting that Barnaby should have been chosen to bear the banner of King Arthur, riding in a black coat, as one of the nine youthful henchmen at King Henry's funeral.

'I hope Barney won't mind my showing this place to you,' he continued rather doubtfully, to Bess's surprise, for he was not wont to be so careful of the feelings of others, 'but anyway I am glad you made me think of it. I am sick of being treated like a baby—'

'Like a prisoner,' said Bess.

He shot her a quick look. 'So it is. Let them wait, that's all. I'll show them something when I'm really King.'

'You're that now. Look how you sent those Peeping Toms packing. It was just like our father.'

He flushed with pleasure. The ogre for whom even Edward had felt some fear and repulsion as well as unwilling fascination was already becoming a legend, a symbol for superb power. 'You think I'll ever be like him?' he asked wistfully.

'Not as fat, I hope!' she laughed.

'Hush! Someone might come near enough to hear you. Oh Bess, it's good to hear you laugh again.'

'Why, at Chelsea we are always laughing, and so would you if you were there. Why shouldn't you be allowed to see your own sister?'

'Or my stepmother or my own uncle?' he capped her, with an indignant wriggle that had disastrous consequences, for a bole in the wood caught and tore his beautiful silk trunk-hose, but they neither of them bothered about that.

'Look,' he said urgently; 'the Admiral often goes to visit the Queen at Chelsea, doesn't he?'

'Oh, once or twice he's been, I think,' said Bess airily.

Edward took this very coolly. 'I expect he goes, and you must see them there, so when next you do, give him this. It's surer than sending it by Fowler as I'd meant to do. You can read them.' And he thrust into Bess's hand two rather crumpled, dirty scraps of paper on which he had scrawled in haste, unlike Edward's usual tidy writing, except for the upright precise signature, with the flourish like a whip at top of the final 'd':

'My Lord, send me per Fowler, as much as you think good. Edward'; and

'My Lord, I thank you and pray you have me commended to the Queen.'

'Better,' he observed, 'to send 'em per you.'

'Per-haps.'

'Oh well,' he chuckled, 'I've made good use of old Fowler, leaving notes to the Admiral for him to find under the carpet in the dining-room.'

It struck Bess that it was the Admiral who was making use of Fowler.

'Does he send you money by Fowler?' she asked, trying not to sound astonished.

'Yes, it was he who thought of it – my Uncle Tom, I mean.
Oh, I know it doesn't seem very kingly,' and the boy's fair
face went a deep pink, 'but am I treated like a King? I've so
little pocket-money, I've none to give presents to my servants
– not even to Barney when he gets a thrashing for me. Why,
do you know what the Admiral said when he heard that, the
first time I had a chance to talk to him? He laughed and
said, "It's a very beggarly King you are! Not a penny to
play with nor give to your servants!" And he handed me
forty pounds straight off.'

'How like him!' exclaimed Bess, glowing.

'Yes, he's given me a deal more. And I've shown him
favour in return. I've insisted he shall attend me sometimes
at Court, and I'm going to see him when I wish, by myself,
and I will not be interrupted.'

The royal favour seemed of a dubious nature to Bess if his
interviews with his uncle were only to produce pocket-
money for himself. 'That will make the Protector jealous of
him,' she said. 'You may have to stand up for one uncle
against the other.'

'I am doing so,' said Edward magnificently, and suddenly
she was struck by the significance of that second bit of
scrubby paper. Edward had written a message for the Queen
expressly for the Admiral to give her; then had the Admiral
confided his secret plan of marriage to the child so as to get
his backing for it? It was an odd conspiracy, between a man
of thirty-five and a boy of nine and a half. She wished she
knew how much Edward knew; but she would at least be on
safe ground if she spoke of Queen Catherine's love for
Edward himself, how she missed him, wished she were still
supervising his lessons and seeing to it that he did not work
too hard. Edward conceded placidly that he knew the Queen
was very fond of him; he added that he was very fond of her,
and would much rather be with her than his Aunt Anne, the
Duchess, who was always saying nasty things about her, and
about the Admiral too.

They had been talking very fast, but now already they
heard voices in the distance calling in search of them, and
Edward spoke still more quickly, gripping his sister's knee
with his thin little hand. 'I want Uncle Tom to be my guar-

dian instead of Uncle Edward, and to be Protector too. He'd be a much finer one. Then I could live with him and the Queen when they marry, and do as I like. Why shouldn't I? I'm the King.'

'When they marry . . . ?'

'Yes, it's my wish. I told him so and he seemed quite willing. Then I could live with her and him and you, and we'd all be together and I could get rid of Uncle Edward. Don't you think it a good idea of mine?'

'Very good,' said Bess rather soberly, 'if it can be done.' So the Admiral had been clever enough to make Edward suggest the marriage himself and think it all his own plan!

He was evidently preening himself as a match-maker. '*I'll* help them and stand by them. *They* are sure to try and stop it. How dare they, if I give my consent? Tell her I give it, that I want her to marry him. I'll write to her when I get the chance.'

Bess wondered how she could warn him tactfully to be careful. The Admiral did not seem to have done it at all.

'The Protector is very powerful,' she said.

Edward suddenly flared up. 'Who is he, I'd like to know? Just Edward Seymour, that's all. He'd be nobody if he wasn't *my* uncle; everything he's got is through me, and yet he behaves as though he were King and I nobody. Nothing is as I want, only as he wants. I'll show him who he is some day, by God's soul I will!'

Nothing could have more displayed the influence Tom Seymour had already won over the child in his brief stolen interviews than his favourite oath piping out of the prim little mouth. Edward swearing was like Jane talking about her parents' company as hell; people were often oddly unlike themselves. An Uncle Tom's Edward might become something very different and, to Bess anyway, far more attractive than the Uncle Ned's Edward, even though in revolt, which was all he had the chance to be at present.

The seeking voices had died away, calling in the distance. Edward cautiously reared his head above the logs. 'The coast's clear. Better take our chance before the search thickens. We'll go by Barney's secret way.'

Bess clambered after him; they crept along by a wall,

climbed in through a little window, ran along a passage, her heart thumping at the sound of scullions' voices in the kitchens, and her ironic sense telling her that it was an odd entry into his palace for the absolute monarch that Edward had just so proudly shown himself.

A minute later they were seated on the window-sill of the room where they had first met, and, as the door opened, conversing brightly in Latin on the advanced views of Bishop Hooper of Gloucester, that surplices, like copes and chasubles, were 'the rags of the Harlot of Babylon'.

It was not only the tutors who entered and Mrs Ashley, sniffing atrociously, either in continued pretence of her cold or in genuine tears, for with them was that redoubtable lady the Protector's wife, the new Duchess of Somerset, her fine eyes snapping in fury and alarm, her tall elegant form wire-drawn with agitation. To her torrent of angry questions Edward replied calmly that he had wearied of waiting for the shuttlecocks and returned to the Palace for a little religious discussion 'with my sweet sister, Temperance'.

The Duchess only just suppressed rapping out one of the oaths that were familiar to all who knew her in the hunting-field, and demanded the reason for this preposterous new name for the Princess Elizabeth.

'It suits her,' said Edward. 'Temperance is a fair and godly thing in women. I would more of them had it.'

Bess held her hands together to keep from clapping. The Duchess's thin face was nearly purple, all its hard beauty had gone from it – 'she looks like a meat-chopper,' thought Bess – and then the Duchess's voice rang out on a new icy note of rage as she enquired if it were in godly conversation that the King had torn his stockings? Edward looked down at his legs, baffled, but his sister came to his defence.

'There is a nail sticking out on that chair,' she said; 'that is why we came over to the window-seat.'

The nail could not be found. The Duchess fumed. Bess, watching her in delight, said in a voice of soft concern, 'Perhaps, Madam, the King my brother might wear some of the late Lord Surrey's stockings?'

'And now,' she sobbed out to Queen Catherine, when she had got home and told her adventures and already counted the cost of that delicious rapier-thrust, 'now she will never allow me to see him again if she can help it.'

*   *   *

Edward did write to his stepmother, who between tears and laughter showed the letters to Elizabeth. They were extremely fatherly; they gave his blessing on her marriage and exhorted her to 'persevere in always reading the Scriptures, for in so doing you show the duty of a good wife and a good subject'; they thanked her heartily for her gentle obedience to his royal advice to accept the Admiral as a wooer, and assured her that 'he is of so good a nature that he will not be troublesome to you'. And he promised the lovers his protection and to 'so provide for you both that if hereafter any grief befall, I shall be sufficient succour to you'.

'And he will not have his tenth birthday for four months yet!' exclaimed Catherine.

In contrast with his elderly style, the Princess Mary's blunt refusal to the Admiral to use her influence in their favour seemed quite schoolgirlish.

'I refuse in any way to be a meddler in this matter,' she wrote to him, though glad to help him in anything else, *'wooing matters set apart, wherein, being a maid, I am not cunning'* (even the emphatic underlining suggested the raw girl). She showed very plainly that she was both shocked and hurt that Catherine could contemplate marriage so soon, undeterred by 'the remembrance of the King's Majesty, my father . . . who is as yet very rife in my own remembrance'.

That was Mary all over, prudish, sentimental, clinging to the past, blind to facts (for no one had better reason to know what horror the remembrance of the King held for his widow), but doggedly honest. No one would ever get a promise out of Mary that she did not mean to keep. 'Poor lady,' sighed Catherine while her lover swore at Mary for a rude old maid : ' "To be plain with you"! – hardly necessary to tell us that, when she can never be anything else!' he growled.

Mary maintained her tone when at last the marriage was made public by the end of June, and presently wrote to Elizabeth begging her to come and live with her at her manor-house of Kenninghall in Norfolk, so that the two royal sisters should join together in showing their disapproval of the behaviour of their father's widow.

Elizabeth giggled. Nothing would induce her to leave the delights of her homes in or near London, now grown so gay and exciting with the Admiral as their acknowledged head, for the dank marshy misty place in the wilds of the Norfolk fens, with her strict elderly sister in charge of her instead of the easy-going Catherine. But whatever happened, she must not offend Mary; every time Edward had a cold or a bad headache, the behaviour of the Court to Mary, as heir to the throne, showed her that.

So she had to pass her first real test in diplomatic correspondence, and settled down to it at her little escritoire with such lively enjoyment that her tongue kept stealing out all the time she was writing, and curling round the corners of her smiling mouth so that, as the Admiral declared on coming into the room, she looked like a sly sandy kitten licking her lips over stolen cream.

'And what is it you're writing? Your first love-letter, I'll be bound, to make you so smug! Come, confess, which of the pages have you seduced?'

He looked over her shoulder, but she had put her hands over the paper; he pulled them away, the inkstand overturned, she shrieked in indignation, snatching up the precious letter, and he chased her round the room for it. Catherine came running at her cries and scolded them both like a pair of naughty children, and the Admiral defended himself, saying he had got to supervise their ward's conduct and how could he, if she carried on a clandestine correspondence with the grooms?

'I don't!' shrieked Bess; 'the letter's to my sister Mary.'

'Tell that to the Beef-eaters! Would anyone write to your sister Mary grinning all over their face? Let's see what merry jests you've put in it!'

'No, no, the jest's to me only. No one else can see it. No one *shall* see it. Give it back, give it me!'

She was chasing him now, for he'd snatched the paper out of her hand and was holding it at arm's length above his head far out of her reach while he dodged round the furniture and finally behind the Queen, darting out first on one side of her, then the other, while Bess put her arms round her step-mother's plump little figure to try and catch him behind it.

'Ouch! You're squeezing me to death between you,' Catherine gasped out, laughing. 'Stop teasing the child and give her back her letter.'

'Read it yourself then first, Cathy, or I'll not be respon-sible!'

'No, no!' shouted Bess, stamping her foot in a real rage by now. 'She's not to, nor you. It's my letter. Give it back.'

He fluttered it above her head, making her jump for it like a dog; at last he let her snatch it from him and she fled from the room clasping it to her breast. He turned to Catherine, suddenly dropping his fooling.

'Is it safe to let her send it without our reading it? We've got to be careful with Mary – so has Bess. It's a ticklish position.'

'Dear heart,' said Catherine, smiling at him as though he were a cross between God and her imbecile child, 'I'd trust Bess to deal with a ticklish position rather better than yourself!'

Bess, reading her letter in the beautiful flowing handwriting that her tutors had taught her, would have concurred. She had pretended entire agreement with her 'very dear sister' while refusing to do anything she asked; shared her 'just grief in seeing the ashes or rather the scarcely cold body of the King our father so shamefully dishonoured' by their step-mother's marriage. (Yes it would have been awkward if Catherine had read that! though she would have understood why Bess had to write it.)

And now came the cream of the jest, though, as she had just said, for herself alone: – 'I cannot express to you how much affliction I suffered when I was first informed of this marriage.' (True enough that, in all conscience! No wonder she had grinned as she wrote in amused appreciation of her insincere candour.) Sincerity broke in also when she wrote of the Queen's 'so great affection and so many kind offices' to herself, but these were advanced only in excuse for Bess having to 'use much tact in manœuvring with her for fear of appearing ungrateful for her benefits'. It was the nearest she dared get to reminding Mary that she, too, owed her step-mother gratitude for her kindness.

But she did manage with consummate aplomb to warn her 'dearest sister' (why did that look so much more affectionate when it came in the middle of a letter?) of the folly of 'running heavy risk of making our own lot much worse than it is; at least, so I think. We have to deal with too powerful a party, who have got all authority into their hands, while we, deprived of power, cut a very poor figure at Court,' – a pathetic picture of two royal Cinderellas that made its writer, in the midst of a whirl of festivities, chuckle happily.

And here Bess did make a bad slip, carried away by her own worldly advice to the woman of over thirty. 'I think, then,' she wrote, 'that the best course we can take is that of dissimulation. . . . If our silence does us no honour, at least it will not draw down upon us such disasters as our lamentations might induce.'

The letter was a perfect piece of diplomacy – if only it had been addressed to the right person. But a letter is a joint affair, depending almost as much upon its reader as its writer. The determined honesty, the loathing of compromise, that Mary had inherited from her mother, without any of her mother's tact, made her quite incapable of taking warning from Bess's reminders of the harm her protests might do to herself.

But the warning she did take was of Bess herself, that inscrutably smiling girl, just on fourteen, who could so complacently accept it 'if our silence do us no honour'; who could so cynically plan, 'the best course we can take is that of dissimulation'.

And Mary would remember that warning to the end of her life.

Chapter Seven

YOUNG EDWARD, not content with writing good advice and assurances of his patronage to his elders, and terse demands for cash to be slipped under carpets, also kept a Journal.

It was Mr Cheke's idea, and it gave him a pleasing sense of importance to write it, sitting at his little desk which was covered with black velvet, so as not to show the inkstains (an economical notion of the Duchess); it contained fascinating inner compartments and secret drawers where he could store his treasures; some buttons of agate and gold, some strange new instruments that showed the signs of the zodiac and the movements of the stars (Edward liked stars); a cormorant's egg which Barnaby had brought him from the Donegal cliffs; and half a dozen dog collars of red and white leather, a present from Cuthbert Vaughan, his Master of the Dogs.

There he sat in 'the Kynge's secret studie' at Westminster, the only place where he could feel himself in undisputed command of a kingdom, looking out on the busy river and on the further shore the gardens and towers of Lambeth Palace where Archbishop Cranmer sat writing, just as busily as himself, at the new English Prayer Book, that staggering innovation that was to make a new religion, a new England, and all the great men in the land would contribute something to it; Edward would himself. Already his only title for it was 'the Book of my proceedings'.

Meanwhile he wrote his Journal. And on the same page as his account of the 'great preparation mad to goe into Scotland' by the Lord Protector and other great nobles, to carry out King Henry's dying wishes to have the Scots finally and thoroughly smashed, he put the briefest of records of his uncle Tom Seymour's marriage to the Queen, 'with wich mariag' (spelling was not yet stabilized, especially Edward's) 'the Lord Protectour was much offended'.

But as the Scottish campaign was carrying the Lord Protector away from this domestic scene of action, he had at first to leave hostilities to that keen lieutenant, his wife. The Duchess instantly attacked with full batteries of abuse which did not spare even that national monument the late King.

'Did not King Henry marry Catherine Parr in his doting days, when he had brought himself so low by his lust and cruelty that no lady that stood on her honour would venture on him?' Whereas she herself was not only the wife of the Duke of Somerset and Lord Protector of England, but the great-great-granddaughter, on her mother's side, of the tenth son of Edward III. It was nothing to her that the progeny of that enormous family would soon make it quite difficult for any gentry *not* to be descended from Edward III; she looked on herself as the one and only Plantagenet, and it was a gross personal insult that she should have to bear the train of the Queen Dowager who was really only Catherine Parr, a nobody, 'now casting herself for support on a younger brother. If Master Admiral teach his wife no better manners, I am she that will.'

And that Impossible She proceeded to teach her new sister-in-law manners by jostling her in the doorway at State functions and fairly stampeding out of the room so as to take precedence of her and avoid bearing her train. 'Exceeding violent' was the verdict of the astonished witnesses, and, in the opinion of one sly observer, this business of the Queen's train was kicking up so much dust that it might well end in smothering both their husbands.

For Tom could also be exceeding violent; he swore with loud and terrible oaths that 'no one should speak ill of the Queen, or he would take his fist to the ears of those who did, from the lowest to the highest.' Which gave to many a reasonable hope of seeing him box the Duchess's ears, or perhaps even the Duke's.

The Court was beginning to take sides, and furiously. Nearly everybody there was finding the Duchess's 'many imperfections intolerable, her pride monstrous'. Ned Seymour had always been an almost oppressively upright and conscientious man; but no one could trust a man ruled by such a wife, and many said that in his quieter way he was becoming almost as bad. He had set aside the conditions of the late King's will almost before the breath was out of his body and taken his supreme power by a *coup d'état*; he was destroying churches, even parts of St Paul's, to build himself Somerset House, – the churches did not matter, they were fair game and everyone was doing it, but St Paul's was more than a church, it was the City, it was London itself; and Somerset House was more than a house, it was a palace bigger than anybody else, even a King, had ever had.

Worst of all, the fellow would make speeches; beautiful speeches, which nobody could make head or tail of; speeches about liberty and freedom of speech for all men, about religious toleration and free discussion as the best way to settle all problems, and not merely of religion either. He had not only repealed all the laws against heresy but most of those against treason too; a man might now even impugn the Royal Supremacy in speech, though not in writing. It was plain asking for trouble and rebellion, and as if this were not enough, he was actually going against his own class, encouraging discontent among the common people, for that was what would come of his taking their side against their landlords in his attempts to give them back their common lands. For centuries they had been allowed to graze their sheep and cattle on them, but they had now been enclosed for the use of the big landowners, who were bristling like hedgehogs at the idea of giving them back to the people.

Let him try out his fool notions on religion if he must; but property, that was another matter, that was sacred.

And now here he was doing his youngest brother out of the property that was rightly, even legally, his and his wife Catherine's. A fellow that could trick his younger brother out of his own, that showed you what the fellow was really like.

For in the midst of all these mutterings and growlings was heard that magnificent voice of Tom Seymour.

'My brother is wondrous hot in helping every man to his right, save me! He makes a great matter of preventing my having the Queen's jewels, which you see by the whole opinion of the lawyers ought to belong to me, and all under pretence that he would not the King should lose so much, — as if it were a loss to the King to let me have mine own!'

Even the Queen's wedding ring had been robbed from her, he told Fowler as he sat drinking in the privy buttery; and Mr Fowler sighed piously and said (or said afterwards that he said), 'Alas, my lord, that ever jewels or muck of this world should make you begin a new matter between my Lord Protector and you!' At which my lord roared for his boots and rode away.

And his wife Catherine, who had been so careless of the 'muck of this world' when she had fled the Palace of Whitehall in those haunted days of last January, was now as eager and indignant about the jewels as he. To her they were no capricious gift of King Henry's doting days, but her just wages for three and a half years' devoted service as his sick-nurse, a job that few women would indeed have willingly ventured on.

And it was not only the jewels, and not only King Henry's gifts. Catherine's favourite country manor of Fasterne had been grabbed by methods even more flagrant. The Protector, or again his Duchess had without its owner's consent, coolly installed a tenant in it who paid the bare minimum of rent (and presently ceased doing even that) and refused even to allow her to graze her cattle in its park, so that she had to pay farmers for their pasturage, — and this at the same time that the Protector was proposing to reform the grievance of the enclosures and to give the grazing lands back to the people! Charity, or rather justice, should begin at home, said Tom loudly; and even his gentle Cathy wrote to her husband that it was lucky his elder brother was away at the moment, 'for else I believe I should have bitten him'.

But she fully intended to utter all her rage against the Protector to him in front of the King, 'if you do not give me advice to the contrary,' — as if it were likely Tom should ever give her such advice! Now that she was married to him she was so deep in love that she was coming to rely utterly on him in all matters, with the abandonment of a woman entirely happy and satisfied for the first time in thirty-five years and four marriages. Any doubts she had ever felt as to his perfect moderation in temper or judgment had been cast to the winds; she was now young for the first time, young and foolish, glorying in feeling so and in looking up to the finest man in England as her arbiter in all things.

Others did not altogether endorse her opinion; that of the more discriminating of his fellows was that 'the Lord Sudley was fierce in courage, courtly in fashion, in personage stately, in voice magnificent, but somewhat empty in matter.'

But he was extremely popular with them; they agreed that his little wife, after all she had been through, deserved her luck, for it was plain that they were really lovers. And if all the world loves a lover, it also loves a younger son, who has to make his own way in the world, as Tom had done triumphantly, and no thanks to his elder brother. And now that that supremely fortunate elder brother was actually trying to hinder him, it was not only base, it was unnatural.

They all liked the little Queen and they liked Tom, even if he did brag and wag his beard a bit – in fact, all the more for doing so; he was so wildly, gloriously indiscreet, generous not only with his money and his sumptuous entertaining, his royal banquets, his gaming parties and water parties and sports of every kind, but also with himself, talking so freely and openly without any shadow of suspicion or even caution of his hearers, taking them all for granted as his friends, certain that they would feel just as he did about the wrongs he had to endure from his brother, and quite reckless lest such talk might lay up occasion for yet worse wrongs. And, however angry, he was never tedious nor doleful, would shrug it off with a laugh and 'Oh well, "more was lost on Mohacs' field," as they still say in Hungary!'

The common people too adored him. Every time he went out they roared for him as they had done for King Hal when at the height of his popularity, and there were many who said he was more like that King when young than the pale little Prince ever showed a sign of becoming; as kingly, and with a finer beauty than even that giant had once worn; and the hearty carefree laugh that rang out from him as he scattered coins among the crowd sounded in all older ears as the echo of that great laugh of Bluff King Hal in his golden youth.

Free with his money he was, like Hal, and saw to it that

the conduits ran wine in the Strand when he gave some grand show at his house there – which was more than his elder brother did, for all that he called himself the Protector. Solemn as a judge *he* was; he might talk big about reform, but reforms never did anybody much good, there was always a catch somewhere, and the rich managed to make themselves richer by them while the poor came off worse than before. A lot of fine talk cost him nothing, and did nothing for anyone else; hot air never warmed anybody – but what everyone could see and hear for themselves was that he was busy feathering his own nest, with hundreds of workmen hammering all day at that vast new house to be called by his name.

Altogether Tom had good reason to be pleased with the way things were going. The Protector went up to Scotland at the head of his army and left his younger brother as his Lieutenant-General in charge of the South Ports, and this gave him more scope. Which he used rather mysteriously when he went to dislodge a notorious pirate called Jack Thompson who had seized the Scilly Isles, and came back apparently well satisfied although he had not dislodged him. Was it because he had agreed to share the swag with Mr Thompson?

His friends chuckled and said they always knew Tom was a born buccaneer; but agreed it looked serious when he protected pirates even in the Admiralty Courts, and complaints began to come in from foreign Powers of the loss of their ships.

He was playing with fire, too, among papers, hunting up all the old records he could find to prove that when a boy-King had two uncles, one of them should be Protector of the Realm and the other the Governor of the King's Person. There was no doubt that the King himself would eagerly welcome it. 'If only he were five or six years older!' Tom would exclaim, 'then it would all be plain sailing.' Still, he had got the boy eating out of his hand, eating up a lot of cash certainly, but it should pay good interest.

In his brother's absence he now had more chance to see him by himself, though they still had to resort to the underhand tricks of truant schoolboys to get in touch, but that too was all to the good, since it was breeding in Edward a contained fury of discontent against his present guardians. Nor did it seem to be only self-interest that bound the child to his younger uncle; he was obviously dazzled by him and would stare, almost awed, when he heard his jolly laugh, as at something so alien to his cold restricted life that he did not know how to meet it.

For his stepmother his feelings were simpler and more certain : for four years she had taken the place of the mother he had never known, and as naturally and lovingly as if she were indeed his mother : he missed her badly, and deeply resented that he was still being kept apart from her except for the briefest of formal visits. Even when she stayed at St James's Palace and he at Whitehall within a stone's throw, he found he could only write to her although 'I was so near to you and expected to see you every day'.

But the Admiral promised he would make it all come right. The Admiral said it was ridiculous that he should have to sit at his books all day. A King ought to be a good fellow, and mix with other good fellows – 'Look at your father, he was hail-fellow-well-met with everyone at sight and it served him a deal better than writing treaties against Luther and getting dubbed Defender of the Faith by the Pope,' – an unfortunate example, for the small face beneath him at once looked huffy and his nephew hastened to say that *he* was writing a comedy against the Pope, called 'The Whore of Babylon'.

'Very sound, very sound,' said his uncle, 'though you'd do it better later when you know more about—'

'I know all about the Pope.'

'—more about whores then.' But he found it safer to step off the subject, for Edward took his position as Supreme Head of the English Church very seriously. So he talked to him of his other duties as King. He ought to go on board the splendid ships that his father and grandfather had built, and tell the sailors that he would build more, to down the Spaniards and conquer the New World beyond the Western Ocean. All true Englishmen were growing sick and tired of sitting at home, watching the smoke of their firesides, now that they no longer went out in every generation to fight in the wars in France. Agincourt was now only an old song –

'Our King went forth to Normandy
With grace and might of chivalry' –

and England had shrunk from a Continental Empire to a little island (and only half of that). But a fine navy might still make her a world power.

And Edward ought to go hunting and hawking and prepare to lead his armies in the field; in Hungary a man did not count himself a man unless he were on a horse—

'Yet the Turks beat them at Mohacs,' Edward interpolated – odious child, he knew everything : but his uncle had a better answer this time.

'And well I know why, as Master Gunner of England, who am seeing to it that it shall never happen to an English army. The Turks were the first to use this stinking new artillery in full force, and the finest chivalry in Europe went down before it. It happened once, it will happen again, but not to us while *I'm* in command of the Ordnance, – if I have the right backing.'

'*I'll* back you,' said the child, suddenly lighting into enthusiasm.

'You'll be a fine King,' said Tom, patting the fair head, but again came the petulant jut of Edward's full under-lip, that so reminded one of his father.

'I am King *now*,' he said.

'You ought to be more of one. You can't always be tied to your Uncle Ned's leading-strings, you know, and he's a bit of an old woman, far too old for you anyway.'

The under-lip stuck out further in a ferocious pout.

'I wish he were dead,' it said.

This was going further than Ned's brother had dreamed of. Edward saw his uncle's astonishment, sucked in his lip so that his mouth became a tiny red button, and repeated with cold, considered obstinacy, 'it would be better if he died.'

It was too much for the hardy buccaneer, who had only been tentatively feeling his way to the suggestion of a joint guardianship with his brother, and now felt a slight shiver at this 'sweet gentle child', as everybody called him.

He told his wife that he was a little monster, whereat his

Cathy indignantly told him that he did not understand children and that it was all because Edward had been taken away from her own motherly care. Tom scoffed at the notion that he did not understand his nephew; anyway, the boy understood *him* and what he wanted, which was the important thing. Edward was going to write out a list of his complaints against his Uncle Somerset, and sign it with the royal signature, telling exactly what he felt about being kept so strictly in hand and so short of cash, and so entirely unsuitably for a great King who had just had his tenth birthday. Tom was going to read it out at that autumn's Parliament, 'and,' said he, 'if they don't do as I want about it, then by God's teeth I'll make it the blackest Parliament ever known in England!'

Even Cathy was startled into alarm and begged him not to oppose his brother so openly; but he only laughed at her fears; and then, before the scheme was ripe, the Protector, Duke of Somerset, came home from Scotland in the autumn, a conquering hero, his position greatly strengthened by his having won a tremendous victory at some place with the absurd name of Pinkie. The soldiers said it was really his second-in-command, John Dudley, Earl of Warwick, who won it. In any case, everybody said that this time the Scots would certainly never be able to lift their heads again; though a few seemed to remember much the same thing being said five years ago after the battle of Solway; and some old croakers went so far as to remember that there had been even more reason to say it over thirty years ago, after Flodden.

The conquering hero himself felt his success oddly clouded, though it was only by a dream, which he recounted to his secretary Mr Patten on the morning of the battle as they walked on the ramparts, looking towards Scotland; and told him to write it down, though, as Mr Patten objected, it was only an idle dream.

'Dreams should not be idle,' said his master; 'they should be the busy servants of those statesmen who have the courage to dream wisely.'

So the secretary shrugged imperceptibly and noted down how the Protector had dreamed of his triumphant return to

Court after the campaign, and the hearty thanks expressed to him by the King and all the country: 'but yet he thought he had done nothing at all in this voyage: which, when he considered the King's Highness' great costs and great travail of the great men and soldiers all to have been done in vain, the very care and shamefast abashment of the thing did waken him out of his dream.'

What could be the point in noting such moonshine, thought Mr Patten, when it had been directly followed by his winning a stupendous victory in which he had killed thousands of the enemy, laid waste their country and destroyed their harvest; and his troops, mainly hired mercenaries from Germany and Spain, had kindled such furious hatred among the Scots that there was no hope of their accepting his very reasonable and conciliatory offer of peace and union.

He omitted all King Henry's arrogant claim to Scotland as a vassal state, and based it only on an equal union through marriage of her Queen and England's King, with Free Trade between the countries, and both England and Scotland to be renamed together with Wales as Great Britain; an island empire 'having the sea for a wall, mutual love for a garrison, and no need in peace to be ashamed, or in war to be afraid of any worldly power.'

Which put it beautifully; but, as Tom said, it wasn't much use to preach mutual love when you'd let loose the German landsknechts and Spanish ruffians under the Italian condottiere Malatesta to loot and rape, burn and murder through the countryside. With their aid he'd won the war but lost the peace, for Scotland was more determined than ever to get their little Queen over in safety to France and betroth her to the Dauphin before she should be captured by force and taken to England. A French fleet had been known to have been hovering off the Scottish shores this summer; now they would have to wait for the spring, since no good seaman would trust so precious a freight to the dangers of a voyage between St Simon's and St Jude's Day and Candlemas, when storms were at their worst, and by seaman's law no ships should then sail the Northern Seas. But they were only biding their time, and then Scotland would be driven deeper into the arms of France than ever before, and England would have to face the prospect of encirclement on south, north and west by France, and by French armies in Scotland, with Ireland as a third base for invasion, easy to capture from Scotland – the very danger that Somerset had recognized and striven so hard to avoid.

It was his fate to have to work by force when he would far rather use persuasion. He tried to use it now, and set in train an immense invasion of another sort – to wit, thousands of religious leaflets and hundreds of Bibles in English, printed in Geneva. For he saw clearly that Scotland could only be united to England if she shared her new Reformed Religion, and that this was the best lever to use against her alliance with Roman Catholic France.

Another propaganda weapon lay in the prisoners he had taken, who were to buy their freedom, also pensions and promises of important marriages, by undertaking to work for English interests in Scotland. The Scots Lord Chancellor himself was one of these, the Earl of Huntly, a fat, talkative fellow who thought he ruled Scotland; and the fickle flimsy Fair Earl of Bothwell, tall and stooping rather from his slight shoulders, very vain of his delicate colouring that betokened consumption, and of his wavering blue eyes. He insisted on marriage to either of the Princesses, Mary or Elizabeth (he hadn't seen either and didn't mind which) as his price; and was fobbed off instead with the usual promise of Anne of Cleves – a promise that nobody, least of all the lady in question, intended to keep. The Fair Lord Francis had a wife at home (and a schoolboy son, James, as dark as he himself was fair), but he had just managed to divorce her, having had the intention of marrying his own Queen-Regent, the mother of the little Queen of Scots. A royal marriage was evidently his *idée fixe*.

The citizens of London wanted to express their loyal gratitude to the victorious Duke of Somerset by giving him a triumphal procession through the city, but this he modestly refused, – to their annoyance, for if one had the expense of a war, one might as well have the fun of it. But the eldest Seymour's lonely spirit was too aloof to see how a gorgeous spectacle and free drinks running in the gutters would en-hance his popularity: just as he never saw that his modesty was first credited as parsimony, and then hypocrisy, for he now placed himself in Parliament on a throne high up and apart from all the other lords, to their intense exasperation.

If *this* were modesty, give them Old Harry's pride! Their offended dignity was only aggravated by his piety, for in his prayer at the opening of Parliament he spoke of himself as 'called by Providence to rule' – but Providence never offered him that upper seat!

The newly self-made Duke then complained of his parvenu Council as a lot of 'lords sprung from the dunghill'; after that, a good many of them said they would prefer Tom as Protector. And Somerset put the final edge on Tom's own grievances against him by writing him a long and solemn letter urging him 'to receive poor men's complaints, that find themselves injured or grieved, for it is our duty and office so to do'.

Tom's roar of rage as he read it brought his household running to hear his blasphemously and indecently expressed opinion of an elder brother who had never helped him to anything, but withheld his wife's possessions, down to her wedding ring, and then lectured him on brotherly duty to his neighbour!

His furious laughter went rolling and roaring through the house; he kicked a chair across the hall and picked up another and broke it in his hands; he swore he would go and see our Pulpit Ned on the instant and ram his canting letter down his throat; he would ask him how he had the face to talk about the Rights or Wrongs of the poor, when he had done his own son and heir out of his inheritance and was now cheating his own brother out of his goods; he was an unnatural father and an unnatural brother, in fact there was nothing natural about him, and he accused his own mother, as she came tottering and quavering down the stairs, of having conceived him of the Devil.

A birdlike little old lady, usually spry and dapper as a water-wagtail, Lady Seymour now twittered about the hall, fluttering her hands and uttering disconsolate chirps such as 'Now, now, now!' 'Another quarrel!' 'Not again!' 'Always fighting as boys, I thought they'd kill each other, and now, now—'

His wife sobbed, the servants peeped awestruck round doorways, Bess took a gallery seat at the top of the stairs to watch the row, and little Jane Grey peeped over her shoulder and wondered if all grown-ups were mad.

The quarrel raged its way into the Protector's palace, and as usual it took the Protector some time to understand what Tom was making all this noise about. He had been meaning himself to get in first with his own grievances.

His nervous eyebrows went fidgeting half-way up the furrowed dome of his forehead as he complained how he had to cut short his campaign in Scotland to hurry home and enquire into all manner of disturbing reports of his brother. Surely the welfare of the State mattered more than petty personal affairs, women's toys, trinkets.

What was this about the Lord High Admiral countenancing piracy? It had even been suggested that he meant to establish a naval base for himself in the Scilly Isles.

But here the Admiral blew away the suggestion like a gale at sea.

'Piracy, pooh! The pirates of today are the pioneers of tomorrow. You'll see! England will owe more to her pirates than to her Protectors.'

The Protector hastily abandoned pirates. Tom had been unsettling the King's mind, taking him out hunting when he should have been at his lessons, thrusting himself into his favour—

'God's blood, and isn't he my nephew as much as yours? Why should you have the right to work the poor little brat to death at his books when his head's spinning so that he can hardly see? I'll swear you don't even know that his eyes are weak and have to be bathed with Mother Jack's foul mixtures—' (The Protector didn't; nor did the Admiral till his wife had told him.) 'Suit you finely to have a blind King, so that you can carry on your Protection – God save the mark!—'

The younger brother shouted; the elder compressed his lips; the Duchess swept in and told Master Admiral what she thought of younger brothers and their wives, and the Admiral told her what he thought of her; the Protector slid away to compose a prayer to 'the Granter of all peace and quietness, the Defender of all Nations, who has willed all men to be accounted as our neighbours, and commanded us to love them as ourselves; and not to hate our enemies, but rather to wish them, yea and also to do them good if we can . . . to give unto all men a speedy wearisomeness of all war, hostility and enmity . . . and grant in Thy days Thy great gift of unity'.

It was perhaps the most moving and perfect prayer ever addressed on behalf of a conquered enemy, for it was a prayer for Union with Scotland; but, for once, 'petty personal affairs' may have also tinged those austere desires for the welfare of the State.

The brothers' quarrel was patched up somehow, as it had to be to avoid a hideous open scandal: the Lord High Admiral's income was increased by £800 a year; and then the Duke of Somerset settled down with a sigh of relief to the enormous but congenial burden of the reform of religion and organization of the Church as an efficient branch of the Civil Service; the direction of all England's foreign diplomatic correspondence (with only two secretaries to help him); the supervising of every meeting of the Council and of Parliament; and a host of far-reaching but not always practicable schemes for the freedom of speech and the Press, and for social reforms to check the rise in prices and the debasement of the currency, to stop land-grabbing by the New Rich and unemployment of the poor; he even had a Court of Requests set up in his own house so that the humblest suppliant who came to complain of any wrong or oppression might get the ear of the great Duke himself, the Good Duke, as the poor now called him.

But the Duchess still wore the Queen Dowager's jewels.

Chapter Eight

THE ADMIRAL LOST his chance to make that autumn's Parliament the blackest ever seen, not because of the power of the greatest statesman in England, but because of the intractability of a small boy.

Edward had never supplied him with that signed list of complaints that was to win him his freedom and his Uncle Tom's ascendancy; instead, he had asked his tutor about it, and 'Mr Cheke said I had better not write it,' he said in his cool little even voice, as dispassionately as if he had been let off writing a Latin prose.

For the second time the reckless adventurer felt a slight shiver as he looked down at the pretty, rather mulish little face. *Did* he – or anyone else – understand children, their secret and incalculable life, governed by no one knew what obscure impulses and caprice?

Young Edward had certainly seemed to resent his elder uncle's domination even to the point of hating him and wishing his death; but now he appeared to have forgotten all about it, or at any rate did not wish to be bothered with it, but only to be left alone.

This was indeed something of the case, for Edward's weak vitality had begun to shrink from his overpowering younger uncle; he vaguely felt that he could never be the sort of King that Uncle Tom expected him to be – but if he couldn't be a mixture of Christopher Columbus, Richard Cœur de Lion and Saint George (silly, that story of Saint George, he was sure there had never been any Dragons in England), at least he could be the wisest, most learned and most religious King England had ever had. A deal of people thought he would be, too.

The learned refugee, Dr Bucer from Germany, said how lucky his subjects were to have a philosopher for their Prince. (Dr Bucer was lucky too, for Edward had sent the cash for him to have a German stove in his house at Cambridge as he couldn't get warm with the English open fires.)

But his Uncle Tom wouldn't think anything of a philosopher King. His Uncle Somerset would.

The Admiral could tell him exciting stories of the heathen Turks, how their janissaries dipped the horsehair plumes of their lances in blood as a sign of war, and for years now those lances were pointing further and further into Europe; the Sultan's dashing incendiaries had plundered Austria and hammered on the walls of Vienna while his Crescent still flew from the citadel of Buda Pest, where Tom himself had feasted and talked with him in his dark gleaming coat of mail, with heron plumes waving in his turban, fastened by a diamond named the Eye of Heaven.

Edward listened with interest, but considered that the Turk was still a long way off, and Europe wasn't England, there was all the sea between; and moreover England was his, and Scotland ought to be too, his father had always said so; and his Uncle Somerset was fighting this Scottish war, not just for Europe or Christendom, but for *him*.

So that it was with a thrill of personal pride that he wrote in his Journal a full account, almost as clear and vivid as if he had been there himself, of the battle of Pinkie, how 10,000 Scots were slain, and 1,000 lords (he wrote 2,000 in his first enthusiasm but punctiliously altered it to the more modest estimate); how the Scots strove for the higher ground 'and almost gott it', but Somerset rallied the English horse so that 'the Scotts stood amasid'; how Somerset was challenged by the pompous Earl of Huntly to single combat but refused him for the excellent reason that he was in charge of so precious a jewel as the governance of his King's person, and how John Dudley, Earl of Warwick, chased that plump Scottish braggart and was almost taken prisoner himself by riding slap into an ambush, but was rescued by a French knight Berteville who got 'hurt in the buttok', but, as Edward finished with a flourish that turned his final 'y' into a horse-whip, 'the ambush ran away'.

And he rubbed his eyes, which were smarting again, and sent for Mother Jack, who clucked like an angry hen at all these books – 'Aren't there enough in the world as it is and

116

enough trouble caused by them?' (she disapproved of the new English Bible) 'but you too must go scribble, scribble, scribble?' – and delicately painted his sore eyes with a feather dipped into a precious water compounded of fennel, rue, pimpernel, sage, celandine, honey, and fifteen peppercorns, boiled in a pint of white wine to which was added five spoons of 'the water of a man-child'that is an innocent.'

But the precious water didn't do as much good as usual, and Edward swore at his nurse with a few of the Admiral's thundering oaths, and the Protector, who never used a brutal or coarse expression in the whole of his life, heard them and demanded which of the King's playfellows had taught him those shocking words. Edward was just going to tell their origin when young Barnaby Fitzpatrick, rolling up his blue eyes with the look of a repentant cherub, admitted to having taught his King to swear.

'And why did you so abuse your trust?' demanded the Protector sternly, while Edward stared, too astonished to speak.

Barnaby was plainly perplexed, but only for the instant. 'I thought,' he said presently, now casting down his eyes in an even more specious humility, 'that it was the proper thing for a King to do.'

There was a moment's hush in which all there seemed to hear the echoed roar of King Harry's monstrous blasphemies. Then the Protector hurriedly ordered the Irish boy to be whipped in Edward's presence, and rubbed it well into his nephew that the same should be done to him too if he were not the King. Edward, white and sullenly furious, watched his friend's punishment, and as soon as they were alone, demanded indignantly why he had courted it.

'Ah, and why wouldn't I?' said young Barnaby carelessly. 'You don't want another fight between your uncles, do you?'

'I have too many uncles,' said Edward ominously.

*   *   *

Christmas brought the first full reunion of the royal family since their father's death. Even Mary accepted the invitation to Court, though it involved her in long arguments with the Protector, who attacked her right to have Mass said privately in her own house; and she counter-attacked the way in which he was setting aside all the terms of her father's Will.

Somerset's attempts to prove that his late Sacred Majesty's intentions were entirely Protestant landed him in a mass of self-contradictions; it was the Admiral who, as he crudely said, 'took the cow by the horns' and pointed out to Mary that King Henry's words and actions had been so inconsistent that it was impossible to base a settled policy upon them. Oddly enough, the Princess seemed to prefer this to his brother's justifications; in spite of the snubbing she had given Tom over his marriage a few months before, they grew very friendly together over music; and when she sighed over her lack of practice in the virginals he lent her his best musician to give her lessons.

He had brought a band of gipsies from Vienna who delighted both the Princesses by playing to them the music they considered appropriate to their charms; Elizabeth's was a wild Hungarian dance, and Mary's a tender mournful ballad about the wanderings of the Magyars in search of their Promised Land, which brought tears to her eyes.

She was in a genial mood, very new to those who had not seen her since she kept her own household, free of the Court and her father's domination. Even her religion seemed to be sitting more loosely on her, for she lost a bet of £10 to Dr Bill, one of the leading theological lights of the Protestant Church; and could not refrain from going a pleased pink when told that her translation of Erasmus's Paraphrases of St John had been issued to all the churches in England as a companion volume to the new English Bible.

'We'll be having you as good a Protestant as any of us,' Tom said, and she only gave her great gruff laugh that reminded one of her father and sounded so oddly from her small, rather shrunken figure. As usual, it was much too showily dressed; ermine stripes ran in every direction like an erratic zebra, and the shoulder-puffs on her sleeves reached her ears, her face poking forward between them, shortsighted, peering, vaguely bewildered but determined.

The dances and romping games, the fooling and practical jokes were as fast and furious as they had been a year ago under the glazed eye of the huge figure that had sat glittering and moribund in the chair worked by his devoted daughter.

This was not because the Protector had the same simple enjoyment in games of Snapdragon, Forfeits, Kiss-in-the-Ring, and Hunt-the-Slipper (indeed, he was barely conscious that they were going on), but because the Admiral had by common consent been appointed Lord of Misrule.

Even the little King took part in a Masque of Cats, and was gravely pleased with his tabby coat and furry mask with whiskers a foot long. He had to enter on the shoulders of John Dudley, the Earl of Warwick, dressed as a dog, according to the curious Natural History of masques. The famous soldier capered about behind the scenes, barking beautifully, then ducked before Edward, but the boy, small even for his age, looked round for a stool to help him to mount; there was none, so Tom placed a massive brass-bound Bible on the floor, but his nephew was shocked at the idea of standing on the Word of God.

'Half the fellows at Court have risen by it,' said Tom with a wink at John Dudley, but the joke went too near home, for the new Earl had made an enormous fortune out of the Reformation and the sale of Church lands, and had testified to the new piety *à la mode* by christening one of his sons Guildford, the first time anyone had been christened after a town and not a saint. Since Henry's death, with the Reformation coming out into the open, he had risen rapidly. So he naturally found Tom's joke in the worst of taste. 'A fine figure of a man,' he drawled in an audible aside; 'pity it wants a head, – may do so in earnest before long.'

There would have been a duel had not the Protector been determined to put down that 'heathenish custom'. Tom told him he was a fool to be so scrupulous as to miss a chance to get Dudley out of the way. 'He's a dark horse and will be in the running against you before long, you can take my word for it,' – nor did it strike him as odd to expect his brother to take his word for it, when he himself had so openly entered the running against him.

*   *   *

Elizabeth had lost a forfeit to the Admiral; she was indignant, for he had taken the unfair advantage of bursting into her room in the morning, putting his head through the bed-curtains and shouting 'Bonjour, Philippine!' before she was awake. He was always up early and generally looked in on his way from Catherine's room before Bess was up, or he himself more than half dressed. 'Now then, Slug-a-bed!' he would call, and pull off the bed-clothes and tickle or smack her to make her get up, and tell her she was an idle slut and sing:

> 'See-saw, Margery Daw
> Sold her bed to lie upon straw.
> Wasn't she an idle slut!'

Bess found these sudden surprises very exciting, sometimes rather alarming, but even that was pleasant. One moment she would be sound asleep, and then crashing into her dreams would come a deep gay voice, a thrill of expectation, – what was it that was going to happen? and she woke to see his face laughing down on her, and this time it was saying, 'Bonjour, Philippine! And now what forfeit will you pay me?'

'Bread and cheese! You've got everything you want.'

'Not everything. Pay me a kiss to start with.'

She had kissed him often, leaping up and flinging her arms round his neck, but now suddenly she shied at it, slid out at the other side of the bed, and ran through the open doorway into the next room where her maids were preparing her bath. He gave chase, there was a wild scurry and giggling, she dodged behind first one girl and then another, she ran round the wide tub of porphyry and he leaped over it, dropping a slipper splash into the steaming scented water, stubbed his bare foot against the marble side of the tub, sprawled forward, dealt her a resounding smack from behind, caught at the flying skirt of her shift and gave it a tug which pulled her backwards plump into the bath with a mighty splash that emptied half the water on to the floor, drenched her hair and all the furniture near. The laughing shrieks brought Mrs Ashley running; she shrieked a little too, in camaraderie, but not with the same conviction; she was shocked at the Admiral's deshabille, at his bare foot, at his romping with the Princess and her maids in her bedroom. People might talk, they might even blame herself.

She pointed this out to him later and asked him to stop his morning visits: she owed it to herself, as she was in charge.

The Admiral did not care what she owed to herself, an interfering cackling busybody, making a storm in a posset-cup! He was genuinely astonished, for he not only swore, to show the purity of his intentions – 'God's precious soul, where's the harm? I mean none, so I'll not leave off!' – but he actually burst out that if there were any more of this meddling he would tell the Protector how he was being slandered, – as certain of Ned's partisanship as if they were still at school, and Ned the much elder brother who would lecture him gravely on his faults but be sure to take his side against anyone else.

So the Admiral did not leave off, and out of bravado made the fun even more outrageous; sometimes Bess ran from him among her maids, sometimes hid from him in the bed-curtains or cupboards and was punished with a slap or tickling that made her wriggle and giggle and hit out at him and shriek for mercy or for help from the giggling maids, and enjoy it all thoroughly. All very well, thought Mrs Ashley, to say it was nothing but a childish frolic, but there were none of these frolics with the child Jane Grey – indeed, one couldn't imagine her, though only eleven, taking part in them. But there was no question of it, for she had her separate apartments, servants, and tutors.

Mrs Ashley, not the wisest of women, and terrified of tackling the Admiral again, tried warning her charge, reminding her that she was now nearly fourteen and a half, and growing very like her mother in some ways, and ought to begin to behave with the dignity and decorum of a young lady.

'Did my mother?' asked Bess demurely.

Her governess wished she had the Admiral's privilege of smacking her. She said she was very pert and silly, that men were fools in not recognizing when a girl was no longer a child, but that they did not really like hoydens, and that of all people a Princess should not behave like a romping milkmaid.

This began to go well; Bess felt uncomfortable and looked

furious; but Mrs Ashley, afraid of provoking one of the girl's rages, which always reduced her to a shaking fit of nerves, then spoilt all chance of real effect from these snubs by making mysterious hints.

Bess's mother, Nan Bullen, had driven men mad for her; she had been betrothed when only fifteen to the poor young Percy, Lord of Northumberland, who had never got over it, 'and your eyes are like hers, though *they* were black as sloes, – but I'll swear the Admiral sees it too. If you knew all I could tell you, you'd see I'm not making a fuss for nothing, but there are things you don't know and you must take my word for it, and be very careful with that man.'

Thus darkly nodding and pursing her lips, Cat Ashley overshot her mark, and knew no peace till Bess had coaxed and bullied the secret out of her.

'The Queen was only second-best to him; he'd have had you if he could. But the Council wouldn't hear of it, so he fell back on his old sweetheart, – Oh, he's very fond of her, all the world can see that—'

Yes, Bess could see that; but she was seeing other things too; the garden at Chelsea nearly a year ago, and the Admiral standing watching her as she played at ball with her pomander; he had asked her to marry him, he had taken her chin in his hand, he had been just going to kiss her, and not, she was sure, in the casual hearty way he had so often kissed her since, as one kisses a child, – and then his Cathy, her Pussy-Cat Purr, came out, and he turned it all into a joke. Watching them together, straight on top of that moment in the garden, she had been quite sure it had only been a joke; and then within four days had come the dreadful damning confirmation of it, when Catherine told her she had just been formally betrothed to him. Bess had shrugged it off, of course, she owed it to herself (but she owed the phrase to the Ash-Cat, she realized in sudden annoyance at its vulgarity): she had laughed and played with him all this year; but, as she was now suddenly aware, all the time her heart had been broken.

She made up her mind to be very grave and dignified with him, rather distant, but not in obvious displeasure, only wistfully aloof. The result was that the Admiral asked her if she had a stomach-ache. And it was impossible to go on being wistfully aloof when you were tickled almost into hysterics.

Mrs Ashley had to look round for a third person to whom to complain; and ended, where she had better have begun, with the Admiral's wife.

Here naturally she dropped no dark hints (she had indeed been doubtful of their prudence the moment she had uttered them to Bess), but based her warning on the danger of tittle-tattle from the maids; people would say she oughtn't to allow the Admiral to come into her young mistress's room in his bedgown and with bare legs, and the Princess herself in bed. She knew, of course, that he saw no harm in it; she knew what sailors were; she knew – but she did not need to know any more, for Catherine at once agreed quietly and said she would see to it.

It was very tiresome, Catherine thought; she had been so delighted with the jolly easy friendship between Tom and Bess, who had almost stopped being that odd difficult girl since he had come into their household, and become more of a real child than Catherine had ever seen her; indeed, that was why she had failed to realize that she was beginning to grow up.

Now she looked at her with awakened eyes and saw how much taller she had grown lately and prettier, and how the curves of her breasts just showed like small apples above the stiff front of her bodice. The girl was in her fifteenth year – and she herself was thirty-five. That gave her a shock, for it was the first time she had ever thought of comparing herself with Bess.

A plague on these women and their solemn unctuous airs, they spoiled everything. It was not that Cat Ashley had spoken any evil, nor probably thought any, but she had made her conscious of herself, of her husband, of Bess. Once a thing was thought, you could not stop it; it was like throwing a stone into a pond, the ripples went further and further out and must go on till they reached the very edge.

And what should she do? What could she do that would not look suspicious, jealous, the very things she most hated? 'Nothing will ever be the same again,' she told herself miserably, as she held her mirror close to her face and wondered

123

if it had not begun to look thinner lately, even rather hollow under the eyes. But there might be a happier reason for that than her age: it might well be that at last, after all these years, she had begun to be with child. The hope restored all her happiness and confidence, and she knew suddenly what she should do.

Next morning when the Admiral came into Bess's room Catherine came too, and together they woke her, laughing, together they tickled and teased her while she defended herself with the bolster and there was a brief pillow-fight.

But it was not nearly so exciting for Bess.

After that, Catherine was nearly always there as a third partner in the romps, and a very lively one, even destructive on one bright morning in early February, when Bess came out with great dignity towards them as they walked by the little fishpond in the Chelsea garden, came slowly, like the tragedy Queen Herodias, down the terrace steps, attired in a black silk dress.

Her mother, she knew, had had a penchant for black; it was French and chic, and emphatically grown-up; it would remind the Admiral both of Nan Bullen, who had driven men mad for her, and of her own advancing age.

But it did not seem to do any of these things. He stood with his legs apart and his thumbs in his belt and rocked backwards and forwards roaring with laughter, until at last he had breath enough to ask her why on earth she was play-acting in that hideous dress. And Catherine said, 'It doesn't suit you at all, my darling. Do go and take it off.'

She stamped with rage. 'I won't. It's a most suitable dress. Why shouldn't I wear black? I'm in mourning for—' but black was not the royal mourning, and the Admiral finished it for her. 'For your poor dear husband, I'll be bound. You look a brisk young widow.'

Bess went more tragic than ever, for it was all too true, she was indeed a widow, in mourning for the husband she had never had. How heartless and obtuse he was not to see it! Instead, he snatched the scissors that dangled from his wife's girdle, and chased her round the pond, swearing he would cut that preposterous frumpery into ribbons. All her indignant sorrow went to the winds; she picked up her solemn skirts and ran squealing, plump into Catherine's arms, who in fits of laughter held her while Tom slit up the dress this way and that.

'Now go and take it off, you monkey,' said Catherine, kissing her, 'and put on your prettiest colours for this spring day.'

She ran back into the house, laughing now as much as they, to meet Cat Ashley's horrified exclamations and scoldings at the damage to her new dress, 'and such beautiful stuff'.

'It's not, it's hideous,' said Bess airily, 'and anyway it's not my fault. It was two against one, for the Queen held me while the Admiral cut it up.'

'*Well!!*' said Mrs Ashley, looking unutterable things and then apparently swallowing them, for she jerked her head back, then forward, like a hen with a large pea, and pursed her lips tight as if to prevent anything ever escaping through them again. What did at last emerge was a very dry thin note: 'The Queen knows her own business best, I suppose.'

'She does,' said her charge, suddenly flaming, 'and that business is not yours, you prying, prowling old Ash-Cat. Get out of my sight, I'm sick to death of your mimsey face.'

Her governess took the hint.

Chapter Nine

THE STONE HAD fallen into the pond, the ripples were spreading, and not all Catherine's gallantry could stay them.

But she did not know this at once. For her hopes of being with child had become certainty and Tom's delight was uproarious. He was very careful of her and gave her tender instructions as solemnly as a village midwife, so she told him, mocking him with equal tenderness. She must go walks every day to strengthen their boy (they never doubted it would be a boy and all his names were chosen), but she must not get tired, and plenty of country air would be good for her. So they moved about from house to house, and Bess went too.

She too was delighted that there would be a new baby step-stepbrother for her to play with, and she would embroider a shirt for him too. She kept Catherine amused, reading Italian romances to her or playing her lute or the virginals; she had a real ear for music and a delicate light touch. Then, suddenly bored and cramped with sitting still, she would spring up and go running down the garden paths with her greyhound and break into the steps of a gipsy dance, she and Catherine both singing the tune.

Tom, hot and dusty after riding back from London, Court life, and a fresh quarrel with his brother, would come upon some such idyllic scene and reflect anew on the advantages of domestic life among the Turks. 'When I was in Buda Pest' became a rather frequent note of nostalgia. They managed these things better in Hungary; it was reasonable and natural for a man to have at least two wives, so as to amuse himself with the one while the other was occupied with bearing his child. He adored his Cathy, there was no other woman like her, but Bess was not a woman, she had all the contrast of crude, budding girlhood, the sharp sweet flavour of a not quite ripe apple. 'Lord, how I wish I had an apple! Have you such a thing as an apple about you, my sweet Tom?' He had such a thing about him, and he must not taste it.

One evening at Chelsea when a soft gusty wind was tossing the pear blossom over the red brick wall, and the new moon had just begun to show like a ghostly flower caught in the topmost branches, he came back from Westminster in a teasing mood that had a tang in it of bad temper, and chaffed Bess on her matrimonial prospects. Had she any fancy for a cold climate, for sleighing and skating, and a moody young Northern giant for a husband?

For the Protector had decided to marry her either to the Danish or Swedish prince, – 'good for trade,' said Tom; also of course she must take a Protestant, and that narrowed the field; best of all, it would get her out of England and lessen her chances of ever becoming Queen of it.

Catherine looked up, startled, for no one spoke of those chances; the loyal notion was that Edward, though possibly rather delicate, would grow up, marry and have children; and even if he did not, there was Mary. But Bess took it very coolly. She only said in a low tone as though to herself, 'I shall not leave England, however many husbands I may marry.'

He tweaked her ear. 'Here's a large-hearted lass. How many are on the list?'

'I've no list. It's you, my Lord Admiral, who should have a wife in every port.'

'And a port in every storm?'

'Not you! But you make a storm in every posset-cup.'

'She's put you down!' exclaimed his wife.

'If I put her, she'd give birth to vixens. Her tongue's sharper than a tooth, even her hair's aflame with malice. Go and quench that foxy red brush of yours or I'll cut it off and hang it in the hall as a trophy among the other wild beasts' heads.'

It flashed on Catherine that people were sometimes rude like this when they had begun to fall in love but did not yet know it, – yes, and looked at each other like that, with a curious new awareness, their eyes casual and mocking on the surface, yet with a stranger lurking in their depths, intent, watchful, defiant, as though a challenge had gone out between them and had been accepted.

There was nothing she could do; she sat stunned, feeling a little sick, and did not dare look at them again. She heard nothing more that they said, her mind was talking too loud to herself, arguing, disputing.

'But he loves me, I know it. He loves me *now*, not merely in the past, nor in the future as the mother of his child.'

'Fool! That man could love several at the same time, it's his nature to make any number of women happy. And at the moment you are not his lover, only the mother of his child.'

'But she's not fifteen yet, not for five months.'

'Fool! She's older at times than you have ever been. Do you ever know what she's thinking, feeling, deep down beneath her pert chatter, her budding airs and graces? – they are those of a child pretending to be a woman; but all the time beneath them there is a mind at work, the mind of a woman pretending to be a child.'

A wave of hysteria was surging up over her; in another moment she would scream her thoughts aloud, make wild and horrible accusations. Whatever happened, *that* must not. She murmured that it was getting chilly and slid away.

Tom did not notice her going. Bess did, and thought that she ought to run after her, but had an odd fear of doing so. She had not seen Catherine's face, but had felt that someone quite different had risen silently from the bench beside her and stolen away into the chill evening air.

She shivered and told herself that she did not want to go after her, so why should she? She was sick of doing what she ought to do, of being the good little girl. Besides, she was no longer a little girl; princes were making offers for her hand; they had done so since she was a few years old, but then it had not mattered personally to anyone; now it did. It mattered to Tom Seymour, she was sure of it; and it mattered much more to herself. Her pert answers to his banter had served to gain time while she turned this new project over in her mind and discovered what she thought of it. She discovered that it had put her in a smouldering rage. Not for worlds would she show this to Tom, who had so lightly betrayed his own anger at the plan; so she appeared to consider it with pleased curiosity, while she longed to order the Protector to the block for daring to dispose of her without even consulting her first. How dared he, or any man, treat her as a mere property of the State, an appanage of the Crown, a bargaining asset? It was what all princesses were, as a matter of course, yet her knowledge of this made no odds to her; *she* was different.

But to Tom she only laughed when he said she might as well marry a turnip as a Swede. 'And why not?' she said. 'There ought to be roots in matrimony. Perhaps I'll strike mine in new soil after all, and see the world.'

He looked quite hurt as he answered, 'But you said just now you didn't want to leave England.'

He had taken that to mean that she didn't want to leave him! A delicious new sense of power thrilled through her as

she realized it; she too could tease him, then, more ex-
quisitely than he had ever teased her, and she flung back her
head and laughed.

He stared; a slow flush was mounting to his forehead; she
had never seen him look like this. He said, 'You are like your
mother when you laugh.'

'*Oh!*' came on a pettish note of disappointment. 'Was all
the world in love with my mother?'

'Half of it was. The other half hated her.'

'Will that be like me too? And you—?' she paused, looking
at him sidelong in desperate coquetry, then said breathlessly,
'Of which half are you? I think you do not hate me.'

'No, Bess, I don't hate you.'

His voice sounded thick, he looked at her as though he did
not see her, the Bess he had always known, but some thought
of her that lay within his mind. And it was she who had done
this, had laughed and looked and spoken so as to make him
lose hold of that moment; she too, then, like her mother,
might drive men mad for her, and had begun even earlier to
do it. She felt drunk with triumph. This moment was hers;
he should do what she wished with it.

She stood up, with a gesture of command rather than
invitation, and said, 'You were going to kiss me once, in this
garden, it was over a year ago. Will you do it now?'

Did he hear her – see her even? It seemed he was staring
too hard to see her. Her heart thumped furiously against the
whaleboned case of her bodice as though it were trying to
get out; panic swept over her, it was all she could do to keep
from turning and running headlong into the house, but no,
she must not, she would not lose this moment, it was hers,
and she clenched her hands together as if to clutch it to her.

But it was no use, she was going to lose it, she was losing
it, something was happening that would tear it away, a
sound, a movement seen in the tail of her eye.

Little Jane Grey was walking sedately down the path towards them, her freckled face composed into a set pattern of
solemnity.

'I have just returned from Westminster,' she told Bess on
a note of anxious awe, 'and have a message for you from the
King. Mr Cheke is very ill.'

Bess slipped her a look full of loathing. 'Is that all?' she said.

'But it's Mr *Cheke*. He's ill.'

'Well, I can't help it. Why have you got to come running to tell me at once? – you're always thrusting yourself in everywhere – little nuisance!'

This brutal attack on top of her cousin's astounding heartlessness was too much for Jane.

'It's not fair – I *wasn't* running – I *don't* thrust in – I'm always trying to keep out of everybody's way—' two large tears rolled down her cheeks.

'Cry-baby! You'll always say everything isn't fair – you'll never love anyone but old dons and tutors – you – *Ow!*' she ended on a yelp, for the Admiral had lunged forward and dealt her a thumping smack, and there was nothing exciting or tantalizing about it. It hurt.

'You young bully,' he roared, 'I won't have you unkind to my Jane.'

He sat on the bench and took the little girl on his knee, and she put her head on his chest and sobbed. Bess knew he had fallen clean out of love with her; she was only a child to him again, and an unpleasant child at that. She could have killed her small cousin.

Jane conscientiously raised her tearful face from the Admiral's waistcoat and gave Edward's message – 'The King told me – to tell you – "tell my sweet sister Temperance," he said—' Pause for effect, Bess was certain, but again unfairly, for Jane was choking back her sobs, – 'the doctors thought Mr Cheke will die, but Edward has prayed for him and knows his prayer will be answered. He asks you to pray too.'

She drew a deep sniff and laid her head down against the Admiral's arm.

'There, there, my pretty,' he said, 'all will be well, you'll see. God's sure to listen to our sweet sister Temperance.'

Bess walked past them with her nose in the air, and as she passed gave a vicious tug at Jane's long hair that hung over the Admiral's arm, then ran for her life.

*   *   *

She would never speak to her cousin again, nor the Admiral; she would marry the Swede or the Dane and leave England for ever and never see any of them again; and when she heard Catherine was feeling ill and had had to go to bed she was not a bit sorry. Catherine had the Admiral to love her and would soon have a jolly baby to play with, his baby, – Catherine had everything, it wasn't fair, but no, only silly little girls thought that, and *she* wasn't going to be a crybaby, so she only sulked like a thundercloud all the next day, until suddenly she remembered that there was going to be a banquet that evening, and scampered off to choose her prettiest dress for it.

It was a grand affair, though informal; Tom was entertaining the King and all the important people at Court, to commemorate another reconciliation with his brother. Catherine came down again for it, looking so gay and pretty that Bess was sure she had only been shamming, until she was close enough to see that she had put on more rouge than usual.

Edward came up the water-steps in a white and yellow suit by the side of his uncle, like a canary under the wing of an eagle. The Duke was looking very noble and forgiving this evening. The Duchess looked like a peacock, her handsome head poised above her glittering robes. But her face was ravaged, insatiable. Surrey would not write poems to her now. She was with child again, as though even in that she must enter into rivalry with her sister-in-law.

The food was delicious though strange, for among all the usual great roasted birds and pies the Admiral's Viennese cook gave them goulash and thin slices of pumpernickel dotted with little white and scarlet toadstools made of cream cheese sprinkled with red sweet peppers, and radishes cut in the shape of Tudor roses; and they drank a rich golden wine of heady sweetness which their host had brought from the sun-baked mountain plateau of Tokay. Even Somerset thawed under it and told his brother with a complimentary bow that it was like drinking liquid sunshine.

The music was always good at the Admiral's house, but tonight his gipsy players and singers seemed to have Tokay in their veins (as in fact they had); their strange tunes were as intoxicating as the wine, and when they played behind Bess's chair the music appropriate to her charms, they chose this time, not a lively dance, but a love-song with a wild call in its refrain that came again and again, tingling and throbbing through the hot buzz of talk and smell of food and wine. Why had they chosen this for her tonight? Was the little dark-faced monkey of a man, capering in his gorgeous embroidered coat behind her chair, a magician as well as a musician, with power to see into her heart?

Or had the Admiral told him to play this? The second possibility was even more exciting, for if it were so, he had then forgotten their quarrel – not forgiven it, for Tom would never bother to forgive, though he might easily forget, – which was far better. Then he did not love Jane best, 'his Jane' indeed! He did not think herself an unpleasant child, he—

'Why do they play this tune for you?' said Edward, who as usual sat with his sister, the next highest in the land (since Mary was absent), on his right hand; 'it's not a bit like you.'

'What tune is like me, then?' she demanded tartly; she was sure he had no idea, and had only said that to be tiresome.

Edward replied promptly, 'Jumping Joan.'

His friend Barnaby, coming forward at that moment to serve him on bended knee, gave a sidelong glance of adoration at the Princess Elizabeth and wondered why she looked so cross.

After the banquet they danced, and after they had danced the formal Court dances that everybody knew, Tom said he would show them something new, and as old as the Magyars' Covenant of Blood, and that was the Palace Dance.

His Bohemians thrummed out a rhythmic measure in which there was hardly any tune but an endless throbbing, drumming movement, as compelling as if it were the procession of a sacrificial victim; they led the way ahead of the company, Tom gave his hand to his hated sister-in-law and told her to give hers to the gentleman of her choice, and so on, each taking a partner by the hand and pacing, slowly at first, then faster and faster, following those little dark foreign men who were dancing, prancing, fiddling, twiddling ahead of them, through the hall and the great staircase, down the long passages, up the odd little flights of stairs and down others, through room after room of the rambling manor-house, 'upstairs and downstairs and in my lady's chamber,' laughing and talking and glittering they went, and all the time some couples kept dropping out, getting left behind, while the rest linked up to new partners.

And so, for a few moments, Barney's dream came true, and he danced hand-in-hand with the Princess Elizabeth.

She did not look cross now. She smiled at him with sera-phic ecstasy induced by the Hungarian music and Tokay; the torches knocked bright sparks out of her hair; and to his bewildered delight she swung him out of the procession to an alcove in one of the downstairs rooms and sat on a win-dow-seat while he leaned against it. Even her explanation for this, that her new shoes were too tight, made as she kicked them off, could not dim the romance of such a mo-ment to Barney, who remained silent with awe, even about the shoes.

She said casually, 'We are cousins, aren't we? You are a connexion of the Butlers of Ormonde, I think, and my mother's grandmother was one of them, – I very nearly was myself'; and then as the boy stammered with astonishment she told him how the Bullens had tried to marry Anne to the Earl of Ormonde of that day but she had flatly refused. 'Think of it! If she had not been so staunch, I'd have been born in Kilkenny Castle, and my only glimpse of town life a visit to Dublin!'

He burst out laughing at thought of this radiant creature among the thatched roofs of that primitive city. It was easily seen how such a prospect had driven her mother, that gay Frenchified coquette, to the perilous pursuit of King Henry that ended in her death. But he naturally did not speak this thought aloud, only–'Kilkenny! After six years at the French Court! Your Highness's mother could never have stood that!'

'I wish I could see the French Court,' sighed Bess.

'And I,' said the page, 'I mean to, too.'

'Do you, Barney? You must not mind me calling you that, for you see my brother always does when he speaks of you.'

'Mind!' When the flattery of her using his intimate home-name sent his blood tingling into his head!

She saw it with delight. So she could use her power on him too, a boy she had scarcely spoken to before. But he was only a boy, perhaps no older than herself, though already so tall (and, yes, he was very good-looking) and shy, so she was careful not to show that she saw it, but asked him with easy friendliness why he wanted to go to the French Court. Barney in a burst of confidence told her that it was not the Court he wanted to see, but something of the French wars, – 'but I wouldn't know how I can leave himself, not till he can shake a loose leg a bit more—'

'Shake the Protector off his back, you mean!'

And she laughed with delicious, daring camaraderie, for well she knew she was mad to speak so of Somerset, – 'but not to you,' she said, and he drew nearer in the proud joy of sharing an indiscretion. It was not the only one they shared, for she had put up her hand with that half appeal to him, and he had taken it in his, and she did not know how to draw it away, though she knew she ought to; she was of the blood royal, second in succession to the throne of England, and more, she was in love with the most magnificent man in the kingdom, a man three times the age and ten times the power and experience and worldly knowledge of this young page, the son of an Irish Chieftain, who came from the hills and bogs of a savage country where no Englishman went, except to lose honour and die.

'I may never hold your hand again,' he said, 'I may never look at you again except from across the hall and I carrying some pompous dish that no one wants to eat, and you with some great English lord looking into your eyes the way he'd drink the honey from them as if they were the blue flowers of heaven itself. But this moment is mine, and not even God can take it from me, that I'm holding your slight hand in mine, and your eyes are looking at me. I'll never ask it of you again. I ask only this, to be true to you and yours from this hour on. Wherever I am across the seas, whatever I am doing there, I swear to leave it on the instant that I know I can be of service to you or yours, so help me God and His Mother.'

He bent his smooth dark head and kissed her hand, so hard

that it hurt. As he looked up, Bess flung her arms round his neck and kissed him.

Behind her the window was open to the soft spring night, and she heard the faint crunch of gravel on the path. She swung round, but the steps had passed on. Frightened, she put on her shoes, caught Barney's hand and swung him back into the procession and they danced on.

There was another break in it, and this time her hand was in her brother's; it was hot and clammy as it pulled her aside.

'Let's stop a moment,' he said, coughing. 'Look, here's a cool corner. Did Jane give you my message?'

'What message?' ('the blue flowers of heaven itself' – had Barney really said that about her eyes?).

'About Mr Cheke?'

'Oh – that!'

'What do you mean? Did you forget to pray as I asked?'

'Oh no,' said Bess with glib haste, 'I prayed – hard.'

'It didn't really matter.' Edward's voice sounded rather smug. 'I'd done it, and God heard me. I knew He would. I told them all so, this morning when I came down to breakfast, and it's happened just as I said it would. At midday he took a turn for the better. The doctors say now he will live.'

'Flounder, flounder in the sea—' sang Bess, to her brother's astonishment; 'do you too think you are God?'

'Of course I don't,' said Edward, hurt. 'God heard me, that's all. Don't you believe in prayers?'

'Not half as much as our sister Mary does, and yet you are dead against her.'

'She,' said Edward with masterly simplicity, 'prays in the wrong way.'

'How do you know which is the right one?'

'The best brains in the kingdom are finding out. Listen, I've just heard this from the Archbishop, it's to be the final blessing to the service of Communion – that's what it's to be called now, you know, instead of the old Mass. Cranmer won't truckle to that.'

'Well, *he* ought to know all about truckling, – perhaps even how to avoid it!'

'What do you mean?' demanded Edward sternly, but was too eager with his information to wait to reprove her. 'He's made everything perfectly clear in it. "The piece of God, that passeth, – all understanding." You see? Who wants to tear God's flesh in his teeth and drink His blood? The blood and wine are only a symbol of remembrance, – a piece of God that passes through men's minds, all men understanding that it is but a symbol. *Do* you understand?' he added anxiously, for women, even the cleverest, were sometimes curiously obtuse.

Bess was thinking it out. At last she said, 'I should give more attention to spelling and less to theology if I were you. I believe it might help.'

But as she looked down at the flushed face and saw through it into the childish, precocious, literal mind that was so determined, like his father's, to build for himself a cast-iron set of theories that should prove himself always in the right, a sudden trembling wave of pity caught her up. Why should he not think himself in the right? He was so small and frail, he might not have very long in which to do it. Something of Barney's protective passion for his little King had communicated itself to her, though she could not know, as did his constant companion, how much he needed it; only that, where his father's sense of self-rightness had blazed like the sun at noonday, Edward's was like a pale slip of moonlight, steady but cold, cold and lonely.

A great heat had gone out of the world with the passing of King Henry, stupendous rascal as he may have been. That vehement and earthy heat seemed to have burnt out all the life round it; both Edward and the Protector were shadows in comparison, conscientious, earnest, cold.

The music was dying away through the house – a long tingling sigh, and then it ceased, as if giving up the competition with the enormous buzz of voices that drummed from every corner of the manor like the humming from a monstrous hive. The noise converged from every side and surged into the hall; the guests were gathering together and taking their leave in order of precedence; the Duke of Somerset approached his royal nephew respectfully and reminded him of the speech of thanks he must make to his other uncle; the King came down into the hall with his sister, and his gentlemen-in-waiting lined up behind him. His page Barnaby

Fitzpatrick came forward with his monarch's fur-lined cloak over his arm to protect him from the night air on the river, bent to put it round the younger boy, then straightened himself, stood back tall and slim and dark behind the fair child, and his glowing eyes fastened once more on his Princess.

She thought he looked like a supple water-reed among all these stiff-coated cabbages. She gave a swift glance round; no one that she could see was looking at her; and placed the tips of her fingers to her lips.

They were all going away down the water-steps; the King had entered his royal barge, the rest were following. Catherine said, 'I cannot stay on my feet one moment longer. I am going to bed,' and her husband tenderly pressed her to do so.

'I'll see to the rest. There's no need for you to worry. Go to bed and sleep sound. I'll not wake you by coming in to say good-night.'

Catherine went.

Bess stayed beside Tom, still saying goodbye to all the lesser guests. He turned to her in a pause between the leave-takings and said, quick and low and furious, 'I must speak to you, tonight. Come out on the water-steps as soon as all these poultry have clucked away. I'll have my barge ready; we'll go on the river.'

'What am I to say to Mrs Ashley?'

'Tell her to go to the devil along with the rest of these old hens. Do I need to tell you what to say?'

'No,' said Bess.

She ran upstairs. Cat Ashley was waiting for her, laying out her night-shift.

'Go away,' said Bess.

'But—your Highness!'

'Didn't you hear what I said? Well, if you must stay, give me my cloak—*any* cloak, woman! What are you havering for?'

'A cloak—*now*? A *cloak*!'

'Stop clucking! I'm accompanying His Majesty on his barge.'

137

'The royal barge left a quarter of an hour ago,' said Mrs Ashley, slowly stiffening.

'What the devil do I care? Give me my cloak.'

'I dare not.'

But in a paroxysm of nervous agitation Mrs Ashley had already reached it down. Bess snatched it from her, dealt a resounding smack on her governess's cheek which sent her staggering into a chair, and whisked out of the room.

Sitting up, a little stunned, her hand groping doubtfully, unbelievingly, to her face, Mrs Ashley heard the bedroom door being locked on her.

Chapter Ten

'I TELL YOU I looked in through the window as I passed, and I saw you fling your arms round a man's neck and kiss him.'

'I have kissed no man tonight,' said Bess.

Well, it was true, wasn't it? Barnaby Fitzpatrick was no man yet; he was probably no older than herself. But it was delightful that the Admiral should think she had kissed a man tonight, a real grown man; that he should mind so much that she felt a delicious qualm of terror as to what he might do next.

He could not do much, he reflected, not with his watermen rowing the barge within a few yards of them, and their heads facing the canopy under which he and the girl sat on their cushions. Fortunately the fellows could not understand English, or so he chose to believe. He slipped his arm round her under her cloak and pressed her lithe young body against his own. There was nothing tender or yielding in it, but he felt it tingling with life.

'God's living soul!' he breathed in her ear, 'if only you were not a virgin!'

In answer came a shocked gasp that turned to a desperate little laugh, and then a whisper: 'How do you know?'

'You devil's strumpet! Have you given your body to any man? Who was that fellow tonight? *Answer* me!' he commanded, while his hand gripped her arm.

But she did not cry out. 'Now I shall have to hide my arm from my waiting-women,' she breathed softly.

'Only from your women? Has no man seen them?'

'Oh yes!'

'Which? You witch! You bitch!'

'Who? Tu whit, tu whoo! Why you! you!' she gave back on a mocking call that answered the big white owl as it went skimming past them over the dark waters to its nest in the old trees round Lambeth Palace.

Bess leaned forward from the canopy to watch its flight. The moonlight fell on her face, a pale oval in the darkness; it glittered on her eyes. Her lips parted in a smile of ecstasy that chilled the man beside her as though he had no part in it, for it was self-contained, the bliss of suddenly awakened vanity. She had no room at the moment to think of Tom himself; she was too full of the discovery that can only come once in a lifetime, if it come at all, the discovery that she, like her mother, was the kind to drive men mad for her. Barney had been mad to speak to her as he had done tonight, the Admiral was mad to take her out in his barge, and she herself mad to box her governess's ears and rush out to join him. 'This is the happiest night of my life,' she told herself, for never before had a man told her that he loved her, and tonight two men – well, a man and a boy – had done so.

The river flowed past below them, gleaming dark and pale together, the ripples lapping and hissing against the sides of the barge; rippling in secret laughter, it flowed on beside them, past them, away into the darkness of the sleeping city, a river tireless as time itself, bearing on its shores this mighty stream of human life all unknowing of its future, even as she was of hers, with all her life rippling away before her into the undiscovered darkness.

'London is breathing all round us,' she said.

'Its breath stinks, then,' said Tom.

But he could not prick her ecstatic bubble. Of course

the river smelt, but so did the ghostly shapes of white may trees flowering on its banks. The dark towers of Whitehall Palace glided past them, and she giggled in delight to think what the Protector and his wife, shut up there in the stuffy dark, would say if they knew who was outside in the barge. The jagged unfinished walls of Somerset House rose beside them; the old houses on London Bridge flung a dark pall shadow upon them as they shot one of its arches; in the distance a lighted window shone out high up among the trees.

'There is a light in Lambeth Palace,' said Bess on a pious note. 'My brother says the Archbishop is working night after night at this new religion.'

'There's something in it,' said the Admiral reflectively. 'Some of these Reformers suggest making it legal to have two wives.'

'I'd never make one of a pair!'

'Not you! You'd be as jealous as the Sultan.'

'Or as yourself. Some of them say a woman should have two husbands, but you don't mention that!'

'God's death, who *was* that man?'

'There *was* no man.'

'Liar!'

Bess hugged herself with enjoyment. 'What will you become?' he had once asked her, and this was what she had become, a woman with the power to tease him into a rage while she kept her head. She spoke in a cool detached voice, only spoilt by a slight breathlessness. 'Some of them want to do away with marriage altogether. It isn't only religion is in the melting-pot, it's the whole of society. Nobody knows what will happen – to any of us – but then – nobody ever did.'

And her unusual philosophic speculation relapsed into a high-pitched giggle of excitement.

It exasperated him. Why the devil had he been such a fool as to bring her out? Virgins were raw as unripe fruit. She was not yet ripe enough even to be excited by a man, only by the admiration and desire that she excited. She was a pert affected chit – not a patch on her mother, and never would be. He told her so, and she longed to scream with rage but became very grown-up and distant and told him it was nothing to her that he had plainly been in love with her mother – as no doubt it had been nothing to her mother either.

He roared to the boatmen to turn about and take them home.

Bess sat stiff with fury. She told herself she cared less than a hoot of the white owl what the Admiral thought of her, or any other man. She would never care for him, or any man. What pleasure was there in seeing them get hot and excited, beyond the pleasure that she could make them do so? That was all they should ever be to her – tributes to her power.

The river flowed against them now, the ripples flopping louder against the barge as they were rowed up-stream, the rowlocks giving their steady rhythmic click in answer. The sleeping houses slid past again, but the awe she had felt of the stream of unknown life was now tinged with both pity and envy – so many little humdrum lives sleeping all round her, people going home from work every night, maids that she had seen this morning hanging out their summer smocks to bleach in the sun, lads she had seen last week in the dawn of May Day bearing green branches from the woods to deck their homes, hovels though they might be, – all these people lay sleeping helplessly round her, poor, pinched, and ugly perhaps, yet all had been intent on getting home to something or someone that made it home to them. But for whom was she going back, in Catherine's house?

She would not think of Catherine.

The moments were slipping past them in the dark, sliding along as fast as the ripples below them. The river-bank rose beside them; tall reeds swayed in the night breeze and shadowy willows drooped towards them; wild swans lay asleep like patches of moonlight, and the white saucer shapes of hemlock starred the darkness. They passed the square stone tower of Chelsea Church, they were just coming to Chelsea Place, the moments were slipping away faster and faster, and she had wasted them all in teasing; this was the happiest night of her life and she had thrown it away, she had driven away the man who sat beside her. She tried desperately to recall him. In a sudden jerky voice she said :

'Soon it will be strawberry-time again. Do you remember them dipped in wine on board the *Great Harry*? I was a little girl then.'

'You are now,' he replied sourly. 'The more fool I for wasting time on such a flutterpate!'

It was no good. The barge had stopped. He was holding out his hand to help her out on to the water-steps. She had let it all slide past her, instead of telling him how she loved him. Next time she would tell him.

She huddled her cloak round her and pretended to yawn.

'And now I must let out my governess,' she said. 'Heigh-ho for hell let loose!'

Chapter Eleven

'HELL LET LOOSE!' said the Duke to himself, looking sideways across the velvet counterpane at his Duchess. He had been thinking it some time. Aloud he said in a carefully gentle tone, 'Well, it's time we both got some sleep.'

It only started her off again. Up sprang all the different heads to her wrath, as many as the hydra-headed monster's.

Imprimis: Her brother-in-law's party this evening; it's showy, its sumptuous, its positively vulgar display, for there was no state, no dignity about it, a hoydenish romp led by a pack of prancing foreigners. And where did he get the money for it, a mere younger brother? By all sorts of vile practices, she'd be bound, – commerce with pirates, taking bribes, false coinage, – there was a deal of debased money going about.

'King Henry started debasing it long ago,' the Duke murmured. The Duchess kicked the sheet.

Item: Her sister-in-law's appearance this evening, its showy, sumptuous, positively vulgar, etc., as before : Far too much rouge, which only showed up how wan and peaked looking her face had grown. The folly of starting a first child at her age! And if she did succeed in bearing it, 'Look at the danger to *us*! A son and heir of theirs starting a rival royal house!'

'Well, I can't prevent their having one,' said the Duke.

'When did you ever prevent anything? You should have prevented the marriage. But you can't even prevent her taking precedence of me.'

'You did that, my love.'

The Duchess actually hooted. The Duke thankfully forbore to tell her how the guests had grinned and nudged each other as the two ladies, both great with child, had collided and all but stuck in the doorway.

Item: On the same matter of this treasonable marriage. Yes, it was sheer treason. For it had taken place so indecently soon after the King's death that if Catherine had had a child at once by the Admiral it might have been in doubt as to whether it were not by the late King, – and so treasonably, have endangered the succession to the throne.

'But she didn't, so it couldn't,' he replied.

'But she might have, and then it would have,' was the answer.

The Duke gave it up.

Item: 'Another matter.' (The Duke drew breath in relief. He drew it too soon.)

'This matter of my eldest son – *our* eldest son. It is he who should be heir to your titles and estates.'

'You ask me,' said the suffocated voice in the rosy gloom of the bed-curtains, 'to set aside my legitimate eldest son and heir by my first wife, for no other reason than that you want your own to inherit. It is impossible, and you know it. The law—'

'Pah, don't weary me with lawyer's stuff. I know that you can do what you like with the laws. You are altering them and bringing in fresh ones every day to suit yourself. King Henry himself never did such preposterous things as you are doing. *He* would never allow the clergy to marry – he always said they'd breed like rabbits and over-populate the island. Besides, look at Mrs Cheke!'

'Cheke's not a clergyman.'

'A tutor then, it's all the same. But why are you dragging in clergymen—'

'I was not.'

'—when I'm talking of my son – our son – whom you want to dispossess? Don't you love me better than you did your first wife? You must, or you wouldn't have divorced her for me.'

He supposed he had. He really couldn't think now how it had happened.

'Well then,' continued the inexorable voice, 'while you're fiddling with the law to please your own whims, you can do this one little thing for me.'

He *could* not do it.

But he knew that he would.

Item: They must have more than empty titles and lands to leave to her son – their son. Would those lazy hounds of workmen never finish Somerset House? And the mansion he proposed to build near his old home, Wolf Hall, barely started! No really suitable place of their own to live in when in town, Richmond and Sion House so out of the way. Master Admiral had *his* town house all ready; being only a younger son, he would of course get Seymour Place and the best of everything, while they themselves at this moment were boxed up in this untidy rabbit-warren of Whitehall.

'It was good enough for King Henry.'

'That old man! So old-fashioned. Never minded even about water laid on.'

'If a conduit 1,600 feet long and 15 feet deep will satisfy you,' came an exhausted whisper, 'the foundations for it are already laid down at Wolf Hall. I had a letter from my brother Henry about it this evening, just before we started for Seymour Place. I believe I have it in this room.'

His voice had quite revived at the hope of finding something to stave off the other. He got out of bed, and turned up the lamp. It was a warm night. He padded barefoot across the room and drew back the window-curtains and saw the light up the river in the Archbishop's study, as Bess had seen it from the Admiral's barge. But he did not draw the same pious conclusion.

'Cantuar is going the pace. There he is sitting up at cards again. Last week when I supped at Lambeth Palace I won thirty-five shillings off him. A lot of money for an Archbishop.'

'But you lost one and fourpence to the Bishop of Rochester at his shooting-match at Guildford yesterday,' came in accusing reminder from behind him.

The Duke hastily turned to the table where he had left the papers concerning the new place he was going to build near his old home of Wolf Hall. His brother Henry, the stolid country squire, was seeing to it all for him; it was all he was good for. And he lived now at the old timbered house of Wolf Hall; it was all it was good for. Not worth adding to, a poky little place, his Duchess had called it; and when his sister Jane had married King Henry they had had to convert the great barn into a banqueting hall for the festivities, since there was no room in the house for all the Court. King Hal in high good humour, having just beheaded Nan Bullen, had twitted Jane with their marriage revels in a barn, like any pair of gipsies. She had smiled dutifully. But her eldest brother had felt it deeply.

Now he was making up for it. Neglecting Wolf Hall itself, he had bought up vast new estates all round it. The mere names of the manor-houses on them filled nearly three columns. He had dissolved a priory near Pewsey to furnish himself with a country house, but that would only be temporary. An enormous palace would rise on the two wooded hills of Bedwyn Brail, already cleared of trees for the purpose, commanding a spacious view of the Vale of Pewsey. He had enclosed huge parks for hunting and stocked them with game. He had ordered caravans of Purbeck stone to be quarried in the Isle of Purbeck and brought all those miles in an endless procession of straining oxen carts. He had (or Henry had) got the brickmakers digging clay for ninety thousand bricks. Four hundred workmen had been at work on the place for a year.

And today had come from Henry the magic message: 'The plumber is getting ready.' He read it out in triumph.

'Is that all? What of the new lake?'

'He says, "The pond, thanks be to God, will hold water."'

'As it should at a cost of £43. 15s. 10d.'

'But he won't compass the bottom.'

'Whose bottom?'

'Ramphries Bottom. If that's brought within the compass of the pond—'

'Lake.'

'Yes, lake – "then," he says, "the Tenants of Wilton should have no maner of common for their rudder beasts, which would be to their utter undoing, for they kept before this tyme in their common, as they say, 180 rudder beasts, and if the whole wood and bottom aforesaid shoald be taken from them, then they would kepe none. And as it is an Old Saying, 'Enough is as good as a feste,' I pray God so we may finde urne."'

'What in the name of God are "rudder beaste"? And "urne"?'

'Urne is "ours" – "ouren," as he would say. And rudder is the rude Saxon word, "hruther" or "hryther," for horned cattle.'

The Duchess lay back on the satin pillows apparently in a dead faint, from which she presently recovered sufficiently to demand of her lord how this rustic had been begotten in his family, and what had given him the notion that he could so identify himself with the Lord Protector as to speak of "ouren," "urne," or "ours"? lecture him with old sayings? and consider the interests of the cottage tenants as of superior importance to the Lord Protector's?

The Protector tried to point out that it would not look well for him to enclose common grazing land that had belonged for centuries to the people, merely to enlarge an ornamental lake, and at the very moment that he was bringing in an Act of Parliament against the enclosures of the Common lands. But his difficulty in doing so made him wonder, not for the first time, whether any man could be a reformer who was not a bachelor.

He beat a retreat to Henry's letter. Henry had stocked Fasterne Park with 500 deer, a piece of news that gave the Duchess some satisfaction, for the Admiral and Catherine were still vainly petitioning for Fasterne, her family property, to be restored to her. The Duke had not told that to Henry. Nor did he tell his wife that he had not told him.

Encouraged by her approval, he handed on Henry's information that 'the work will get on faster if God send fayre wether, as hitherto we have none, but always extremity of rayne.' 'Curious thing,' added the Duke, 'he told me the workmen say it's never stopped raining since Thomas More was beheaded. You wouldn't think they'd still care about the death of a scholar.'

The Duchess didn't care what they cared about. She remarked that Henry was 'a proper hayseed, always grumbling about the weather!'

'He grumbles about more than that.' The Duke got back into bed, pulling back the curtain for the light as he added, 'Barwick seems to be a slack paymaster. Henry asks me to write to him direct to pay the wages punctually – "or els" – where is it now? Oh yes – "or els shure our men will not aply ther works so well as els: for the poor men here do much complayn—"'

'No news in *that*!' barked the Duchess, but he went on unswervingly, '"although they be delayed but from Satterday to Monday next following, yet somewhat it hyndereth and the poor men can not forebeare, because they must take the advantage of the market, or els they can not live with their wages; for where an ox selleth for XX nobles ther will but small penyworths arise, and when it is bought out of the market then it is worse. This do the poor men alledge unto me with such an exclamacion that I can do no lesse than write the same unto ye."'

The Duke laid down the letter. 'How like Henry!' he said indulgently.

'*Just* like Henry! Making their exclamation to him indeed! That shows what sort of master he makes. They can speak to him as to one of themselves.'

'That is how it should be, surely.'

'Oh, leave all that for your speeches! You are not in Parliament now. We'd best go down and see to it or nothing will get done.'

'But – the press of my work! I have five new Bills to introduce at this session.'

'Surely you can manage a "Satterday to Monday next following"?'

'Well – it would be very pleasant.'

But would it? He wasn't sure. Nor was she. Last time they had gone, a herd of little pigs had been cluttering up the drive just as she was alighting from her coach, and when at her command the Duke had complained to his brother, Henry had only grinned and held up one of them in his arms. "A pig can look at a Protector," he had said. That was Homely Harry's idea of a joke. No, she decided, they would not go down for a Satterday to Monday.

'Pray Heaven he never come to town again to disgrace us!'

'He never will, you can rest assured of that. It was hard enough to make him come up for his knighthood at the Coronation – and then complained his new boots were too tight and that he'd rather be fox-hunting.'

'That plebeian sport! He might at least make it hares. The upkeep of that old house at Wolf Hall is absurdly expensive. £2 a year for the Chaplain – the same wage as the Grubber. It is simply throwing money away, as we are never in residence.'

'But Henry is, on my account.'

'Then let him pay it, if he has need of one, which he has not, for I'll swear he goes to the village church with the other yokels. Has he no more to say?'

'Only that he ends as usual, "praying you that I may be most hartely commended unto my good lady your bedfellow." '

The Duchess yelped. 'Of all odious coarse old-fashioned expressions! Is it not enough to have a scoundrel for one brother-in-law but I must have a simpleton for the other?'

He tried to soothe her with a sleepy laugh that ended abruptly in a yawn.

'But, my dove, you *are* my bedfellow.' And he put an arm round her to demonstrate the fact, but his dove clawed it. Pained, he withdrew it.

'My first Duchess would never have dared do that. And she was a Fillol.'

'I am a Plantagenet.'

'Only on the distaff side.'

'What odds? At least it ensures legitimacy.'

'She was no bastard,' he said haughtily.

'And no duchess either. You forget how raw your title is.'

'And you, that I gave you yours.'

'What need have I of your upstart Tudor titles, I whose mother was a daughter of the great-grandson of a son of Edward III?'

'The youngest son – of thirteen. In a few generations there'll be precious few of our families who can't claim descent from a son of Edward III.'

The Protector always took long views. But his tact in propounding them was short-sighted. The storm that followed raged hysterically over every cause for grievance he had ever given her.

'I am wretched, wretched, wretched,' she cried. 'I don't know what is wrong – only everything in the world. I only know that I am the most wretched creature alive and I wish I were dead.'

He tried desperately to comfort her, while he wondered how he had ever become enslaved to this strident woman. She reminded him that she was with child by him, of all the painful symptoms of her condition, of her certainty that she would not survive its birth, for she had never felt as bad as this time.

But she would survive it; she would survive him; she would live to be nearly a hundred, and marry again and make others as wretched as himself. He knew it all. He could not escape. He could only agree to all her terms of unconditional surrender.

'You will make my son your heir?'

'Yes,' he said faintly.

'You will never give in to the odious woman and her demands for Fasterne?'

'No,' he said fretfully.

'Nor for her – for the King's jewels?'

'No.' It was almost a whisper by now. He added after a hesitant pause, 'Not even – don't you think we might send back her wedding ring?'

'Most certainly not. It's the principle that counts. Admit that she has the right to one thing, then she has it to all.'

He saw the conclusion only too well. He even agreed to it. But not aloud.

The voice continued: 'You will look into those extraordinary practices of the Admiral – piracy – false coinage – his quite open working up of a party against you? And his seduction of the Princess Elizabeth.'

'What!' The exhausted voice was startled into life again.

Oh yes, the Duchess had had it on the best authority from her maid. Or, at least, if the Admiral had not already seduced the Princess, he soon would. An offence not merely against morals but against the throne.

Her tongue darted hither and thither. If he could see it (but he had put out the light) it surely would be forked.

It hissed the word 'treason'.

'Do you understand what you are demanding of me?' he said. 'You are wishing me to prove my own brother guilty of high treason. To condemn him to the block.'

'It would not be you. It would be the law.'

'Which you have already asked me to twist to your purposes.'

He did not hear her answer. He felt he was suffocating. And it was now near morning, and if he got no sleep, how could he work tomorrow? He promised to do all she had asked, and at last her tongue was still, and they lay still, the woman still within the man's arms, taut, wide-awake, staring with hot eyes into the dark.

A consuming envy seemed to burn away her vitals; envy of her hosts this evening, who had been so much in love that they could not wait to marry at the prudent time; of the Princess Elizabeth sitting upright and bright-eyed beside her brother at the banquet, so very young; of the way she had looked across the table at the Admiral's genial jokes, meeting his quick glances, startled yet unaware, her eager childish hands stretched out so greedily to life, all unknowing what they might take.

So she herself had been – once.

What had happened since to make everything so different? If she had had a man in love with her like the Admiral, scoundrel as he might be, would she not be different now? But he hated her, as she hated him, hated, hated.

Her life was nothing. She too had clutched at it with both hands, and it had crumbled in them to dust and ashes. All her beauty, her radiant strength of will and purpose, strength to love or hate (it was the same thing really) – all wasted on this man beside her, a fine figure, but only a figure, a figure-head rather, dry as dust, cold as ashes; while his youngest brother glowed and vibrated with the warmth and splendour of life. And she had wasted herself on this poor weak creature, whom she could twist round her little finger.

Yet in her despair she turned and clung to him like a thing drowning.

He had fallen into an uneasy dream, and felt she was dragging him down, down, into the uttermost depths of what black and icy sea?

He floundered this way and that in those dreadful waters, dragged down, down, down by his frantic burden, floundered and floundered. A huge fish floated towards him and stared at him with gaping mouth and eyes.

'Flounder, flounder in the sea,' he heard his mother say, and through the black engulfing water all round him he could see her perched by his little carved wood bed in the old nursery at Wolf Hall, telling a bed-time story to him alone; when he was still the only boy, and no interloping baby brothers as yet, only docile, adoring sisters. He could see his mother's peaked cap, her small hands gesturing as she told the story; he tried to reach her through the choking waves, to call to her to save him. 'Come to me,' he shrieked. 'Come and save me.'

But she never saw nor turned her head; only her voice went on inexorably:

> 'Come, for my wife Isabel
> Wishes what I dare not tell.'

Chapter Twelve

THE LIGHT BURNED all night in Lambeth Palace, where Archbishop Cranmer sat, writing the new English Prayer Book that was to make a new land of saints from this old sinful England.

He wrote in his window, never seeing the soft spring night outside, but only the balancing phrases that took shape on the blank paper beneath his fingers, phrases that responded to each other, built themselves up like the rungs of a ladder up to heaven, into the most perfect prose ever yet written in English.

And it was he who was writing it, he who was creating this great work, imperfect, tremulous man that he was, an arrant coward, as he had always known whenever he had entered the presence of that Sun of Man, that majestic, rollicking, bewildering, baffling Master, who had passed away only a little over a year ago, though it seemed like three or four centuries, and left the world this tired dim place, peopled by shadows.

He fingered the two grey prongs of straggling beard that were growing as long as a gnome's in a German fairy-tale.

He had never cut nor trimmed it since King Henry died. His Gretchen did not like it. She did not see why he should look like an old goat as a protest against shaven priests, – nor as a token of affection to his late master. Women had no sense of loyalty. They had no sense of proportion. She was mistress of Lambeth Palace, she was wife of the Archbishop of Canterbury, a thing no woman had ever been before.

Yet she could worry about his beard. Was it, after all, a mistake to combine the clerical office with matrimony? He had never intended to do so himself; in fact, he had intended neither.

He had been frightened from women as a young man when he had been tricked and bullied into marrying the bouncing black-eyed niece of the landlady of the Dolphin Inn at

Cambridge, and had therefore had to resign his new-won Fellowship. It had been a bitter pill to swallow along with the 'raw, small and windy ale' that Erasmus had so complained of as they sat and drank together at the Dolphin.

Lucky for him, said his friends, that his Black Joan died in childbed within the year, and he was promptly re-elected as Fellow. He also took Orders, a safeguard against further assaults. And ever after at Cambridge he frequented only the White Horse, where there were no dangerous women though plenty of dangerous talk; for the inn was so well known as a meeting-place for Lutheran reformers that it was nicknamed Little Germany.

But when much later he visited their headquarters in Germany itself, he fell in love, at forty-five, with the daughter of a scholar at Nuremberg, a maiden as fair, pliable and docile, as devoted to himself, as Joan had been dark and flashy and shrilly intent on her own way. He felt safe with Margarete Hosmer – Gretchen she liked him to call her – who was young enough to be his daughter, but cared and cooked and sewed for him as though she were his mother. After more than twenty years the widower remarried, intending never to settle permanently again in England, certainly never to hold office there.

But no sooner had he acquired a wife than King Henry required him to help get rid of his; no sooner had he resolved to slip quietly into retirement than King Henry ordered him to become Archbishop of Canterbury. He was plunged into action for the first time in his life, and in middle life. His friends showered congratulations on him; he would be the King's greatest servant, as Wolsey had been, now cast away. But Cranmer did not want honours and preferment and riches; he wanted peace and quiet.

Henry promised it to him; he even liked to share it; often he would come to visit him at Lambeth, look at his books, ask to see what he was writing now, and walk with him in the garden, even in winter, where as he said he could find rest as nowhere else, in its 'singular quiet.'

The Archbishop's hand paused in its writing as the rhythmic thumping click of rowlocks floated up through his open window at this late hour. He went to the window and his eyes absently followed the dark form of a barge gliding past; then turned and rested on the moon-washed spaces of the lawns directly below him, the black shapes of trees, the ghostly bushes of white may that wafted their scent out on the cool air.

It had not always known peace. He could see the sharp shadow cast by the little shed where Sir Thomas More had sat and awaited the verdict of the Commissioners that was to be his doom; while at a little distance 'boisterous Latimer' had walked up and down with various doctors and chaplains, joking and jollying them, flinging his arms about their necks.

And there was the pretty summer-house that Cranmer himself had built, now turned to a glimmering temple by the magic rays of the moon. He used to love to sit there, sometimes dozing a little in the sun; until that night in May before Nan Bullen's execution. Then he could find no sleep in his bed, and wandered out into the garden, up and down, up and down, remembering how More had prophesied this very thing: 'her sporting and dancing will spurn our heads off like footballs, yet it will not be long before hers will dance the same dance.'

It had not been long. Just a year after the King beheaded More to secure the legality of his marriage to Nan, he ordered Cranmer to prove the marriage illegal: and struck off the lovely head for which he had spurned the wisest and noblest in England.

'Is there in good faith no more difference between you and me,' More had asked her, 'but that I shall die today, and you tomorrow?'

The question had echoed in Cranmer's heart ever since, but addressed to himself.

Never since that night had he been able to find rest in the little summer-house where at last, worn out by wandering aimlessly up and down, he had sat breathing in the scent of the white may, while the birds began their first faint songs and the dawnlight turned the river pale as a corpse; and he knew that his love for his great master was full of horror and fear.

Yet this love was somehow enhanced by it. The King had

never been cruel to *him*, so that his adoration had in it something of the pride of a favourite pupil. He needed that, for his schooldays had been tortured by a savage bully of a master who, as Cranmer frequently explained, had 'dulled and daunted the fine wits of his scholars.' Every time he forgot anything he said this, lamenting that he had lost 'both memory and audacity' from his cruel treatment and could never recover from it. Every time he did so he knew his old complaint was boring his friends, who thought it high time to outgrow his childish troubles; and what was there to complain of anyway, since More himself had been astounded by the subtlety of Cranmer's mind?

Surprisingly, it was a master still more savage who restored his self-respect by making him his friend. And absorbing the singular quiet that Henry had loved like himself, Cranmer felt that he alone knew what it was to miss the King.

Chapter Thirteen

'I LOVE YOU. You think I am a child, that I don't know what that means, but I do, I *do*. I want to be yours, now, wholly and for ever.'

'Bess, you're mad, we're both mad I think—'

'Does my Lord Admiral preach sanity, safety to me now? Will you of all men trim your sails to the wind?'

'You devil's brat! You've bewitched me clean out of my senses.'

'But I want you too. I am longing – Oh, for what? I do not know, and if you do not give it me, I shall never know.'

'Child!' he cried, but it was no child he held in his arms.

The wind outside the little arbour in the pleached alley was tearing the clouds and the fruit trees and flowering shrubs to pieces; long strips of white scudded across the brilliant sky, clouds of blossom blew up in the air, separated into pink and white snowflakes to be tossed here and there over the prim walks; butterflies were blown as helplessly as the flying petals, and a pair of blackbirds went fluttering up, this way and that, as light as scraps of burnt paper in the wind, screaming and chattering because their nest had been blown over and their silly fat fledgelings were now each opening a squawking orange beak and rolling an indignant eye in so many different parts of the garden. The boatmen were shouting to each other on the river beyond the garden walls as their slight craft drove headlong before the half-gale; from their cockney, jeering cries one could not guess what danger they were in, but certainly they were trimming their sails to the wind.

Which the Admiral, of all men, could not do. He looked down at this young witch that had flung herself across his knees, a thin scrap of a girl whose arms felt brittle enough to break in his grasp.

How on earth, or in hell rather, had she come to get this hold on him? He had thought he was amusing himself with a little girl, crude, yet sharp as a small stiletto, and sure enough she had stabbed him to the heart.

Her face looked up at him, all the lines immature, yet a white flame in the red of her hair; he bent his head to quench it, and kissed her.

There came another sound among all the crying noises in the wind, a crunching sound on the gravel of short high-heeled steps that kept hurrying and then checking, steps that were accustomed to be faster and lighter than they now had to go. Catherine came down the pleached alley, stopped dead, turned round as if to go back, then turned again, and came slowly on to them.

Quickly the Admiral gave Bess a shake, told her jokingly to get to her feet for a brazen hussy, told Catherine he'd been scolding her, for he'd looked through the window and seen her kissing some man, but now all was forgiven.

Bess babbled nervously. 'It's not true. What man could I have kissed? I never see any man alone but my tutor, and *would* I kiss Mr Grindal?' and finished on a frightened giggle.

But neither of them was listening; nor looked at her; and Catherine's face staring up at her husband was grey and pinched; she opened her mouth to speak, but no sound came out; she was twisting her hands together and suddenly she flung them open as though throwing something away, and turned and ran back down the pleached alley, ran blindly, clumsily, heavily, so differently from her usual light dancing step that Bess saw for the first time what it must be to her to be carrying the burden of a child.

The Admiral brushed straight past her and ran after Catherine.

She was left standing alone in the flickering pale green light under the leaves. She felt that she would now be alone for ever.

*   *   *

'You must go away,' said Catherine. 'What else can I do? I am responsible for you, and if any harm comes to you while under my charge, I should have betrayed my trust.'

'Madam—' began Bess, but Catherine put up her hand.

'I know what you would say, and I too, that my lord intends you no harm. But we have to think of harm in other terms than those of actual fact. The harm done you by gossip and slander might endanger not only your reputation but your whole position in the country, perhaps even your life. And I am certain that, if no bad twist should happen to your fate, you will one day be Queen of England.'

She spoke so quietly, casually almost, that Bess wondered for a moment if she had indeed heard her, or if it were her own voice that had at last uttered this thing that she had said to herself so long: 'You will one day be Queen of England.'

She had never believed that she would ever hear anyone else say it, and now here was the Queen herself saying it, at the very moment when her pain and humiliation were so acute that she could not believe she would ever outlive it; all her life she would be standing in front of her stepmother, staring down at the black and white marble tiles, unable ever again to lift her eyes and look Catherine in the face.

Yet Catherine had not spoken harshly; there was a distressed, almost an apologetic note in her 'I *must* send you away,' as though wondering whether she were wrong in doing so, whether there were anything else she could possibly do, or have done in the past, 'I have thought of you as a child,' she said, 'but you are that no longer. You have great responsibilities and dangers ahead of you, and I should only add to them if I kept you here. What are you thinking?' she added suddenly, for there had been no change in the masked face since she began to speak to her. But now at last Bess raised those long white lids that veiled her eyes, and looked full at her.

'That you said, Madam, I should one day be Queen of England.'

She must hear her say it again. Not till then could she believe that she had already heard her say it. Elizabeth of England – how impossible it was that she should ever be called that! Why, there had never been a Queen of England in her own right before, except that one unfortunate example, four and a half centuries ago, of Queen Matilda (enough reason in herself why there had never been another), and even she had to share her title with her enemy cousin King Stephen.

Yet Catherine's quiet voice was considering the matter as coolly as if it were the most ordinary thing in the world.

'I think it very likely. Your brother is delicate, more so than those now in charge of him trouble to consider. Your sister would never hold the people as you could do. For, remember, that is the whole crux of the matter. Kings here in England do not rule by divine right but by the will of the people. It was the people who put your grandfather on the throne when he defeated and killed Richard Crookback. Your father never forgot that, not even after thirty-eight years of such power and popularity as an English King has not known for centuries. "Would I be such a fool as to kick away the ladder that mounted my family to the throne?" Yes, he said that to me. But now it is the third generation, and neither your brother nor sister will, I think, keep that same sense of what the goodwill of the people has done for their family; or of what it may cease to do, if they are not careful of it.'

'I thought my father ruled more absolutely than any King has dared do here for generations.' Bess spoke eagerly, snatching at this generous chance that Catherine had given to get both their minds away from her present disgrace.

Catherine was indeed determined she should think of the future rather than the present. Her conviction of what that future would be had come to her long since. 'But don't you be the little fool I was when my future was told me as a child,' she said, with a gallant effort at her old gaiety, 'for when a fortune-teller told me I should one day sit on a throne and wear a crown, I refused to do any more sewing, for my hands, I said, were reserved for royal actions – and well slapped I got for it.'

'But it came true,' said Bess. 'The future is already written for those who can read it in the stars.' She yearned to consult an astrologer, but even in this unguarded moment of relief knew she would be scolded for saying so. But Catherine saw her wish clear enough; she leaned forward and took her hands, speaking again with an urgency that sounded rather desperate even to herself, for why should she have to say everything now at this moment, as though there would never be another chance to do so? And suddenly it came into her mind that there might never be one, and that she loved as her own child this girl who had given her more bitter agony of heart than ever her cruel father had done; and that that love mattered more to both of them, and would last when the agony had long since passed away.

'The future is written,' she said, 'but it's in our hands to blot it if we will. The future is for you to make, as you will. The people of England will never keep a wanton for their Queen. They hated your mother as one; it may have been unjustly, but whether so or not, that hate brought her downfall. Their love will bring you greater strength than any army. Treasure it as you would your life, for it will be your life. Why do you cry?'

'You speak so strangely – it's as though we were never to meet again.'

'I did not mean to frighten you. We shall meet again – yes, of course we shall. But how can one count on anything as certain among "the changes and chances of this mortal life" – have you heard that phrase of the Archbishop's? He should be one of our famous poets, yet no man will know what share was his in this Book of Common Prayer – common to all England, its writers unnamed, with all the holy beauty of their words in common.'

But what was the use of her going on about old yellow-faced Mumpsy-mouse and his precious book, when she had spoken as though they might never meet again, as though she might die? 'I cannot bear it,' sobbed Bess, crying as Catherine had never seen her do – 'to go away, and you ill, and it is all my own fault.'

'Not all,' said Catherine sadly.

      *   *   *

That obscure and sudden disease, the sweating sickness, was killing off people within a few days of their getting it. Edward's tutor, Mr Cheke, had recovered, but Bess's tutor, Mr Grindal, had caught it and died, and there was all the question of a new tutor for her. Her repentant mood did not lead her to any meek acceptance of her guardians' choice; she flatly refused to learn from the Oxford scholar whom both Catherine and the Admiral wished to appoint; Oxford was old-fashioned, behind the times; all the Princess Mary's tutors had come from Oxford; and Bess insisted on a Cambridge man.

Mr Roger Ascham had been Greek reader at St John's, had set all Cambridge reading and acting Greek plays; he had been Mr Cheke's favourite pupil and supported his theory of modern Greek pronunciation, which was denounced at Oxford as rabidly as heresy. Greek was in itself a kind of heresy; religious reformers based their authority on the newly discovered Greek texts and manuscripts; and this rage for the New Learning had all the excitement of revolt against the tedious old Latin that the monks had used and everyone was tired of.

If you read Greek you were not only clever, you were modern, you were advanced, you were in the fashion.

And Bess was as determined to flaunt the New Learning as new clothes; she would have this coming Cambridge man, and nobody else. She had already started a correspondence with him, in Latin of course. He was as eager for the post of her tutor as herself, he pulled wires, he wrote charming letters to Mrs Ashley and sent her a silver pen of exquisite Italian workmanship. In the end, as usual, Bess got her way.

This triumph gave a fillip to her departure and took away a little from the uncomfortable sense of being sent off in disgrace. Catherine had done her best to avoid that; but she was deep in love, ill, and frightened, and could not always control her temper. It would flash out at moments in little sub-acid remarks, and then she would be sorry and try to make up for it, and that made it worse.

And Tom had gone off on one of his frequent sudden expeditions to some island or other – Wight or Lundy or the Scillies – murmuring mysterious boasts in his beard: 'Easy to run down the office of Lord Admiral as a show-title, but I tell you it means something. I've now got the rule over a good sort of ships and men. It's a good thing to have the rule of men,' he had added, glowering rather belligerently at his household of women and little girls, and off he had gone without even saying goodbye to Bess. But it was certainly easier with Catherine when he had gone.

*   *   *

Before he came back, Bess too was gone, in the week after Whitsun, riding off down the sun-baked rutted white lanes with the dust rising in clouds under her pony's hoofs and powdering the round pink faces of the campion on the hedges, swirling up over the white clusters of heavy-scented may, up, up, as though to chase the larks that soared, shrilling their songs into the blue sky.

It was good to be riding away from disgrace and scoldings, however gentle; yes, and even from the Admiral and the storms he brewed. All her life lay before her on this springtime journey. Anything might happen. She might run away with Barney, and Edward would make him Lord of Ireland, and she would wear a green kirtle and coat of cloth of gold, such as her mother had so nearly done, in a painted palace built of clay and timber where on winter nights one could hear the howling of wolves on the wind.

She might run even further westward, sailing for months towards the sunset, towards the strange lands that had lain there undiscovered since the beginning of time and now were newly opened to them. The Admiral sometimes spoke in his wild half-joking way of ousting the Spaniards there and founding an empire of his own – and then his eyes had rested on her, and she knew now that when he saw himself as its King he had thought of her as its Queen. Why hadn't she known it at the time? Not even when he told her once that she wore the sunset in her hair and the barbaric gold of the Incas!

She drew in her breath sharply at the memory, then jerked herself awake from her daydreams. Anything might happen, but these things would not happen.

But no, what might really happen was that she would be Queen of England.

She had flatly refused to sit in the stuffy coach with Cat Ashley, declaring its jolting made her sick, but there was another reason beside her enjoyment in the ride, and that was the strange new pride thrilling up in her, that she was riding through the country, showing herself to the people, *her* people, – so she had believed, and now Catherine had said they might be one day.

At the least, she could smile and flourish her whip as they ran from their fields and barns and cottage-doors to stare at the young Princess Elizabeth riding by in her white dress with the sunlight on her hair; at the most, she could find some pretext to stop and talk with them, pretended her pony's shoe was loose, or that she wanted a drink of new milk from the pail that some sturdy bare-armed girl was carrying home ('How enchanting to be a milkmaid!' she said, while the girl's shy glances told her how enchanting she would find it to be a princess).

Her escort found it impossible to hurry her through the little country towns, especially if a market were going on, or a travelling fair; then she must buy this or watch that; it was all they could do to stop her getting her fortune told, and always she would talk with any and everybody, however unsuitable. 'Why not, if my father did, and he was King of England?'

Old men told her that it would never be a merry England again till they heard the church bells ringing through the day and night at the hours of prayer, reminding the sick and sorry that they could always go up to the kindly monks for a bite and sup. Bess listened sympathetically to them; as also to the young men on the extreme left of Reform, who insisted that God Himself should be abolished; and that the country would never be right till ruled by 'communistic law'.

But what everybody told her, and far more eagerly than matters of religion or politics, was that in spite of the new laws wages were sinking, since men would work for next to nothing to avoid unemployment; prices were rising, for, though fixed in name, one could always pass something under the counter; and that for all the money you spent you only got rotten imitation goods, – leather falsely curried and tanned; 'feather' beds stuffed with rubbish; and even, worst of all, beer made without true malt.

Things were bad, but they might be worse, and one mustn't grumble, said they, grumbling hard, but generally finding something they could make a joke of.

This, and the dogged courage of their patience, made her feel akin to them, though she did not recognize it, only that she was interested and pleased, especially in that they liked her.

She saw a rabble of beggars, alarming as a troop of marauding robbers – which indeed they were; her escort closed in round her, church bells clashed out a warning, and the gates of the little country town she had just left clanged to against them.

> '*Hark, hark, the dogs do bark,*
> *The beggars are coming to town.*'

She saw a little boy led by a chain, and a man with an iron ring round his neck and the letter S branded on his forehead to show that he was his master's slave for ever, to be sold or bequeathed at his will; for the new law against unemployment had made it legal for vagabonds and their children to be sold into slavery. This then was what lay behind the cheerful remark, – 'might be worse'.

A chill fell on all her high spirits; she rode under the great oaks of Hatfield Park knowing suddenly, irrevocably, that she must not love Tom, nor Tom her, that she was going away where she would not hear his jolly laugh nor deep teasing voice, nor look up at the swaggering shoulders and catch his mocking glance, that had lately grown heavy with desire as he looked at her.

How could she, even half in fun, as a game of 'Let's pretend', have imagined herself with the boy Barney in his remote and savage island? If she could not love Tom, she would never love anybody else, never, never.

But she must not love Tom, and, almost worse than this, she might not have her Pussy-Cat Purr's loving tenderness round her any more.

Nonsense, Catherine had said, of course she would see her again, and very soon; wait till her child was born, and then everything would be the same as before. But would it? Bess could not quite believe it. She too had had her glimpse, though she tried not to recognize it, into what was written in the stars.

In this sudden depression at the end of her long ride she sat down to write her departed-guest letter, giving thanks for the manifold kindnesses received from her late hostess. With an unusual and pathetic humility she assured Catherine that 'although I answered little, I weighed it all the more deeply when you said you would warn me of all evil that you should hear of me. For if you had not a good opinion of me, you would not have offered friendship to me that way at all. But what may I more say than thank God for providing such friends to me?'

Chapter Fourteen

THE NEW TUTOR was a success, especially in his pupil's opinion. At thirty-three, Roger Ascham was one of the foremost Greek scholars of the day, but he was by no means only a scholar; he was an accomplished musician, and a keen and knowledgeable sportsman. Bess remembered her father's pleasure in the Treatise on Archery which the young Cambridge don had published and presented to King Henry shortly before his death; it was in English, which showed his originality and freedom from pedantry; in fact, he valued the writing of good English prose as highly as that of Greek or Latin, and foretold a magnificent future for it. The new Bible, the new prayers in the churches, showed, as the poets had already shown, what the English language could do. But it must not stay only in the pulpit, nor in poetry; it must come down into the world and express the common life and simple pleasures of humanity, – yes, not only of the science of the long bow, that backbone of England, but of such lesser sports as cock-fighting. And his mild brown eyes glowed as he sketched his plans to the Princess for a Book of the Cockpit which should be his best offering to English sport and prose.

He was full of praise for Bess's own writing, the simplicity and directness she could command when she chose, letting the style grow out of the subject. Unfortunately she was apt to forget this when anxious to write brilliantly, and would never quite believe him when he told her that good style knew no tricks.

He encouraged her dancing and music, which previous tutors had condemned as a waste of time, played and sang duets with her, taught her to shoot with the long bow as her father had taught her mother; and of course, when she discovered from Mrs Ashley that Nan Bullen had had a special shooting-costume made for her, she had to have one too and a saucy green hat with feathers and long elegant shooting-gloves. He told her of cockfighting matches and dicing parties at Cambridge in which he had so nearly made his fortune, but managed instead to lose all his spare cash. All this was surprising in so learned and gentle a scholar, but was very far from meaning that lessons were neglected.

She worked at Greek with him in the mornings and at Latin in the afternoons, on his system of double translation, turning the originals into English and then back into Greek and Latin; she even worked a little at what he called, rather contemptuously, 'Euclid's pricks and lines', since mathematics were also fashionable, though they could never, he assured her, be of the same value to human intelligence as the classics. And he was enchanted with her skill and speed and the fiery intentness of her concentration. Bess collected compliments

165

on her brains as greedily as her mother had done those on her charms. Not but what she would have liked those too. But that would come.

There were encouraging signs of it even now, when Mr Ascham sought to inflame her with his own passion for this new world of ancient Greece, to which her own nature was, he suggested, as much akin as if she were a nymph or goddess born anew from that shadowless tireless dawn of the world, with the dew of that dawn still glistening on her brow, and the spear of the huntress Diana poised in her hand. Indeed, the fancy sometimes affected him almost with fear, as he watched her across the study table, her face, intent and pale in the bright aureole of her hair, lighting suddenly into a smile that was not of any christened soul, but inscrutably aware of her strange power.

So had he seen a marble goddess smile, made by a man who had never heard of Christ.

In excuse for these pagan fancies he would remind himself and tell his pupil that the world was coming out of its old dark cramped preoccupation with Heaven and Hell, with the Earth wedged unalterably between them; that Copernicus had proved the Earth to be no longer the centre of the universe but one of a myriad stars circling round the sun, 'like courtiers round their Sovereign,' said he, thinking of a vast red face and a hot hand that had slapped him on the back, and a mighty voice saying his treatise on archery had scored a bull's eye! 'And as they will circle round your royal father's daughter, should Divine Providence ever place you on the throne.'

Bess's smile was certainly pagan now. It was all very well for an upstart Protector to make a modest claim for Providence putting *him* in power, but when she got there she would know what to thank for it – her father's blood and her own wits.

At present those last were well occupied, and she herself content to stay quiet and work, but not as her cousin Jane was working with her grave young tutor Mr Aylmer, a scholar of the conventional pattern and no sportsman, for the sheer disinterested love of abstract learning. For Bess never lost sight of the aim and object for which she worked:

166

to make herself as fit to be on the throne of England as ever her learned young brother would be.

And in the meantime Mr Ascham's admiration (was it perhaps, sometimes something more? She had caught him looking at her rather oddly across the study table) was a faint compensation for the Admiral's exciting companionship; it served to pass the time, and it provided her with useful counter-thrusts against Cat Ashley.

That much-tried governess was not unnaturally in a twitter of nerves at their expulsion from Catherine's household, and the construction that might be put on it; she was for ever warning Bess against making eyes at men, against making pert answers, against a score of new-found faults in her behaviour.

Never before had Mrs Ashley seen so clearly, in watching her charge, that her mother had not been a lady. What was it that Queen Nan had said when Cat Ashley was going to see the Princess Mary? 'Give her a box on the ears now and then for the cursed bastard she is!'

No, much as she had admired her husband's cousin, even in her flashes of dangerous temper, Mrs Ashley could not but reflect on looking back through the years that that had *not* been the remark of a lady.

'How can you hope to be Queen' (the girl had let that out) 'when you chatter with every stable-boy and take no care of your dignity?'

'Mr Ascham says my dignity and gentleness are wonderful.'

Or – 'Women should be modest and remember their weakness. They can't be the equal of man.'

'They can, and I am. Mr Ascham says my mind has no womanly weakness, and my perseverance is equal to a man's.'

Mrs Ashley began to think her silver pen rather dearly bought. At this rate there would soon be no holding her young mistress. It was clear that she had captivated her new tutor as she had the last, and the greater the scholar, the less his sense.

The sight of Bess preening herself on her dignity and gentleness, who so short a time ago had locked her into her room while she went gallivanting on the river at night alone with the Admiral, was the last straw.

'I tell you what it is, my young Madam,' she flared out, 'you are like the cat in the fairy-tale who was turned into the form of a lady and could behave as such perfectly – as long as she did not see a mouse! Mice or men it's all the same, – the moment you catch sight of one, hey presto! away go all your fine manners and you must pounce!'

And the scolding ended in fits of laughter from them both.

But Bess was not entirely as confident as she seemed. She was anxious about Catherine, who she heard was not at all well, and at last realized that it was a serious matter for her to be having her first child at thirty-five. And Catherine's generosity made her ashamed and embarrassed; she had actually encouraged her husband to write to her, and sent messages by him as she did not feel up to writing herself, and told Bess how she missed her companionship and wished she were there with them at Sudley Castle, where they had gone for her to bear her child in the peace and quiet of their Gloucestershire home.

Determined to be as prudent as possible, Bess wrote her answer to Catherine, not Tom, but asked tentatively that he should continue to 'give me knowledge from time to time how his busy child does', and added with a sad little attempt at a joke, 'if I were at his birth no doubt I would have him beaten for the trouble he has put you to.'

'Him' and 'he'; no one thought of the coming baby in any other terms. Catherine made his sex a particular point in the petitions she offered up for his safe arrival, in the family prayers that she held for her household – a new development which her husband complained was adding fresh revolutionary terrors to the Reformed Religion, since the servants would be wanting their wages raised for having to troop into the hall and pray twice daily. He himself generally found he had to attend to some earnest business at the bottom of the garden at just those moments, and would stroll off, singing a popular street song in parody of the New Religion, which, he declared, was one of hate.

> 'Hate a cross, hate a surplice,
> Mitres, copes and rochets.
> Come hear me pray
> Nine times a day
> And fill your head with crochets.'

Pity the best of women had to have crochets, he told Cathy, laughing at her pet preachers and her enthusiasm over the higher education for women. She was only a little hurt, for she knew she would not like her Tom any the better if he held advanced views like his brother. She told herself they were so happy that they could afford the jolts that might have broken a more brittle happiness, – differences of opinion, downright quarrels, even bitter moments of jealousy.

Until, when it came to that last, the image of Bess's darting glance, the dragonfly swiftness of her turn of head, would rise before her, and she could not feel her happiness so secure.

But her child would safeguard it.

Tom did his own part towards the coming event by visiting all the best astrologers and fortune-tellers, and they all gave him certain assurance that his child would be a son – just as they had done to King Henry before his daughter Elizabeth was born, but nobody was going to remember that now. It would make all the difference to Tom's position, his ambitious hopes and intrigues, if he had a son and heir to be their focal point for the future.

At the end of July, just a month before Catherine's time was due, the Duchess gave birth to a son, 'and let *that* spur you to a strapping boy!' Tom told his wife. He was full of gay confidence, and as long as he was there she was too; but in his absence she drooped and was beset with nervous fears and melancholy. That was easily remedied, he told her; he would not leave her till the child was born and all well again.

He refused Somerset's offered command of the fleet in this summer's campaign against the Scots armies who had been annihilated last summer at Pinkie. But in spite of that, the Protector had to appeal to the Emperor for help, and march against his conquered enemy with the German troops, paid for in advance – a difficult matter with the Treasury bankrupt from the debts and debased coinage left over from the old King's reign; and Somerset could not help thinking it an uneconomic measure, when thousands of unemployed Englishmen were wandering homeless on the roads, and the magistrates could find no remedy except to flog and imprison them for their failure to find work. Though they knew well that no work was to be had, since they themselves were mostly employing one shepherd boy to mind their new flocks, where their fathers had given work to fifty ploughboys and farm labourers.

Still, there was no doubt that unemployed men quickly became unemployable, and these wretched vagrants would be no use as soldiers compared with the German mercenaries; moreover, they were apt to fraternize with the Scots, and particularly, as fellow-peasants, to dislike firing their harvest and ripening crops.

The German mercenaries had no such scruples; they were a race apart, bred only for war, heavy and inhuman as their armour: 'Find some means of making it move without 'em inside it, and you'd never know the difference!' said Tom, who hated the Germans from what he had seen of them in Hungary where they had spied and wormed their way in for centuries, and now treated the Magyars like slaves in their own country, holding them to the law passed over a hundred years before, that no one should have any position of importance unless he could produce a testimonial of Purity of Race, proving that all his four grandparents belonged to the ruling German nation.

Ned asked what the – he nearly said 'the devil' but changed it to 'on earth' – the four German grandparents had to do with his mercenaries?

'Why, this, you fool, – yes, you can look down your long nose at me and think you're always right, but you don't know everything, nobody here knows what the Germans are like. Ask the Magyars. Ask the Poles. Ask that old fellow I met in Cracow – only he died last year – you know who I mean – old fellow with a beard like a furze bush and a bumpy nose turned up at the end from poking it so high into the heavens – God's light, what *was* his name? – who wrote that the sun doesn't move but that we all go whizzing round it instead.'

'If you mean the Polish heretic Copernicus—'

'Why heretic? He dedicated his book to the Pope, who accepted it. Are you Reformers going to be more pernickety than the Pope? But whatever Copernicus wrote of the stars, he was sound on the Teutons, and the way they've ravaged Poland year after year. He told me himself, "we can scarcely dwell in our own houses for an hour." And all because the Germans think they are made by God to conquer the world. Their Emperor is not the Emperor of Germany, he's the German Emperor – of the World. But you'll never understand that here, you think it's just an empty traditional title. One has to have lived on the Continent to see it. And it's this Master Race of mechanic monsters that you're bringing into this island to fight your battles for you, against fellows who speak the same language as ourselves – and to do the dirty work you can't get Englishmen to do. You hire German hogs while our decayed yeomen rot in idleness on the roads. And *then* you complain that the Scots won't listen to your fine speeches about brotherly love and Free Trade!'

His elder brother said that Tom entirely failed to understand the Scottish question. Extreme measures had unfortunately been made necessary by this final outrage of the Scots, for they had at last shipped off their little Queen safely to France. Even Tom's shallow brain should grasp the danger to England of a Scottish-French encirclement.

But Tom only howled in exasperated boredom. He said that a lot of long words didn't alter facts; that Ned thought he could make the Devil himself sound respectable by speaking of his 'extreme measures'; that the Scots ought not to object to having their people slaughtered, their wives ravished in their sight, their fields burned, their churches, towns and villages razed to the ground, as long as he left the words 'English Sovereignty' out of his peace terms: – that in all his life Ned had never grasped a single fact, – only words, words, words.

The argument, as so often happens in the inconsequence of family quarrels, wandered far afield in a furious comparison of the 'ordered and disciplined' German rulers in Hungary with the dispossessed Magyar nobles who, having been left no other means of subsistence, would swoop down from their mountain fortresses on the market-place and carry off goods or, better, someone for ransom – preferably a Jew, for that was worth a bag of ducats where even a rich merchant would only fetch a reasonable sum. Good fellows, those Robber Knights, and no one in the world so handy with horseflesh.

Tom, glowing with nostalgic appreciation, wondered whether it wouldn't be a good plan to kidnap his royal nephew and ransom him for his own Protectorship of him. It was a bright notion and would be thought nothing of in Hungary, but here in England everyone was so conventional.

He swung off to visit his nephew and consider him from the point of view of this possibility. He found Edward ruffled as an angry kitten because Mary had written to him (on the eternal vexed question of having the Mass in her household) that 'although he was of great understanding, yet experience would teach him more yet'; an elder-sister touch far more irritating than the friendly equal arguing and wrangling between him and Bess. He showed his uncle with some pride his prompt retort to Mary that *she* 'might have something to learn, and no one was too old for that!'

But what chiefly infuriated him was that the German Emperor, her mother's nephew, was throwing out hints that if Mary were not allowed her own way, he would withdraw his Ambassador.

'Just because he is her first cousin and was once betrothed to her, how dare he think that gives him any right to interfere with *me*? I'd have declared war on him by now, only my Uncle Somerset is such a slug and won't set about it.'

Tom heartily encouraged him to 'pull the Emperor's nose', – in spite of the fact that he had always said it was a shame to bother the Princess Mary about her private worship, and that 'Live and let live' was the only sound course in religion. He disliked the Reformers, if anything, rather more than the priests; he complained that they made far more fuss about religion in their determination to prove themselves in the right; in fact, he had only joined them for professional purposes, since it was politically necessary to be on their side, and also because, like the rest of the nobles, he had made a good thing out of the plunder of the Church lands and property.

But questions of consistency never troubled him. It was enough that his brother was letting in an advance guard of the Emperor's troops, that the Emperor wanted to interfere in England as he had done practically everywhere on the Continent, and worst of all, that he was the Princess Mary's first cousin.

'The Hapsburgs don't need to fight, – they marry. They've got a hold over half Europe by that, and they'll get it here if we don't look out. Peaceful penetration – allies in the family – paid troops to fight our battles and act as spies in our country! Show him you won't stand any of it.'

'I will,' said Edward, squaring his elbows and clenching his inky fist round his pen as he bent over his black velvet desk to write a belligerent letter to the terrible Charles V, Imperator Mundi.

Tom, standing behind his chair, suddenly swept him up out of it, tossed him up in his arms just as though he were a baby, and hugged him. 'You're the living spit of your mother – just Jane's prim little determined air!'

'Put me down!' exclaimed the King in a squeak of astonished indignation. 'I'm like my father, – they all say so.'

'Oh, you're old Harry's own, sure enough, a chip of the old block. By Christ's soul, you'll make a King to match himself, and not all these canting snivelling book-learned old women shall keep you from it! I'll get you away from them, never fear.'

'Put me *down*!'

At last Tom heard him, put him down and knelt to him with exaggerated deference, humbly craving his dread Sire's pardon for his familiar treatment of him. Edward pulled down his waistcoat, smoothed his hair, and said in aggrieved tones, 'Now I shall have to get it brushed again.'

It wasn't until he had left that Tom remembered the prime motive of his visit, which was to consider his nephew's kidnapping.

Well, that could come later.

Chapter Fifteen

THE GOOD DUKE sat looking down his long nose at the letter, in Latin, of King Edward of England to the Emperor of the World. There were three mistakes in the syntax. It was time young Barnaby was whipped again. It was the only thing that had any real effect on Edward. He made a note of it and leaned across the table to stick it in a stand.

His eye fell on his last letter from his brother Henry at Wolf Hall.

'Further ye sent us downe such a lewde company of Frenchmen masons as I never sawe the lyke. I assure you they be the worst condicyoned people that ever I sawe and the dronkenest; for they will drynke more in one day than 3 dayes wages will come to, and then lye lyke beasts on the flore not able to stande. They are well nigh XXXs in debt for beer, victuals and other borrowed money. Praying you that I may be most hartely commendyed—' but here the Duke's eye instinctively averted from the fateful word 'bedfellowe'.

What a welter of things he had to see to, and all himself, for no one else ever did them properly. Was it even worth the trouble, all this accumulation of vast estates which he never had time to ride over, – of palaces spreading over the earth, towering to the sky, which he might never live even to see finished?

But this would never do. He made a shuddering guess at what his Duchess would say if she had heard his thought. He was not building for himself (nothing that he did was for himself) but for his son – and hers. Not for his eldest son, by Katrine Fillol; *he* had already been dispossessed of his birthright; and his younger stepbrother was to inherit his father's titles and estates. The Good Duke did not care to think of that.

It was narrow to consider one's own flesh and blood, or even one's own countrymen, as of prime importance. His public prayer to the Defender of All Nations showed a new and nobler view. And he had given practical testimony to it by opening a settlement of Flemish weavers, exiled for their religious beliefs, on his own estates at Glastonbury; the Somerset Weavers they were called, after him, a lasting tribute to his tolerance and foresight.

He took long views, in private as well as public matters. It was a fine instinct that made him take his pleasure, not in momentary self-indulgence, but in planting great trees that he would never see full-grown, in building palaces such as Somerset House that would dominate the untidy huddle of London's wooden buildings like an eagle brooding over a nest of sparrows.

The only idle moments he knew were those in which he stood watching his workmen, as busy as a swarm of ants, at work on that enormous ant-heap. He even sometimes watched them during sermon-time. The new Scottish preacher, Mr John Knox, whom he had imported as the latest of the Royal Chaplains, had actually dared raise complaints about it.

But then Mr Knox raised complaints about everything. His first sermon at Court had been a frenzied diatribe against the iniquity of kneeling at Communion. The Archbishop thought it went too far. The Duke had appointed him for his Protestant zeal, to which he had earlier testified by his share in the murder of Cardinal Beton in Scotland. King Henry had rewarded that deed with good money; but the French had imprisoned him in their galleys for it. You would have thought that after two years as a galley-slave the man would be pleased with the post of King's Chaplain in the now most firmly Protestant country in Europe. But he spent most of his time in bitter quarrels with his fellow-Reformers, with half the Court officials, and even, when he could, with his new patron the Protector. It was plain he could bear no authority but his own. Yet the Duke hesitated to get rid of him. The fellow was a powerful preacher. He had a vein of shrill nagging invective that was all the more telling because of its feminine quality – in fact, it had something in common with the Duchess's.

'What do you think of the new Chaplain – John Knox?' he demanded abruptly of John Dudley, Earl of Warwick, who had just entered, twirling a minute nosegay of single clove pinks, lad's love and balm of Gilead, in a slender silver flower-holder.

'Neither grateful nor pleasable,' replied the Earl promptly. He strolled over to the window and looked out. 'Besides,' he added over his shoulder, 'he called me Achitophel in his last sermon.'

The Duke exclaimed 'Tsa!' so violently that it sounded like an oath. 'It's sheer blasphemy to use the Bible as a stalking-horse for opposition to the Government!'

'He'll always be in opposition to any Government.'

'Yes. He's best as a revolutionary agent. I might send him later into Scotland to stir up revolt against the Government there.'

'Must it be later?'

The Earl's voice was low and pleasant; it sounded always as though he were smiling, though he did not in fact often smile. His hair and slight fringe of beard were cut very short, his moustaches very thin in a curved pencilled line. He did not look in the least like a famous soldier, but a fastidious dandy; his clothes of exquisite simplicity, almost monastic in style, no jewels, not even a ring; his delicate eyebrows and fine eyes fixed in a cool stare that held a hint of mockery.

Nor did the new Earl look like one of the 'Lords sprung from the dunghill', as the new Duke had unkindly stigma-tized him and his fellows. As a matter of fact, his remote ancestry was rather more illustrious than the Duke's; and his air of patrician calm would never lead one to suppose that his father, Edmund Dudley, had been a clever shady lawyer who made a lot of money for King Henry's father by hunting up obsolete old laws and imposing huge fines on all who were, quite unconsciously, breaking them. Henry VIII, on coming to the throne as a bright lad of eighteen, had promptly executed him, as a popularity measure; but there was no ill feeling about it. Edmund's son, John Dudley, had risen steadily at Court; Henry had a high opinion of his ability, created him Viscount Lisle, appointed him Lord High Admiral, and nominated him as one of the Lords of the Council of Regency for his son. On the King's death, when most people moved one up, John Dudley was created Earl of

Warwick and handed over his post as Lord High Admiral to Tom Seymour, then Admiral of the Fleet.

He was by far the most important figure on the Council after Somerset, and had managed the Scottish campaign rather better than he, but the Duke felt no uneasiness on that score; he had long ago labelled him in his mind as an old friend, and his labels were apt to remain unchanged.

But he was annoyed by the fellow's idle air; here he was lounging into his room, apparently only to sniff at his posy and remark on the stifling August heat and the stinking steam of the vapours exhaled by the river that wound like a decaying dragon below the open windows. With a curious glee in his gentle voice he called Somerset's attention to the oily glitter on old Thames' dark scales, too sluggish for ripples, a slimy pewter colour under the thunder-grey of the sky.

'Look at the old serpent gliding down to Tower Bridge and Traitors' Gate,' he said, 'so rotten that she is phosphorescent, and faugh!' he twiddled the miniature bouquet at his nose, 'yet she's swallowed finer bodies than yours or mine, and will swallow more yet, that old serpent.'

The Good Duke flung down his pen. 'Your fancies may be poetic,' he rapped out in the tone of an irritable schoolmaster, 'but I have no time for them. Can you not see that I am engaged on business of the State?'

Dudley flicked a glance across the writing-table; it came to rest on the note Somerset had just written and stuck up in the stand before him : 'Barnaby to be whipped.'

A slow bluish flush crept up above the Good Duke's beard. 'The King's learning,' he said, 'is the prime business of the State. We can't have him writing to foreign princes with mistakes in his Latin syntax.'

He tossed Edward's letter over to Dudley, who read it with an eyebrow up. 'We can't have him writing to foreign princes with declarations of war either,' he remarked softly.

'Oh – that! I shall tear it up, naturally.'

'Then why trouble about the syntax?'

The Good Duke groaned. It was impossible to explain a principle. Nobody but himself was capable of understanding one.

He curtly offered his visitor a seat, in the manner of one who has made up his mind to endure interruption, and demanded the reason for it.

'An unwelcome one, I fear,' said the suave voice by the window. 'The House of Commons has just thrown out your Act against the Enclosures of the common lands.'

The Protector was silent. Then he reached for his copy of his Proclamation on the Enclosures and began to read it out. John Dudley sat down. He had heard it before. 'The pitiful complaints of His Majesty's poor subjects' left him cold. In what far Eden had they not complained?

' "In time past,' " read the Protector, ' "ten, twenty, yes and in some places an hundred or two hundred Christian people have inhabited and kept household, to the replenishing and fulfilling of His Majesty's realm with faithful subjects for its defence, where now there is nothing kept but sheep and bullocks. All that land which heretofore was tilled and occupied with so many men is now gotten by insatiable greediness of mind unto one or two men's hands and scarcely dwelled upon with one poor shepherd. Men are eaten up and devoured and driven from their houses by sheep and bullocks." '

'Not original,' murmured Dudley. 'Sir Thomas More wrote back in the 'twenties that sheep are eating men.'

'Even that tax I put on, of 2d. on every sheep owned, hasn't stopped it.'

'You can't put back the clock. The wool trade's been going on "in time past" for a long time. And it gave England her wealth.'

'What's the use of wealth?'

The Earl of Warwick cocked an ear to listen to the hammering of the hundreds of workmen engaged on the building of Somerset House. The Duke of Somerset heard it too. He tapped nervously on the table as though to cover the sound. The Earl coughed sympathetically.

'Look at the final result!' said the Duke. He picked up his Proclamation again. Dudley hastily agreed that the final result was deplorable. Hoping to forestall a renewed reading, he remarked that one result was the shortage of man-power in this Scottish war; but the Duke instantly capped it from the Proclamation, – ' "this realm must be defended against the enemy with force of men, not with flocks of sheep and droves of brute beasts." '

'The Italian and German troops make a good substitute,' soothed Dudley.

The Protector, mindful of his talk with Tom, said curtly, 'I've had quite enough of that.'

'Let's hope the Scots will too.' Dudley got up and added sympathetically, 'It has not been a lucky session for all of your Reform measures.'

'For not one of them! The House of Commons have thrown out my Bills to provide for poor children in each town, and to prevent farmers being unjustly turned out of their own land; while the House of Lords reject my Act to prevent the decay of ploughing and growing of crops. Most important of all, my project for the Reform of the Common Law didn't even reach a second reading in the Commons. Every one of my schemes to provide for the poor has failed.'

'You are forgetting your Act of Slavery.'

The Protector's eyes rolled round at him with the look of a wounded stag.

'Yes. The only one to be passed unanimously by both Houses! The only way in which Parliament would consent to provide for the unemployed.' And he began to quote his Slavery Act, by heart.

The Earl pulled a scrap of paper on the table towards him and drew a gargoyle face. 'I know,' he said, 'but there have been slaves here in England before now.'

But the Duke went on quoting. The Earl began to scribble.

The Duke never noticed it. 'At least,' he said presently, 'it only applies to the able-bodied. The Act provides for the aged and impotent by collections in church every Sunday. *They* are not slaves.'

'They'd be no use,' said the Earl. In a minute or two this fellow would argue himself round, as usual, into self-justification.

But instead, 'Liberty, liberty!' cried the Duke in a great voice. 'Is this to be the end of all my hopes to make England a land where nothing can be profitable that is not godly and honest; nor nothing godly and honest whereby our neighbours and Christian brethren are harmed? But these fat newly rich fellows in Parliament care nothing for their brethren. Is there indeed one honest man amongst them except myself? And you,' he remembered to add.

'Parliament represent the rich. Why should they care about the poor?'

'Then by Heaven!' (the Protector had actually made an oath) 'I will not rest until the poor too are represented. I will reform Parliament so that the yeoman, yes and his labourer, shall find a mouthpiece in it.'

Dudley repressed a shudder of that contemptuous distaste with which one recognizes symptoms of an abnormal state of mind. Really, Somerset was becoming a public danger as well as nuisance. Reform always led to revolt. And the fellow was working the Duke himself into a frenzy.

With lips white with rage, the Duke burst out, 'In spite of the devil, of private profit, self-love, money, and such-like devil's instruments, *it shall go forward*.'

'Would you go against your own class?' Dudley asked in carefully gentle reproof. 'The new landed gentry are making still stronger distinctions between rich and poor. Even the universities are becoming conscious of rank; they are growing so expensive that the yeomen and labourers can no longer afford to send their sons. Absurd as it may seem, I believe that very soon Oxford and Cambridge, yes, and even Eton, will be only for the sons of gentry. Regrettable, but one can't put back the clock. Your hopes for the future are really only dreams of the past, when any labourer's son could get the learning that is now the privilege of the rich. But we must forget all that and live in the present.'

The Duke sighed heavily. There was no time he liked so little.

'Whatever makes the past or future predominate over the vulgar present,' he pronounced, 'advances us in the dignity of thinking beings.'

Dudley laid a friendly hand on his shoulder. Poor old Somerset, he should have been the celibate Master of some college, a thinker, dreamer, idealist.

'You drive yourself too hard,' he said; 'there are limits to what one man can do, though you will never recognize it. Think less of your brethren – and more of your brother.'

Somerset started as if stung. 'What of my brother? I've had enough of him and to spare. He was here just now, haranguing me like a tornado.'

'It's in the family,' thought Dudley, and aloud: 'Will he take the command of the fleet you've offered him?'

'Not he! Nor would I urge it now after the fantastic way he's just been talking to me about the Scots, as though it were a crime to lead foreign troops against them. You'd think they were his brothers!'

'That's dangerous.'

'When was Tom ever anything but dangerous? Well, he can't do much harm now, for he's gone back to his wife – says he'd rather stay at home to make merry with his friends in the country.'

'Hmm. I don't like that. Sounds as though he means to go on working against you in your absence. He's getting up a stout following among the squires and yeomen – a following of ten thousand if one's to believe his own boast. Old Squire Dodrington has been up in town for the lawsuit on his lands, and tells me that Master Admiral was mighty sympathetic telling him how *he* would get him justice, – this when Tom came to dinner at Dodrington Hall bringing a couple of flagons of good wine and a venison pasty and roast sucking-pig or two – no wonder he's a popular guest! He does it all round the country, dining with his inferiors, but not at their expense. Tells his friends to do it too. At least half a dozen fellows in the House have told me of it.'

'It isn't treasonable to be a good diner-out,' said the Duke uncomfortably.

'Depends on the after-dinner talk. He makes no secret of his discontent, that he is not allowed his share of power – meaning, no doubt, the lion's share. He has always been accustomed to it, hasn't he – at home?'

The Protector winced. So it was common knowledge that Tom had always been their mother's favourite! He tried to think of some scathing reply that would show his complete indifference to the matter; but Dudley, with an airy flick of his flower-holder, had already passed on to another. What of the pirate, Jack Thompson, and the Admiral's obscure dealings with him? Fishy he called them, very fishy, – 'Have you taxed him with them?'

'I have,' said the Protector shortly. He had heard enough of pirates and their virtues from his brother.

Dudley then spoke of this notorious scandal about the Princess Elizabeth.

The Protector said nothing. He had heard too much of the Princess and her vices from his wife.

'The whole country knows why she was sent away from the Queen's household. There are some who say they know more, – that it was because she was found to be with child by him.'

The Good Duke looked at him. 'She won't be fifteen till next month.'

'It is still possible.'

Even the Good Duke noticed something of ironic pity in the other's cool gaze. In another minute he would be telling him the facts of life. He was determined to snub him.

'You talk like a woman,' he said in pained disgust.

The Earl recognized his mistake in entering into competition with the Duchess. But he stuck to his guns on the practical issue. 'The Princess is only second heir to the throne, but it's not a bad second, with a delicate child and a sickly woman in her thirties between. An heir to her and the Admiral would put him in a paramount position.'

'A bastard would not be an heir.'

'It's not so long since the Princess herself was referred to as the Little Bastard, even by her sire. It's a position easily remedied nowadays, when divorce is becoming so common – and so respectable.'

The Good Duke cleared his throat. He had had a divorce himself. The Wicked Earl (as some were inclined to think him) was, on the other hand, a faithfully devoted husband and father to twelve children. He was walking up and down the room on a soft measured tread, his hands behind his back twirling that miniature bouquet like a budding tail.

'It's not any one particular prank of the Admiral's that makes me anxious,' he said slowly, as though considering aloud; 'it is that everything he does, kissing that little red-haired wretch, currying favour with the King and telling him you're too hard a task-master, dining with country squires, encouraging pirates, – in all this he is helping to rock the ship of State – and that in foul enough weather already, God knows. The whole country's in a smoulder of discontent, any breeze may blow it into a fire of revolt. Even at best there is only a quivering quiet. Remember those attempted risings this spring in half a dozen counties. They never gathered head, for they were not united. They may yet unite.'

'The base ingratitude of the people!' Somerset exclaimed. 'I've done more for them in eighteen months than the old King in the whole of his reign. Do they *want* tyranny? Do they *hate* liberty? I have given them freedom of speech – of opinion—'

'One has to be full fed to care about opinion.'

'I have swept away all the monstrous new Treason and Heresy Acts of the last reign, that Act of Six Articles which they called the Whip with Six Strings. Royal Proclamations can no longer become law of themselves. I have removed the restrictions on the printing of the English Bible.'

'Do they care about the Bible?'

'What in God's name *do* they care about? I have minimized executions, refused to employ the torture-chamber. Do they care nothing for that?'

'No one cares if others have been tortured and executed. Those who have been, aren't alive to thank you.' And Dudley turned on his heel with a flourish of his flowery tail.

Somerset slammed his hands down on the table. 'You are telling me that all they care about is hard cash. It's not my fault the Exchequer was bankrupt at King Henry's death. That the only thing that's cheap is labour. I've brought in laws to raise wages, to lower prices, to prevent the markets being flooded with trashy goods. But no laws can make good men. Men have never been so mad as now to make money at the expense of their neighbour. But that is not a cause, it's a consequence. Debased coinage, debased goods, they're the result of debased ideas. All the old ways are gone. The world is in the melting-pot. We have the chance now to build a far greater and happier State than ever before. But they cannot take that chance; they cannot even see it. They are blind with greed. They are like wasps in a honey jar, never seeing that their neighbours' deaths lead only to their own.'

Dudley led him gently but firmly back to the point. 'Very true. The country is ripe for revolution. I know the tenderness of your feelings for your mother. But in such a case surely your country should come first.'

'What do you mean by speaking of my mother?'

Dudley did not appear to notice the question. 'Those risings this spring failed at the outset because they had no leader. What if they should find one? I would rather your brother were anywhere this summer but at home in Gloucestershire.'

'Where under heaven then should he be, unless he were dead?'

Dudley was silent.

The Protector glanced at him, then looked away.

The silence thickened. It weighed on the room like a thunder-cloud.

Dudley began to whistle a nonchalant tune. 'Well,' he said, 'I must not delay your work for the State any longer.'

He took his leave. The Protector watched him go. He in his turn now walked up and down the room, which had grown even more oppressively hot. He could not settle his thoughts; they chased each other round and round like rats in a trap, chasing the things that Dudley had said, had not said, had looked.

Could he have meant what he looked?

He thought of Tom, that perpetual nuisance of a youngest brother who had always given trouble at home; even as a baby he had been a sturdy rogue, grabbing the others' toys, trotting through the Ladies' Garden and picking off the heads of the flowers, and never smacked nor even scolded by their mother; then later playing truant from his lessons, robbing the apple orchards in Pound and Broom Close and the cherries in Ladelwell-pound; later still, making friends with such low rascals as Gorway's son the shepherd boy and young Wynbolt the undergrubber and going poaching with them at nights. What an uproar there had been when the red-faced old keeper of the Home Park (what *was* his name? Something like an apple – Quince? – no, Vince) had complained to their father, gobbling with rage! And Tom at last got the thrashing he so richly deserved, but only chuckled in triumph because he had padded his breeches with rags. Tom, later, getting into that mess with Edie of the dairy-house and her fellow Audrey Cocks with the bold black eyes (how was it he still remembered *their* names – a couple of dairymaids?). Getting into debt; getting into all sorts of mischief when he went to the French Court in the train of Bryan, whom King Henry had nicknamed the Vicar of Hell, – 'and this young rascal is his best chorister there!' old Foxnose François had said, pinching Tom's ear, so that he only swaggered about his scrapes.

And it was the same with the Hapsburgs in Hungary; and in the Netherlands with the Emperor's sister, the Regent there; and even with that grave and dignified Oriental Potentate, Suliman the Magnificent. It was the same everywhere; people only liked him the better for being a showy daredevil adventurer. And most of all, King Henry.

With a sudden unhappy little yelp he began to move things restlessly about on his table as he remembered that enormous laughter of their royal brother-in-law while he read out bits of Tom's letters from the Turkish wars.

Henry had made endless use of 'Good Ned', had worked him to death and barely grunted his appreciation.

But he would stand anything from Tom. When privately betrothed to their sister Jane (with Nan Bullen still alive), he had proudly told them how she was working the tapestry pictures for their nuptial bed-curtains herself, and Tom had asked with that impudent cock of his eyebrow, 'What's the subject? Bathsheba?'

That would have been the end of any other man. Yet the King had still liked Tom best.

And always their mother had loved him best, her precious youngest boy, the mother's spoilt darling, and had taken his side in the furious quarrels of his boyhood (the Wolf Cubs at Wolf Hall the neighbours had called them); and when their father was away, told Ned he must take care of his little brother and be like a father to him, which was impossible and unfair, for she never told Tom to treat him with the respect due to a father, or even to a so much elder brother. She never backed up his authority for all she kept saying, 'You're so much older and wiser, dear Ned'; she only said that to coax him into pulling Tom out of his scrapes; it was all he was there for.

And Tom himself thought it quite enough reward to clap. him on the shoulder with that insufferably jolly air and say, 'Good old Ned, I knew you'd always stand by me.'

Yes, he'd always stood by him; he supposed he would always have to, even now, even though Tom was now deliberately working against him, undermining his authority, disloyal to the core, imperilling all these disinterested, farsighted schemes of his, any one of which was worth a deal more than that young Tom Fool.

Yet all were imperilled by this braggart, this *farceur*, this unnatural brother, whom he had got to try and get out of the trouble he was making for himself, as though that, and that alone, were his perpetual job in life.

He would not think of that. He would think of his plans for the future of the people, which would, which *should* go forward, in spite of the devil, or private profit, self-love, money, and such-like devil's instruments – yes, and in spite of Tom.

So he tried to think of all he was doing for the people, and of what he must do next; but always he kept seeing that raw foggy night in his boyhood when he and Tom had been out shooting birds in the Forest of Savernake with their crossbows, and lost their way in the sudden thick mist, and had met a wild boar face to face and he had struck up Tom's bow just in time to prevent the young ass stinging it up with an arrow. And he had driven off the boar and at last found their way and brought them both safely home. And as they came near Wolf Hall their little mother came flitting out of the broad lighted doorway like a frightened bird, and down into the dark towards them, crying, 'Tom! Tom! Is he there? Is he safe?'

She had thanked and praised him afterwards, explained that she had asked first for Tom 'because, you see, Ned, he is such a little boy,' but it made no odds: she had not cried out for him; and that raw foggy night had struck a chill damp on his spirit ever since.

* * *

The stifling smelly mist from the river was creeping into the room, dulling the light. How long had he been pacing up and down, doing nothing?

His restless eye, roving over the floor, caught sight of a small white object. It was a tight paper ball. He remembered now that Dudley had scribbled something on a scrap of paper which he had been crumpling in his hand as he talked, and must have dropped. He picked it up, smoothed it out, saw a rough drawing of a gargoyle head, and some lines of verse. He read:

> 'Observe: 'tis the mild Idealists
> Who plan our social Revolutions;
> Then come the brutal Realists
> And turn them into – Executions!
>
> And, first and foremost on their lists,
> Appear the mild Idealists!!'

Chapter Sixteen

SO THE DUKE went up to Scotland with his German troops and without his brother, and people said that for a fighter like Tom to choose to stay at home with a sick wife at this juncture looked extremely sinister, and his friends warned him to become 'a new sort of man, for the world began to talk very unfavourably of him, both for his slothfulness to serve and his greediness to get.'

The joke of it to Tom was that for once, in the burning August heat, he was really eager to escape from the stifling smelly town, and to ride back to Gloucestershire through cornfields splashed with scarlet poppies, back to the cool gardens of Sudley, where for the moment all his care was to cheer and hearten his Cathy and plan with her the nurseries for their child.

He had hung her room, where the baby would be born, with new tapestries showing the story of Daphne; even the wet-nurse's bed was to be decorated with gay colours 'to please the babe.' The day nursery led out of it, all ready furnished even to the minute chair of state upholstered in cloth of gold where the baby should receive his first visitors when he was old enough to sit on a chair at all.

Jane Grey helped with all the preparations in grave delight, and Bess nearly cried with envy when she heard of them, to think that Jane was there and not herself. However badly she had behaved, Catherine had always liked her best, she was certain, and would rather have her there now than her good little cousin.

And her other little cousin, Mary Queen of Scots, now five and a half years old, had eluded all the efforts of the English fleet to capture her, and arrived in France, where the King and his wife, Queen Catherine de Medici, and, far more important, his *maîtresse en titre*, Diane de Poictiers, all declared her the loveliest child they had ever seen, and treated her publicly as the prospective bride of their small son, the Dauphin. So she would be Queen of France some day as well as Queen of Scotland – a very convenient base for her French armies to undertake their long-planned invasion of England.

For Bess never forgot for long that summer day on board her father's flagship when the French Armada, three hundred strong, was sighted sailing towards Portsmouth.

She never forgot that her father had called the baby Scottish Queen the most dangerous person in Europe; and now that Mary was in France, playing with a still younger baby boy, Bess understood why. And her precocious fear of her was sharpened by childish envy, as of her cousin Jane; for if Jane were safe and happy, cosseted by Catherine and planning baby clothes and nursery furniture with her, Mary was surely the luckiest child in the world, the most important, with a life already as adventurous as a fairytale, and now the spoilt and petted guest of the glittering Court of France.

But she herself, the eldest of the three cousins, was left out of everything, out of cosy domesticity and thrilling triumph alike; banished, disgraced, and with no one to admire her but Mr Ascham.

* * *

On the last day of August, hot and still and bright, when the Cotswold hills lay as soft and purple as ripe plums in the hazy sunshine, Catherine's baby was born, and it was a girl.

The midwife, being the best that money could hire, was the one who had helped the Princess Elizabeth into the world, and had had to break the news of her sex to her expectant sire. Never would she forget the tremendous figure striding up and down the gallery at Greenwich Palace, stopping short at sight of her, swinging round and stiffening taut as a lion crouched to spring, in the suspense of his unspoken question. She had felt her answer freezing on her lips, could hardly herself hear the words she faltered, 'Your Majesty – a beautiful little – daughter.'

The bellow of a maddened bull had replied. Yet even that moment, which the midwife had thought her last, had not been as terrifying as the one a little later when the King had stood by his wife's bedside, looking down at the infant Elizabeth, stood in silence worse than any roar of rage, and said at last in a low and dreadful voice, 'I see that God does not wish to give me male children.'

Now it was all to do again. Now it was Tom Seymour, Lord High Admiral, striding up and down the long gallery in that castle of pleasant golden Cotswold stone at Sudley, and to him too a male child had been promised by prophecy, as important to his reckless gamble with ambition as ever it had been to the Tudor dynasty. And to him too went the now doubly nervous midwife, taught by experience what the disappointed sire was like.

But there was never any counting on Tom. Yet again the midwife stammered, 'a beautiful little – daughter,' but he seemed to have forgotten all about the sex question, he demanded only how the mother and child were doing, and he rushed up to see them as soon as he was allowed; and when he was given a glimpse of the daughter that had as shockingly betrayed his trust in God as ever King Henry's had done, he was as delighted and proud as if a daughter had been just what he had hoped and prayed for from the beginning.

He even had to dash off a letter at once to his brother the Protector with a full description of the baby's beauties and asking him to rejoice with him, quite forgetting that this was just what Somerset and his Duchess were certain to do, since the birth of a mere daughter rendered him so much less dangerous.

Clearly Ned had been right to call Tom shallow, but what a mercy it was to find him as shallow as this! It thawed the elder brother, who had just finished writing a long and well-deserved lecture, into adding a very kindly postscript, congratulating him on the birth of 'so pretty a daughter.'

In his relief he found he could take real pleasure in the latest news from his other brother; in the furzes that Henry had planted in the new hare warren; 'the wild bore and 500 dere shal be sent next week; there be pasture ynough for them, for the grounde was never so well before-hande yn grasse thys tyme of the yere as yt is nowe.'

The Duke even pulled a philosophical smile over Henry's explanation that 'It was not possible to devyde the bucks from the rascalls, but we wyl put all yn together.' It was a forester speaking of the difficulty of dividing the full-grown deer from the lean and inferior, – but so perhaps God might speak of men.

And he did not fall into one of his fretful storms of nervous rage with the messenger when he read that the lewd company of Frenchmen 'be departid and stoln away like themselves'; for his head was full of the old days when he and Henry and Tom used to go hawking in Collingbourne woods and hunting the wild boar in Savernake Forest, and, when the day of reckoning came round, toss a penny for who should pay the necessary fourpence to buy hempen halters to bind their quarry's legs to a pole and carry him home in triumph.

'*Gear may come and gear may go,*
But three brothers again we'll never be.'

But they would be. They would leave their womenfolk behind and all three go hunting together as in the old days.

Brotherly love was once again possible – even between brothers.

He was so far carried away that he sent a message from his Duchess (there was no need to be too literal in going to get it from her lips) assuring Tom of both their hopes that now his wife had begun so well she would bear him many more children, sons as well as daughters.

It was a venturesome tempting of Providence. But anything might happen before then.

It did.

By the time that letter reached Gloucestershire all Tom's pride and joy were being dashed to the ground. Catherine had become dangerously ill with puerperal fever. It came on her with such appalling swiftness that it was difficult even for those in attendance on her to grasp what had happened. One moment she was smiling contentedly at her husband's delight and amusement at this absurdly tiny scrap of flesh that waved its pink fists so helplessly in the air; the next, she was frowning and tossing her head from side to side on the pillow and speaking in a high peevish voice quite unlike her own, speaking things that no one, not even herself, had known she thought.

For they did not grasp at once that she was delirious when she complained to her husband that he was really wanting her to die, so that he would be free to marry the Princess Elizabeth.

He did not know how to comfort her, for he soon found that his words could not reach her understanding; he consulted with her friend Lady Tyrwhitt, who was in charge of the sickroom, and as he stood with her in the window, looking anxiously towards the bed, that strained unnatural voice called out, saying he was standing there laughing at her misery, and that he had given her 'many shrewd taunts.'

Was this the end of all their joking and playing, all his teasing of her, and her calling him brute and bully in fun – that it should be thus monstrously translated?

'Christ's soul!' he cried, 'I cannot bear it. Cathy, Cathy, my sweet fool, when did I ever want to hurt you?'

He flung down on the bed beside her and took her in his arms, pushing her hair back from her hot face with furious tender hands, until at last his love communicated itself to her, and she lay quiet.

Presently she recovered consciousness enough to say that she would make her will, leaving all her lands and money to her husband and 'wishing that it were a thousand times more in value.' But she never mentioned the baby on which all her thoughts and hopes had been set for so long; she seemed to have forgotten its very existence; and her ladies shook their heads over this, taking it as a sure symptom of approaching death.

They were right, for two days later she was dead.

Chapter Seventeen

THE FIRST Protestant royal funeral took place in England with the Lady Jane Grey as chief female mourner, and Mr Coverdale, the translator of the Bible, to preach the sermon and explain that all the alms and offerings given were not 'to benefit the dead, but for the poor only'; nor were the prayers and lighted candles for 'any other intent or purpose than to do honour' (but no benefit) 'to the deceased.'

'The new Church,' said Elizabeth bitterly when she heard of it, 'deserts her children at the grave.'

Jane Grey, who was visiting her on her way to her home at Bradgate in Leicestershire, was shocked at her cousin's attitude. 'It is illogical and impious,' she said, 'to pray for the dead.'

'Would you say that if you yourself were at the point of death?'

'I would, and shall. I shall ask people to pray for me as long as I am still living, but the moment I am dead it would be wrong.'

Yes, she would hold by that. Whatever Jane said, she would stand by. Bess gave a laugh which startled the younger girl, who had, however, some glimmering of what she was feeling.

'She often wished you were there,' Jane said, 'she would

rather have had you with her than me, I know. She has left you half her jewels.'

Bess turned sharply away, and Jane, looking sadly after her, wondered why her cousin could not take her grief in a more Christian spirit. It seemed to make her harsh and mocking.

Jane had been so looking forward to her comfort and guidance; and Bess had just had her fifteenth birthday, which made her practically a grown-up woman; Jane would not have her twelfth for three weeks yet, but her parents seemed to think that made her one also, for they were saying it was not suitable for her to stay on in the Admiral's household now that his wife was dead. She thought this absurd, for her great difficulty was to make the Admiral realize she was as old as she was. He still gave her dolls and spoke to her as though she were about six, and when she protested, said it was her own fault for being so small, she grew downwards like a cow's tail.

But Bess, instead of agreeing how silly and tiresome Jane's parents were being, only said that she wasn't going to answer for the Admiral. And finding her so unsympathetic, Jane could not bring herself to tell her real sorrow; which was that it was the Admiral himself who had sent her away.

So shocked and stunned had he been by his wife's death that all his far-reaching plans and ambitions had gone clean out of his head; he would not even keep his household, but talked of dismissing the lot and going right away, he did not know nor care where; and packed Jane straight off home to her parents as though she were a puppy he had tired of training.

And now Bess said she was lucky to have parents and a home to go to, where she would be safe and be told what to do. Really she must be ill!

Mrs Ashley also thought her charge's behaviour odd; the girl had been utterly bewildered and aghast at first at the news of Catherine's death, yet seemed even more angry than sorry, and went about with a white face and shut set mouth when she did not fly into sudden and unreasonable rages.

The Admiral's servant who brought the news told them of

his master's passionate grief; but Bess showed no sympathy, and when Mrs Ashley told her it would be only right and proper for her to write him a letter of condolence, she flew out at her governess like a spitfire and snapped out, 'I will not. He doesn't need it.'

Mrs Ashley told her she was monstrously unfeeling. What was worse, it looked so marked. *Someone* from the Princess's household must write; 'if Your Grace will not,' she said in coldly formal remonstrance, 'then I will.'

So she did, but when she showed the letter, Her Grace gave it an indifferent glance and said not one word about it, one way or the other.

Mrs Ashley's conclusion was that the Princess did not believe in the Admiral's grief for his wife; perhaps did not wish to believe it.

'Your old husband is free again now,' she said lightly one evening, when the girl's fierce tension had for some time relaxed and she had flown suddenly into a wildly silly mood that seemed to welcome chaff and badinage, – and whatever she might welcome, Mrs Ashley must try and give. 'Oh yes,' she continued, nodding her head, 'you can have him if you will, and well you know it. If the Protector and the Council give their consent, would you be so cruel as to deny him? You were his first choice, you know . . .'

Bess had clapped her hand over her governess's mouth. 'If you don't stop talking,' said a small clear deadly voice, 'I'll thrust you out of the room.'

One could never be sure what she would welcome.

But certainly she listened with both ears when people spoke to each other, not to her, about the Admiral, especially if they spoke praise, which made her flush with pleasure. Mr Parry the cofferer, who kept all the household accounts, was a great friend of Mrs Ashley's, and the two of them would casually remind each other, in front of their young mistress, what a great man the Admiral was clearly born to be; how he had begun to win position and notice entirely on his own merits, as a younger son, and before any of his sisters had made important marriages; how the sumptuous state he kept abroad for the honour of his country came as naturally to him as to any of the great princes of the House of Valois and of Hapsburg, and how his popularity with them had made his success as a diplomat.

'A King among kings, he was their fellow from the first,' Mrs Ashley declared, rolling up her eyes, and Mr Parry, turning his down modestly, said, 'Ah, but what did he care for that, whenever there was a chance to prove himself a man among men? Off he dashed in the middle of all his success and splendour at the Hungarian Court, to fight in their quarrel against the cruel Turk. "A lion in battle," so the King of Hungary wrote of him to King Henry.'

Mrs Ashley took up the antiphony.

'And as great a sailor as soldier – look how he drove off the French Armada when they outnumbered us by five to one!'

'And I was there!' Bess thought, hugging herself, while her eyes glowed in the firelight like a cat's.

But she could not contain in silence her pride and glory in that towering figure on the deck of the *Great Harry* as the enemy sails hove into sight over the edge of the bright sea. She laughed aloud, yet her laughter had a secret sound; they pressed her for its reason, and then she said in airy tones, 'Three hundred tall ships sailing to invade England – and then "Pouf! the wind blew them away!" That was all that happened, so the Admiral said; "we'd the luck of the wind." What would have happened if the wind *hadn't* changed just then? But no, he was certain that England would always have luck, and the wind, on her side – on his side too,' she added tentatively.

Mrs Ashley quickly assured her that the Admiral was born to be lucky, the youngest son of three, as in the fairytales. Hadn't he proved himself lucky in Court and camp, and, she hoped, (with a sly look) in love? Bess leaned forward and nonchalantly touched a log of wood. She thought nobody would notice, but the tutor did.

Mr Ascham's brain was whirling in a vortex of emotions; jealousy was shot through with pride, and a new awareness of what he himself was capable, as well as that bold and handsome conqueror of his Princess's thoughts. Yes, they were both of them men of this new many-coloured, fast-moving age, when a man was not content to be one thing merely, but was often courtier, soldier, statesman, sportsman, all in one.

He had just had a grave warning from his former tutor that his passion for dice and the cockpit would be his ruin. But would it? He had put his best writing into this new book he was doing on the Cockpit; he was making English prose, a new thing, the thing that Englishmen would write in future instead of the old monkish musty Latin.

Those two bawds were chuckling now over the Admiral's pranks that had made him the favourite of King Henry and the playboy of Europe; 'but of course his elder brother can never understand that. *He* can only see him as the bad boy of the family!'

The tutor unexpectedly chimed in on an acid note; only Englishmen were so stupid as to think that to be solemn, dull and unpleasant was a sure criterion of solid worth and intellect. King Hal had known better, because the joy he took in living had been more French than English, and the keenness of his wits more Italian than either. 'He was not content merely to govern with a strong hand such as England needed; he has made her excel in music, in singing and dancing above all other countries, and encouraged plays to be written in English – light and transient toys they are called by the solemn dullards, but there's no knowing what those plays might become in the hands of some great poet. He wrote himself, was musician and composer, dancer and draughtsman, the best of our sportsmen – and our greatest ruler!'

'And *my* father,' Bess murmured.

They spoke of King Hal, while she thought of the Admiral, and Mr Ascham of himself.

'Man is a microcosm,' he cried, 'the full man should take all life for his province.'

'What's this about a full man?' came a great voice from the doorway. 'Here's one that's empty as an old can.'

Bess half rose from her chair, then sat down again, gripping its arms. All the resentment that had been surging in her against the Admiral these past weeks was whirling away. She tried to clutch on to it. She had forgotten Catherine while she listened to praise of him; now she told herself,

'Catherine is dead and he doesn't care. Catherine is dead, and he and I made her unhappy. Catherine is dead, and it's her I loved, not him. Oh God, make me go on loving her and not him.'

It was no good. He was there at the end of the hall flinging off his cloak, he was striding across to her, lifting her hand to kiss it, and how warm and strong his grasp was round her fingers, how warm and strong his voice. His eyes were laughing into hers again, – how dared he ever laugh at her again? She had told herself she would never laugh with him again – you might as well tell the grass not to grow nor the birds sing. She raised those drooping white-lidded eyes and looked full at him.

'Why have you come, my lord?' She tried hard to make the question sound casual and matter of fact.

'Don't you know, my Lady Bess?'

There was no attempt to make the answer sound casual.

*   *   *

Tom in fact had recovered. Which does not mean that he had never been sick – sick unto death, for that was what his soul had been, a ship that had lost its rudder and was veering wildly to the winds of despair and utter weariness of all ambition. He had been within an ace of killing himself in the days that followed Cathy's death.

But his body simply would not let him stay sad; the unthinking high spirits of sheer physical vigour would keep tingling through his veins, reminding him even in the very midst of his stormy grief that it was good to be alive. Being miserable was no use to anyone, least of all to Cathy. If he did not kill himself he must go on living; and if he went on living he must be busy, active, make plans, take chances, run risks, or he would be blue-moulded with misery; he must have bustle, music, the flickering light of hundreds of candles and torches, the noise of people coming and going, of people talking, courting him, discussing gay and desperate ventures, and of his own voice laughing away their fears.

He caught again at all the old schemes that he had begun to let fall through his fingers in the first shock of his despair; countermanded the disposal of his household; sent for his everwilling old mother to come and take charge of the female part of it; and wrote off to Jane's parents to have her returned to his care and his mother's chaperonage, explaining that he had only sent her away because he had been 'so amazed that I had small regard either to myself or my doings.'

They hesitated; the Admiral was still dangling that prize of the Crown of England for their daughter, but *was* he a suitable match-maker? There were all sorts of stories about him and Elizabeth even while his wife was alive and the Princess a schoolgirl under his roof; and now he was a widower, with only old Lady Seymour to hold him in check, – and when would she ever do, had ever done such a thing?

Their timid half-denials put more life into the bereaved widower than all the beautiful letters of condolence he had received. Now he had something to do; he must ride off on the instant and put some spunk into these Grey creep-mice, and off he went to lead Henry Grey once more up and down the garden path. He told the old gentleman that if he backed out now he would lose all hope of ever getting a King for a son-in-law. Since there was no longer any chance of marrying the little Queen of Scots to King Edward, the Protector had now the single aim of pushing forward his own daughter, Janet Seymour, as his bride; Tom had certain knowledge of this, he declared, thumping Henry Grey's top waistcoat button as the little man hummed and hawed and Tom had to bite his lip to keep from whistling 'How shall I make this ass to go?'

In fact, he only agreed to 'go' after the irresistible argument of ready cash. Tom paid the more pressing of his debts; and Jane Grey was told to write a nice letter to the Admiral telling him she would be glad to return to his guardianship.

She needed no telling; the Lady Frances, reading her daughter's letter, felt that Jane had rather overdone her 'thanks for the gentle letters which I received from you' and 'your great goodness toward me . . . as you have been unto me a loving and kind father, so I shall be always most ready to obey your godly monitions and good instructions.'

'God's blood, I hope not!' rapped out her anxious mother, slapping her riding-whip against her fat thigh. 'And why sign yourself his "most humble servant during my life"?'

'Because I could not be it after my death,' said Jane. The logic was unanswerable. And since even the threat of a whipping would not make Jane write her letter again, or even scratch out the last three emphatic words, it was despatched 'this 1st of October 1548.'

Through the great woods that spread for miles round Bradgate the Admiral and his retinue again came riding, the golden leaves falling round them; again he dined and wined, walked and talked, hunted and made merry with the Greys. But this time when he left, Jane rode back with him to his house in the Strand, – a long ride, they had to stop at more than one town *en route* for cold beef and beer for themselves and their numerous escort, and Jane was astonished at the gusto with which he ate it, and, for the matter, at her own. On this lovely changing autumn day the world seemed to be beginning all over again.

Yet only a month ago she had followed Queen Catherine's corpse to the grave, her long black robes trailing behind her, and this splendid figure in the sunlight beside her, filling the keen air with his talk and laughter, had then been a great dumb beast, his face the dark shadow of what it now was. And Catherine would not be there to run out with little cries of greeting when they reached Seymour Place.

'Oh God,' Jane sighed to herself, 'if only everything could always stay the same!'

But in one respect change was welcome; her cousin Bess would not be at Seymour Place.

*   *   *

Jane was only a side-line. Bess was the Admiral's main ambition – and unfortunately for him, not only an ambition. He knew that to pursue her in haste was to imperil all his hopes, not only of her but of personal safety for them both; yet he could not help it. He was mad, but not blind; seeing the danger, yet remembering only the warmth of her lithe body tucked down beside him in the barge, of her pointed face dimly white in the luminous darkness of that night last May; of her evasive mocking answers to his furious questions.

She had never told him who the man had been that he had

seen merely as a shadowy form against the light as the girl leaped up to it, her arms outflung in a wild movement of childish abandon. She was growing up so fast; who was she seeing, falling in love with perhaps, even at this moment? There could be no one but the tutor; but these tutors were dangerous fellows, they were there all the time, and this one was young, a sportsman who taught her to shoot and play and sing as well as read Greek.

Never trust a music master – he knew! He'd given music lessons himself, though not for money. But he'd got his reward. Was this Mr Ask-'em (that's bad) – Mr At'em (that's worse) getting his?

The possibility took him headlong down to Hatfield.

The sight of Mr Ascham's pleasant smile and square shoulders (a bookworm ought to stoop and frown) did not encourage him; nor did the way he sang praises of his pupil when the Admiral, as was right and proper, enquired about the Princess's progress in her lessons. Sang was the word, for Mr Ascham became positively lyrical when he mentioned the beauties even of Elizabeth's handwriting – true, he was forming it himself. And when he spoke of the grace and 'grandity' of her deportment, the Admiral, amused by this odd tribute to her budding queenliness, was seriously alarmed by the light that glowed in those mild brown eyes as they turned to follow the swift and resolute movements of his pupil. She went past them in the stiff embroidery of her clothes as though walking on Mount Gargaros on 'new grass and dewy lotus and crocus and hyacinth' bringing sunshine in her wake. Aloud, the tutor spoke the words of the old blind poet, and the Princess, turning her head, flashed him a smile and called something back as if capping his quotation. This Greek, the Admiral decided, gave them an unfair advantage.

And of course he could get nothing out of Elizabeth when he questioned her. Yes, Mr Ascham was charming; he made her lessons much more interesting than poor Mr Grindal had done; yes, it was an advantage that he was not only learned but a keen sportsman and musician.

It was not the first time he had been baffled by this imper-

tinent chit. Would he ever get the better of her till he held
her in his arms and made her his own? Would he even
then?

He took her by the elbows and told her he was mad for
her; and she looked up into his eyes and laughed.

'You need not be so coy,' he said, 'the report goes now
that I am to marry little Lady Jane.'

She tore herself out of his hands and whisked away like a
whirlwind. 'So you've two strings to your bow! Then you'll
never shoot straight.'

He gave a roar of delight at her sudden white fury. 'You
little fool, it's a joke, that's all. I'll not have her if you'll
have me.'

'Nor my sister Mary? Nor that unfailing stopgap, Anne of
Cleves? Report has married you to both these lately. It says
indeed that you don't care whom you marry as long as it's a
princess and her dowry.'

'So much the better,' he answered casually, 'the more
they guess, the less likely to guess right.'

'Is that why you've been making enquiries into their
lands and inheritance as well as mine?'

'Of course. Has it made you jealous? It has! Come,
admit it!'

'I'll admit nothing,' she cried in rage, 'it's nothing to me
whom you marry.'

'Not if it's yourself?'

'I won't marry you, or anyone. I'll not be tied and bound.
A wedding ring is a yoke ring.'

'Not between friends. Aren't we good friends?'

'Very good.'

'And don't you love me?'

'I love a friend as myself. But I should love a husband
more than myself, since I should be giving myself to him.'

'And will you not give yourself to me?'

He caught her to him, he kissed her again and again until
she took fire from his lips and kissed him back suddenly,
savagely, then tore herself away, darted across the room,
picked up a comfit-box and started cramming her mouth
with sweets as if to besiege it against further kissing, and
mumbled with her mouth full, 'You can't marry me without

the Council's consent, or you'll marry nothing. And that you'd never do.'

'Would *you*?'

Almost – when he looked at her like that, and his voice dropped on to that deep note – almost she thought she would give up anything she had to be his. Anything she had, yes perhaps, – but anything she might have? Even that future that had been written for her in the stars? One could alter that future, for man had free will to disrupt his own fate if he would. Would she?

She looked at him, and her eyes were not mocking now, nor angry; they were clear and blank as water in a glass. She swallowed hard, gulping down the last of the sweets.

'No,' she said.

Chapter Eighteen

THE ADMIRAL DECIDED to attend to business. He had already been doing so on the lines that had annoyed Elizabeth, enquiring into her lands and income and, disappointed with the results, comparing them with those of the other female legatees of King Henry's Will, to make sure that she was not being cheated. He also tried to set about an exchange of her lands for those in the same area as his own in the west, and suggested to her that she should ask the Duchess to help work this with the Protector. Bess could hardly believe her ears. *She* ask the Duchess for anything?

'I will *not*. I'll not begin to flatter and sue now.'

It was awkward. He could not explain that he was already fortifying his castle of Holt in Cheshire in case of a possible revolt, and that in that case it would be well to have her lands in line with his. A female conspirator just fifteen was not a good choice of ally.

He fell back on his friends, and he had plenty of them; asked them about their lands, how near they marched with his own, what power they had in them, urging them to increase it, and not merely with the gentry – 'for *they* are not the fellows that count, they're too cautious and heavy; the little they have hangs round their necks like a millstone, they're for ever fearing they'll lose it. No, the men for my money are the yeomen, the true leaders of the countryside, in touch with all the peasants as we can never be. Shake hands with the yeomen of England, and you have your hand on England itself.'

And he urged on his friends those Rules for a Perfect Guest that had alarmed the Earl of Warwick: to take your own wine and victuals and leave them to your hosts while declaring their tough mutton and home-brewed ale and cider the best you ever tasted. By these simple means he would soon have the best part of the country with him; and as Lord High Admiral he had the sea, with the islands as naval bases at his back.

When he had all that power in his hands, the Council would have to consent to his marrying Elizabeth. And of her own consent he was now pretty certain.

Even he knew that he must not go and see her too often at this juncture, but the Ash-Cat was working steadily for him, and Parry, the cofferer and steward, – 'stout fellow Parry,' and loyal to the bone to them both.

He wrote frequently to her and gave the messengers orders to wait while the Princess wrote her answers; and write she did, always very properly and circumspectly : but she did not keep the messenger waiting. And he felt he could read between the lines.

'I am a friend not won with trifles, nor lost with the like.'

What a queer solemn assurance from the chit who had just been flirting so lightly with him!

And to assuage (or was it to arouse?) his jealousy at some. fresh plan of the Protector's for a foreign alliance for her: 'It has been said that I have only refused you because I was thinking of someone else. I therefore entreat you, my lord, to set your mind at rest on this subject; up to this time I have not the slightest intention of being married, and if ever I should think of it (which I do not believe is possible) you would be the first to whom I should make known my resolution.'

His head jerked back in a crack of laughter as he read that. He would indeed be the first, and not so long now, to whom she should make known her resolution.

As for those coy protestations about never marrying, she was an absurd minx to think them worth the writing.

He had to ride down just once more to tell her so, and had the luck to meet her out riding through the beech-woods round Hatfield that dull late November afternoon.

'What do you know about marriage?' he said as their servants promptly dropped behind – 'or about yourself either? You're a child, though an intelligent one – too much so, one would think, to write such stuff.'

'I've learnt about marriage from my stepmothers,' she said, sliding a look at him.

'God forbid! D'you think, then, we all play Old Harry with our wives?'

'You've not all got his opportunities.'

'No, but seriously—'

'Seriously, my lord, my first stepmother, Jane, died in childbed, and so was the only past wife he spoke of with respect; my second, big Anne Cleves, he shoved out of the way for my pretty cousin Cat Howard, whom he beheaded, – and my last one gave me a step-stepfather,' she finished, and this time she did not look at him.

He stared at the white profile against the grey misty beech-trunks, their horses' hoofs squelching the thick wet fallen leaves of the road through the woods. There was no colour anywhere except in her hair, which flamed like a belated autumn leaf beside him. They said red hair showed a passionate nature; she had shown him that too. But how much else was there in her that she did not show?

They were having her portrait painted now, a stiff unchild-like thing (pity old Holbein was dead) and not much like her except for the childishly thin erect shoulders and beautiful hands, carefully displayed, and the level eyes that could look at you so coolly with that wicked little hint of mockery in one of them, – he'd always told her they didn't match! The lips were shut tight, compressed into a thin line as if to let no secret escape them. 'Cross at being made to stand still so long, weren't you?' he had chaffed her as he looked.

at it. But yes, there *was* something in it that was like her, the gaze so direct, yet baffling.

'Elizabeth the Enigma,' he had once called her years ago when she was quite a child, called her that to tease her as he had stood watching a pattern of wavering watery light flickering up under her soft yet resolute little chin. Where had that been?

It did not matter. His name for her had come true. He never could be sure of her.

'Say it!' he roared suddenly. 'Why do you never say what you think?'

'I do not say all that I think. But at least I never say anything I do not think. What is it you wish me to say?'

'All – yes, all that you think. What is this grudge, or fear against me – why the "stepfather"? Catherine is dead and I cannot help that. I loved her.'

'And loved me.'

'I could not help that either. Nor could you.'

'Nor may you help loving others. And that would be hell on earth to me.'

She whipped up her horse and galloped ahead. He rode after her, he caught at her rein, his eyes were blazing with anger, he said he would never love, never had loved, any woman as he loved her. Still holding her bridle, he leaped from his saddle and pulled her down from hers, letting her horse go.

'I'll show you how I love you,' he said between his teeth as she fell forward into his arms and they closed round her, hugging the breath out of her.

His startled horse veered round and began to canter back down the ride. A heavier, more regular thudding of horses' hoofs came towards it, – 'God's soul!' Tom exploded in incredulous fury that their escort should dare to catch them up.

But the gaunt old man with the long white beard flowing over his chest now riding through the woods towards them, like the approach of winter, was none of their escort. It was the Lord Privy Seal, Father Russell, as Tom always called him.

'I feared frost and here's snow,' said Bess to herself.

Chapter Nineteen

'My Lord Admiral,' said the Lord Privy Seal that evening, 'there are certain rumours about you which I am very sorry to hear.'

'What are they?'

'That you mean to marry with' – he coughed a little – 'the Lady Mary, or else – ahem – with the Lady Elizabeth.'

'Oh, *that*!' observed Tom casually. 'Surely you'll throw in Anne of Cleves?'

'That too is said,' said Russell stiffly, 'and the Lady Jane Grey has also been mentioned. It makes little odds which of them it is, since all are royal; except that, naturally, the King's sisters are the most royal of all.'

'Father Russell, you are very suspicious of me. Who's been telling you these tales?'

Father Russell would not say, except that those who had done so were the Admiral's very good friends and advised him, as he himself did, 'to make no suit of marriage *that way*,' as though it were too dangerous even to repeat the names of the prospective brides. But Tom showed no such caution.

'Even a King's sisters may marry,' was his modest answer, 'and better for them to marry within the realm than outside it; so why might not I, or any other man, raised by the King their father, marry one of them?'

It sounded a fair and honest question. But Father Russell's face was nearly as long as his beard as he replied to it.

'My lord, if either you or any other within this realm shall match himself in marriage either with my Lady Mary or my Lady Elizabeth, he shall undoubtedly procure unto himself the occasion of his own utter undoing, – and you especially, being of so near alliance to the King's Majesty.'

A deep silence followed the warning. Their steps went on and on, up and down, heavy, padded, measured steps in velvet slippers on the black and white marbled flags of the hall floor, while the rain fell outside the shuttered windows that rattled and creaked in the wintry gale.

Tom's Austrian boar-hound pricked an ear and stirred in his sleep by the fire as a gust and spatter of rain blew down the wide chimney and hissed on the burning logs.

He raised his head and listened to the footsteps going up and down behind him. His master was not wont to walk so, in silence, with any man. He rose heavily, stretched himself and shaking off the dreams of hunting that had been enchanting him as he lay in blissful warmth with his nose to the fire: he went and walked beside his master, up and down, up and down, to tell him that he was there, and that if he uttered the word he would be delighted to fly at the throat of this skinny man who smelt old and dry, who walked cautiously, who spoke coldly, who had made his master silent.

And he gave a preliminary yearning sniff at his bony ankles.

'What's your dog doing?' asked the Lord Privy Seal.

'Reminding me that there are better friends than humans,' said the Lord High Admiral.

It was Privy Seal's turn to sniff.

'And what would you get out of it?' he asked suddenly – 'how much do you think you'd have with either of them?'

'Three thousand a year,' said Tom coolly.

'You're wrong. Not a farthing more than ten thousand down, in money, plate and goods – and no land. And what's that to a man who's got to keep up the estate of a Princess's husband?'

'They *must* have £3,000 a year as well,' said Tom.

'God's body, they will *not*.'

'God's soul, they will! God's life, I tell you—'

'God's death, I tell you, *no*.'

The Lord High Admiral, outsworn by that aged and venerable man, Lord Privy Seal, was silent again. Only his hound gave a hungry yawn.

*   *   *

Upstairs in her little closet, with the firelight winking on the silver candlesticks and the gilded carving of the ceiling, and the icy rain drumming against the windows where padded blue velvet curtains shut out the draughts, Mrs Ashley was having a long cosy chat with Mr Parry, the steward, over a nice hot brandy posset of her own brewing.

'Oh, it's true enough,' said Mrs Ashley, 'there's – well, what shall I say? – put it at its lowest, there's goodwill between the Lord Admiral and Her Grace – but I had such a charge of secrecy in it that I dare say nothing about it, except that I would wish her his wife of all men living. And I dare say he might bring off the matter with the Council well enough.'

'But do you think he will with her?' asked Mr Parry. 'I once was bold enough to ask her whether she'd marry him if the Council liked it, and all she would say was, "When that comes to pass, I will do as God shall put into my mind." '

'That's Her Grace all over,' chuckled Mrs Ashley; 'fobbed me off too, she did – or tried to. "What's the news from London?" she asked after my last visit. "Why," said I, "the voice goes there that you are to marry the Lord Admiral." Such a look she gave me – and then laughed – you know her laugh, clear as all the birds in the air. "Get out!" said she, "that's only London news!" Oh, she's deep – deep as a well, but she'll never take *me* in. I know too much.' And she took another sip at her posset and wagged her head, then two or three more sips and wagged her head two or three more times; then set down the empty cup and pursed her lips as though not another drop nor word should pass either way.

It was clearly incumbent on Mr Parry to do something about it. He leaned forward and filled her cup with a carefully steady hand, then sank back with a comfortable sigh and said, 'Ah, she's got a true friend in you.'

'That she has,' said Mrs Ashley, 'too true, maybe. I've tried to shield her when it's done no good to her, but harm to me. *That* woman, the Duchess, I mean, must have as many eyes in her tail as a peacock. The things she's nosed out!'

'What things?' enquired Mr Parry, as his colleague showed further signs of pursing.

'Things that I never breathed to a soul – and never will.'

'Come, if the Duchess knows them, what matter who else does?'

'She doesn't know all, thank heaven, and what she does is all crooked, like her own nasty mind. Told me I wasn't worthy to have the governance of a King's daughter! Because I permitted – *permitted*, mark you! – that's a nice one, if she only knew! – *permitted* my young lady to go out at night on the Thames in a barge with the Admiral. And other light parts.'

'Which parts?'

'Just parts,' said Mrs Ashley vaguely.

'Well, there's no harm in a barge,' said Mr Parry; 'can't be, with the oarsmen facing the canopy. If it were a gondola, now! I knew a man who'd been in Venice,' he began reminiscently.

The spur acted quickly. Mrs Ashley, determined to prevent his anecdote, hastily assured him that there were other light parts besides barges. There were garden walks, benches in pleached alleys, and there the late Queen Catherine had come on her stepdaughter in her husband's arms.

'*No!*' said the steward.

'*Yes!*' said the governess.

'And that's why,' said the governess with finality.

'Why what?' asked the steward.

'Why we had to go away and have a separate establishment for Her Grace. It wasn't the first time the Queen had been jealous, I'm sure of that, and she was getting near her time, which made things worse.'

She emptied her cup absent-mindedly.

'What was I saying?' she asked.

'That it made things worse.'

'What things? Oh yes, the Queen's jealousy, poor soul. I can tell you, Mr Parry, it's been no easy business among the lot of them.'

Mr Parry made sympathetic noises and filled up his own cup.

'No easy bus-i-ness,' repeated Mrs Ashley, determined to get those s's quite distinct. It was the consonants that were the trouble. She would talk more freely if there weren't so many tiresome consonants in the words she wanted to use. No one could say she was drunk. She had seen Nan Bullen reeling about the room and swearing, but *she* was never like that. She might not be a queen, but she was a lady. And Mr Parry was a gentleman, a nice safe quiet dependable gentleman. It could not matter what one said to him. He understood.

'Women,' said Mr Parry.

'Yes, women,' said Mrs Ashley, 'and one of them hardly a girl, but the most difficult of the lot. After all, she's—' she rushed her consonants – 'she's old-Harry's-daughter.'

'Eh?' said Mr Parry.

'Red hair,' explained Mrs Ashley. 'Not pretty, but—'

'Ah,' said Mr Parry.

'The Admiral was always wild for her. Only married the Queen because he couldn't get the Princess.'

'Oh!' said Mr Parry. He filled up both their cups.

'And then,' said Mrs Ashley, looking at her cup, surprised to find it still so full and sipping a little to rectify this, 'then, of course, with her in the house, there was the devil – ahem! shall I say, Old Harry? – to pay!'

She laughed, and so did Mr Parry. After all, it was a long time since she had had such an enjoyable evening, such a companionable evening. She wanted to say so, but companionable was a difficult word. It was better to stick to facts.

She stuck to them. All that about the Admiral coming into the Princess's room in the mornings. Bare legs. Bed-curtains. Smacking. Tickling. They were all quite simple words. And didn't mean any – he hadn't meant any harm. He had sworn so, on God's mosht precioush shoul. But when Queen Catherine had found her alone in his arms, – well that was another matter.

Mr Parry quite agreed.

'Well, all that's over now,' said Mrs Ashley. 'Poor lady! He's free now. And I'd wish her his wife of all men living. For it's my belief, if she doesn't marry him, she'll marry no one.'

She sighed deeply and picked up her cup, but it was empty.

Mr Parry leaned forward again.

But he never filled the cup. He sat there with his eyes on Mrs Ashley, and hers on his, and between them a cry went shivering through the air, splintering up that cosy friendly warmth into thin particles of ice, a cry that froze them both sober, a cry not of this world nor of any that they knew.

Mrs Ashley sprang up, knocking the jug out of Mr Parry's hand over her gown and never noticing it; she picked up her wet skirt, never noticing that it dripped with brandy posset, and ran, straight as a die, to the room of her charge, the Princess Elizabeth.

She burst open the door and drew the bed-curtains. The light of the candles and the fire poured into the dark cave of the curtained bed, over a slight figure sitting bolt upright, and red hair rippling over the bare shoulders, and a small white face aghast, with staring eyes and open, shrieking mouth.

'My lamb,' cried Mrs Ashley, 'my sweet, my treasure, what's the matter? There's no harm near you, there's nothing here, I tell you, nothing but your old Ash-Cat.'

She hugged the staring face to her thin bosom, stroking the rough hair over and over, feeling the young bones of the skull beneath, and now feeling, almost with relief, the long sobs that came welling up, shaking the childish shoulders.

'You've been dreaming, my lamb, that is all, a hateful dream. You've been riding the night mare, – where to? Tell your old Ash-Cat. It's better to tell and have done with it so.'

'Oh Cat, my old Ash-Cat, you're right – if only I could tell it, Cat, my Ash-Cat.'

What was it there at the end of the corridor that had been so terrible, so strange, yet somehow familiar? The rain on the roof, the icy winter wind, they had drummed in her sleep now for years – no, only two, – the years since her father died. The night he died, just two years ago, she had got out of her bed in the Palace at Whitehall and run along the corridor, until she fell plump into the arms of the Lord Admiral. Ever since she had dreamed of running along the corridor, into his arms.

Tonight again she had done so, but this time the door at the end of the corridor was closed. She had hammered on it with both fists, knowing that if it did not open at once she would be too late – too late for what? Too late for her life, or his, or both?

The door would not open, but she could see through it.

She saw the Admiral sitting on a stone bench in a small bare room, taking off his shoes. He was looking into them, plucking something out of them, and then beginning to write with it. He was writing to her. But whatever he wrote she knew she would never see it. She tried to call to him through the door. But he could not hear her, and she could not see what he was writing.

'I shall never see it,' she cried to Cat Ashley, ' I shall never, never see it!'

The dream was fading. Even as she thought of it, she could not think what had so terrified her. The things that had affected her conscious mind came forward instead. So that all Cat Ashley heard of what she had *not* dreamed was this: 'What reproaches did Queen Catherine whisper to her husband on her death-bed? What misery did she know through marrying the man she loved?'

Said Cat Ashley stoutly, 'She knew great happiness with him. Let that content you, as it did her. There was no bitterness in her end.'

Bess answered her, 'Because there never was in her life. It would not be so with me. If my husband did not love me alone, it would be worse than death, it would be perpetual hell.'

'Sweetheart, is this the dream that troubled you so?'

'No,' said she. 'I dreamed of the Admiral taking off his shoes.'

Her laugh terrified Mrs Ashley more than her cries had done.

Suddenly the girl sniffed long and searchingly. 'Fie, Ash-Cat,' said she, 'how you stink of brandy!'

*　　　*　　　*

Bess was asleep. Light tawny eyelashes lay on the pale cheeks like two ruddy half-moons in a summer dusk. Mrs Ashley whispered to her charge, waited, heard no answer but long regular breathing, and the rain drumming on the roof.

She ran back down the passage to her own little closet. The candles were low in their candlesticks. The fire was dim and red. Mr Parry, that silent fat man, lay stretched in his chair, his hands folded piously across his stomach. He looked extremely dependable, even in his sleep.

'Mr Parry!' said Mrs Ashley.

Mr Parry sat up. He kicked a log. A bright flame-light filled the small room. All the gilded carving in the ceiling leaped to life, the silver candlesticks gleamed red.

'Mr Parry!' said Mrs Ashley, and there was agony in her voice. She had forgotten all about her consonants. It did not matter how she spoke, as long as she said what she must say. 'Mr Parry, I spoke unwisely just now. I wish I had not said all that I said to you of her Grace the Lady Elizabeth and the late Queen and the Lord Admiral.'

'You can depend on me,' said Mr Parry. 'Not another soul shall ever hear of it, not if they were to drag me in pieces by wild horses. No,' said he, sitting up and looking straight before him with solemn unctuous eyes at the winking silver candlesticks, and then all round him on the small room filled to the ceiling with bright firelight, 'not if I were dragged in pieces – by wild horses.'

Chapter Twenty

HIS MOTHER AND little Jane Grey were in the house when they came to arrest the Admiral.

Old Lady Seymour did not twitter and flutter, nor even cry. She stood like a small statue of grey stone; her lips moved a little but no one heard what she said, except Jane, who thought she was praying and crept to her side to join her. But the words she heard, over and over again, were – 'I knew it. I knew it. I knew it. One of them would kill the other.'

The frightened tears began to run in silence down Jane's face.

But the Admiral was as gay and unworried as if it had been a summons to Court.

'You'll see me back again in no time, never fear,' he told

them; 'they'll never dare do anything really against me. And if they did, Ned wouldn't let 'em.'

But even as he said it, an uncomfortable echo sounded in his mind from Ned's last solemn warning and lecture, uttered after Father Russell's had so signally failed. 'I may not be able to save you,' he had said. 'Only yourself can do that now for certain.' And he had begged him – yes, his urgency had really amounted to that – begged him to go on a mission to Boulogne to see to the defences there – to get him out of England, that was patent; but for the first time Tom wondered if Ned hadn't after all been sincere when he pressed it on Tom's account rather than his own.

He had so nearly gone to Boulogne. He had even begun to pack for it. And then – Mr Parry had come up from Hatfield. He had brought a letter from Elizabeth; nothing much, as usual, to be got from that. But he could tell the Admiral a deal about her, and his plump smiles and sympathetic glances had told still more.

The Princess changed colour very noticeably if the Admiral were but mentioned; and if anything praising or admiring were said, 'she drinks it in as a flower does the rain, lifting her head to it, and you can see the little pulse in her throat throbbing with pride.' He had then remarked discreetly on the arrangements for a town house for her so as to visit the Court and her brother this winter.

'That won't be till after I've gone to Boulogne, – they'll see to that!' said the Admiral bitterly.

And after Mr Parry had left he had sat trying to think out his plans, but he could only think of the pulse throbbing in that childishly bony little hollow at the base of her long throat – a pulse that throbbed even at hearing him mentioned. He thought how he could make it beat; how he could make every inch of her body tingle with longing for him, as it had never yet known that it could do.

His steward had come in with a pile of papers for him to sign, giving powers to various persons to act for him at home while he was in Boulogne.

'Take them away,' said the Admiral. 'I'm not going.'

And so now he was not in Boulogne, he was in his own house of Seymour Place in the Strand, and they had come to arrest him. A stupid business, he'd never forgive Ned for frightening his mother like this. Ned had got frightened himself, that was why he'd done it; he was as nervous as a cat, and cowards were always cruel.

'They can't do anything,' he told his mother, 'they've got nothing really against me. You'll see me back sooner than if I'd gone to Boulogne. Give me your blessing, little Mam.'

As he knelt to receive it, the sense of that hurried muttering whisper struck chill on his heart.

'I knew it. I knew it. One of them would kill the other.'

He sprang up and flung his arms round her, swept her up from the ground and tried to kiss warmth into that cold old face.

The Captain of the Guard reminded him that they must go. He went, not looking back. A small figure came pattering after him.

'My lord, my lord,' cried Jane's voice, 'say goodbye to me too!'

He stooped and kissed her, and she clung to him. 'You are going to the Tower!' she said, and shuddered.

'What of that? You'll go to the Tower too one day.' And he whispered, smiling at her, 'The night before your Coronation, when you marry the King.'

'That is different,' sobbed Jane. 'I shan't go by the Traitors' Gate.'

'Don't be too sure,' he chaffed her. But she would not be coaxed into a smile.

'You have been a true father to me,' she said, 'better than my own.'

'That's easy!' He added hastily, '—to such a daughter. Come, you must stop crying or your eyelashes will fall out. Look after my mother and make her laugh.'

And then he went.

Chapter Twenty-One

SIR ROBERT TYRWHITT dismounted at Hatfield House at the head of a considerable body of servants, and demanded to see the Princess Elizabeth. He was told that she was at lessons and could never be disturbed till they were finished. Sir Robert, tugging at his short scrubby greying beard, showed an order signed by the Council.

He was promptly ushered into the study, where Bess sat opposite Mr Ascham and a maid-in-waiting yawned over her embroidery-frame in the corner. Usually this was Mrs Ashley's occupation, but she had had to go up to town in answer to another summons from the Duchess, and departed with many wry anticipations of another wigging, slightly mollified by the company of Mr Parry, who was making one of his rather mysterious visits to the Admiral. So a young girl sat in Ashley's place and pretended great interest in the lesson, until she found she could not catch Mr Ascham's eye.

Mr Ascham shut his books slowly, looking across the table at his Princess. He saw terror leap at the back of her clear eyes, and then they seemed to cloud over, deliberately, as though she were pulling a veil across her face while she summoned all her forces of courage and deception beneath it.

The thought flashed through his mind, – 'Is this perhaps the last time I shall see her?'

Then he had to go, and she was left alone, facing the little man who had always disliked her and had now suddenly become a powerful enemy. What could have happened to place him in this position?

'The Lord High Admiral,' said Sir Robert slowly, and then waited a moment, watching her intently, as a cat watches the mouse just beyond its paws. She knew it, and though a sick cold wave crept up over her flesh, turning everything dark round her, she did not stir a hair's-breadth, and her eyes faced his, still veiled and inscrutable.

'The Lord High Admiral,' he repeated, 'has just been arrested by order of the Council and taken to the Tower.'

She still did not move, nor did her eyes flicker.

It was unwomanly, inhuman. He had banked everything on this first shock. But he had others in store.

'Mrs Ashley and Mr Parry,' he began, and again paused before finishing his sentence, – 'are also under arrest.'

Still she stared, and her eyes looked more blank than before. Then suddenly they flashed open in a green flame, she leaped forward, her hand swung up and out, and she would have struck Sir Robert full in the face if he had not stepped back so abruptly that his heel slipped on the marble tiles and he sat down on them suddenly and painfully.

A gleam of delight shot through the Princess's eyes as she looked down on him, her clenched fist still raised so that he fancied she was going to hit him as he sat on the floor; but she thought better of it, put her hand resolutely behind her back, and shouted in a voice that surprisingly resembled her father's, 'God death, how dare you arrest *my* governess and steward?'

Sir Roger got up, carefully refraining from feeling himself behind. His face was crimson, his eyes glazed with fury. He said, 'Mr Parry, the pandar, and your bawd are in the Tower by now, giving a full account of Your Highness's relations with the Admiral, and how you plotted to marry him against the will of the Council.'

She laughed, at first wildly, on an unmistakable note of hysteria. Tyrwhitt heard it, hopefully, but she heard it too and controlled it, though now shaking all over, and went on laughing, but deliberately, scornfully.

'Take care,' she said; 'you are not very wise. I am second to the throne.'

'Ha, you've thought of that, have you?'

'I am neither an idiot nor a child.'

'Married to the Admiral, you thought you would be able to take the throne for yourself.'

'By God,' she cried, 'you go too far.'

'Not as far as I may yet go. It is said that Your Grace is with child by the Admiral.'

She was silent, staring at him; then, 'You will answer for this with your head,' she said softly.

'Ah! Already you think you have Sovereign power. I advise Your Grace to remember your honour, and the danger you are in, for—' he paused again, and then said with ominous weight. 'You are but a subject – as was Your Grace's mother.'

All colour seemed to drain from her eyes; the pupils narrowed to pin-points like those of a cat – or a lion about to spring. At last she spoke wildly, in terror as well as rage.

'I appeal to the King my brother. I appeal to the Protector. I will go to them and answer any charges made against me. I will not stay here to be abused so traitorously.'

She made for the door, but he stood against it. 'I have to inform Your Grace that the Protector's orders are that you remain here under strict watch.'

'Am I a prisoner?' Her voice faltered at that.

'Virtually. Your Grace will not be put to the indignity of being under lock and key – unless it becomes necessary.'

He bowed low, went out and shut but did not lock the door, then waited. She did not rush out. He ducked down, looked through the wide keyhole, and had the satisfaction of seeing that unwomanly inhuman girl fling herself on the floor in a passion of frantic weeping.

But that moment of pleasure died in him as he walked thoughtfully away to write his report to the Protector. He would have to admit that he had got absolutely nothing out of the Princess. Shock tactics had proved useless. It looked as though he would have to change them.

'She has a very good wit,' he wrote, 'and nothing can be gotten from her except by great policy.'

He would have to try it.

He did. Next day he sent a respectful message asking the Princess to grant him another interview, which of course she had no power to refuse; and then apologized, frankly and humorously, for having lost his temper in such an unwarrantable fashion – it was all because he had sat down so hard and she had looked so pleased, he said, smiling ruefully as he tenderly felt the part affected.

Then he began to coax and excuse her. She had not always behaved as properly as a young lady should, – come, she must admit that, for everybody knew that she had been sent away from Queen Catherine's household because of her conduct with the Lord Admiral.

'If Queen Catherine were here *she* would answer for me,' Bess interpolated on a strangled sob, and then the forlornness of her position broke her down. She had no heart now to defy Sir Robert. He had told her she was but a subject – as her mother had been; had hinted that as her mother had died, so might she. Was it true that he had only spoken so in a rage? Certainly he seemed gentler now, and he grew still gentler when she cried.

So she cried a good deal.

He was then very fatherly, he patted her head and seemed even to like doing so, for he went on stroking her hair while she gritted her teeth to keep herself from shaking off his hand; he told her she was not to worry too much. 'You are very young,' he kept saying, and it was not really her fault as much as that of her elders who ought to have looked after her better; if only she 'would open all things to him, all the evil and shame will be ascribed to them, and your youth taken into consideration by His Majesty,' the Protector and the whole Council.'

But she would only open her mouth to cry – and her eyes, after rubbing them, just in time to catch Sir Robert's eager glance at her as she seemed about to speak.

'Come, come,' he said as she hesitated, 'what's the odds? Your servants have told everything, so it cannot matter what you say.'

Then why should he want her to say it?

She said a great deal, but nothing that Tyrwhitt wanted.

Again he had to write to the Protector – 'in no way will she confess any practice by Mrs Ashley or the cofferer Parry concerning my Lord Admiral.'

It was infuriating: what sort of a fool would his master

think him that he could not force the girl to speak? He dug the pen into the ink so angrily that it splashed on to the paper, and added:

'Yet I do see it in her face that she is guilty, and yet I do perceive that she will abide more storms ere she will accuse Mrs Ashley.'

He tried more storms. He tried gentle persuasion and complacently assured the Protector that he was 'beginning to grow with her in credit' – but unfortunately he could give no tangible proofs of it.

He tried a formal commission to put her under cross-examination and take down her evidence.

He tried a false letter from the Protector to himself which they agreed that he should show her as if at some danger to himself, 'with a great protestation that I would not for £1,000 to be known of it'; this confidence trick, to make her confide in him in return, produced much polite gratitude for his trust in her, but 'notwithstanding, I cannot frame her to all points.'

He tried a false friend, the Lady Browne, *née* Fitzgerald, who had been Surrey's Fair Geraldine, and Surrey had written poems to her, – but then so he had to the Duchess. His taste in women had not been as good as in dress; so Bess decided after the Fair Geraldine had coaxed and condoled with her, and said a thousand sympathetic, teasing, complimentary things which nevertheless left Bess with only one consideration, – what was it exactly that she had said to Lady Browne?

She had seen no one of her own household since Tyrwhitt's arrival, but only him and his accomplices, his wife and her servants. Lady Tyrwhitt's affection for Catherine made her take a very hard view of the bright young girl who had disturbed Catherine's married happiness. Bess was not bright now, but neither was she humbled, nor conciliatory, nor frank. She regarded Lady Tyrwhitt with more undisguised hostility than she had dared show any of the others; her tone to her, prisoner though she was, speaking to her gaoler's wife, flicked a whiplash of contempt. Yet she was well aware how desperate was her position.

Parry had rushed to his wife when he heard he was to go to London and be questioned; had torn off his chain of office, wrung his hands and thrown away his rings, sobbed out that he wished he had never been born for now he was utterly undone; and several servants had witnessed his panic.

They told this to the Princess, who spat. Certainly she needed a new governess, said Lady Tyrwhitt. But Bess knew the stakes were for more than that. In this struggle, which might be for her life, and, as she was beginning to understand, was most certainly for the life of the man she loved, she had no one whose advice she could ask; no one to whom she dared speak without guarding her every word, her every look; no one near her who was not her enemy, watching, listening, waiting to trap her unawares.

The hard frost that was imprisoning earth and air outside her windows, so that sometimes as she stood staring out through them she saw a starved bird fall to the ground like a stone falling, was shutting down on her spirit. Did they mean to freeze her too to death, with terror?

She turned with a shudder from the window and crouched down by the fire, holding out her long hands to the warmth which glowed through them, showing the pink flesh translucent and the shadowy thin bones encased in it. So easy would it be to become a skeleton; already you could see its narrow framework. Instinctively her hands went up and round her slender throat: 'I have a little neck,' her mother had said, 'it will not be hard work for the executioner.'

There she sat with her fingers round her throat, staring into the fire. There was a fox in the fire, a flaming red fox in a black cave, peering out at her with winking glowing eyes, the wicked eyes of a fox caught in a trap, but they were the eyes of a fellow-conspirator, perhaps of herself, and they bade her beware.

Lady Browne came flurrying in and knelt down beside her and flung her warm arms round her. 'My child,' said that soft imploring Irish voice, 'my darling child, I've run here to warn you, – Sir Robert is on his way to you – he has the statements, signed statements made by your servants in the Tower – they have confessed everything.'

'*What* have they confessed?'

Lady Browne, already in tears, became rather incoherent, but kept on urging, 'No time to lose – he's on his way here. Think what you'd better say and tell me quickly, then I'll tell you if it's safe to say to him.'

Bess was crying with fright. Her voice could just be heard in a thin squeak.

'Have they confessed? *What* have they confessed?'

'Everything. I've told you, everything. Their statements are here, signed by them. It was Parry did it first.'

'Parry! The traitor!'

'Yes, yes,' agreed Lady Browne eagerly.

'The liar!'

'Oh,' said Lady Browne more dubiously. She waited, but nothing more came from the girl, and she ran back to Sir Robert and told him what the Princess had said. Sir Robert noticed rather what she had not said. But he hoped more from the signed statements.

They were thrust into her hands, while he and two or three other gentlemen hovered round her, hunched uneasy shadows hanging over her, at which she dared not look. She choked back her tears.

She looked down on the papers and at all the black marks of the writing that wriggled and squirmed over them like small black snakes. They would not keep still. She could not read what they said if they would not keep still. She heard a voice that sounded a long way off – 'Look! She is going to faint!'

If she did that, it would be a sign of guilt. If she did that, she might say something incriminating while she was unconscious. She dragged her senses back under control, focussed her eyes until the snakes became still. But that was worse, for now scattered words and sentences swam up from the paper and struck at her eyes so that she reeled under first one blow and then another.

Humiliating things they were, all written down for everyone to see, and looking so much worse in words. She turned her head to avoid seeing them, but she must see them, everybody here knew what they were, and was watching to see how she would take them. Those morning romps when Tom would swing into her room and if she were up, 'strike her upon the back or buttocks familiarly and so go forth' (how low it sounded, but nothing in it – they *must* see there was nothing), 'and sometimes go through to the maids and play with them and so go forth.' (Well, that proved there was nothing.) But here was something about her being in bed, and how 'he would open the curtains and bid her good-morrow and make as though he would come at her, and she would go further in the bed so that he could not come at her' – and more about his chasing her and her running to her maids and getting them to hide her – it all looked so shocking written down in solemn words, read by these shocked solemn elderly faces all round her – a herd of old bearded goats, she longed to call them. She *could* not read further with all their wall-eyes on her. She must gain time somehow, hold up some sort of mask.

She tried to say, 'How do I know these are not forgeries?' but her breath would not come, nor her voice except in a ridiculous squeak; her face was flaming hot while all the rest of her body seemed to be turning to ice, and her heart hammered so loud against her stiff bodice that surely every-one there must be hearing it.

It seemed a long time before she managed to gasp out that she must examine the signatures carefully to make sure they were genuine.

Tyrwhitt took this insulting suggestion very coolly and saw its intention.

'Your Grace knows your governess's and steward's signatures with half an eye,' he remarked scornfully.

But Bess was not to be stampeded. She pretended to pore over the signatures while her glance shot here and there over the papers, taking in the worst that she could see.

Parry's was the danger-point; Cat Ashley would never give away anything that he had not; and so it was his report that she scanned in swift sweeping glances. It seemed to be all about a long gossip he had had with Cat Ashley full of 'she saids' and 'I saids'; and Parry had evidently seized his chance to curry favour with the Protector by abusing the man whom he had been serving so assiduously as go-between, for he had written : 'Then I chanced to say to her that I had heard much evil report of the Lord Admiral. ... and how cruelly and dishonourably he had used the Queen.'

This from Parry who was always trying to get kind messages out of her for the Admiral and running up to town with them as often as he could! Parry the pandar – Parry the traitor!

And out of all this tittle-tattle there were other sentences sticking up like swords – 'I do remember also that she told me that the Admiral loved the Lady Elizabeth but too well, and had done so a good while: and that the Queen was jealous of her and him. – "Why," said I, "has there been such familiarity indeed between them?" And with that she sighed and said, "I will tell you more another time." But afterwards she seemed to repent that she had gone so far with me and prayed me that I would not disclose these matters, and I said that I would not. And again she prayed me not to open it, for Her Grace would be dishonoured for ever and she likewise undone. And I said I would not; and I said I had rather be pulled with horses.'

The silence was filling the room. She would have to speak. She said, still gasping for breath, and every word seemed to come with a gulp, 'This man – has proved himself false – through and through. I do not believe – my governess ever said such things to him.'

Tyrwhitt answered her. 'She denied them and would say nothing on her own account, until they were brought face to face, and Parry stood fast to all this that he has written. Then she burst out against him and called him a false wretch and reminded him that he had promised he would never confess till death. That proved his words.'

Again the silence came creeping out of all the corners and crannies of the room. The eyes round her were boring through her like screws, further and further inside her head, until soon all inside it would lie open for them to read.

At last she looked up; she stared full at Sir Robert with eyes that did not shift, though everything at which they looked seemed to waver.

She spoke in a voice that no longer shook. 'It was a great matter for him to promise such a promise, and to break it.'

Chapter Twenty-Two

SIR HENRY SEYMOUR rode to London for the second time in his forty years of life. The first time had been just two years ago when Brother Ned had made such a pother about his going up for the Coronation to be made a knight because his little nephew was being made King; though for the life of him Henry could not see what that had to do with him. He had flatly refused to be made a peer; if they must make a fool of him they must, but they should not carry it on to his children.

Though he knew, of course, that it wasn't always Coronation-time, he had ever since pictured London as a crammed shrieking whirligig of a fair-ground, where people drank and danced in the streets and sang and shouted like madmen and jostled and trampled each other into the mud, and you couldn't see the sky because of a lot of mummers and jugglers played their foolery on platforms or ropes high over your head; and he'd got a cricked neck looking at them, and his ears dinged with noise till they buzzed, and his pocket was picked. Nothing in his life, he thought, would ever get him to London again.

Yet here he was on Dapple's back, going at a steady jog-trot down the long wintry rides of Savernake Forest, with the brown interlacing pattern of the bare branches overhead, and the crackling of the horse's hoofs through the frosty crust on the mud underfoot, jogging once again to London town, to see Brother Ned.

He rode through some of Ned's vast new estates, past his splendid mansion that was rising higher and higher, brick by brick, till all the ninety hundred thousand of them should be placed on top of each other; and even then it would not be the summit, for dozens of newfangled chimneys were to go on the roofs, wriggling up higher and higher as if to vie with the Tower of Babel.

Henry didn't fancy all the bright red brick and white stone facings and windows wide as walls, glittering with brittle glass. To his mind, the shining surfaces of the modern houses were harsh and garish, like the modern people who live in them, all for show. Even the land was for show nowadays, a desecration in Henry's eyes equal to blasphemy.

Rich tradesmen were buying country estates so that their sons should be brought up on them as gentry! And those who already had land must have more. But the more land they got, the more they lost touch with it, and with the people on it; cut off from it by their own climbing ambition, climbing after fame and gold, climbing to the top of the tree, spending their vast new wealth only on fine feathers and feathering their own nests with them, never caring what other nests crumbled and fell to the ground.

'Charity died when chimneys were built,' the villagers said, for the poor never got such good fare under them as they had been given in the smoke-raftered, draughty old halls of the old gentry.

Had Brother Ned also lost all sense of charity as his chimneys rose? Well, he would soon see.

But he did not, for he did not see Brother Ned nearly as soon nor as easily as he had imagined. The Lord Protector sent word that he would be glad to see his brother Henry as soon as his press of business gave him a moment's leisure; as soon as that happened he would send word again.

But word did not come. It was Henry who sent word again, and got the same answer.

Henry began to hang about the precincts of the Duke's palace. Others were doing the same thing, quite a crowd of them. He talked with them in the casual manner with which he talked with neighbouring farmers at a cattle-sale, and found they were waiting to enter the Court of Requests which the Good Duke had set up in his own house to hear the complaints of the poor who could not afford the expense and delay of the law courts, or who had already tried them and been dissatisfied with the results.

For the Good Duke often overruled the decisions of the magistrates, and made them repair the wrongs they had done, so they told Henry gleefully. 'The law is ended as a man is friended,' – that was true enough of most of the judges, since if a man could not afford to bribe he had better not go to law at all; but it wasn't true of the Good Duke. He was told the case of the poor widow who had been defrauded of her lands by Paulet, Lord St John, and how that great lord had been forced to redress the injury done her. 'The Good Duke doesn't only bring in laws against the rich, he sees to it that they're carried out. That's how he makes the mare bite their thumbs,' they chuckled; 'he sees that justice is done and the wrong righted.'

Very good, thought Henry, as long as Brother Ned were always right himself. But it struck him as an extraordinary instance of arbitrary power to reverse the magistrates' decisions entirely on his own judgement.

And he heard other things, not so much to the credit of the Good Duke. He learned how he had pulled down two parish churches, St Mary-le-Strand and Pardon Church, and a chapel, to provide further building materials for his Somerset House, and had begun to pull down St Margaret's Church at Westminster as well, but there the cockneys themselves rose in protest and prevented it by mobbing his workmen and driving them away.

' 'Tisn't right,' said the waiting suppliants; 'pulled down part of St Paul's too, he did. Might as well pull down Westminster Abbey next.'

'Ar,' said Henry.

He made no claim to priority through his kinship to the Protector, gave his name simply as Squire Seymour (he pronounced it Semmor, and Wolf Hall as Ulfall) and waited his turn in the queue of plaintiffs.

Waiting never troubled Henry. He could stand for an hour or more leaning over a gate staring at his pigs or his brood mares. Here he sat stolidly on a bench along with the other clods of English earth, waiting patiently for his turn and staring at the floor or at his fellows, who stared back at a man like many of themselves, dressed in simple country

227

clothes, a leather jerkin, and long heavy riding-boots, and his face ruddy, wrinkled and tanned, itself a square of weather-beaten leather within its tawny fringe of short beard, like the yellow lichen on a red brick wall. His eyes when he raised them from the ground were as clear and direct in gaze as those of a boy.

You might think that no thoughts stirred behind those placid brown orbs – and perhaps they did not stir much; but they were there, lying deep and still, reflecting the things that he heard spoken round him, reflecting others that he had heard before.

Strange things he had heard told in dropped tones over the wassail cups of this Christmastide, things that sounded like the old wives' tales told by his nurse in his childhood, and so for the most part he believed them to be, – rehashed and served up in a modern setting.

A wise woman, a midwife, living in a neighbouring county, not a hundred miles from London, was awakened on a night of this winter by a strange horseman who wore a mask of black velvet. She was made to mount behind him and ride off with him through the night. Before reaching their destination, the horseman put a bandage over her eyes and tied her hands that she might not raise it. He then lifted her down from the horse and led her into a house which must, she knew, be very large, for she counted her steps going through the hall and then up one staircase, down another, along one, two, three passages, then into a very warm room where the bandage was taken from off her eyes and she saw an enormous fire blazing on a great stone hearth. A carved and gilded bed hung with bright tapestry was at one side of the room, and by it stood a very tall man, richly clothed, and he also was masked and said no word.

In the bed lay a very young and very fair lady, her red-gold hair falling loose over the pillows, who was in labour. The midwife helped her bear the child, all things being put there necessary, and all the time not a word spoken. When the baby was delivered, the tall man took it from her hands and threw it on the fire. She was then given a bag of gold, her eyes bandaged as before, and she was taken back to her cottage, the horseman making her swear never to say what she had done that night.

But while she had been at work on her task she had contrived, unseen, to cut a small piece from the tapestry hangings of the bed, – and if you were to go to Hatfield, where was the Princess Elizabeth, you would find that a certain bed there in a certain room had a piece cut out of its hangings.

At this point the narrative, told invariably by someone who had met – well, not the midwife herself, but a most reliably unimaginative applewoman, laundrymaid, housekeeper, or, in the best instance, one of the new parsons' wives, not of the flighty young kind that were setting their husbands' parishes by the ears, but quite a respectable body, who knew the said midwife intimately, – at this point the narrative in a lowered voice would draw to its impressive close in the firelight, followed by an awed silence and a few shocked 'Ohs!' and 'Ahs!'

'I always liked that tale,' Henry had said when they turned to him.

And to their protestations of its truth as testified by the aforesaid parsons' wives, housekeepers, laundrymaids, and applewoman, he would only add, 'Ar. Reckon feminine kind have always known it for true.'

*　　*　　*

His turn came at last. He was led into a small room where three men sat at a table, and the centre one was his eldest brother, in a dark velvet coat with a broad fur collar, his face longer, thinner, and more lined than Henry had known it, the lips more tightly compressed within the drooping moustaches that flowed down into the little pointed beard. The narrow, rather hesitating glance the Protector gave at the sturdy countryman who had just entered flashed into disconcerted surprise; his eyebrows shot up into his forehead, making a network of new furrows; the liverish yellow-whites of the eyeballs swerved like those of a shying horse. Henry felt an instant's most unusual satisfaction, that there was no one he could meet who could make himself look like that.

'He-ey, brother,' he said, on exactly the note he would have said, 'Whoa there, whoa.' 'Well met, brother, at last.'

'But why – why – what have you come for?'

As if to stave off the real answer to this question, the Duke hurriedly followed it with others: 'Is it the Purbeck stone or the conduit? I've told you about 1,600 feet is not an inch too long for it – if I want water brought to my house I must have it, whatever the cost. I said you need not try to recover the French workmen—'

'It's not the Frenchies,' came the answer, slow and sure as doom, '*nor* the conduit, *nor* the marble, that I've come to see you about. Reckoned I'd better come, as I never had word from you.'

'But this is the Court of Requests.'

'Can't a brother make a request?' asked Henry a trifle grimly.

'I'll see you later, you can't stay here now. There are people waiting their turn.'

'I've been waiting *my* turn. Now I've got it.'

And Henry planted himself on a chair as four-square as a billet of wood, quite unaware of the gasps round him at his seating himself before the Lord Protector. But the Protector himself did not seem to notice. His tone became hesitant, almost apologetic.

'The fools never told me it was you. Did you say you were my brother?'

'Why, no. I reckoned it might be easier to see you if I didn't.'

The Protector hastily suggested their talking in private, and led the way into another room, where he offered Henry refreshments after his journey, and Henry had to remind him that that had been over three weeks ago. Pitiful the way living in London dulled the wits.

He thought so the more when Ned remembered to ask after his wife and children but had obvious difficulty with their names. Henry then asked after Ned's good bedfellow and Ned's nine children, one by his first wife and eight by his present, by name, from the eldest to the youngest. He mentioned that his sisters, Elizabeth Cromwell and Dorothy

Smith, were in good health, and he then asked after Brother Tom.

Again there came that startled swerve of the yellow eyeballs. 'But – you know about him!' exclaimed Ned incredulously.

'I know he's in the Tower. That's not to say he's well.'

'It's not indeed. You'd best know it at once. There's no chance for him. There are thirty-three charges of treason against him.'

'What did Tom say to the witnesses?'

'The prisoner under Bill of Attainder is not allowed to speak in his own defence.'

'Hey, what's this? Thought you'd abolished the new treason laws and gone back to the good old laws of the Plantagenets – aye, and better. Haven't you brought it in that there must be two sufficient witnesses against a man, and that they must be confronted with the accused?'

'Yes, yes, but you don't understand. That is for the ordinary prisoner at law. This is a Bill of Attainder.'

'And why deny to your brother the justice you'd give to the ordinary prisoner?'

'Attainder is a perfectly constitutional proceeding. It is part of the course of the law.'

'Then dang and blast the law! I want justice.'

The Protector shifted his ground.

'You asked me what the prisoner has said. The whole Council waited on him in the Tower, with the exception of Archbishop Cranmer and myself, and told him the charges against him, and he refused to say one word in answer to them – except in open trial.'

'Why didn't you go?'

'I? But – naturally – it would have been too painful – for both of us.'

'Not as painful as getting beheaded.'

There was a stunned pause. Then Henry added, 'Why won't you give him a fair chance in open trial?'

'I? I? It is not my doing, I took no part in drawing up the articles against him. Nor at his examination in the Tower – I told you I was not there.'

'And again I say, why not? Tom might ha' spoken to you.'

'I spoke to him before. I gave him full warning again and again. So did others. Old Russell warned him. He wouldn't listen.'

'I'm not asking what was said before the trial—'

'I tell you, it wasn't a trial.'

'And in God's name, brother,' roared Henry, rising slowly to his feet and leaning over the little table behind which Somerset had entrenched himself, '*why not?*'

'The Council decided against it, for the better avoidance of scandal. It is doubtful whether an open trial would have given him any better chance. Anyway, the Government decided against it.'

'The Government – the Council—' Henry repeated slowly. 'What then are *you*? You sit on a high seat above all the rest of the Council. You act at times without consulting them. This Court of Requests is set up by you, and judged by you alone. You try cases without any other judge. You reverse decisions made by other judges. Yet, when it is a case of life and death for your own brother, you make as if to wash your hands of it, like Pontius Pilate. It can mean but one thing – that you want Tom's death. You alone gain from it. No one else gains anything.'

'The whole country gains, if the country is at peace.'

'It will not have peace. Nor will you. Hark'ee, Ned, this is but a feather of your own goose. Kill Tom, and you'll put a rope round your neck. The country calls you the Good Duke. They won't if you kill your brother. No one will stand by a man who doesn't stand by his own kith and kin. They've heard how your guards took him at Mother's house, with her there. They don't like that.'

The Duke looked at him as though he neither saw nor heard him. Henry spoke a little louder, but gently, for his brother's face was white and piteous. 'Taking him at Mother's house, and she standing by. You shouldn't ha' done that, Ned.'

Ned sat quite still, staring before him. What was he seeing? Henry felt anxious. Was Ned, as they say, himself? There was a queer look on him, the look, it might be, of a man whose horse was riding straight for a precipice, and he with no power and perhaps no will to stop it.

When at last he began to speak it was in a different voice, no longer low and measured, disdainfully impersonal. It was sharp and querulous, the voice of a complaining schoolboy who at any minute will burst into tears.

'Mother this and Mother that,' he cried. 'Is Master Tom always to shelter under her petticoats? Precious little mother's darling, *he's* shown how he stands by kith and kin, hasn't he? Working against me all these two years, doing his best to pull me down, and she – *she* never sees it. Oh no, she wouldn't! Tom can make mincemeat of me for all she cares. All she cares about – all – all – is that he shall be safe, her spoilt brat, and that is all she's ever cared about. You know it too. *We* were never anything to her, as soon as she'd got Tom.'

It was utterly bewildering. There was Ned gone clean back to being a child again, sobbing his fury under the old apple tree in Broom Close because he had been blamed for something that he said was all Tom's fault. These clever fellows who came to the top and ruled the Kingdom didn't ever know how to grow up, seemingly.

'Well, but in nature she loved him best.' Henry spoke carefully, as to a child. 'He was the youngest and always gave her a deal more trouble than the rest of us. Feminine kind are like that. And they like Tom. Men do too. It's in nature.'

He wished he could make it plain to Ned. He had always seen it so plain.

All of romance he had ever known had been bound up in that babbling baby creature who had always rushed into danger as soon as he could toddle, into the green duck-pond or the bright fire, straight up to the fierce stallions or mastiffs or the ring-nosed bull, all of which Henry had always known he must not touch, and at once dragged Tom away, – but so soon was Tom standing up to Henry himself or to anyone who opposed him, so soon he shot up taller and handsomer and livelier than any of them, so soon he had darted away from home out into the world, and brought Henry back a whiff of the scent and colour of strange countries and foreign wars, had talked with the Sultan and cracked jokes with the

233

King of France, and sent Henry strange treasures fashioned by dark heathens who wore petticoats.

Henry's hunting-cap at home rested on a round hat-stand of blue and white pottery with Arabic inscriptions; on his sideboard was a Persian dish five hundred years old, with a gay little bird on it sprouting into a serpent's tail at one end and at the other a smiling woman's face in jaunty cap and collar as modern as a lass of today. Tom had told Henry with a dig in the ribs that he sent him his rarest finds for the pleasure he had in hearing him say 'Ar, mighty feat and pretty.'

If he lived as long as Methuselah he'd never cram as much into his years as Tom had done in even one of his dazzling kingfisher flights across the Continent.

Henry had always been rather awed by his elder brother, had adored his younger, and taken it for granted that he himself was the stupid one who did not count – but not so stupid that he couldn't see that the women would love Tom best. Odd that the clever ones should be so stupid.

But nothing of this could he say to Ned, for the poor fellow was fair beside himself, mouthing his face all awry as he talked, and it white to the lips, rolling his eyes round the room and grabbing at one unhelpful thing after another on the table, just as he had done in those queer unchancy rages he had had as a boy.

But now he was not a boy, and Henry felt deep in his bones that he was witnessing that terrifying thing, the rage of a weak man in mortal fear.

It was a case of Tom's life or his, Ned said; there could not be two Protectors, nor even two brothers in power; for himself he cared nothing, – but Tom would ruin his great work for England. *He* worked for the future and for others, – but Tom only for the present moment and himself. Tom would always undermine his authority; the country was not big enough for them both, and that was the plain fact of it, – and why should he show any consideration for Tom, who had never in all his life shown any for him?

Henry waited till the storm spent itself out and a shaken yellow-faced old man had shrunk back, cold and exhausted, into his huddled furs.

Then he said, ''Tisn't right, Ned, that's all that matters. Take it that Tom's not done right by you, – well, you can't help that. But you can help this. Bible says you should forgive your brother, not seven times only, but seventy times seven.'

The Protector passed a feverish hand over his brow. It came away damp. Mechanically he murmured, as he had often found it well to do, 'That may be a mistake in the translation.'

'It's God's holy word, isn't it?' persisted Henry.

'Oh yes, yes, and a dozen fellows at work on it. Miles Coverdale isn't the only Hebrew and Greek scholar in England. Miles acknowledges himself that he's used five other translations in it.' He began to wonder wearily if he had been wise to push forward this business of the English Bible, – you couldn't tell where it might lead to, when every ploughman, however simple and ignorant, started quoting it to suit his purposes, profaning the Sacred Word in every ale-house and tavern, just as the old King had complained, and rightly, Ned now thought.

He *would* not doubt it; he would not lose faith and hope in himself, nor yet in the humblest of his brethren, – but how could he believe in himself or anything else while this clod stood and gaped at him and preached to him, yes, to *him*, of his duty to his brother?

'Go back,' he shouted suddenly, 'back to your stables and your pigsties! What can such as you understand of me, and of the work I have been called upon to do?'

As if in answer to that hoarse strained shout, a servant entered hurriedly, looking rather aghast. But it was to announce an unexpected visit of King Edward, and with him John Dudley, Earl of Warwick.

They came in, leaving their gentlemen-in-waiting outside, and with only Barnaby Fitzpatrick still in attendance at the royal elbow. The Protector rose in haste, and bowed very low, so Henry did too, though, dear Lord! it seemed a queer way to go on to a small boy who was your nephew when all's said and done, and in a private room and no affair of State.

He took a good look at the lad, who was complaining

235

about something in a high fretful pipe; he wasn't shaping as well as Henry had hoped, not much taller nor sturdier than at his Coronation two years ago, and he'd been small even for a nine year old then. Peaky too. Kept too hard at his books by the look of him. Young plants never grew well indoors. He'd like to turn him out to grass for a year or two to kick up his heels and run wild, and loosen that set small mouth that shut like a trap as he finished speaking.

By which time Henry had heard what his nephew had been saying.

'It's intolerable. Why don't you stop it? The people shout at me in the streets, they yell "Justice for the Admiral!" A woman called out that I was an unnatural nephew, and she wished she had the jerking of me – *me*! And look at that!' He stuck out his foot and the Protector backed as though suspecting a kick. 'Mud! Mud on my stocking. Someone threw that – at *me*!'

'One cannot prevent people calling out in the street, Your Grace.'

'Why not? My father would have. Is this your freedom of speech for all? There's been too much of it.'

John Dudley's cool voice slid between the child's angry treble and the exasperated answer that his uncle was just beginning. 'Indeed, my lord, His Majesty has grave cause for his annoyance if the people are encouraged to think they can insult the Crown with impunity.'

The Protector's hands began to twitch with nervous rage – (How well Henry knew that clenching of the fists, blue-white at the knuckles. If you touched them they would be as cold as frogs.) 'What does Your Lordship suggest I should do?' he rasped. 'Order out the guard to fire on them because some street urchin, who's probably no longer there, threw a clod of mud some time before? Will that impress them with the royal justice?'

He turned sharply on his nephew, 'I have yet to learn how it is Your Majesty is out riding with the Earl of Warwick when you should be at your Hebrew with Mr Cheke?'

Edward drew back from him. 'There's the match of Rovers

and Prisoners' Base in ten days' time. How am I to have a chance of winning if I never practise?'

He looked appealingly at Dudley, who smilingly said: 'Mea culpa! Let me be His Majesty's whipping-boy instead of young Barney this time. The day was fine, the royal head ached, and it is certain the King needs practice to give him a fair chance in the match I've arranged. He draws no strong bow as yet, though a very pretty shot.'

Edward flushed with pleasure, then turned to his uncle with his upper lip sucked in and his under stuck out. For two pins, it seemed to say, his tongue would follow it.

It began to dawn on Henry that if the King had been turned against his youngest uncle by his eldest, he did not like his eldest any the better for it.

The Protector burst out, 'Am I the King's guardian or am I not? How can I have any authority if the moment my back is turned every Tom, Dick, and Harry works against it?'

'My name is not Tom,' said Dudley softly. 'I trust you will not confuse the matter. It is not I who am in the Tower on charges of undermining your authority.'

'With as little reason, maybe,' came an unexpected voice. Something had boiled up in Henry's head, and boiled over. They turned and stared at him, those fine gentlemen, as mum and mim as a couple of calves. As for the little lad, he looked at him as though a piece of the furniture had given tongue.

'Who is this – gentleman?' Edward asked with a slight emphasis on the last word.

As Ned didn't seem able to collect his wits or his words, Henry answered: 'Your Uncle Henry, Your Grace, up from Wolf Hall.'

'Another uncle!' The boy turned away.

But Henry wasn't going to let go of his chance. 'You've a finer uncle than me in the Tower. Have justice done to your own flesh and blood. Give him a fair and open trial. You are the King. Show it.'

The King and the Protector spoke at once. But Henry only heard the boy's voice shrilling hysterically above the man's expostulations.

'Uncles – uncles everywhere – always quarrelling – bullying me – keeping me from my bow, wanting to make me a butter-fingers. And Uncle Tom's a bad man, he's dishonoured my sister, he poisoned my stepmother so as to marry her, he—'

'Christ have pity!' shouted Henry, silencing both boy and man. 'Are these the lies they've been telling you? Even a child should see their falseness. The Queen's own brothers are almost the only loyal friends to stand by Tom now. Would they do so if he'd poisoned their sister? Let Tom confront his accusers. Give him the chance you'd give to any common thief or murderer.'

The Protector had got his hand on his shoulder and was trying to shove him out of the room, while the Earl of Warwick stared with an expression of detached interest.

Henry knocked off the hand as though it were a fly. 'Hark'ee, brother, you shall hear me, aye and the lad too, before you're rid of me. "Whoso causeth one of these little ones to stumble, it were better for him that a millstone were tied about his neck and he were cast into the uttermost depths of the sea." '

Then he went. The Earl of Warwick's eyebrows rose slightly as he looked at his colleague.

'Is that another mistake in the translation?' he asked.

*   *   *

Edward, alone with Barney at last, was fuming at him. Barney had shown him respectfully that he hadn't liked Edward's manners to his Uncle Henry. Edward said that he was sick to death of all his uncles, a lot of nobodies who wouldn't be anybody but for *him*, but just lumps of Wiltshire mud and he wished to heaven they'd stayed there – 'that oaf, that clod, to thrust his way into my presence and speak to me like that – *he* my uncle! They're all alike, – knaves, bullies, upstarts. *These Seymours!*'

Barney felt it better not to stress the King's own half of Seymour blood. He said, 'In my country the lords of the land treat humbler people, even peasants and servants, with as much courtesy and friendliness as those of their own kind.'

'Yes, dine at the same table, feed out of the same dish, don't they? We English had to pass a law against it. In your country they live like savages.'

The King swung out of the room and slammed the door. Barney stood looking after him.

'*These Tudors!*' he said.

Chapter Twenty-Three

LADY TYRWHITT had been appointed by the Council as the Princess Elizabeth's new governess: an awkward position for the lady, for the Princess herself flatly refused to recognize her as such. Haughtily she declared that Mrs Ashley was her governess; she had not so demeaned herself that she needed any other set over her. In fact, she would rather have none at all. Sir Robert Tyrwhitt's opinion was that she needed two! But he had to admit to his master that 'she cannot digest such advice in no way'.

His wife told him that the girl sulked all day and wept all night. It was all the result they could boast, though she had now been under their constant supervision for more than a month. The confessions of her servants had led to none of any value by herself. She wrote a deposition that echoed theirs, and went no further – except for her bright assurance at the end that this was all she could remember at the moment of her dealings with the Admiral, but if anything came into her head that she had forgotten, she would promptly add it! It sounded far too good to be true. So did the close resemblance between her account and that of her servants. 'They all sing the same song,' wrote Sir Robert glumly, 'which they would not do unless they had set the note before.'

But he grew more hopeful as he reported, 'She begins now to droop a little'; this when he had let her know that things were going badly for the Admiral, his horses already given away, his property plundered, his servants discharged.

But she did not droop if anyone spoke against him; she

239

flared out then in his defence as passionately imperious as a reigning Princess. Could nothing teach her that she was a helpless prisoner, in danger even of her life?

The Protector wrote to impress her with the fact, and demanded an answer; Tyrwhitt wrote a rough draft for her to copy and send as her own, admitting her faults and submitting herself to his merciful forgiveness.

She scarcely looked at it. She would write to the Protector, certainly, but she needed nobody's suggestions as to what to say.

She sat down, pen in hand, a tight determined smile on her face, the smile of a fighter. And not in mere defence. She would carry the war straight into the enemy's camp.

'Master Tyrwhitt and others have told me that there are rumours abroad that I am with child by my Lord Admiral. My Lord, these are shameful slanders. I shall most heartily desire Your Lordship that I may come to the Court, that I may show myself there as I am.
　　Written in haste, from Hatfield,
　　　　　Your assured friend to my little power,
　　　　　　　　　　　　　　ELIZABETH.'

The Protector blinked as he read the upright beautifully shaped hand. Never surely did a fifteen-year-old Princess dispose of so base a charge in so brief and businesslike a manner. Nothing here of the proper outraged modesty and ignorance of a very young lady, – but a sound medical knowledge, and the courage to stand upon it. They said she was with child. Let them prove it then; she was perfectly ready to come to Court to be medically examined and to outface all the prying whispering gossip of the women who would know why she had come.

The Good Duke was scandalized. Why, at her age his sister Jane would not even have known such things. And the bold accusation (for it plainly accused him too), 'My Lord, these are shameful slanders', was like a blow straight between his eyes. Almost he could hear it thundered out in King Harry's voice with one of his tremendous oaths.

There was finesse in the letter too; she thanked him at the

beginning for his 'great gentleness and goodwill' to her, and told him that she was only writing to him because he had told her to. (So whatever he got from her, he had asked for it!)

She even insinuated a subtle defence of the Admiral by quoting an almost too innocent question of his, 'Why he might not visit me as well as my sister?'; and of Mrs Ashley, by declaring that her governess had always said 'she would never have me marry without the consent of the King's Majesty, Your Grace's, and the Council's'.

And the only pathetic note in this letter from an utterly friendless child in a desperate position, was that she had altered the conventional closing, 'Your assured friend to my power', with the addition 'to my little power'.

It did not impress the Duke, who wrote in sharp retort that she was too well assured of herself; as to these shameful slanders, let her but name the author of them, and the Council would take up the matter.

Again he got more than he bargained for. She was very sorry he took her letter 'in evil part', but coolly observed that 'I do not see that Your Grace has made any direct answer'. As to naming the scandal-mongers, 'I can easily do it, but I would be loth to do, because it is mine own cause', and she had no wish to punish anyone in that cause, 'and so get the ill will of the people'.

But she told him with uncompromising directness what *he* ought to do, and that was 'to send forth a Proclamation declaring how the tales be but lies'.

The Duchess, reading it over the Duke's shoulder, gave a squeal of exasperation. 'Telling *you* what Proclamations to issue! Who the devil does she think she is?'

The letter told them. She was 'The King's Majesty's sister'. It would be well for the Protector and the Council to show the people that they remembered this, and that they had some regard for her honour.

The Duchess screamed. This bastard, this wanton, was giving herself all the airs of a future Queen. All her talk of the people (it was a marvel she did not write '*my* people'!) and their will towards her, good or ill, showed her sinister intentions. She was determined to play for popularity, to work up a following in the country, as her seducer had tried to do. There would not be a moment's peace in England till she met the same fate as he.

And why, she demanded, was that fate so long in coming to him?

It was over a month now since the Admiral had been sent to the Tower, and every week, day, hour while the Duke delayed, hesitated, prevaricated, hummed and hawed and made tedious speeches, was giving his equally traitorous brother Henry time to work up more and more opposition to the execution.

She swept out of the room. A servant entering just after was surprised to get an inkpot thrown at his head, and hurriedly departed, to tell his fellows that the Protector was not the same man since he had started hounding his brother to the scaffold. He was growing quite irritable.

The Protector raged round the room, hurling books on to the floor, flinging papers into the fire. The airy, erect handwriting of the Princess looked up at him as he was about to destroy that too. It was very like her; the fantastic looped lines of the signature that twirled into a little arabesque at the end were those of an artist longing to draw rather than write; even the two large sploshy blots on the other side of it, which she had ignored rather than write her letter again, were characteristic. But the words were quite unlike the hard frivolous young thing he believed her to be.

'They are most deceived that trust most in themselves.'

That had been in answer to his reproof of her over-confidence; but seeing the sentence apart from the rest, it sounded a warning to himself. Had he, after all, trusted so earnestly in his fine resolves, his noble desires for humanity, only to be deceived by a traitor within his own breast?

He looked again. He saw, 'I know I have a soul to be saved as well as other folk have.' Its simplicity seemed utterly forlorn; yet there was a true pride in it that no humiliation could crush.

Was this girl indeed a contemptible wanton? Her dealings with him and his servants were showing sparks of unexpected greatness. He laid down the letters, still looking searchingly at the writing as at a portrait: then inward at himself.

He too had a soul. What had become of it? Always he had regarded himself as morally superior to the run of men. He never swore, nor drank too much; nor felt any temptation to lechery; his greed for money and property was too cold a lust for him to recognize it as that. How should it be a personal lust when he was building his possessions for the future, laying up treasure, honourable position and power for his sons' sons rather than himself?

That sophistry had crumbled. It would not even be his true heir who would inherit his titles, his eagerly grasped lands and gold, – a little mud and metal, that was what it had turned to now in his eyes. Yet he had been no greedier nor more ambitious than many others; and no vices stained his private character.

But for all that, he knew now that for many years his soul had been in hell.

He hoped that death would release it.

*   *   *

Bess got her Proclamation. The Protector issued one as she had requested, stating that the scandals against her were lies, and forbidding the people to repeat them, on pain of severe punishment.

Whereupon she promptly made another request: that the Protector and the Council should be good to her governess in the Tower, 'because she has been with me a long time, and has taken great labour and pains in bringing me up in learning and honesty'.

There were many tales of poor Ashley's pains in bringing Bess up; the Protector almost suspected that baffling smile of the Princess behind the words. Yet it was a touchingly loyal appeal. It made no reference to any other subject, though she wrote it only three days after the Bill of Attainder against the Admiral had passed its third reading in the House of Lords. She could make no appeal for him; it would only harm him, since his courtship of her was one of the chief charges against him.

She could only plead for her old Ash-Cat, – a poor

substitute, and in her agony of anxiety she did not think at first that she could drive herself to do it. But Cat was her old friend and she must do the best she could for her. She did.

The letter was full of a faithful and passionate tenderness, – perhaps not all for Ashley. But Ashley was the only person for whom she could admit it.

She walked, these first cold days of March, under the great oaks of Hatfield Park, where she had been so glad to run out and listen to the nightingale on the early summer evenings when she had first come here with Mr Ascham, – and Queen Catherine was still alive. There was the old tree scarred with her arrows where she had shot at a mark and her tutor had told her she drew as pretty a bow as the goddess Diana.

Was she indeed walking in the very same place, under the self-same trees? Was she here at all, and was she the same self? Or was there nothing round her, the world nothing, and she herself nobody?

'Thus in no place, this nobody, in no time I met
Where no man, nor naught was, nor nothing did appear.'

The world seemed to have dropped into a vast silence, and yet there were birds shrilly piping their first songs, dogs barking, and the chatter and rustle of female voices and movement all round her.

Lady Tyrwhitt and her women walked with her, talking, talking, watching her, trying to make her talk too. Of what was Her Grace thinking? Why did her lips move and yet say nothing?

'Because I can say nothing,' she said.

And still she said, only to herself:

'He said he was little John Nobody that durst not once speak.'

Chapter Twenty-Four

IN THOSE FIRST days after his arrest, Tom walked up
and down his room in the Tower and talked, while his friend
and servant Sir John Harington sat by the fire and stared at
it in silence. He listened sympathetically to every word his
lord was saying, while the back of his mind, which was irre-
pressibly given to statistics, computed the number of miles
Tom must have already walked that day. He would verify
the measurement of the room presently, but he must be
doing a good average of twenty-five miles a day. At this rate
he could have walked to the South Coast by now and got on
one of Jack Thompson's ships for France; in a fortnight he
could walk across the Border to Scotland and freedom.

But at every few steps the Tower walls turned his footsteps sharp round and back again. Would he ever walk
straight on, out into the air, except to his grave?

The subject of these gloomy fancies was far from indulg-
ing in them.

Tom was blazingly angry, but he still had no notion that
there was anything to be really afraid of – except of the
shock that his sudden arrest must have given his mother.
He'd never forgive Ned for that – he'd let him know it too,
the damned clumsy heavy-footed brute, so full of his own
importance that he'd got blunted to everything and everyone
else – 'he can only think in terms of Council speeches, he's
forgotten that the People are made up of persons. No wonder
his wife is sick of the sight and in especial the sound of him,
– much good it does her to have a fellow like that in bed
with her – if it weren't for the loathing I've got for the bad-
tempered bitch I'd cuckold Ned myself to show her what a
Seymour can do.'

Three turns in silence, only two steps off four, then out he
broke again, – 'This is to give me a jerk, that's all. They've
not a thing they can really hold against me. I'll be out in no
time, and by God if he thinks I'll keep the peace the better

245

for this brotherly hint, he'll soon find his mistake! I'll make him sorry he ever did such a damn fool thing as to clap me into the Tower. *Who* can be behind it? That's what worries me. Ned would never have done this of himself.'

Another turn, then a sharp swing-round on his heel and a thump on Harington's shoulder that nearly spun him into the fire. 'By God, Jack, I've got it! I always knew it really, but I was too hot with Ned to think of anyone else. I'll swear this is Dudley's doing. I've always distrusted that fellow. Didn't I say he's a dark horse, hasn't shown his form yet, but I'll bet a thousand pounds he's keeping something back that will show when it comes to a race for power. And that blind jackass Ned doesn't see it, for all his conceit about his brains – but you know the Spaniard Chapuys always said Ned was "not very intelligent and rather haughty"!' He interrupted himself with a roar of delighted mirth. 'Sure enough, our Ned isn't intelligent enough to see that this dainty fop the Earl of Warwick is making trouble between us for his own ends – the old tag, "divide et impera", and so come in for the pickings. Isn't it clear as mud?'

'Clearer,' said Harington, 'if it's clear that Dudley is in this thing. There's nothing to show it yet.'

'But someone must be, and if not he, who is it? Who else would gain?'

Harington hesitated. Then he said, 'Your brother would gain, or thinks so, or he wouldn't have done it.'

Tom stared at him, really shocked. 'You bloody-minded old cynic, you don't really think Ned did this of himself!'

'I don't know. What is the use of thinking, till one knows?'

'There's the mathematician! But we'll soon know, for it's bound to come out at the trial. That's the best of a trial, everything comes out at it – you can see who's against you, answer their accusations and show how piffling they are. And by God, I'll show 'em a few things on the other side! I'll bring it all out in the open about Ned stealing my wife's wedding ring! And Fasterne – her own family lands. What's he got against me compared with *that*? He'll wish he'd never given me the chance to speak in public. And mark you, I'm going to get that chance. I'm not going to be let out with a warning after a few weeks in the Tower and told to take my medicine like a good boy and go quietly and not make a fuss. I shall insist on a trial. I'll make it so hot for them all, they'll wish to God they'd never touched me.'

And for several more miles he went over and over all the things that he would bring up against Ned at the trial.

He had walked nearly as far as the Welsh Border before he heard that there was not going to be any open trial; but not because he was to be set free without one. It was because they were bringing a Bill of Attainder against him.

He stopped walking. He stopped talking. He stood dead still and stared before him. It was Harington who could no longer bear the silence, though a man discreetly trained to it. He had married a bastard daughter of King Henry's, oddly named Ethelred, and with masterly lack of snobbery in a snobbish age never let it be supposed that she was anything but the bastard of Henry's tailor. And in these last weeks the Council had tried their utmost by bribes and threats to get out of him any incriminating evidence on the Admiral's relations with the Princess Elizabeth – but all in vain.

Short and sturdy, he glanced uneasily up at that magnificent figure of his patron, like an unhappy dog, and at last murmured, 'I'm afraid this looks bad.'

But Tom did not hear him.

A Bill of Attainder was the surest and deadliest weapon they could bring against him. Thomas Cromwell had used it again and again to rid King Henry of anyone he wished out of the way without the inconvenience of an open trial – until the King turned it on Cromwell himself. And now the Protector had turned it on his brother.

'So – Ned – *is* in it!' He spoke as though he had seen a ghost.

Harington looked at his watch. It was twenty-five minutes since the Admiral had last spoken. And still he had not moved.

Ten minutes later he said, 'Then there'll be no trial. I'll not get a hearing.'

Five minutes, and he said, 'Ned *must* be in it.'

Two minutes, and he moved in a mad rush across the room, sweeping everything off the table with a stroke of his arm, kicking over a heavy chair, and gripped Harington by the shoulders till the fingers seemed to meet through his flesh.

'He *can't* do this thing. He's my own brother, he's stood by me again and again – in a damned superior priggish way if you like, but – he *can't* mean to kill me.'

'Let *go*!' said Harington.

Tom dropped him. 'It would kill Mother. He must know that. If he doesn't mind killing me, he'd mind *that*, wouldn't he? Answer me!' he roared.

'He won't let himself think he's killed her,' Harington replied, feeling his shoulder tenderly.

'By God, I believe you're right. He has my head under his belt.'

*　　*　　*

But still he could not believe that Ned would keep it there, – still less, put it on a spike. From his nursery days he had been brought up to think of his eldest brother as good. Why, even the common people were now all calling him the Good Duke.

There must be some compensation for being good, and now he would find what it was: a good man did not cut off his brother's head. Ned would still stand by him, somehow or other. Ned would find a way to get him out.

But then the Governor of the Tower, who was very friendly, especially after sharing a bottle or two of Tom's wine, brought him news of the proceedings in Parliament. There were many who objected to a Bill of Attainder being brought instead of an open trial; there were speeches against it in both Houses, especially in the Commons.

But the Lord Protector, 'declaring how sorrowful a case this was for him, did yet regard his bounden duty more than his own son or brother'.

' "His own son" – the Roman father, hey? He's getting on his toga for the rôle. By Christ's soul, he means to do it! Once Ned starts talking about duty, anything may happen. He'll talk himself into being good enough to kill his brother,

yes, and his own mother. And never see that he's an unnatural monster – only a man who does his duty – the
damned inhuman conceited swab of dirty cotton mopping
up the mess that his own injustice has got him into, mopping
it with his own flesh and blood. "His bounden duty" – "Foy
pour devoir" – that our father used to preach to us, the fine
old man, shouting the family motto out like a battle-cry, –
and Ned the good boy of the family lapping it up like a cat
with cream, – to see what use he could put it to. If *he* were
living now, he'd have strangled Ned in his cradle to prevent
it coming to this, – to kill me and "my Margery" as he always
called her, and used to say the verse that was written to her,
and watch her blush –

> "With margerain gentle,
>   The flower of goodlihead."

"To Mistress Margery Wentworth" – yes, old John Skelton
wrote that to her when they were both young.

> "Benign, courteous and meek,
>   With wordes well devised"––

She's using them now, no doubt – on her Ned. And small
good they'll do her – or me. For she's using them on a stone,
a clod of earth long since fossilized, a man who's never
known what it is to be one, who's wrapped himself round
with a cloud of "wordes well devised" so that he sees and
hears nothing but what he says himself. So that he can call
it his bounden duty to kill me! My God, I'll kill *him*!
Just let me get my hands on his scrawny throat when I get
out!'

He forgot that he would not get out.

The Council came, to remind him.

His eyes like a hungry wolf's sought Ned among them.
But he was not there.

They read him the thirty-three charges against him. He
demanded to hear them from the witnesses themselves, in
open trial. He was told he could have no open trial, he could
call no witnesses in his defence. He could answer to the
charges against him now, by himself, or not at all.

'Then not at all,' he said. What was the use if he could not answer the men who made them? They had risen up against him as fast as daws rising up from corn at the shot of a gun, – 'Caw, caw, caw,' they cried, flapping forward, croaking their accusations, clawing and pecking at his eyes, – and nearly all were those he had thought his friends, fellows he had dined and drunk with and talked to freely, who had nodded in agreement and then chimed in with lists of their own grievances. But now they had all come forward to quote his words as heinous treason, and not a hint of the eagerness they had shown to join in the intrigues they now exposed.

Even Henry Grey whose debts he had paid, whose daughter was under his roof, even Grey had pulled his long melancholy moustaches and turned informer against him.

And Tom could not answer back, to him or any of them.

But talking over the charges afterwards with Harington he was cheered again.

'There's not enough to hang a cat among the lot of them. Their worst charge is slackness in dealing with pirates. But they've not attempted to prove it, and if they did, the punishment can only be dismissal from my post as Admiral, with a large fine. There's not a thing that amounts to treason. It's not treason to want to marry the Princess Elizabeth, and they've made that the principal charge. But they've got no change out of it – not one word to help them from the girl herself, bless her stout little heart!'

Bess would prove a match for Ned any day; she had done so since she was four years old. Hilariously he reminded Jack Harington how she had to bear the christening robe for the baby Prince Edward when she herself had been too small to walk all the way in the Procession, and so Ned had been given the doubtful honour of carrying her – to his intense discomfiture, for she had grabbed off his cap and plucked at his beard and all but wriggled herself out of his arms, and everybody had laughed at him – him, Ned, – who could not bear to be laughed at!

'And still she's as slippery as an eel. "Wild for to hold" – she'll always be that.'

His pride was sharpened with regret, for he himself had

250

not yet held her, only begun to do so, only enough to know how exquisite would be the triumph when he did.

He swerved sharply to other charges against him – plentiful as blackberries, but as waterlogged as those picked in November.

'Was there ever such blether as to call it treason because I married Cathy so soon after the King's death that *if* she'd had a child at once, it *might* have been thought to be the King's. Confuse the issue, hey?' he suddenly shot at Harington, who gaped in amazement that he could still joke. 'Well, if that's treason, why did no one say it then, instead of waiting two years? Because no man thought such piffle – nor does now. It's the cloven hoof of the Duchess kicking that bit of mud out from her petticoats!'

'There's more mud from the pulpits,' murmured Harington.

For the preachers were carrying on a furious campaign to work up public opinion against the Admiral. The Bishop of Worcester, Dr Latimer, thundered out sermon after sermon to prove his wickedness. But his proofs could not be said to justify the death penalty.

Imprimis. A woman executed for robbery nine years ago had said her bad life was due to having been seduced by the Admiral about ten years before that.

Item: The Admiral had not attended family prayers regularly twice daily when at home with his wife, but was apt to 'get himself out of the way like a mole digging in the earth.'

Item: He had said this brand new Prayer Book was not really God's holy word, but old man Cranmer's.

Item: He had tried to get his King away from his lessons and out to sports in the open air; – 'Now woe,' cried the Bishop, 'to him, or anyone else, that would have my Sovereign not brought up in learning, and would pluck him from his book!'

This list of his crimes brought the heartiest roar of laughter Harington had heard from his master since he entered the Tower. 'What's the use of turning the pulpit into a dungheap if that's the worst they can rake up against me? They nose out muck near a score of years old, and all they can find is a drab's word for it. And it's treason to care for the King's health and pleasure! Just wait and hear what the boy himself will say to that!'

He still held his trump card – the King himself. They could set justice and even the law at naught, but they could not carry out the death-warrant without the King's own signature. It did his heart good to describe the miniature roar from the lion cub when told to sign away the life of his favourite uncle – he could be as royal in his rage as his father, a chip of the old block as he had called him, and as he would prove. The living spit of his mother too – loyal little Janey, who had stood by her friends, stood up for them even against Old Harry himself.

And he reminded Harington of those days a dozen years ago when King Hal was visiting Wolf Hall to woo their Janey and complain of Nan Bullen – 'I was seduced into this marriage' – and little Jane, while so sorry for him and certain that he could never have loved That Woman, was still devoted to the memory of his first wife, Katherine of Aragon, whom she had served, and her daughter the Princess Mary, Jane's best friend at Court, and insisted that he should reinstate her.

'You are a fool,' King Hal had growled, 'you ought to plead for the advancement of the children *we* will have, not any others.'

But 'Foy pour devoir' was really Jane Seymour's motto; she even risked her neck for it (and so he threatened her) when she implored him to restore the Abbeys and told him the rebellions against him were a judgment on him for seizing them.

'A woman who could do that,' Tom said proudly, 'would stand up for a blind puppy against a tiger.'

And he remembered her nice kind little ways to the people at home, – making endless babyclothes for the wife of John Wynbolt the undergrubber ('her fifteenth, isn't it, Janey,' he would tease her, 'or have I lost count?'); compounding lozenges of 'Manus Christi' in the stillroom, of white sugar and rosewater and powder of pearls, as a sovereign remedy for the old shepherd John Gorway's quotidian fever, the daily ague, and explaining with flushed earnestness that she was not really being extravagant as they were only the seed pearls off her old blue bodice. Kind, prim, serious, tactless little Janey; nobody thought she had much beauty, and that cynical Spaniard Chapuys marvelled that an Englishwoman should have been so long at Court and still a maid (she was twenty-five when she married the King). But she was true as steel; she was the only one of his wives to do her duty to the King, she gave him a son and died of it, – and he forgot her in a week, 'as merry as a widower may be,' one of his Councillors said slyly; and as if to mock her demure memory, all the College of Heralds disgraced themselves getting dead drunk after her funeral, – Clarencieux falling downstairs on top of the Garter King-at-Arms, Chester trying to ravish a maid of the house and all but strangling her, and Rouge Dragon, with his three wives all living, the worst of the lot.

So Tom poured out his memories of his sister to John Harington as he walked up and back again, up and back again, and Harington said a word here and there to keep him thinking of her, – and not of her son King Edward.

But back and back again Tom came to Edward.

'Of course her boy will stand by me – just as I've always stood by him, given him pocket money, helped him cut a dash with his fellows, taken his side against his domineering old bully of a guardian. Hasn't he said a hundred times – shown it anyway – that he wanted *me* for his guardian and not Ned? He'd never let me down.'

*   *   *

Less than a mile away the Lords of the Council listened to a clear monotonous voice, as dispassionate as if it were saying a lesson, telling to his uncle's enemies his uncle's hopes to make it the 'blackest Parliament ever,' with the King's complaints.

'The Lord Admiral came to me and desired me to write a thing for him. I desired him to let me alone. Cheke said afterwards to me, "You did best not to write." ...

'The Lord Admiral said of the Lord Protector, "Your uncle is old and I trust will not live long."

253

'I answered, "It were better that he should die." ...

'Then he said he would give Fowler money for me, and so he did. And he gave Cheke money, as I bade him; and also to a book-binder; and to others at that time, I remember not to whom. ...

'The Lord Admiral said I was too bashful in my own matters and asked me why I did not bear rule, as other Kings do; I said I needed not, for I was well enough.'

They then produced his servants' account-books of 'such sums of money as I Fowler have disbursed by the King's Majesty's Commandment.'

First. Delivered to His Highness to give to Mr Cheke, at sundry times. £xx

Item, to Mr Barnaby by the King's commandment at sundry times. xx^s

Item, at Greenwich, to certain tumblers that played, His Grace looked out upon them. xl^s

Item, to my Lord Privy Seal's trumpet at Hampton Court when his Highness skirmished in the garden at sundry times. xl^s

That account-book had been Tom's answer to his own jocular comments, 'You are a very beggarly King; you have no money to play with nor give to your servants.' He had given him the money to play with, to give to his friend Barney, to his tutor, to the tumblers that the child had watched, delighted at their skill and daring, to the trumpeters of old Father Russell of the snowy beard at Hampton Court when Edward had skirmished in the gardens, playing at soldiers with his favourite uncle, the Lord High Admiral.

But now the source of all these childish games, this royal boyish generosity, was revealed – in the guise of treason. He who had helped the King to it was a traitor. Why then was the King not a traitor also, who had said of the Lord Protector of his realm, 'It were better that he should die'?

But Kings were not traitors – not yet.

'If this goes on,' said Tom when he heard of it, 'in another hundred years they will find the King himself guilty of high treason and cut off his head.'

'A hundred years?' said Harington statistically. 'That would be in 1649.'

'God damn your dates, you old mathematician!' Tom had stopped walking, he had actually sat down, to take it in.

So, then, the boy was handing him over to his enemies as coolly as Henry Grey, as Ned himself. Tom had bribed him, as he had bribed the bankrupt Grey, in vain. Owing to him, they were both now 'well enough.' And so they could now do without him.

His nephew would not lift a finger to save him.

His head sank into his hands. At last he had broken down.

'The rat, the rat!' he sobbed. 'The little white rat – with Janey's face. And I loved the boy. I was sorry for him.'

His own fate was as yet nothing to him. It was his betrayal by Jane's own son, a boy of eleven and a half, that had crushed him.

But sitting there with his fingers pressed against his eyeballs so that red suns came whirling up out of the blackness, he began to know that the impossible nightmare was coming true. The walls of his prison were closing in on him, as they did in that torture-chamber of the Inquisition, taking forty days to crush their victim out of life.

It had taken about as long with him. One hope after another had died, and now he knew. His brother intended his death. And his nephew consented to it.

He leaped up, his arms flung high about his head, his fists clenched, his laughter hurling about the little room.

'A chip of the old block, I said, and so he's proved it. He's handed me over to my enemies as Hal handed Crum, whom he called the best of his servants. I loved the boy and he knows it, yet he's handed me over to Ned whom he hates – hates – and will bring to death, as he has brought me. He said it were better Ned should die, – he'll do it too, – God, let him do it, let him kill Ned as he's killing me. Let Ned kill him too! The rats will devour their own flesh and blood down to the ends of their tails. God, if I could kill them myself! – but I'll do it, alive or dead. I'll drag Ned down, down. He'll curse the day he killed me – he'll long for death – and he'll get it, the same way as he's killed me.'

He would go down fighting and drag his brother with him. England would never stand being ruled by a man who had killed his own brother. King Hal killing his wives was another matter. But to kill one's own mother's son, that was against nature. He himself would raise revolution against Ned.

He sent Harington away, and his voice was surprisingly calm. Then he sat down on the stone bench by the fire and pulled off his shoes. There was paper secreted in them; he drew it out, and pulled a quill from their aigrette ornament. He had ink as cunningly and secretly prepared. He wrote two letters, one to the Princess Mary, the other to the Princess Elizabeth. He told them that his brother the Protector was murdering him in killing him without a fair trial; he told them what the Protector would do to them if they suffered him to live and work his own ends against them. Let them rise up against him while yet there was time, and make the throne safe for their brother, perhaps for themselves. Let them raise the country against this usurper.

He wrote faster and faster, and then in the midst of the second letter, to the Princess Elizabeth, he stopped. He saw her in his mind as clear as if she were there before him, saw her sitting up in bed with that startled, suddenly awakened air that made her look like a wild deer standing at gaze for an instant before it fled into the forest. So he had seen her a dozen times when he had woken her for a romp on those bright mornings in Chelsea Place when she had been a rosy sleep-tumbled child – not quite a child. But never had she looked at him so, in this strained agony and terror, as though awakening from a ghastly dream of him, to find it true.

She must know by now that it was all up with him. Soon there would be no more to know but that he was dead. She was very young, very impressionable, as wild a coquette as her mother. She would forget him for others – but oh, not yet, not yet!

He finished the letter, but no longer saw the words he wrote, for still he was dazzled with his vision of the slight figure sitting up in bed, the red hair rippling over the bare shoulders, the small white face aghast, with staring eyes, staring at him, and open mouth that shrieked, calling his name.

He sent for his valet, gave him the letters, told him to hide them in his shoes and immediately after his execution to give them in secret to the Princesses.

But all the time that he was pushing forward his last desperate project the refrain was echoing in his head, 'Forget not yet.'

Tom Wyatt had written that song; a gay reckless lover like himself, he had written it to that black-eyed witch, Bess's mother, and been imprisoned in the Tower along with the five other men who were executed for her, but Tom Wyatt had been let off.

'Have you such a thing as an apple about you, my sweet Tom? Lord, I have such an incredible fierce desire to eat an apple! Do you know what King Henry says? He says it means I am with child!'

And the child was Bess, the love-apple for whom he himself had had such incredible fierce desire.

There was no more to do. He sent away his valet. He refused to have a jolly supper with the Governor to drown the fact that it was his last night on earth; he would not even spend it with his old friend Jack Harington.

It did not matter now that death was waiting for him on the morrow. Death had always been there waiting for him, ever since he had been born, as it waited for every man : to strike him down, in battle or on the block, of the plague or moribund old age, at the height of the Christmas feast as it had struck down King Hal, looking out with glazed eyes at his vanishing greatness.

And through all the dancing whirligig of his own life, his feasting and fighting and jollity and popularity with women and kings; through all of it that grisly skeleton had been coming nearer. Now, after the mocking, torturing delay of weeks, days, hours, he could feel on his cheek the cold breath of his pursuer in this relentless game of Blind Man's Buff.

Music was going from him, his lute, his magnificent voice. In so few hours it would be dumb for ever; dust would choke his mouth and close his eyes. He would see no more of pleasure nor sing its praise. The hour had come when he must die.

He had loved a Queen, he loved a Princess, he had loved his little King, and put his trust in him. Put not your trust in princes. He had forgotten God. And now there was so short time to remember Him. So soon would no living man nor boy nor girl matter to him any more, but only God.

He dipped the quill again into the ink and wrote on a torn off scrap of paper:

> 'Forgetting God to love a King
> Hath been my rod.'

That had been his own fault, not the King's. He wished now he had not cursed Janey's boy; he was frail like her, and would have a hard time of it now.

He wrote,

> 'Yet God did call me in my pride,'

but though he tried hard to think of God and how He would judge him, he was still thinking of the King. Rhymes did not come easily with him as with Tom Wyatt, but he must leave something behind to wipe out that curse. He wrote:

> 'Lord send the King in years as Noe,
> In governing this realm with joy,
> And after this frail life such grace,
> That in thy bliss he may find place.'

He flung down the quill in relief. Rhymes were the devil, especially to 'Noe.' But he had got down what he wanted; he had wished long life and happiness to Janey's boy. Now he was free to die.

But he went down fighting. He refused consolations of religion from Dr Latimer, and even from any other preacher. He refused to make a penitent speech on the scaffold acknowledging his crimes and the justice of his punishment. The executioner, frightened by the defiance of that towering figure, struck a feeble blow with his axe so that it slipped on to the victim's shoulder and a great spurt of blood gushed up.

Tom saw red; this was Ned himself striking at him, as Ned had always wanted to do. He leaped up and grappled with the man, dragging him down, down, but it was Ned he was dragging down with him to hell. A dozen hands tore them apart and flung him on to the block, and again the axe hacked at him, but, not yet dead, he struggled to rise again.

The third blow killed him.

Chapter Twenty-Five

THE BRIGHT LATE March sunlight shone into the King's garden where Bishop Latimer was preaching his next Sunday's sermon to the King who sat looking out of the window at the end of the gallery, and to the lords and ladies and servants of the Court, who walked up and down in the garden, an annoyingly restless practice, apt to distract the preacher.

Dr Latimer shouted suddenly, 'This I say, if they ask me what I think of the Lord Admiral's death, that he died very dangerously, irksomely and horribly.'

It worked. The shuffling and whispering stopped; no more of his congregation slid away up side-paths; some who had begun to, turned back. Old Latimer was off again on the Admiral, even though he was now in his grave in the Tower.

'He was a covetous man, a horrible covetous man.' The preacher's eyes rolled round his congregation and his voice dropped a semi-tone: '*I would there were no more in England.*'

Now, whom did he mean by that? Sly glances slid among the crowd, at the elegant Earl of Warwick whose blank ironic stare was fixed upward at the preacher; at the Protector himself, who was gnawing at his lip.

'He was an ambitious man. *I would there were no more in England.*'

'He was a seditious man, a contemner of the Common Prayer. *I would there were no more in England.*'

259

('Latimer's new Litany!' murmured the Earl of Warwick to his neighbour.)

'He is gone. *I would he had left none behind him.*'

And with this generic curse on all men still left alive, the Bishop stepped down from the pulpit. There was no doubt about the effectiveness of *this* sermon.

But the effect was not what he intended. People were soon saying that these snarling curs of the clergy worried even the dead in their graves. And if one did attend to his text, why then it was true enough that there were more men left alive in England as covetous, ambitious, and seditious as ever the Admiral had been – yet he had had to die, while they still pranked it.

Immediately after the execution, men who had been paid by the Council ran among the crowds of waiting citizens, crying that a traitor had died. But they had met no enthusiastic response and many had turned away. 'The man died very boldly,' they said; 'he would not have done so had he not died in a just quarrel.' The Protector himself must have thought so, they said, else why did he not let him be heard in his own defence? There were mutterings about the curse of Cain. The Good Duke had killed his brother. It would do him no good. Soon people were quoting a verse, made, it was said, by one of the Duke's own Council:

> 'But ever since I thought him sure a beast,
> That causeless laboured to defile his nest.'

And the following line exonerated the Admiral (though not the poet), declaring:

> 'Thus guiltless he, through malice, went to pot.'

Poetry was not what it had been a few years ago when Surrey and Wyatt were writing; there were no coming young men to take their place, said the critics. Sir John Harington's Muse did only a little better, when praising his patron's 'strong limbs and manly shape,' his 'sumptuous generosity' and 'in war-skill great bold hand.' That last was in actual and vivid touch, it called up the Admiral at once to those who knew him.

His servant had been searched; the letters to the Princesses Mary and Elizabeth discovered in the soles of his shoes and instantly burnt; the man himself hanged.

They told this to Bess, still a prisoner at Hatfield; they told her how her lover had died, 'very dangerously, irksomely and horribly'; to the last instigating her to rebellion against his brother.

They asked questions. They were watching her. She had to speak. At last she said,

'This day died a man of great wit but little judgment.'

After that there was no more for her to say or do.

They had burnt his last letter to her; she would never know what he had written. The nightmare she had dreamed had come true; and she was living it.

She went to bed and did not get up again for a long time. For many weeks she was too ill to know clearly what was happening in the country round her, certainly too ill to care, – so ill that the doctors thought at first she would not live, though they could find no definite cause of disease. But she had lost the will to live. She had lost the only two people she had really loved in her short life; and perhaps Cathy's death as well as Tom's had been in part due to her. She had lost her good name; she was beggared of love, of character, and of her health; before she was sixteen, it seemed there was nothing left to live for.

But one thing no fate could take from her, her fierce loyalty, not only to a person but to an intention. The first got Cat Ashley out of prison and back to her side; the second set her to work, with the almost blind force of instinct, to recover the ground she had lost; to win 'the goodwill of the people' that had been so jeopardized by scandal. They thought her a wanton; they should see that she was not.

There was still, then, something for her to do, and at once; it just saved her nerves, perhaps her reason, from shipwreck. As soon as she could leave her bed she began her lessons again, though her hand was still so shaky that she had to dictate her letters to a secretary since her writing was 'not now so good as she trusts it will be.' In those last three words lay all her indomitable resolution. Her handwriting '*will*' be good again. She '*will*' work; and with a fury that now allowed itself no alleviation of flirting with Mr Ascham, not even when her always ready jealousy was roused by his admiration of little Jane Grey's industry in learning.

For there were three children in England just then driving at their lessons with ferocious intensity, and with the same object, the Crown of England.

Edward must work to make himself a good King. Jane, though herself working for sheer love of it, was being urged by her parents in order to make herself a suitable consort for him.

Elizabeth was working to fit herself for her far more remote chance of becoming Queen. Now that there was nothing left for her to live for, she was free to live only for that. She did. She worked, – or someone else did, whom she had ceased to recognize as herself.

She saw this other self sit at her books and write, heard it give the right answers, a shadow moved by some strange mechanism, while all the time she stood apart. Very rarely her own self stirred; once it took up her jewelled pen and wrote words that had nothing to do with her lessons:

> '*I love and yet am forced to seem to hate,*
> *I seem stark mute, yet inwardly do prate;*
> *I am, and am not – freeze and yet I burn,*
> *Since from myself my other self I turn.*

> . . . . . .

> *My care is like my shadow in the sun –*
> *Follows my flying – flies when I pursue it;*
> *Stands and lives by me, does what I have done*

> . . . . . .

> *Or let me live with some more sweet content*
> *Or die and so forget what love e'er meant.*'

She stared astonished at the lines. Why had she written them? She had no need to pray to forget what love e'er meant. She had forgotten.

* * *

She worked not only at languages ancient and modern, insisting on beginning to learn Spanish as well as Italian (was not Spain the most powerful country in the world and therefore the most important to understand in all the finer shades of political meaning?); not only at history and mathematics and music and dancing; but at acting a part completely alien to her nature. She wore dresses of nun-like severity, refused to wear or even look at jewels, strained her hair straight and smooth, avoided company whenever possible, and in the presence of men kept her eyes downcast and spoke scarcely at all.

But she listened. In her secluded shell of quiet she heard echoes of the world without, and brooded over them, at first in a dull despair that tried to pass as indifference, for what could anything matter now?

Yet it did begin to matter a little when the sun shone more brightly at her archery practice, and her fingers as she drew her bow were no longer stiff with cold inside the long elegant gloves. The silly shout of the cuckoos in the towering trees in Hatfield Park only mocked her unhappiness.

But then came the time when she first heard the nightingale in the hot bright silence of noonday in early June. It mattered too much; she flung down her bow and rushed headlong into the house in a passion of tears.

The sun must not shine, the birds not sing, or she would never dare go out again. She would sit always in a cool dim room, drowning her heart in dead languages. She pulled the books towards her, – but a wild leaping tune of the Tartar tribes that Tom had often whistled came into her head; she beat her hands against the table to shut it out, but they were beating to the same rhythm. It was no use to try and read, to deafen her thoughts.

It had all come back, the agonized longing for the sound of Tom's voice, of his quick firm step that made the world his own; for the touch of the 'great bold hand' on her

263

shoulder, on her face, lifting it to meet his, – but here the pain became unbearable, she uttered little sharp cries aloud to herself, she seized the papers before her on the table, all the careful work on which she had been laboriously engaged for the past weeks, and tore them into shreds, her hands shaking, her lips trembling, muttering, 'Fool, fool, fool!' to herself, and to him; all her unwilling anger against him burning up again, scorching and withering her heart to ashes.

Why could he not have managed things better, plotted more secretly, played his hand more cunningly, as even she could have done?

He had loved too much, hated too much, talked too much, – thought too little. 'Much wit but little judgment,' so little, – less than a child's, a young girl's. Why couldn't he have been more like herself?

But if he had been, she would never have loved him, as now she did; loved him just because he had been so gaily reckless of consequences, because, though they could kill him, no one could make him cautious; loved him so that the thought of him was tearing her in two, – tearing – tearing – as she tore these senseless scraps of paper.

Why couldn't she forget him?

But she would never forget.

*   *   *

'No, she'll never forget,' said Mrs Ashley to Mr Parry (for the two of them were both out again). 'Love someone else? Why, yes, I should hope so, and she all but a child still. But mark my words, she'll only love men who'll remind her of the Admiral.'

Wherein Mrs Ashley showed that, though lacking in prudence she had her own wisdom.

*   *   *

Something else woke in Bess in those June days, the hope of revenge.

The house was a-buzz with reports confirming the vague rumours of weeks past, rumours of discontent, of insurrections coming to a head in different parts of England against her rulers. Bess's interest, which she had curbed against hope (the people were always rising, and it led to nothing but their own hurt, poor wretches), now galloped forward into fierce excitement.

The mills of God were grinding, not slowly, but exceeding fast. Retribution was coming quickly on the man who had killed her lover and her good name. Within only three or four months of Tom Seymour's death there were rebellions all over the country against the Lord Protector.

This time they had found a leader; a man called Robert Kett who preached 'communistic law' from the branches of an oak tree, and told his followers to keep the peace and harm no man, and share all property in common. As they themselves had none, this meant sharing other people's property; they tore up the palings of the gentry's parks, levelled the hedges, and drove off their deer and cattle to feed on. The Council sent the German and Italian troops against the rebels, under near a score of noble commanders. But Kett's rabble defeated them and took some of the noble commanders prisoner.

So this, said the Council, was the result of the Protector's Reform measures!

He had to forswear them all; to enforce the Land Enclosures that he had tried to abolish, and follow the hated policy of his colleagues. But he still told them what he thought of it – and of them: it was their covetousness that had caused the revolt, and though it must be put down, he would not himself lead a force against it. Characteristically he ended his bitter speech to all those sneering faces, with a crumb of still bitter comfort, to himself. 'Better that they should die fighting than live to die of lack of a living.'

Death was beginning to wear a desirable aspect to him; no grisly pursuing skeleton through the dance of life, but an angel with welcoming arms and a smile of infinite understanding. When he himself was dead, then only perhaps would the people begin to know how he had wanted to help them. But now a quick death instead of a slow one was the boundary of his hopes for them.

So John Dudley, Earl of Warwick, marched against the

rebels, hanged Kett from his Oak of Reformation, put the landlords firmly in power, and returned in triumph, strong enough to move openly against the Protector.

Danger is the best antidote to despair. The Duke at once retorted with a far-flung attack of pamphlets; they were scattered among the people, most of whom were unable to read them at all, and those who began were too bored to finish.

He descended upon Hampton Court, barricaded it, got the little King, who had a heavy cold, out of his bed, and made him address the uneasy populace through the bars of the great gates, with a petition to them 'to be good to me and to my uncle.' Edward did not like it at all. His dignity was ruffled and his cold got worse. And the pathetic effect of his childish appeal was entirely spoilt by the Protector's speech which followed it, asserting that if he went down, the King would go down with him.

The people did not see it. Nor did the King.

And the next night his uncle made him get out of bed again, this time at midnight, and go a long cold tiring ride through the autumn river mist. They rode out of those gates where Nan Bullen's initials, intertwined with King Hal's, had been defaced for Jane Seymour's. Now the servants at Hampton Court were saying that Jane Seymour's ghost came out from the doorway on to the Silver Stick Gallery with a lighted taper in her hand. And Nan Bullen's cousin, pretty Catherine Howard, beheaded in her teens, was heard at nights shrieking in the Long Gallery that led to the Chapel. Bloated red spiders five inches wide had appeared in the Cardinal's palace, which King Henry had looted from him for his own pleasure, and from which his enormous body could not be moved in those last months of his life without the help of machinery. He who had boasted that he never spared a man in his anger (he might have added, in his greed), or a woman in his lust, was no longer spared.

From this haunted pleasure palace on the river his little son rode away at midnight, frail as a feather on his pony, and coughing fretfully in the dark dank October fog. He had to ride all the way to Windsor, – for his safety, the Protector said, though of that Edward was sceptical. It seemed to be entirely for his uncle's safety.

There at Windsor the Earl of Warwick found him, more disgruntled and becolded than ever.

'I bight as well be in prison,' he said; 'there are do galleries here or gardens to play in.'

Dudley took him out of prison. He gave him his friends to play with again, especially Barney. He gave him sports and Christmas parties and mummings, he took him hunting and shooting and made him feel that soon he would be a man among men. The boy was delighted at the change; he flung himself into sports and exercises – with rather too sudden energy in fact for his delicate physique; and sometimes even cut his church attendance so that the Court preacher was disgusted to find himself preaching to an empty royal chair.

But still that nasty cough, that Edward had caught on the long cold night-ride to Windsor, hung on. Dudley told him not to bother about it, he would soon shake it off, as he had at last shaken off his oppressive guardian uncle.

For the Duke of Somerset was no longer the Protector. Dudley, now created Duke of Northumberland, reigned in his stead.

The Seymours' mother, the poet Skelton's Mistress Margery Wentworth, the 'flower of goodlihead,' died only a few months after Tom's death. It was decided not to give her a royal funeral. This was done in order to insult the Duke of Somerset's mother; nobody seemed to notice that it also insulted the King's grandmother, – not even the King. He did not even record her death in his Journal. And the Duke himself took it meekly, as he took most things now; people said he was a changed man since his brother's death, not now in his increased nervous irritability but in his broken spirit.

There was enough, without remorse, to break it, for he had to stand by and watch the utter ruin of all his hopes of social and economic reform, of liberty and religious tolerance, destroyed by the greedy tyranny of Dudley and the new landlords. He had lost not only the power, but much of the will to act. But whether he acted or not, he was naturally the focus point of any opposition to the new rule. And the common people, who had been shocked by his executing his own brother, could now consider that he had paid for it in his swift downfall from power, and remember that the Good Duke had been on their side. So were they now on his side. But they had no power; it was all in the hands of the rich, who were on the side of Dudley, a sensible fellow, especially in his sense of property. And Dudley had the sense to see that an ex-Protector was a danger. Even if he didn't do anything, he was always stirring up the people with his talk of liberty.

To secure his position, Dudley had to strike again, this time to kill. And so, less than two years after Tom Seymour was beheaded, his brother Ned laid down his head on the same block. There was a trial of him on some flimsy charges; he was accused, rather oddly, of trying to secure his position against possible enemies; and of plotting against Dudley, even as Dudley had plotted against him. Dudley himself dared not call this 'treason.' But it made no odds. From the first it was clear that the Duke would share the fate to which he had sent his brother.

He met it very differently. Tom died like a tiger, Ned like a gentleman. He behaved perfectly throughout, thanked the Council on his knees for having given him the open trial that he had denied his brother, – though indeed it was only the show of justice that was granted him, for the House had been carefully packed. And he made a beautiful before-execution speech which moved all the watching crowds to a passion of pity, both for him and for themselves.

They surged forward; a deep muttering growl rose and thickened the air. He had them in his sway in this hour of death as he had never had them in his life. They knew now whatever his faults, crimes even, he had taken thought for them, had wished them well; as none had done of the pack of greedy wolves who were now pulling him down. He had but to lift his hand in sign to them and they would rescue him.

But he did not do it. Why should he give the signal that would lead many of them to their deaths, in order to escape his own? It was little he had been able to do for them, prevented by the greed and ambition of others; but also by his own. 'Let me alone' – yes, alone to die – 'for I am not better than my fathers.'

And he did not even remember in that hour that he had at least wished to be better.

*   *   *

Jan. 22. 'The Duke of Somerset had his head cut off upon Tower Hill between eight and nine this morning,' wrote King Edward briskly in his Journal.

Earlier he had entered all the charges against his eldest uncle with considerable satisfaction, especially his 'following his own opinion and doing all by his authority.'

He had shown indifference over his Uncle Tom's fate; this time it was an active animosity, for the Duke's execution was both suggested and warranted under Edward's own hand. The whirligig of time had brought a strange revenge for King Edward V and his brother, the two small princes murdered by their uncle in the Tower, whose fate King Henry had remembered with dread for his own son.

Edward VI, nearly seventy years later, brought about the death of his two uncles.

It did not weigh on him. At a shooting-match shortly after, when Dudley shouted, 'Good shot, my liege!' the boy brightly answered, 'Not as good as yours, when you shot off my Uncle Somerset's head.'

He was painted standing with his legs rather apart, both thumbs in his belt and the fingers of one hand resting on his dagger, in exactly the same stance as his father, with the same argumentative stare, the same thrust of the dogmatic under-lip. This conscious likeness between the slight boy and his tremendous sire gave amusement to many, but also some alarm.

He was enjoying life: the matches and tourneys that his new guardian arranged to dispel any 'dampy thoughts' about his former guardian's fall (but after that shooting-match Dudley realized he need not have worried); the visit of the little Queen of Scots' mother, the stately and gracious Queen Dowager, whom Mr Knox in his rugged fashion called 'an old cow,' and Edward with schoolboy wit amplified it

269

to the Dow Cow. He showed off his music and dancing to her, and, which he enjoyed still more, his performance on horseback at Prisoners' Base and Running at the Ring, and in shooting, where he was able to record proudly that though he lost at Rounds he won at Rovers.

To Barney he wrote gleefully of musters of a thousand men-at-arms, 'so horsed as was never seen. We think you shall see in France none like.'

For now that his little King seemed free at last to enjoy life and apparent health, Barney too had felt free to follow his ambition and go to France. Edward had generously done his utmost for him in this, got him appointed as one of the French King's Gentlemen of the Bedchamber, and made up for his absence by writing him long eager letters into which he put far more of himself than into his Journal.

To Barney indeed he showed what he had never done to anyone else, an affection that could rise to sympathetic imagination. For while Barney went to the French wars, Edward went a delightful royal progress round the country, staying at the houses of his chief nobles, fêted, entertained with dancing and sports and hunting, and 'whereas you have been occupied in killing your enemies, in long marches in extreme heat, in sore skirmishings, we have been occupied in killing of wild beasts, in pleasant journeys, in good fare, in viewing of fair countries ... and goodly houses where we were marvellously, – yea rather excessively banquetted!'

And Barney wrote back about Romish processions with crosses and banners in Paris, and street rows between French and English soldiers; and soothed Edward's anxiety for his morals by promising that 'as for the avoiding of the company of ladies, I will assure your Highness I will not come into their company unless I do wait upon the French King'; and always ended,

> 'Other news have I none.
> The meanest and most obligest of your subjects,
>   BARNABY FITZPATRICK.'

Then the young man got a letter from the boy more reassuring than any other, in the casual cheerful pluck with which Edward dismissed a recent illness: 'we have been a little troubled with smallpox which has prevented us from writing; but now we have shaken that quite away.'

But it was his death-knell. It left him weakened; his persistent cough, that ill legacy from his last ride with his Uncle Somerset, had come back worse than ever; it got no better as summer came on, and it was evident that he was gravely ill. Barney instantly threw up his promising career abroad to hurry back to him.

He found the fifteen-year-old boy, who had had to give up his new-found triumphs in sport, indomitably interested in all the recent marvels of scientific discovery. He had been studying the cause of comets and rainbows; he showed Barney his geographic and astronomic instruments, the magnetic needle and astrolobe which had been explained to him by old Sebastian Cabot, the Emperor's Pilot-Major of the Indies.

Once again Edward was not going to be outdone by the Emperor; he proposed to make Cabot the Grand Pilot of England.

'The New World ought to be English,' he told Barney indignantly; for it was the Sheriff of Bristol, Richard Ameryk, who'd paid a pension to Sebastian's father, John Cabot, for his voyages of discovery, and that was why people were calling the place America, and *not*, as foreigners tried to make out, because a wretched ship's chandler called Amerigo Vespucci had happened to get there too, within a fortnight of old Father Cabot. 'I'll publish the whole facts to the world – the exact sums my grandfather told Ameryk to pay him—'

'Ah, I wouldn't do that,' said Barney with a careless glance at the accounts that Edward was flourishing at him from his bed, '£40, over three years, doesn't sound much these days for a royal pension!'

The boy gave him a weak thump on the arm. 'All you Irish are cynics. I can't help it if my grandfather was a skinflint. My father made up for that. So will I. And I'm showing what *my* discoverers can do to rival the Emperor's.'

This very day he was sending out three ships under Sir Hugh Willoughby and Richard Chancellor to find a

North-East passage through the Arctic to Cathay. It would be a voyage through 'perils of ice, intolerable colds,' but years ago the merchant Robert Thorne had told King Henry that it was possible, for a man might 'sail so far that he came at last to the place where there was no night at all, but a continual light and brightness of the sun shining clearly upon the huge and mighty sea.'

'And,' said the sick boy, flushing with the triumph of man's unconquerable spirit, 'he told my father "there is *no land unhabitable nor sea unnavigable.*" '

He spoke only of Robert Thorne, whom he had not seen. He did not wish to remember his uncle the Lord Admiral and the sunlight flashing on the gold lacing of his coat as he stood there by the window of this very room in the palace of Greenwich, and pointed at the river Thames flowing down below towards the sea; and said, 'There lies the path of England's glory. Take it, and you'll travel far.'

The Admiral had gone, with his great laugh and promise of splendour and power; but the river flowed on.

From its shores a murmur was rising that grew into a distant roar; it came nearer, louder, ripping out in great tearing gusts of sound, echoing up from the water like a drum.

'They're coming downstream. Look out of the windows. Can you see them yet?' Edward was leaning forward from his pillows.

His old nurse Mother Jack came up and patted them and pressed him back on to them again. 'There, there now, don't you get excited. They won't be here yet. Your Highness will know all about it when they come, the brave fellows, though indeed I think they'd better have stayed at home.'

Barney put his head out of the window, rested his elbows on the sill, and looked upstream, the wind behind him from the sea blowing his hair before his eyes. In the brilliant early summer sunshine the Thames glittered like a diamond ribbon, between its shores that were dark with the swarming crowds thronging to see the start of this wild venture into the terrors of the Outland ocean; where no night was, and rocks of ice as high as mountains and gleaming like sapphire and emerald came drifting down to crush the ships that were no bigger than walnut shells beside them.

Nearer and nearer came the hurly-burly of that mighty cheering as the three ships hove into sight, towed down-stream by small boats rowed by mariners in sky-blue cloth. And in answer, more sailors were running up the rigging and shouting till the sky rang with the noise. Now the guns of the Palace were booming out their God-speed to them.

The Courtiers were already clustered on the tops of the towers, the Privy Council had run to the windows of the other rooms in the Palace.

'Hurrah! hurrah!' they all shouted, even old Father Russell of the snowy beard, even the douce quiet secretary Mr Cecil. The King was all but sobbing, 'I *must* see them. It's *my* venture. Their chief ship is called after me, the *Edward Bonaventure.*'

Barney carried him to the window; it was terribly easy, his weight was so light. Mother Jack tut-tutted and fussed with blankets, but they stayed there till the crowds had swept shouting on, leaving the river banks green and bare; and in the distance the three ships grew misty on that sparkl-ing river, broadening out towards the sea. They sailed out on it, to discover, not the passage to Cathay but the White Sea, and then Moscow, where the great Tsar Ivan the Terrible waited to do them honour in a long garment of beaten gold with an imperial crown upon his head.

But only one of the three ships, the *Edward Bonaventure,* was to achieve this and return to England.

The other two were caught in the ice and there found by the Russian fishermen the next spring, the crews all frozen in their transparent coffin, their gear and belongings intact, to be carefully returned to England by the Tsar.

But now it was still the summer of 1553, and the three ships still sailing out, while the two friends by the Palace window strained their eyes into the future.

'When next they go,' said Edward, 'I will go, too. Old Thorne said he "wondered any prince could be content to

273

live quiet within his own dominions." I am not content. I will—' his cough interrupted him,

Barney laid him down again in his bed.

*   *   *

The roses were like lamps filled with the level light of the sunset. Beyond them the river shone dark through the bright trees and their long slanting shadows.

The lawns and flowerbeds of the Palace gardens glowed iridescent and unreal like the transparent scene reflected on the surface of a soap bubble, – a bubble floating on a ripple of tinkling music that drifted from a boat, clear as sounds can only be on the water; lutes were playing and boys' voices singing to comfort the young King lying sick in the Palace.

In this idyllic scene, screened by the trees from any watching windows, Barney met his Princess once again at last.

He did not in the least want to do so.

Alarmed by the serious reports of her brother, she had ridden in haste to Greenwich to see him, but she had not been allowed to do so. Ever since the Admiral's death she had been carefully prevented from seeing anything of her brother in private, and as she had been living a deliberately retired life she had had only an occasional meeting with him even among the crowds of the Court. Now her desperate attempt to force a meeting had failed, and all she had been able to do was to arrange this semi-clandestine interview with his reluctant page.

It was just five years since that night in early summer when Barney had partnered her for a few moments in the Hungarians' Palace-Dance at the Admiral's house and she had swung him aside into the window seat – to take off her tight shoes, she had said, but surely it was for more than that? She had let him take her hand and speak his love for her; she had smiled at him, and her glorious eyes had opened on him as though he alone were there in all the world; she had – he never could believe it afterwards – but she had sprung up into his arms and kissed him.

And later he had learnt, through tittering deviations of

backstairs gossip, that she had gone out that very same night alone with the Admiral in his barge.

Scandal had blackened her far more deeply in the months that followed; and the grudging Proclamation that the Council had at last issued to clear her name had, in the opinion of many, only confirmed it. 'No smoke without a fire,' was a good, knowing proverb. But nothing that he heard later, not even the confident assertion that the Admiral had been beheaded for getting the Princess with child (the clear proof of it being that none of the open charges against him merited the death sentence), nothing that he heard later could hurt Barney as did the memory of that summer night when she had kissed him – and then crept out in secret to the Admiral.

Even at the French Court it had hung about him, giving him a contemptuous distaste for the gay young women who would have been ready enough to flirt with the grave handsome youth. But he had found it easy to obey his little King's anxious injunctions 'for the avoiding of the company of the ladies.'

Now he had to meet the Princess again. She was nineteen by now and had changed much, so he had heard on all sides; she had lived retired from the Court; she was often ill and, though no one could say what exactly was the matter with her, the doctors sometimes despaired even of her life. Yet she worked like a Trojan, she devoted herself to her studies; she had become a paragon, not only of learning and theology, but of maidenly modesty and discretion. If she had been a Roman Catholic like her sister Mary, she would undoubtedly have gone into a nunnery, so they said; and as it was, her dress was so simple and severely plain that it was almost that of a nun's. Even when Mary of Guise, the French Queen Dowager of Scotland, had come to visit King Edward with all her ladies from the French Court, and set all the English Court ladies on fire to follow the French fashions, causing a complete revolution in feminine dress and hairdressing, the Princess Elizabeth had not changed her style one jot, had refused to wear jewels or even to curl her hair.

This had brought loud praise of her 'maiden shamefacedness' from the Reformers, who were busy condemning the new fashions, especially the 'hair frounced, curled and double curled,' – a hit at the Lady Mary, who, a devout Catholic, could never resist new finery, however unbecoming.

The two sisters were regarded as the rival heroines of the two religious creeds. Little Lady Jane Grey, an ardent admirer of her now austere cousin, had flung herself into the controversy with all the eagerness of a schoolgirl in taking sides; she had refused to wear a cloth-of-gold dress that Mary had sent her, – 'it would be a shame to follow my Lady Mary's example, against God's word, and leave my Lady Elizabeth's example, who is a follower of God's word.'

The speech, duly reported, had infuriated (and alarmed) my Lady Elizabeth a good deal more than my Lady Mary; but Barney could not know that; nor would it have altered his firm opinion that in whatever way she dressed or did her hair she did it of set design, for her own ends, – and those far from spiritual. Since in all Papist eyes she was illegitimate, she would naturally plump for the Reformed Religion.

And the total abstinence from coquetry was too good to be true; he had the word of others for that. The new Spanish Ambassador to England had spoken of her as 'a creature full of beguilement.'

Let her be! She would never again find it possible to beguile *him*!

So he waited on that glimmering golden evening that was filled like a crystal cup with light and music. The boys on the river were singing the song that the young Earl of Surrey had composed in his scarlet-coated pride and joy in a sportsman's life. Barney hoped the sick boy would not recognize it, for he never cared to be reminded that his father had cut off Surrey's head.

> *'Summer is come, for every spray now springs,*
> *The hart has hung his old head on the pale,*
> *The buck in brake his winter coat he flings,*
> *The fishes flit with new repaired scale.'*

A slight figure was coming towards him through the trees with swift and resolute tread. Barney found himself looking at a pale girl in a plain dress of dull green, which for all its sober hue showed up marvellously the whiteness of her long bare throat, uncovered by any necklace, and the red-gold glint on her straight, demurely parted hair that was brushed as smooth and shining as satin. Her mouth was wide and the thin lips shut fast as if not to let any secret escape them; she looked sad and strained, a pale girl, rather tall, with no especial beauty, so he kept telling himself, – but then he had to admit that her eyes were really beautiful. They were the colour of the blue dusk in the shadow of the trees; he remembered now how they reflected the lights and colours round them, the pupils contracting or dilating till sometimes the eyes seemed pale almost as water, and at others nearly black.

And they were looking into his eyes, sinking into them, as once they had done on a night of early summer years before – and suddenly he knew that there was only one reason why he had consented to meet her thus; only one thing he wanted to ask of her; – had she, that same night that she had kissed him, given her body to the Admiral.

He had no chance to ask it. In that same instant that he looked at them, those deep blue eyes changed again, the pupils narrowed, they were the colour of steel as she asked the question that she, not he, had chosen.

'What the devil is this foolery of Dudley's? He has just married his son Guildford in hugger-mugger haste to Lady Jane Grey, to her little liking, and to his own purpose only. You must know of it. It can mean but one thing – that he intends to rule England through her; get the King to alter the Succession and appoint Jane his heir to the throne.'

'It must be for the sake of the true religion, Your Grace,' said Barney uncomfortably. 'If the Lady Mary came to the throne now, it would wreck the course of the Reformation.'

But it was difficult to explain why the Lady Elizabeth, so widely regarded as the representative of true religion, should also have been set aside.

She saw his thought and laughed. 'Yes, he approached me first, all in the cause of the true faith! He quickly found I would have nothing to do with it. So he will set both Mary and myself aside, as declared bastards, which is absurd, for

277

if either is a bastard then the other must be legitimate. Jane's a child for all she's sixteen – and a little fool for all her learning. Her villainous parents are pushing her into this, – to her ruin.'

She spoke the more emphatically as she saw the young man's face settle into resistance to her argument. How wooden and conceited and disapproving he had grown, – and she had once thought him so charming!

Barney on his side, having stiffened himself against any attempt to beguile him, was annoyed to find none made. Did she not think it worth while? Frigidly he put Edward's view to her: he disapproved of his sister Mary; all his reign had been clouded by quarrels with her over her observance of the Mass in her private household; it had nearly caused a war with the Emperor, since she had got him to take her side. That was the danger – Rome – foreign interference—

'I think,' she interrupted crisply, 'you must have been listening to Dr Latimer's sermon last Sunday. In his opinion, "God had better remove both the Princesses from this Earth," since we *might* marry foreign princes who *might* endanger God's Church. But if Godly Dudley takes that hint, he'll pull a hornet's nest about his ears. He'll do it in any case by putting Jane on the throne. The throne of England depends ultimately on the consent of the people. And the people will never stand it if the rightful heir is set aside.'

'The consent of the people? Yes, Your Grace, and the people have given their consent to the new religion. Which the Lady Mary has rejected.'

'So that they will reject her? Never think it! I know more of them than you do, – you've been abroad,' she added, to soften this. 'But indeed I know them, the commoners, well. Creeds don't matter to them as much as people, – or as the simple standards of right and wrong. Some of them may think it fun to toss a priest or two in a blanket, but they won't stand seeing an innocent woman done out of her rights. And they like Mary all the better for standing up for them and insisting on her own form of private worship. They tell dozens of good stories about her pluck – how she roared at the Council, "My father made the best part of you out of nothing!" How they bawled back! It could be heard in the street outside! But so was the story. When the English tell stories about anyone it means they've taken him – or her – as their own. And she is not only comedy to them, she is romance. For so many years now she has been a legend, a princess cruelly shut up in Dolorous Guard. I will tell you something I saw myself only this spring; a simpleton of a girl who wandered the countryside, believing herself to be the Princess Mary! She told me that King Henry's sister, the lovely Mary Rose, had appeared to her in a dream – she was sitting in a silver bath! – and told her, "You must go a-begging once in your life, either in your youth or in your age." "And so," said the poor fool, "I have chosen to do it in my youth." You will think this not worth a straw – but straws show the wind – and the hold that my sister's sad state has had on the people's imagination.'

On hers too, it seemed, with such eager sympathy she told the queer little tale – until it occurred to Barney that she too, as well as Mary, had had to go a-begging in her youth; and might well see herself as another ill-used princess in Dolorous Guard.

For the first time it struck him that he himself had not been the only person to be pitied in the affair of the Princess and the Admiral.

He knelt and kissed her hand. 'I will do what I can with His Majesty for Your Grace,' he murmured.

For answer she flicked him on the nose. 'You are impertinent. Who said it was for *my* Grace?'

'For my Lady Mary's then.' At last he was smiling.

But she sighed. 'Why not say, for my Lady Jane's? It's she who would come off worst.'

*   *   *

She went back to Hatfield and wrote telling her brother how she had come to see him and been prevented. It is doubtful if he ever got the letter. He was fast getting worse. Dudley was having to work madly against time. He had married Jane to his son almost as quickly as one bought a cow (but Jane was still refusing to consummate the marriage).

279

Now he bought quantities of arms and was manning the Tower; twenty ships fully manned and gunned rode at anchor in the Thames on the thin pretext of an expedition to Barbary and the Spice Islands, which everyone knew would not take place.

Only one thing remained to secure his position; he must seize the persons of the two Princesses.

Two bodies of horsemen were sent to bring them to London in answer to urgent messages from their dying brother.

Mary started from Hunsdon. Elizabeth, just about to start from Hatfield, had a sudden suspicion that these pathetic appeals might be a trap to take them prisoner. What if they had been sent, not by the King, but by Dudley in his name?

Edward Seymour had kept King Henry's death a secret for three days while he snatched the supreme power. Was John Dudley now playing the same trick?

She promptly went to bed and declared herself too ill to ride to London. It would gain time, but only for a few days, perhaps hours, and sooner or later she would have to declare herself either for Mary or Dudley.

It was an appalling dilemma, for she knew nothing of what had happened to Mary, and if she continued to disobey the summons to London, it might well lead to Dudley sending an armed force to carry her to the Tower, perhaps the block. On the other hand, if she threw in her lot with him, it would bring her into open enmity with Mary, who might even now be fighting his army – and winning.

She lay back on her pillows and knew that she could do nothing more but wait for the next move.

It came with the public announcement of the King's death. The heralds proclaimed Jane as Queen at street corners, and their printed Proclamations, stuck up in market squares and church porches all over the country, justified her succession on the ground that the King's sisters were both bastards.

It was Sunday, and preachers all preached the same doctrine: Jane alone was the true and rightful Queen. A servant rode back from Amersham where he had heard a little man with a beard like a billygoat thump the pulpit and scream, 'Woe! Woe to England!' if she allied herself to the enemies of the Gospel – by which Mr Knox intended Mary.

No one could tell Bess where Mary was, – alive or dead – free or a prisoner – in England or escaped – (as she had often planned) to the Netherlands.

But there was far more that no one could tell her about Mary. She lay by the new open windows, and the clang and peal of church bells acclaiming Jane as Queen of England floated in on the golden early July air. Would the country tamely accept her, or would they rise on behalf of Mary, as she had so boldly assured Barney they would?

She had not felt as bold as she had sounded. Dudley held whatever army there was, and the navy (all those ships lying off London all ready to attack! 'Spice Islands my nose!' she had exclaimed. It had smelt gunpowder, not spices); he held the Tower; and all the great nobles in his pay. He was the greatest soldier England had had for years; he had succeeded in Scotland where Somerset, a sound and ruthless general, had failed; he had succeeded against the revolution.

Would he succeed now? – or would that inveterate bungler, Mary?

And if Mary did succeed, what then?

Dudley was the only man Mary had ever feared, except here father.

Nobody feared Mary. Her gruff good-natured laugh; her overdressing coupled with her simplicity and utter ignorance of the world, ignorance that had begun as a secluded girl's, devoted to her deeply religious mother, and had fixed into an old maid's; her inability to say anything she did not mean ('to be plain with you,' it was always accompanying some fresh gaffe); all these things had made her, among those who knew her, a figure of fun, certainly not of any mystery or alarm.

But Bess, lying in the warm July sunshine, shivered as she thought of her half-sister. Would it be better for herself if Mary won instead of Dudley? Dudley was utterly unscrupulous, ruthlessly bent on his own ambition, and would sweep anyone who interfered with it out of the way without remorse.

But Mary was unpredictable. She would never do anything that she did not feel to be right, – but what might govern those feelings? Her starved emotions, her bitter broodings on the past and the wrong her father had done her mother, had twisted her judgment, of which she had never had much. She could not see nor reason clearly, but acted on impulse, letting her heart govern, and not her head. That ought to be well, since Mary had a good heart. But a female heart rampant could be a terrifying thing.

Under Mary's essential goodness of nature there lay the sickening uncertainty of hysteria. That quagmire, that welter of shifting angry unhappy emotion, blind, bottomless, a bog on a black night, was always there, waiting to engulf her, and anyone who was so unfortunate as to be having any dealings with her at that moment.

Jane might well turn out to be as much of a bigot as Mary.

But Jane was not an hysteric. Jane's fury of righteous indignation would be a deal less dangerous than Mary's sobbing paroxysms of grief over her sainted mother.

'May God preserve me from good women!' sighed Bess.

But there she had to lie, on the horns of a dilemma, between two very good women.

The church bells broke out again into a peal of joyous triumph. A white butterfly fluttered in and flapped about the room. She got out of bed, caught it and let it fly out of the window, watching it join a cluster of its fellows and go dancing all together, up, up, like flecks of light against the green glory of the sunlit trees, until suddenly she remembered she might be seen at the window.

She jumped into bed again, and looked at her face in the little hand-mirror. It was sufficiently white not to need any rubbing with chalk. Her teeth were chattering with fear; but she laughed.

Something in her that had lain numb all these four and a half years, since Tom Seymour's death, was quickening her pulses to a terrified yet heartening throb.

Now at last again, when at any moment she might lose it, she knew how sweet life was, and hope; yes, and fear too, since it had made her want to keep that life, want passionately, with all the wild excitement of a young lover's desire, to live, and to be Queen.

JEAN PLAIDY

Three memorable and exciting novels on the reign of Henry VIII:—

MURDER MOST ROYAL 5/-

The story of Henry's two murdered queens—the vital, fascinating Anne Boleyn, and her lovely cousin Catherine Howard.

ST. THOMAS'S EVE 3/6

Sir Thomas More—man of integrity, sentenced to death as the price of his opposition to the wild desires of the King.

THE SIXTH WIFE 3/6

Katharine Parr survived her royal husband, but was fated to suffer tragic and mysterious death.

Two novels recreate the poignant and fascinating story of Mary, Queen of Scots:—

ROYAL ROAD TO FOTHERINGAY 5/-

Mary Stuart, a generous, desirable woman betrayed by her passions.

THE CAPTIVE QUEEN OF SCOTS 5/-

Mary was a brave woman. She never abandoned hope until the end—her execution.

No family is more notorious than the Borgias, no character more fascinating than Lucrezia:—

MADONNA OF THE SEVEN HILLS 5/-

All of the Borgias are here: Pope Roderigo, 'the most carnal man of his age'; Cesare and Lucrezia whose influences were capable of changing and ending other people's lives.

LIGHT ON LUCREZIA 5/-

With a handsome husband, Lucrezia has hopes of a happy life. But after his murder, she was torn between love for her husband and her brother.

The first in her trilogy about Charles II, the most fascinating rake in England's history.

THE WANDERING PRINCE 5/-

The story of Charles II's years he spent in exile as a young man is seen through the eyes of his sister Minette and his mistress Lucy Water.

All aboard for happiness...

There's not a boy—or his father—who wouldn't swap the family car for the magical, almost human

CHITTY CHITTY BANG BANG 3/6
All the family will enjoy THE STORY OF THE FILM based on the screenplay by Roald Dahl and Ken Hughes — COMPLETE WITH EIGHT PAGES OF FULL COLOUR PICTURES.
Based on the original IAN FLEMING stories, the film is directed by KEN HUGHES and stars DICK VAN DYKE, SALLY ANN HOWES, LIONEL JEFFRIES, with GERT FROBE, ANNA QUAYLE, BENNY HILL and JAMES ROBERTSON JUSTICE and ROBERT HELPMANN. Filmed in Super-Pana-vision 70, Colour by Technicolor for United Artists release.

It's the most fantasmagorical musical ever made!
A Pan Original   By John Burke

CHITTY-CHITTY-BANG-BANG
Ian Fleming   8/6
'... should be immortal ... she can swim and fly, as well as do her ton on a good road.'
Weekend Telegraph.

All three stories in one sumptuous Double Pan with the outstanding John Burningham illustrations in full colour.

A SELECTION OF
POPULAR READING IN PAN

- [ ] **PRIDE AND PREJUDICE** Jane Austen   3/6
- [ ] **PLAY DIRTY** Zeno
- [ ] **THREE INTO TWO WON'T GO** Andrea Newman   5/–
- [ ] **PASSPORT IN SUSPENSE** James Leasor   5/–
- [ ] **THE SOUND OF THUNDER** Wilbur A. Smith   6/–
- [ ] **ONE OF OUR SUBMARINES** Edward Young (illus.) 5/–
- [ ] **ROSEMARY'S BABY** Ira Levin   5/–
- [ ] **EAGLE DAY** Richard Collier (illus.)   6/–
- [ ] **THE MAN WITH THE GOLDEN GUN** Ian Fleming 3/6
- [ ] **THE SPY WHO LOVED ME** Ian Fleming   3/6
- [ ] **THE MAGUS** John Fowles   8/6
- [ ] **FRUIT OF THE POPPY** Robert Wilder   5/–
- [ ] **THE MAN WHO WAS MAGIC** Paul Gallico (illus.) 5/–
- [ ] **THE ROOM UPSTAIRS** Monica Dickens   5/–
- [ ] **THE RIOT** Frank Elli   5/–
- [ ] **ON FORSYTE 'CHANGE** John Galsworthy   5/–
- [ ] **FAR FROM THE MADDING CROWD**
                                                      Thomas Hardy 5/–
- [ ] **FREDERICA** Georgette Heyer   5/–
- [ ] **SPRIG MUSLIN** Georgette Heyer   5/–
- [ ] **STRANGERS ON A TRAIN** Patricia Highsmith   5/–
- [ ] **THE SHOES OF THE FISHERMAN** Morris West   5/–
- [ ] **YOUNG BESS** Margaret Irwin   5/–
- [ ] **A PURPLE PLACE FOR DYING**
                                                      John D. MacDonald 3/6
- [ ] **THE LIFE OF IAN FLEMING** John Pearson (illus.) 7/6
- [ ] **SHAMELADY** James Mayo   3/6
- [ ] **THE WANDERING PRINCE** Jean Plaidy   5/–
- [ ] **ROUND THE BEND** Nevil Shute   5/–
- [ ] **THE BOSTON STRANGLER** Gerold Frank   5/–

Obtainable from all booksellers and newsagents. If you
have any difficulty, please send purchase price plus 6d.
postage to PO Box 11, Falmouth, Cornwall.

I enclose a cheque/postal order for selected titles ticked
above plus 6d. per book to cover packing and postage.

NAME..

ADDRESS ....